Amazing Praise for Clare M~~cHugh's First~~
Novel, *A Most Engl~~ish Princess~~*

"A rich indulgence!"

—~~People~~

"In this sweeping, immersive novel, Clare McHugh draws readers into the mesmerizing world of the eldest daughter of Queen Victoria—Princess Vicky—as she emerges into a powerful force in her own right and ascends to become the first German Empress."

—Marie Benedict, *New York Times* bestselling author of *The Only Woman in the Room*

"With impeccable attention to research, a sense of place, and filled with relatable characters, *A Most English Princess* will sweep you away. A literary triumph with flavors of Daphne du Maurier, Edith Wharton, and *Downton Abbey*, this novel is poised to become a favorite for historical fiction lovers."

—Armando Lucas Correa, bestselling author of *The German Girl* and *The Daughter's Tale*

"The strength of one woman, Crown Princess Victoria, to influence the path of European history during turbulent times is striking in this stunning debut from Clare McHugh."

—Geri Krotow, bestselling author

"The eldest daughter of Queen Victoria and mother of Kaiser Wilhelm, Princess Vicky deserves a novel of her own. Brimming with luxurious detail and vicious court intrigue, this is both a splendid portrait of a royal marriage and a woman whose dreams fell prey to the darkness of German history."

—Mariah Fredericks, author of *Death of an American Beauty*

The Romanov Brides

Also by Clare McHugh

A Most English Princess

The
Romanov
Brides

a novel of the

LAST TSARINA

and

HER SISTERS

CLARE McHUGH

wm

WILLIAM MORROW
An Imprint of HarperCollinsPublishers

THE ROMANOV BRIDES. Copyright © 2024 by Clare McHugh. All rights reserved. Printed in the United States of America. No part of this book may be used or reproduced in any manner whatsoever without written permission except in the case of brief quotations embodied in critical articles and reviews. For information, address HarperCollins Publishers, 195 Broadway, New York, NY 10007.

HarperCollins books may be purchased for educational, business, or sales promotional use. For information, please email the Special Markets Department at SPsales@harpercollins.com.

FIRST EDITION

Designed by Diahann Sturge

Library of Congress Cataloging-in-Publication Data has been applied for.

ISBN 978-0-06-325093-2

24 25 26 27 28 LBC 5 4 3 2 1

For Jean Barlow McHugh

Historical Note

$\mathcal{I}$n 1878, when this story begins, the most important families in Europe were closely intertwined. The Grand Duchy of Hesse and by Rhine was a small German territory, and its capital, Darmstadt, a small, provincial place, but the grand duke, Ludwig, was supremely well connected. He had married Alice, the second daughter of Queen Victoria. His children were the grandchildren of the famous queen, the Prince of Wales was their uncle, and the five Wales children their cousins. Alice's sister Vicky had married the Crown Prince of Prussia, making her son, Prince Wilhelm, later Kaiser Wilhelm II, another first cousin of the Hesse children. Grand Duke Ludwig was also related to the Romanovs—the imperial rulers of Russia—as his aunt Marie had married Tsar Alexander II, with whom she had eight children, six who survived to be adults.

The princesses of Hesse grew up at the very center of a web of royal relations.

Characters

In Darmstadt

Ludwig, the Grand Duke of Hesse and by Rhine (**Papa**)

His wife: Alice, the Grand Duchess (**Mama**)

Their daughters: Princesses **Victoria**, Elisabeth (**Ella**)

Irène, **Alix** (also called **Sunny** or **Alicky**), and Marie (**May**)

Their sons: Princes Ernst Ludwig (**Ernie**), Friedrich (**Frittie**)

The grand duke's uncle: **Uncle Alexander**, Prince of Battenberg

Two of his sons: Princes **Louis** and Henry (**Liko**)

And

Madame Alexandrine de Kolemine

A divorcée

In Berlin

Victoria, Crown Princess of Prussia (**Aunt Vicky**)

Her eldest son: Prince Wilhelm (**William**
or **Willy**, later Kaiser Wilhelm II)

Her second son: Prince Heinrich (**Henry**)

Wilhelm's cousin: Friedrich, Prince of Baden (**Fritz**)

In Britain

Queen Victoria (**Grandmama**)

Her youngest son: Prince Leopold (**Uncle Leo**)

Her youngest daughter: Princess Beatrice (**Aunt Beatrice**)

Her heir and eldest son: Albert Edward,
Prince of Wales (**Uncle Bertie**)

His wife, also a sister of the tsarina: Alexandra,
Princess of Wales (**Aunt Alix**)

Their sons: Princes Albert Victor (**Eddy**) and **George**

Their daughters: Princesses **Louise**, Victoria (**Toria**), and **Maud**

In St. Petersburg

Tsar Alexander III (**Uncle Sasha**)

His wife: Tsarina Maria Feodorovna (**Aunt Minnie**)

His brothers: Grand Duke **Serge**, Grand
Duke **Paul**, Grand Duke **Vladimir**

The tsar's eldest son, the tsarevich: Nicholas (**Nicky**)

The tsar's other children: **Georgy**, **Xenia**,
Michael (**Misha**), and **Olga**

The tsar's cousins: Grand Duke **Sergei** and
Grand Duke Alexander (**Sandro**)

The tsar's sister: Marie, Duchess of Edinburgh (**Aunt Marie**)

Her husband, a son of Queen Victoria: Alfred,
Duke of Edinburgh (**Uncle Affie**)

Their daughter: Princess Victoria Melita (**Ducky**)

Her Majesty's ambassador to the Russian Empire: **Sir Edward Thornton**

A friend of the imperial family: Countess Alexandra Vorontsova-Dashkov (**Sandra**)

And

Matilda Kschessinska

A ballerina

The Family of Queen Victoria

(Simplified)

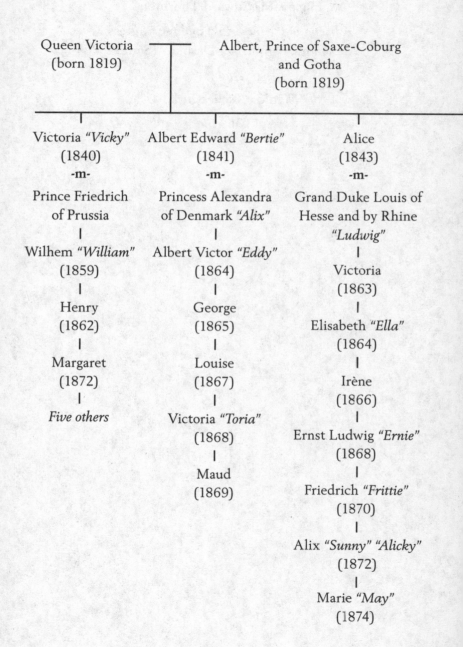

Queen Victoria
(born 1819)
—
Albert, Prince of Saxe-Coburg
and Gotha
(born 1819)

Victoria *"Vicky"* (1840)	Albert Edward *"Bertie"* (1841)	Alice (1843)
-m-	-m-	-m-
Prince Friedrich of Prussia	Princess Alexandra of Denmark *"Alix"*	Grand Duke Louis of Hesse and by Rhine *"Ludwig"*
Wilhem *"William"* (1859)	Albert Victor *"Eddy"* (1864)	Victoria (1863)
Henry (1862)	George (1865)	Elisabeth *"Ella"* (1864)
Margaret (1872)	Louise (1867)	Irène (1866)
Five others	Victoria *"Toria"* (1868)	Ernst Ludwig *"Ernie"* (1868)
	Maud (1869)	Friedrich *"Frittie"* (1870)
		Alix *"Sunny" "Alicky"* (1872)
		Marie *"May"* (1874)

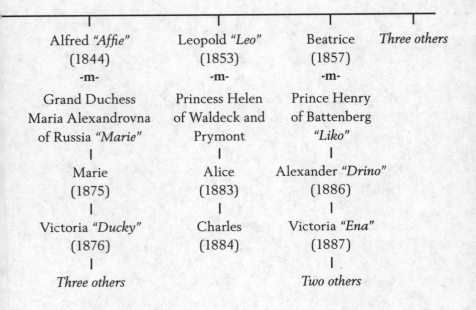

Alfred *"Affie"*
(1844)
-m-
Grand Duchess
Maria Alexandrovna
of Russia *"Marie"*
|
Marie
(1875)
|
Victoria *"Ducky"*
(1876)
|
Three others

Leopold *"Leo"*
(1853)
-m-
Princess Helen
of Waldeck and
Prymont
|
Alice
(1883)
|
Charles
(1884)

Beatrice
(1857)
-m-
Prince Henry
of Battenberg
"Liko"
|
Alexander *"Drino"*
(1886)
|
Victoria *"Ena"*
(1887)
|
Two others

Three others

The Family of Tsar Alexander II
(Simplified)

Tsar Alexander II (born 1818) — Marie, Princess of Hesse and by Rhine (born 1824)

Alexander *"Sasha"*
(1845)
-m-
Princess Dagmar
of Denmark
"Minnie"
|
Nicholas *"Nicky"*
(1868)
|
George *"Georgy"*
(1871)
|
Xenia
(1875)
|
Michael *"Misha"*
(1878)
|
Olga
(1882)

Vladimir
(1847)
-m-
Princess Marie
of Mecklenburg
"Miechen"
|
Kirill
(1876)
|
Four others

Alexei
(1850)
-m-
Alexandra
Zhukovskaya

Maria *"Marie"*	Sergei *"Serge"*	Paul
(1853)	(1857)	(1860)
-m-	-m-	-m-
Prince Alfred	Princess Elisabeth	Princess
of Great Britain	of Hesse and	Alexandra of
"Affie"	by Rhine *"Ella"*	Greece
|		|
Marie		Maria
(1875)		(1890)
|		|
Victoria *"Ducky"*		Dmitri
(1876)		(1891)
|		
Four others		

Prologue

Neues Palais, Darmstadt, November 1878

Wherever Alix is, May is there too. They share a room, a very nice one, with pretty pink paper on the walls and a soft red carpet underfoot, perfect for turning somersaults. They possess a large number of dolls, and a dollhouse with a roof that lifts off. There's one bed, which is Alix's because she is already six. May must sleep in a cot as she's only four.

On this evening, their nurse has gone out and Victoria is in charge at bedtime. Alix never likes this. Their eldest sister finds too much pleasure in issuing orders. She marches into their room, points at the dolls strewn on the red carpet, and says, "Have you thrown them about on purpose? Re-creating a shipwreck? Imagining some dreadful earthquake?"

Alix scowls at Victoria, but May asks: "What's an earthquake?" She's so little there's a lot she doesn't know.

"And the old clothes in a big heap!" Victoria exclaims.

A leather trunk next to the wardrobe is full of gowns Mama doesn't wear any longer. Alix and May love to pull them out by the armful—the blue silk taffeta, the pale-purple wool, the dark-green brocade. All smell pleasantly sweet and dusty. Once the two of them have chosen favorites, wriggling their heads through the high necks and threading their arms down the long sleeves, Alix directs. Up and down the passageway they march, going to a tea party, or to church, or to visit Grandmama in her Windsor Castle far away.

"Set everything to rights now—dresses in the trunk, dolls on the shelves," Victoria demands, fists planted on her hips. "And smooth the bed—I see you've been bouncing."

Alix curls her bottom lip. "My bed can remain rumpled," she announces.

"Don't contradict, Alix," Victoria scolds. "Get into your nightdress and help May with hers. If you're quick, I'll read aloud. From a book you will like with a queen, and animals, and a little girl who has adventures."

IN THE SCHOOLROOM, burning wood pops and snaps in the grate, and Alix hears the soft rasp of wool pulling through linen twill. Ella and Irène sit, heads bent over needlework. Ella looks up and smiles. If only Ella were the eldest, not Victoria. If only Ella played with her and May more often—she's so good at singing and drawing and can make the most cunning little doll's tea set out of acorns. But Ella constantly goes out with Victoria for a walk or a drive. At home, the two disappear together behind the closed door of the bedroom they share. Victoria is fifteen and Ella fourteen—Mama calls them the big pair. Alix and May are the little girlies. Irène, who is twelve, hasn't got a special name. She's just in the middle with Ernie, their brother, who is ten.

Five daughters, one son—Papa says he's rich in ladies, and that's even before he counts Mama.

"On the hearth rug, girlies," says Victoria, bumping a chair out of the corner to set in front of the fire. She sits, hitches her heels on the chair's bottom rung, and opens a red-covered book in her lap.

"Alice was beginning to get very tired . . ."

Alix gasps when Alice follows the rabbit into a hole and falls and falls! Good thing she lands upon sticks and dry leaves, and can run along a passage after the rabbit, into a low hall. Alix leans forward excitedly to hear what comes next.

But Victoria claps the book shut. "That's enough."

"No, more!" Alix protests.

"I have a pain here." Victoria fingers the flesh under her chin. "And my throat hurts when I swallow."

"Don't swallow," says Alix.

Ella comes over to lay a hand across Victoria's forehead. "You're hot."

Victoria shivers. "I feel cold."

Alix stands, and folds her arms in front of her chest. "Victoria, you must never, ever stop right in the middle of a story," she says.

"Silly goose," Ella replies. "It's a long book. Victoria couldn't finish it tonight."

"You read, Ella!" Alix seizes the book from Victoria's lap to hold out to Ella.

"It's late now," says Victoria, taking it back. "Ellie, will you put them in bed?"

Ella nods. "Give Victoria a kiss, Alix. You too, May."

Alix plants a quick kiss on the corner of Victoria's lips, and May, stretching up on tiptoes, does too. Ella leads them away.

"We'll hear more of the Alice book tomorrow?" Alix asks as Ella lifts May into her cot.

"If you promise to go to sleep now, without fuss."

"And you'll sing?"

"Yes, into bed now."

Dear Ella. She's hardly ever cross and her face is as pretty as a bisque doll—pink cheeks, curved lips, very dark lashes, and blue eyes that glow. Alix likes watching Ella as she drifts through the palace, humming dreamily. A young man who came in the summer to learn German—Lord Charles Montague he was called—wrote a poem praising her beauty. Cousin William insists it is he who will marry Ella, although Mama says the big pair are not old enough yet to think about husbands. Anyway, that bellowing, puffed-up Willy with his odd hanging arm isn't right for her lovely sister.

Ella sits down on her bed and Alix rolls on her side, snug against her sister. "Begin!" she demands.

"*Guten Abend, gut' Nacht, mit Rosen bedacht, mit Näglein besteckt, schlupf' unter die Deck*," Ella sings softly. May, gazing solemnly at them through the rails of her cot, sucks her thumb.

May's eyes are shut by the time Ella finishes. "Just one more; it can be a very, very quiet one," Alix wheedles.

"Enough!" Ella playfully pulls Alix's ear. "See you tomorrow, sweet little sister of mine."

MAMA'S DISTANT VOICE wakes Alix. She pads across the passage to find her mother and Orchie, their nurse, standing beside Victoria's bed.

Victoria, sitting up, has drawn the patchwork coverlet up to her shoulders. Her face is bright red, and her throat is swollen out to be as wide as her cheeks.

"Eww," Alix exclaims.

Mama whirls around. "Out of here, Sunny—you mustn't catch what Victoria has."

"Where's Ella?" Alix replies, sulkily. Mama hasn't even said good morning to her. Tall and thin and with a long neck and gentle eyes, her mother is usually very glad to see her Sunny. Alix, Mama says, is like a sunbeam in the house.

Victoria coughs, more like a bark than a cough, and Mama winces.

"Ella went to your Grossmutter Hesse in the Wilhelminen-strasse," Orchie says, steering Alix away, a hand on her back. Mrs. Orchard, to use her proper name, wears her usual gray dress, white apron, and white cap. She resembles a hen, with her broad behind. Also, she clucks.

"But why?'

"Because Ella can't share a room with Victoria when she's ill."

"What's wrong with Victoria?"

"The doctor will say," Orchie tells her. "You and May stay in your room and play quietly."

The dolls come down from the shelves. Some are ill and need imaginary medicine. Next Alix and May go to the window, breathe on the cold glass, and rub designs into the fog clouds with their fingers. After that, bored, they stand side by side in their doorway. Mama walks in and out of Victoria's room. Miss Jackson, the big pair's governess, has her hat on—she is taking Irène to the dentist. Orchie bustles down the passageway, carrying a tray, holding a clay pot with a long spout.

"Is that for Victoria?" Alix asks, pointing.

"Yes, to breathe in steam to soothe her throat."

"Can't we go out?" Alix asks.

"For the short while before luncheon," Orchie says.

Downstairs, she opens the garden door, and Alix and May race across the grass, under bare branches, and around the prickly rosebushes. They circle the pond where the water lilies are all pushed to the center because it's cold. They stretch out their arms and pretend to fly.

Passing the big tree with the V-shaped trunk, Alix stops short.

"Look, May—*Maronen*." On the ground are a scattering of spiky burrs—inside are the shiny-brown triangular nuts that their father loves to eat once they've been roasted in the oven.

"We must bring these to the kitchen," she instructs May.

Alix's sister crouches next to her. Some burrs are partly broken open, others still closed up. "So many," May says.

"Yes," Alix says. "Too many to carry in our hands. Stand up, open your coat, and hold out your skirt."

Alix tosses the burrs into May's outstretched skirt, and minds her sister closely, as step by slow step, they find their way indoors to Frau Schmidt, the cook. She claps in delight, and quickly shovels the *Maronen* out of May's skirt with her large pink hand. "*Danke, kleine Prinzessinnen!*" she says, beaming at them.

Upstairs they find Irène in bed—the dentist noticed she had a fever and sent her home without looking at her teeth. But their brother joins them at the table.

"We're sad without Ella," says Alix.

"We are," May agrees.

"More bread and butter for me," says Ernie, and he snatches two slices off the serving plate, holds one in each hand, and takes a bite out of one and then the other. Back and forth, quicker and quicker. Crumbs fly out of his mouth and Alix and May laugh.

Mama comes in. "Stop that, Ernie, you're making a mess," she scolds. But she smiles. Mama dotes on Ernie, her only boy. They had another brother, little Frittie, but he died long ago.

"Sunny, why aren't you drinking your milk?" Mama asks.

"Mama, me and May found more *Maronen* today, and we collected them for Frau Schmidt!"

"*May and I* found more *chestnuts*," Mama corrects. "What good girlies you are."

"When will Ella come back?" asks Alix.

"When Victoria and Irène are well," Mama says.

ALIX WAKES IN the night and her throat hurts so much she can barely swallow.

She calls for Mama, who comes, and sends Orchie for the little pot. Breathing the steam doesn't help much. Alix sits on Mama's lap, fiddling with the smooth silver cross her mother always wears around her neck, while Mama talks with Orchie over her head. "Little ones, with their little narrow throats, are most at risk. Let's move the baby in with me."

When Orchie lifts May out of her cot, her sister's head dangles backward, her feet and legs hang limp.

"She is sound asleep, Mama, shhh . . ." Alix whispers, and taps a finger against her lips.

"You sleep too now, Sunny," says Mama, helping Alix under the covers.

The next moment, it seems, Mama is shaking her awake. A solemn man with a beaky face, wearing a black coat that smells of the outdoors, stands beside her bed. Alix must sit up and open her mouth.

Holding her tongue down with a spoon, the man looks down her throat. "*Ja, bestimmt, Diphtherie.*"

Orchie's hands fly to her face. Mama is calm. "Come to see the older girls now, Doctor."

By afternoon Alix has the barking cough. Beyond the window, streaming with rain, the branches of a tall tree rise and fall in the wind. If only it were yesterday and she and May were in the garden collecting *Maronen*.

HER FACE BLAZES. The insides of her eyelids burn when she closes her eyes. She's lying down but feels as if she's spinning in the air. She stares at the chintz drapes next to her bed—the nosegays of pink roses with their tiny lime-colored leaves wobble side to side.

Orchie comes in to offer cool water in her favorite silver cup and Alix croaks, "I want Mama."

"She is occupied. Your brother is ill now, and May too," the nurse says sadly. "Your little sister suffers so with high fever."

Orchie wraps warm, wet towels around Alix's neck. After she removes them, Alix puts her hands up and feels her throat has swelled up. She must look as monstrous as Victoria now.

In the afternoon, Mama does come, with two strange maids. After kissing her forehead, Mama instructs the women. "Clean this room thoroughly and take the dolls and that old trunk away," she says, pointing.

Where are you taking everything? Alix would ask, if only her throat wasn't too tight to talk.

Is that Orchie weeping outside in the passageway? Or is it a dream? Alix has so many dreams, with painfully bright colors and bursting shapes. In others she falls down a deep hole to a cellar, where fearsome beasts crouch in the dark corners, ready to strike.

She lies with her hot cheek against the cool pillow, and Papa opens the door. Holding the knob, he stands for a long moment on the threshold, gazing at her. Their Papa has a large head, a broad sun-burnt forehead, and a brown beard. Usually, he's a very smiley person. Mama rules the house, while Papa is the joker. In one game he lets Alix and May push him, and he falls over dramatically, to roll around on the ground pretending to be frightened and shouting, "*Bitte habt Gnade!*" Please have mercy. It's very funny.

But today he looks glum—probably because she's too ill to play.

"Poor little Alix, left alone without her dearest chum," he says softly.

So, bring me May. She still can't make words, and now her head is too heavy to lift.

One morning when Alix puts her hands around her neck, it is no longer swollen. When Orchie comes, Alix asks: "What can I eat?"

Her nurse brings beef broth and bread. She finishes that and asks for more. Alix looks around—how empty the room is. No May, no dolls, no dresses.

"Bring the trunk back, please? I won't put on any of the dresses, just sort through them," Alix pleads.

"Those clothes are all gone," Orchie says.

"Gone where? They are mine—mine and May's." She is indignant. She hasn't been ill so very long.

"The dresses were burned, because the doctor feared they carried infection."

Alix stares at Orchie, in a muddle.

"Did you tell May?" she asks.

Orchie goes for Mama.

Her mother is wearing a black dress, and her face looks odd—white and bare, like the wind blew across it. When she sits on the bed, Alix climbs into her lap.

"May will be very sad about the dresses all burnt, Mama. How shall we tell her?"

Mama says, "May has gone to heaven, darling girl." She hugs Alix tightly.

"Heaven? Where? Above the clouds?" she asks.

"Somewhere like that." Mama is smoothing Alix's hair.

"May doesn't like to go strange places without me."

"One day you will join her there. We all will."

"Together at the same time?"

"No, when God calls each of us—when we die."

"Die? I'm going to die?" Now she's alarmed.

"No, you are getting well, my dearest. Just rest and stay quiet now. Sleep more."

After Mama tucks the covers around her, Alix lies in bed feeling limp and achy. Through the window she can see that it's a bright day. A few puffy white clouds float by. Will May ride on the top of one and look down on the whole world and see Alix? And wave?

THE NEXT DAY, Orchie brings a note from Ernie. She runs her finger under the words to help Alix read it aloud: *"Dear Alix, I am mosh beter & hav iten a vare beg Brakfast."*

"Your brother mixes up English and German spelling," Orchie says, shaking her head.

"Mama always says Ernie must grow up to a proper English gentleman as well as the future Grand Duke of Hesse," Alix reminds her.

"And thus attend closely to his lessons," Orchie says with a small smile. "Look, he has listed his toys. You are to make a stroke under any you wish to borrow."

She chooses Ernie's little bronze animals. The giraffe is best, long neck and tiny, sweet ears. Alix arrays them all around her on the bed.

That afternoon Ernie appears, wearing his nightshirt, but also his heavy shoes, which look silly together. His hair sticks up in the back from lying in his bed for such a long time. He wants to go out into the garden, but Orchie says no. Alix and he sit together on the floor and play with the animals.

Ernie doesn't say anything about May going to heaven. Maybe it's not true. Or it could be true for a short while and then she'll come back. May will want to play with Ernie's animals too.

NOW MAMA IS ill. Orchie says she exhausted herself caring for the whole family.

A special doctor from a place called München comes to see Mama. Papa and Victoria visit her in her room, but Alix is never allowed. She begs every day to see Mama, and finally Orchie takes her in. They find Mama asleep—her thin white arms lying on top of her bedclothes. The curtains are drawn and the air smells sour. Her mother opens her eyes and sees them. She struggles to sit up. She picks up paper and pencil from the bedside table and begins to write, because she can't speak properly for the moment, Orchie explains.

The nurse reads out: "Are you being a good girl and listening to Mrs. Orchard and Victoria?"

Alix nods. What ugly, dark brown circles Mama has around her eyes.

Next note: "I want you to start French lessons. I will instruct Miss Jackson."

Alix doesn't care about French. "When will you get out of bed?" she asks.

Mama writes: "Soon. Let me rest now."

VICTORIA HOLDS HER hand. It's late, after tea, and it's cold standing in the entrance hall with its stone floor. Who moved the pair of tall iron candelabras from the dining room out here? The same men who propped the big box, covered over with a heavy cloth, up on two dining chairs?

The box is called a coffin, Orchie said.

This is a coffin, a coffin for Mama, Alix repeats silently to herself.

But Mama closed up inside? No, not reasonable. This is something Mama likes to say—"Be reasonable!" The world goes on—why wouldn't Mama go on too?

Alix thinks she'd rather be upstairs in her and May's room. She tries to wriggle her hand free, but Victoria clutches harder. "We must wait here for Papa, and the British minister," she whispers.

Ella stands on Victoria's other side. Alix jumped up and down with excitement when Ella came back this morning. But Ella barely speaks, she doesn't smile, and her eyes don't glow. Eyes, it turns out, are like candles, and can be blown out.

The door opens; chill air slithers around Alix's stockinged legs. A sharp tap-tap of boots and Papa is there, with him a man wearing spectacles.

Papa has on his black uniform coat, broad scarlet flaps folded open in front. He clasps to his chest a blue-and-red bundle. His mouth twists when he looks down at the coffin.

Then he nods. "We change it. As she wished. She goes out under the English colors."

Papa puts his bundle aside. He and the man with spectacles go to stand at either end of the coffin. "*Zusammen*," her father says, and the two carefully lift up the cloth, which has a broad white stripe down the middle and red on both sides.

Now Alix sees. It's the flag of the Grand Duchy of Hesse and by Rhine. Papa's flag.

They step sideways and then toward each other, bringing the corners of the flag together like the maids folding up ironed sheets. The man folds it once again, and drapes it over his arm.

The coffin is made of polished dark wood and also has small gold handles on the sides, rather like pulls on a bureau. Victoria, that great big girl, is weeping, and Ella and Irène too. Alix leans forward to see Ernie at the end of their line. He's squeezed his eyes tight shut, balled his fists, and is pressing his arms straight against his sides.

Papa shakes out his bundle. It's another flag—a big red cross, blue triangles and some white. When he throws it open, Alix thinks again of the maids, billowing out the bedclothes when they make up the beds.

In the gust of air, the candle flames sway and then right themselves. It's so still and cold and lonely.

Come back, May.

Papa pulls on one corner of the flag and then the other to make it straight. He strokes it. Then he makes an odd, choking noise, and, resting both hands on the top of the coffin, bows his head. "A few last words, Sir James," he says. "Before we carry her out? For the children?"

The man clears his throat and begins in English: "O heavenly Father, we pray to You for Alice and for all those whom we love but we see no longer . . ."

See no longer? I see Mama.

Alix closes her eyes. Mama walks in the garden, leading the way. The train of her pale purple dress skims over the green, green grass. Mama turns her head to look over her shoulder. When she sees Alix she smiles, and reaches out her hand.

Part I

Chapter One

The Visit of the Russian Cousins

Neues Palais, Darmstadt, October 1882

In Russia, a country very far away, it's nearly always winter. Russia doesn't have a queen or a kaiser but a tsar, who is also their cousin, and he's been in Darmstadt, although not when Alix can remember. Papa describes the tsar—Alexander is his name, although the family calls him Sasha—as a big and burly man, built like a bear. Very suitable for living in all that cold weather.

Papa announces that two of the tsar's younger brothers are stopping for a visit. And he promises that because Alix is ten now, she can dine down whilst the cousins are here. But on the afternoon they arrive, Miss Jackson refuses to let Alix off lessons early. By the time she comes downstairs and approaches the sitting room everyone else is talking happily together. She stands in the doorway. The two young men—one dark, the other with brown-gold hair and a pointed beard, sit side by side on the sofa. They may be relations, but they are still strangers, and she feels shy.

"Look who's here," says Papa heartily.

The young men jump to their feet immediately—both tall as trees.

"What a beauty you have become, little Alix," says the darker cousin, and he steps toward her. Will he chuck her under the chin? No, he bends, takes her hand, and lifts it to his lips to kiss, as if she were as old as Ella and Victoria. Very nice.

The other cousin calls out: "I've seen you in your bath."

She feels her cheeks flame, and scowls, looking down at the carpet.

"You mustn't tease her, Serge," says Victoria.

"Alix, *komm*," Papa beckons, and when she's beside him, he puts an arm around her and whispers in her ear. "Cousin Serge stayed with us for several weeks when you were a baby."

"Please, Alix," this Serge says. "Let me tell you—you were such an adorable little thing."

"Yes," she says coldly. "I imagine."

Everyone laughs, although she didn't mean to be funny.

At the table, the dark-haired brother, who is called Paul, sits beside Alix. When he smiles, he shows many of his teeth. He describes his home in St. Petersburg, which has canals. Cousin Paul and Cousin Serge have recently been to Venice, where all the streets are canals. "Much dirtier than ours," Paul explains. "But in lovely Venice nothing ever freezes. While in Petersburg for nearly half the year the canals are frozen, and also our River Neva, too, that winds through the city." He makes a snaking motion with his hand.

Across the table Serge nods. "On the splendid day in April when, finally, the ice begins to heave and crack and float out to sea, the start of navigation on the Neva is declared. There's a big celebration. Cannons are fired, church bells ring, people dance in the streets."

Alix pictures the crowds—women in kerchiefs, men in fur hats. When you don't have something for a long time, like warm weather, you would miss it especially much.

The talk moves on, and the big girls, as so often, want to discuss Italy, where they visited recently. This is rather dull until

Alix hears Serge say how he's taught himself Italian, and he's reading a very long Italian poem about traveling into the land of the dead.

Alix has her own ideas about meeting the dead. Up in Mama's bedroom, left untouched since the day she died, there's a stained-glass window. Once it was an ordinary window, out of which her small brother, Frittie, leant too far and tumbled down onto the stone terrace below. He bled so much inside he couldn't live any longer. Now instead of a big square of clear glass, there are tiny squares of colored glass that make the shape of an angel with beams of sun around her. Below are the words: *Not lost, only gone before.* Alix likes to stand in front of this window, and with her eyes closed, whisper, "Not lost, only gone before." Then she bids the most hidden part of her—her soul it must be—to float out of her chest, drawing upward toward Mama and Frittie and little May. Alix is rather like an angel then, alive in this world, while wafting into the other—a cloudy, blue-gray place, without roof or floor. There she can sense Mama close. Alix can't remember exactly what her mother's voice sounded like, but she knows it's her saying soft words: "You are my Sunny, my dearest girl."

It's magical when this happens.

"I'd like to read that poem," Alix tells Serge, interrupting.

Her cousin smiles. "Best to learn Italian first and read it in the original."

Alix draws in her chin and looks at him sternly from beneath her fringe. "I have English, German, and some French. I don't need another language."

Everyone laughs again—unbidden!

"In future you need to become more ambitious, Alix. I believe you are up to Italian," says Serge. His smile is not toothy like Paul's, but tilted, with one side higher than the other.

He must be teasing her again. She gives him another frown.

Papa says, "*Meine Kleine*, come sit on my lap. Let Serge and Paul tell us more about their travels."

THE RUSSIAN COUSINS are stopping only two days, and the next afternoon they are eager to visit Grossmutter Hesse in the Wilhelminenstrasse. That white-haired lady is too old and frail to venture out of her home, so they will all go and take tea with her, except Papa, who must do his work.

Navy coat and hat on, Alix waits impatiently by the door. Ernie is clowning with Paul, Irène still searching for her gloves, Victoria speaking with the *Hofmarschall*, Baron Westerweller, about the orders for dinner.

Where is Ella?

Alix finally spots her gliding down the staircase, wearing her hat with the wafting black feather and her new gray coat, draping sleeves trimmed with beaver. Ella tore pages out of a French magazine to show the dressmaker, Frau Hoyer, exactly what she wanted.

Ella is smiling at Serge, who is gazing up at her. Of course he admires her, as so many young men do. Serge is fiddling with a gold ring he has on his little finger, twisting it round and round. Ella looks especially rosy. Then he says something to Ella that Alix is too far away to hear. Ella's smile vanishes, her face tightens, she looks unhappy. When she reaches the foot of the stairs, her eyes dart about.

"Oh, Sunny, good girl, you are ready. Let's go on ahead, shall we?" Ella asks, speeding toward her. Her sister seizes her left hand, and they sweep out together, through the door Gunther the footman holds open.

Alix swings her arm high so Ella's arm will swing too. "Did Serge tell you something?" she asks as the iron gate clangs behind them and they turn into the road.

"When?"

"Just now."

Ella's mind seems to have wandered away.

"When you came down the stairs I saw Serge say something to you," Alix presses.

"Ah, yes, he said—" She pauses.

Alix waits.

"He made a remark about my hat," Ella finishes.

"It's such a nice hat," Alix says, smiling up at her. "You were so clever to sew on that ostrich feather. And I hope he admired your coat? Has Frau Hoyer ever made something so smart?"

Ella smiles back. "I worried that it could never be as I envisioned, but I am pleased."

"The sleeves are lovely, not tight on your arms."

"Dolman sleeves they're called." She squeezes Alix's hand.

But why had Ella wanted to rush out? Alix still doesn't know.

At tea Alix watches Ella attend closely to Grossmutter, making sure her cup is never empty, passing her a second slice of cake. Serge gazes at Ella steadily the whole hour. Meanwhile, Ella pays him no notice at all.

The conversation—about lots of relations she's never met—doesn't interest Alix. She stares at Grossmutter's marvelous tall clock. Behind the numbers and thin black arms, there's a large sailing ship that bobs up and down on a green sea, the waves painted with delicate white crests and gold dots of spray. Where, oh where, is the ship heading? To America? Madagascar? Peru?

The others talk on and on. Alix slides forward on the hard horsehair chair and slumps back, which feels agreeable. Then Victoria snaps: "Alix, you mustn't sit like that!"

She is glad when it's time to go home.

OUTSIDE IN WILHELMINENSTRASSE, Ernie challenges Paul to a foot race. Their cousin says he could not possibly match Ernie's pace, but perhaps Ernie can hop on one foot, as Paul will, and they'll see how far they both can get. Not very far at all, it turns out—Ernie collapses on the ground ten yards along the road. Paul grins, but admits he couldn't have gone on much farther himself. Victoria proposes that they all try running backward. Irène is surprisingly good at this. Paul seems unable to control his tall frame when moving in reverse, and keeps stumbling and falling over. Yet he laughs every time.

Being a Russian grand duke is obviously an impressive thing to be, and these cousins wear glossy, fancy clothes and jeweled rings on their fingers, but Paul is still playful, and Alix admires that.

During all these larks, Alix keeps an eye out for Ella, who is following behind with Cousin Serge. The two walk quite slowly, deep in conversation. What are they talking about? Not hats, as they look so solemn. Gradually they fall farther behind, and by the time Alix and the others reach the palace gate the two are nowhere to be seen.

They've all been in the sitting room recounting their outing to Papa for ten minutes before Ella and Serge turn up. She's rosy and smiling serenely.

Good. Lovely Ella should not be put out. Maybe on their walk Serge was paying her many compliments. As he should.

Chapter Two

Neues Palais, Darmstadt, December 1882

Ella believes she witnessed the precise moment Victoria fell in love with Louis Battenberg—on a warm evening, last July, in the garden of Buckingham Palace.

A rakish man, with a full black beard and twinkly eyes, Louis is one of Papa's cousins, the son of his uncle Alexander. Because he left Darmstadt to join the British navy at fourteen, when Victoria and Ella were still small, they only got to know him properly last summer in London. There, at the request of their grandmother, the queen, Louis acted as their escort for various dinners, parties, and balls. During one tedious palace reception, Louis persuaded them to steal away, promising to take them rowing on the lake. Once in the small boat, he sang sea chanteys and told a few racy stories. Victoria laughed so much the vessel rocked from side to side. Although gripped with terror, sure they would tip over and drown, Ella couldn't miss her sister's elated expression. And after Louis returned to his post on the HMS *Inconstant*, Victoria declared London was dull and they might as well go home.

While Louis is a close friend of Mama's brothers—Uncle Leo and Uncle Bertie, the Prince of Wales—some of their other relations, notably those in Berlin, disdain him. It would not be fitting, in their view, for the Grand Duke of Hesse's eldest daughter to marry a man who works for a living. Moreover, Louis's mother was born a mere countess, which makes Louis only a semi-prince—a Serene Highness not a Royal Highness.

In her letters from Windsor, Grandmama frets over the difference in rank—and Louis's conspicuous want of fortune. But Victoria, the family progressive, is not put off by Louis's unsuitability. It increases her ardor, Ella suspects. And Papa isn't objecting to Louis, although he'll concede it's a great shame the man has no money.

From Italy, where she and Victoria went on tour with Miss Jackson for three weeks, Victoria sent Louis a card every day. Now her sister is clearly impatient for Christmas, because her beloved is due home on leave.

While happy for Victoria, Ella feels wistful too. What of her own future? In former days, when Mama still lived, it was thought she would marry her older cousin William. The son of Mama's sister Aunt Vicky, Willy is heir to the Prussian—and German—thrones. Then, quite soon after Mama died, Willy announced his engagement to Dona, a princess of Schleswig-Holstein. This surprised Grandmama and offended Papa, but Ella didn't mind too terribly. Although fond of Willy—whose enraptured gaze focused always on her, never Victoria—he's a boastful and obstreperous character, not the ideal man. And soon enough, her father declared himself relieved that his daughter would never be Queen of Prussia. After losing a war against Prussia when Ella was a baby, the Grand Duchy of Hesse was absorbed into the German Empire—ruled by Willy's grandfather, Kaiser Wilhelm, and run by the odious Prince Bismarck.

Papa must be polite about Prussians in public, but in private he scorns them for their arrogance and their loutish ways.

Papa reports Grandmama has a new match in mind for Ella: Prince Charles of Sweden. And the Empress of Germany, the Kaiserin, proposes another of her grandsons, Friedrich, Prince of Baden, called Fritz. Do these two sovereign ladies imagine they can just assign her a husband? Ella worries. In any case Papa has so far declined to invite either eligible prince to Darmstadt. Ella turned eighteen only last month, and he tells everyone he is in no hurry to lose his elder daughters. Without Mama, Hesse has no proper *Landesmutter*, so Ella and Victoria appear at state events, help entertain distinguished guests, and run the Alice Frauenvereine, Mama's charity established to train nurses and educate girls.

The only young men Papa has welcomed recently to the Neues Palais were two of his Russian cousins—the Grand Dukes Serge and Paul, whom Ella and Victoria recalled from past visits as sullen and aloof, sitting sprawled on the sofas, and muttering to each other in Russian. On this occasion the brothers proved good company, full of stories from their own just-completed Italian tour.

Paul is a loose-limbed young man with merry brown eyes. His older brother, Serge, is tall, lean, and intent. He converses in a bracing manner. When he and Ella discussed various paintings they had seen, separately, at the Uffizi, he disparaged her favorite, Raphael—"I am left unmoved by his perfect proportions and idealized faces." They did agree the view from Fiesole is the most enchanting of all vistas. And he read aloud to them from *The Divine Comedy*—Serge has decided to teach himself Italian.

Serge also speaks good German and some English, but prefers French, the language of the Russian court. Why, he asked Ella gravely, is her French accent not better? And on the second afternoon of their visit, en route to take tea with Grossmutter in the Wilhelminenstrasse, Serge remarked, "My child, your hat is too disappointing."

Ella felt mortified. Having splurged on a beaver-trimmed winter coat, Ella had no allowance left for a new hat, so she'd revived last winter's felt one by attaching an ostrich feather to the crown. The effect had pleased her until Serge's disdainful comment.

Serge surprised her, after tea, outside on the pavement, when he touched her elbow. "Let Victoria and Paul take care of the children; walk home with me." As they strolled along, he told her a little of his experiences in the Turkish war and his new post, as commander of the Preobrazhensky Life Guards, appointed by his eldest brother, Sasha, now the tsar. In turn, Ella found herself confessing what she rarely tells anyone—four years after Mama's death, she still grieves. Will it be ever thus?

Serge owned that he, too, without his parents, feels an emptiness that nothing can fill. He lost them in quick succession. His mother—the tsarina, Papa's aunt, their great-aunt Marie—died of tuberculosis two years ago, and last year, his father, Tsar Alexander II, was mortally wounded by a bomb hurled at him outside the Winter Palace in St. Petersburg.

Ella knew of the assassination, of course—Papa had gone to the funeral—but hearing Serge's account wrung her heart. Serge's father had escaped five previous attempts on his life, only, on this occasion, to be ambushed in his sleigh. The blast tore off the tsar's lower right leg, shattered his left, ripped open his stomach, and cut his face. His guards carried him inside the palace, to his study, and there he bled to death in front of his family.

"How could God allow it?" Serge asked, his voice harsh, his green eyes flashing. "My father's valiant work for the Russian people answered with a most ghastly end."

Ella struggled for the right words. "Pfarrer Sell, our pastor, preaches that for believers, suffering can be redemptive and bring wisdom."

Serge nodded. "I pray for it. I know Sasha does too. It's been hardest on him, thrust so suddenly into his high position. And aware, as we all are, that the evil impulse is not extinguished—villains continue to plot, eager to spill more Romanov blood."

Ella shuddered. How dreadful that must be, to live shadowed by horrid violence.

At the station the next day, at the conductor's shrill call—*Alle einsteigen!*—Serge and Paul climbed the stairs into the train, and Ella, looking on, felt a wave of tender pity for these two, the orphaned sons of a martyred man.

ON A CHILLY evening a fortnight after the grand dukes' departure, Ella sits with Victoria in front of the fire in the sitting room. Their father is out—precisely where they do not know, although they have their suspicions.

Supper done, the three younger children have gone upstairs, while she and Victoria remain below in hopes Papa might return home in time to bid them good night. As always in the weeks before Christmas, the palace smells of pine—green boughs are woven through the gold balustrade of the main stairs, draped across windows, and laid artfully on the chimney pieces.

Ella slides open her work box, looking for white thread to mend Alix's petticoat while Victoria pulls out of her pocket a letter from Grandmama.

"I could read it aloud," her sister says. "But it comes down to one short message: Ella must not marry a Russian!"

"She writes simply 'Russian'? No name?"

"No name, but she'll mean Serge."

"Goodness! Our cousins stop for two days and she immediately envisions me the wife of one of them? Where did she get this idea?"

"Serge and Paul were to dine with Aunt Vicky and Uncle Fritz when they passed through Berlin."

"Ah, so Aunt Vicky—?"

"Yes, you can imagine," her sister says. "Serge impressed

her—so refined and artistic—the very opposite of those repugnant Junkers our dear aunt is surrounded by. And he must have
told her how he enjoyed your company. Aunt Vicky reported
this to Grandmama, and *voilà*."

Victoria flaps the letter in the air before folding it back into
its envelope.

"Doesn't Grandmama have better things to do than rushing
out instructions to us? Why isn't she instead, I can't think, perhaps consulting with her ministers? Ruling?"

Victoria laughs. "The affairs of state count for so little compared with the affairs of the heart! Especially when the hearts
in question belong to her own relations."

"But jumping to conclusions?"

"You do like Serge," Victoria says.

"I feel for him."

Victoria smiles knowingly. "And?"

"And he's stern. Also, quite old."

"Twenty-five is not so very old; Louis is twenty-seven."

"Serge seems older."

"I predict he will be back to see you before long."

"He's not searching for a wife, if that's what you are implying.
He's taken up with his army command, his art collection, his
study of Italian. And should he marry, he'll choose someone . . ."
She finds herself trailing off.

"Someone?"

"Someone cerebral, very stylish, with better French."

"You? Insufficiently cerebral? Unstylish? How ridiculous!
Ella, your taste is lovely, and don't forget *Lady's Pictorial* described you as possibly the most beautiful princess in Europe."

"Possibly, not certainly!" she protests with a small smile. In
Darmstadt their comings and goings don't attract much attention. But in London, Princess Victoria and Princess Elisabeth,
the Hesse granddaughters of Her Majesty the Queen, earned

regular mention in the Court Circular, and last summer their appearances at teas and balls—even shopping expeditions to Liberty and visits to Carlè the hairdresser in Regent Street— were chronicled by the press.

"Do you know what Madame de Kolemine says?" asks Victoria.

"Madame de Kolemine? Don't you call her Drina now? At her invitation?"

"I'm not prepared to be quite *that* familiar," her sister says, rueful.

Blonde, statuesque Alexandrine de Kolemine first arrived in Darmstadt as the wife of the Russian chargé d'affaires. Now divorced from her husband, she has become, they believe, Papa's mistress. He may never admit this aloud to them, as the liaison cannot be officially acknowledged. Bad enough that Papa prevailed upon his Russian connections to have her husband turfed out of his post and sent home, claiming he was a drunk and a brute who mistreated his wife. That lady now appears regularly at the Neues Palais. Always beautifully dressed, a vivacious talker, she has thick, wheat-colored hair that grows out of a peak on her forehead, and large, far-apart brown eyes. To Ella Madame de Kolemine resembles a very handsome cat, keeping sharp claws sheathed, adept at showering Papa with praise and attention. He looks better than at any time since Mama's death.

Victoria says not to begrudge Papa his happiness. Still, it pains Ella to imagine what their mother would think of the situation.

"Madame de Kolemine tells me that Serge is the rare Romanov with an artistic temperament and true discernment," says Victoria, returning to the subject at hand.

"Those were her very words? How many Romanovs does she know personally?"

"She's met a few, although not probably as many as we have."

Ella sighs. "Do you remember how much Mama pitied poor Great-Aunt Marie?"

"I remember her taking us to Heiligenberg to call on the empress when she visited—and how she looked like a wraith and barely said a word, only coughed. Nothing much imperial about her!"

"Poor thing, an invalid robbed of her health."

"And with such a husband," Victoria says. In his last years, the former tsar, Serge and Paul's father, had a liaison with a younger woman, siring three children with her.

To their grandmother in England, this was more proof, as if any were needed, that Russians can *never* be trusted.

"Why does Grandmama so dislike Russia and Russians—it can't be just the old tsar and his disgraceful goings-on?" Ella asks her sister.

"The Crimean War, to start."

"But that was years ago!"

"The Russians advance now in Afghanistan toward India, and since they won against the Turks, they rattle their swords in the Balkans and declare Constantinople should properly be theirs."

"I don't think Serge cares much about this. He told me battle sickened him, and while devoted to his men, he prays he never has to fight again."

"Unburdening his heart to you then," Victoria says with a knowing smile.

"Hardly! If I were a man, I would feel exactly the same."

"I can't imagine you a man, my dear possibly-the-most-beautiful-princess-in-Europe sister. A model of gracious femininity—a continent awaits your marriage plans breathlessly!"

"Don't tease," Ella says, frowning.

"You really haven't given thought to him? You two looked so engrossed in one another on that walk home."

Ella sighs. Serge is admirably serious, but his sharp opinions and exacting questions nicked at her confidence. And yet when they were strolling along, side by side, conversing privately, she sensed him bending toward her, like a flower bends to the light. Did she only imagine this?

"It makes no difference what I do or do not think," she says, suddenly irked. "I don't like Grandmama feeling free to castigate all Russians while picturing Serge as my future husband. She should leave well enough alone."

"If it's any consolation, she did add a postscript," says Victoria.

"Which is?"

Victoria takes out the letter again and reads: "Remember, dear child, it is impossible for a family to live comfortably on a naval officer's salary."

They laugh. And they head up to bed, too sleepy to wait any longer for Papa.

GRANDMAMA DOES NOT leave well enough alone. She decides the kaiserin is correct, and Fritz of Baden is best for Ella. Under pressure, Papa gives in, and the man comes to visit the Neues Palais on a cold, bright day in January.

Oh, no, he'll never do, Ella thinks within minutes.

Fritz has watery blue eyes, a domed forehead, and a small brown mustache. When he strokes Papa's boxer dog, Tyrus, Ella notices his red hands are large and rather ugly with prominent knuckles. The beast takes to him, leaning against Fritz's knees as the prince sits on the sofa. But Ella senses a nature as bland as semolina pudding without raisins. Papa suggests she show Fritz around the wintery garden; there she struggles to think of topics to discuss.

Art? Fritz doesn't care about painting or sculpture.

Books? Fritz wonders why people waste time reading novels.

Has he been to Italy? No, no interest, but he does enjoy hiking in the Black Forest and sailing on the Obersee.

The family? Cousin Willy, his comrade in the Prussian Foot Guards, is a grand fellow, his best friend. Willy's father, Uncle Fritz, is a great warrior, but Aunt Vicky is too English.

"I am extremely English also," Ella declares, switching to that language. Maybe this will put Fritz off.

"Oh, I don't believe that," Fritz replies, in German. As they walk by the dormant plantings, he extolls Bismarck and the growing power of the German Empire. Ella prefers to let Fritz prate on and on rather than confess that politics bore her.

Back indoors, Victoria waits with the children to be introduced. Ella falls back so she can roll her eyes at her older sister while her suitor steps forward to greet the group.

"Nothing Fritz says is the least bit surprising," she confides to Victoria the next evening, after the prince has taken his leave. "Nor does he seem to care passionately about anything much."

Her sister smiles. "I noticed he liked Tyrus."

"A dog!"

"I also saw him staring at you. He's not indifferent."

"Just what I dreamt of in a husband: a lack of indifference."

Victoria bends over laughing. She's especially jolly these days because Papa has agreed to tell the Darmstadt *Landtag* that she wants to marry Louis, and to negotiate a dowry for her.

"I'm in earnest," Ella continues. "How can life be only about inconsequential things? Meals, and hunts, and trips to the Obersee?"

"I don't think it is," Victoria says, still smiling.

"And shouldn't a young prince endeavor to step back and assess the world, so as to decide how to contribute—rather than accepting his privilege as his due and passing his days complacently?"

"Of course! As Machiavelli says, 'It is not titles which honor men but men who honor titles,'" Victoria replies, and asks, "Have you discussed Fritz with Papa?"

"Tomorrow, I will."

ELLA FINDS HER father in his private study—a small room off the back corridor that smells of pipe tobacco, whiskey, and leather.

"I expected you, *liebe* Ella. What do you make of young Fritz?" He gestures at a chair and she sits down.

"Obviously a pleasant man," she says cautiously.

Papa smiles. "Pleasant?"

"Well, not unpleasant."

He raises his brows and reaches for his pipe.

"What I mean is that Fritz seems nice and good-natured," she says.

"And so?" Papa strikes a match, lights his pipe, and shakes the match out.

"I can't imagine spending my life with him," she says, a slight tremor in her voice. Will Papa find her ungenerous, proclaiming this after such a short acquaintance?

But her father looks untroubled. "I will never compel you girls to marry against your inclination; I promised your mother that before she died."

Ella nods, relieved.

"But young Baden seems quite a fine fellow," Papa continues.

"You like him?"

"I do," he says, waggling his head. "Very decent."

"You believe he's the right husband for me?"

"Your English grandmother certainly does. Yesterday she wrote to say, with ample underlining, how Fritz of Baden is *so good* and *so steady* and offers such a *safe* and *happy* position."

Papa grins—they both recognize that the queen writes much the same way she speaks.

"Although how would she know?" Ella asks. "She's met him maybe twice? Years ago?"

"I've made my own inquiries. Fritz is sound—very popular with his *Kameraden*."

"And I should rely on the endorsement of fellow army officers?" Papa smiles again. "To be the Grand Duchess of Baden one day, that's an excellent thing. To have you living so nearby, I prefer." Baden borders Hesse Darmstadt to the south. "Nor do I imagine you want to move far from the younger ones, as they depend on you still."

Ella sighs. Ernie, now fourteen, and Alix, ten, do look to her for some of the affection they should have had from Mama. Irène at sixteen too. And she loves them all. But they will grow up soon enough.

She shakes her head. "On balance I would rather have married William. At least he is lively."

Papa snorts. "Lively? He's an impudent rascal. By the way, I hear from your aunt Vicky that Dona is expecting again."

"Already? Is their son even a year old?"

He shrugs. "Who remembers? I wager your cousin intends to raise a proper little regiment. To the greater glory of Prussia. You can congratulate Willy when you see him."

"He's coming here?"

"No, no. We've been invited—you and me and Victoria—to a ball in Berlin, in March, to celebrate the silver wedding anniversary of your aunt and uncle. We will go."

Ella nods absently and watches Papa puff on his pipe. If she hadn't so recently become better acquainted with Serge, would Fritz appeal to her more? Not that she's heard anything from her Russian cousin since he left. And Papa wouldn't want her to move as far away as Russia.

It cannot be denied—Fritz has much to recommend him.

He's a German prince, agreeable enough, and residing close by. Still, shouldn't one feel a bit of excitement about one's prospective mate?

"*Hör mal zu*, Ella," Papa says abruptly. "It's not for me to say who is the right person for you to love. Being as I am deeply in love with a woman everyone regards as completely unsuitable."

She stares at her father—astonished that he would acknowledge this.

"It must be obvious to you and Victoria how it is with Drina, *ja?*" he asks.

She blushes and looks down at her hands in her lap. She cannot discuss Papa's intimate life with him. This is beyond her.

She hears him clear his throat. "You and Victoria have been gracious to accept my . . ." A pause. "My choice," he continues. "However, you are a young woman of rank and we must think very carefully about the alliance you make in marriage."

"Because my choices are more limited?" she asks, raising her eyes to meet his.

"Because you are young and inexperienced and your grandmother feels so strongly . . ."

"And you like Fritz too."

"Good-hearted, and bound to be faithful, I'd say."

"You would?"

"Yes. I'd prefer you didn't marry now, as Victoria will likely be engaged soon, but this Fritz is so eager. He'll be thinking of you constantly, he told me. So much so he'll be distracted from his duties. We can't have that!"

Papa chuckles, which irritates Ella. "Will you invite Fritz to visit again?" she asks.

"*Ja.* He's got a fortnight's leave. He's gone off to Heidelberg to stay with some university friends. He thought to come back here afterward."

"So, you've already agreed?" Ella feels another flash of irritation.

"Why not? A chance for you to get to know him better."

WHEN FRITZ RETURNS, Ella does try. She attempts to draw him out, seeking evidence that this most suitable of princes could make a fond and worthy husband. And she supposes some sacrifice will be required—in any marriage, to any man. No one is perfect. She remembers her mother saying this. Only now does Ella wonder: Was Mama truly happy with Papa? She was such a thoughtful, altruistic person, most concerned with the welfare of others, while Papa is neither intellectual nor driven. He enjoys his family, his friends, his gardens, and his sporting pursuits.

But at least Papa feels things deeply. She's not sure Fritz does. None of her conversational efforts flourish. And while she senses Fritz admires her—gazing at her with mouth slightly agape, complimenting her toilette—he never asks her about herself. He opines at length on the subjects within his narrow scope, apparently without fear of boring her. He seems to have no idea how discouraged she is by their give-and-take, and he departs with a salute to Papa and a cheerful *See you in Berlin* called out to her.

THREE WEEKS LATER, she and Victoria, with Papa, board the train to the Prussian capital early on a gray morning.

Ella sits in the corner of the compartment, watching stone walls, narrow tree-lined tracks, and houses with green-painted shutters flash by. The mist slowly lifts off the bare brown fields. A farmer—cap pulled down, collar turned up—drives a cart pulled by a plodding horse. The enormous world, containing thousands upon thousands of lives, every person the main character in their own story—what will be her part to play? She can't bear to think it will be a trivial one. Justly or unjustly, she is already raised above so many others. A princess, an acknowledged beauty, the daughter of a virtuous woman who died too young. With the time granted her she must pursue righteous ends. But how precisely? And with whom?

Ella sighs. It's all very well to turn down a dull and limited young man. She has resolved to do this when Fritz inevitably proposes. Still, refusing an unsatisfactory husband isn't the same as embarking on a laudable life. And how can she even explain her aspirations? Papa would struggle to understand. Victoria might laugh and tell her not to take herself so seriously.

She looks over at her elder sister, absorbed in reading a fat English novel, *A Tale of Two Cities*. Papa stands at the far window, smoking. He's out of sorts this morning because, Ella guesses, Madame de Kolemine isn't with them. Even if she enjoyed higher rank, that lady could never appear in the Berlin court, where divorced persons are not received.

At least Papa isn't pressing Ella. Since Fritz's departure he has said only: "It is for you to choose, my dear."

AUNT VICKY GREETS them in the front hall of the Kronprinzen-palais, her hand resting in the crook of Uncle Fritz's elbow.

"Darlings, I am overjoyed to see you," Aunt Vicky says. Although shorter than Mama was, with darker hair and a rounder face, their aunt's voice sounds exactly as Mama's did. Which is always a small shock.

Uncle Fritz, Crown Prince of Prussia, celebrated hero of the battle of Königgrätz and the siege of Metz, carries himself in the Prussian military manner, shoulders back, chin up. The three Prussian princesses who still live at home—their cousins Moretta, Sophie, and Margaret—wait within. Aunt Vicky announces that Fritz of Baden will call in an hour, impatient to welcome the Darmstadt party to Berlin. Her sister Victoria shoots a significant glance at Ella, and Ella's stomach sinks. All the family must know there's more to Fritz's eagerness than that.

Fritz of Baden arrives at six, and Aunt Vicky has the two of them shown into a small book-lined room. The young man's color is high, his eyes wide—this moment clearly excites him.

He wastes no time. "I believe you and I should marry," Fritz states as soon as a servant closes the door on them.

Despite herself, Ella is offended. He's not going to kneel at her feet, throw open the doors of his heart, confess his deep love?

Fritz barrels on. "And everyone else thinks so too."

She feels a wild instinct to announce: *Such a pity only I disagree.* Instead, she begins the polite response she has prepared, "I am aware of the honor—"

"Even Willy—who I suspect is a bit envious—even he approves!" Fritz cuts in, grinning.

Something stricken about her expression gives him pause.

"What's the matter?" he says.

"Fritz, while I am aware of the honor you do me, I must decline your very gracious proposal," she says in a rush, without pointing out he failed to propose properly.

"What do you mean?" Now he sounds baffled.

"I can't marry you."

"Of course you can."

"I am fond of you and will always regard you as a friend, but I don't believe I will make you happy."

"Of course you will."

He stares at her, both truculent and confused. Then he bites his lower lip. For a long moment they stand together in silence. Embarrassed, she looks away. Through the window she sees carriages passing by on Unter den Linden—if only she were riding in one, rolling away, free and untroubled, no mortifying scene to play out.

"You are refusing me?" he asks finally.

"I am." She forces herself to look him in the eye.

He emits an odd sound—a kind of mutinous guffaw—seizes the leather gloves he had thrown onto a side table, and strides out of the room. Maybe she is mistaken. Maybe Fritz of Baden is not entirely lacking in spirit. But she won't have the opportunity to ascertain this, as most likely he will never speak to her again.

"JUST IMAGINE! THIS is how it feels to be a leper!" declares Victoria, with great good cheer, two nights later, in the Weisser Saal of the Berliner Schloss. The anniversary ball for Aunt Vicky and Uncle Fritz is in full swing, the music soars, couples glide across the floor, hundreds of candles blaze in the imposing chandeliers overhead.

No one has asked Ella or Victoria to dance. The two of them can expect to be shunned for the entire evening. The news that Ella has refused popular Fritz of Baden has swept through the court. Victoria is cold-shouldered, also, because people have learned of her intention to marry a prince not of the blood.

When they are presented to the kaiser and kaiserin, the haughty-eyed empress looks over their heads, as if she hasn't heard their names, as if they are not standing right in front of her. The red-faced old kaiser, heavy in the jowls, smiles absently and murmurs, "Dear Alice's girls, very nice."

From across the room, Cousin William glares at them. He looks the way he did when, as children, they played together and Ella and Victoria refused to follow his orders to the letter. Now here he is again, incensed. His wife, Dona, wears a gorgeous gown of pink crepe de chine. Ella's own dress—last summer's yellow tulle—is drab in comparison. When Dona sweeps past, she looks down her nose at Ella and Victoria, arches her eyebrows, and moves on wordlessly, radiating disapproval.

"Dona must worry if she gets too close, some of our disgracefulness will infect her," whispers Victoria.

"She seems awfully pleased with herself for a princess who is neither pretty, nor, it seems, particularly hospitable," answers Ella.

"Goodness! You've been in Berlin three days and you've already become as poisonous as a Prussian, sister dear."

"Perhaps it's something in the air," Ella answers lightly.

Actually, it's something else—a strange, reckless exhilaration. Ella dreaded turning Fritz down, but now she's done it, she's shocked at how gleeful she feels. Did she believe herself too faint-hearted? Doubt her resolve? Imagine in the end she wouldn't be capable of defying Grandmama, the German empress, and the general expectation that she, just one of the many princesses from inconsequential little Hesse-Darmstadt, must jump at the chance to become the next Grand Duchess of Baden?

Fritz certainly made it easier with his offhand proposal, and his all-around vacuity. Still, she proved herself strong and principled. Maybe on some distant day, she will tell this story about herself to her children. The thought pleases her greatly.

A WEEK LATER, back home, she receives an irate letter from Grandmama. How could Ella possibly reject excellent Fritz of Baden? *Russia I could not wish for you*, the queen adds.

Why is her grandmother so certain that Ella has turned down one offer of marriage to entertain another, from Serge?

"Unless she constantly directs against it, she worries that which she fears most will come to pass," Victoria says.

"You're sure?"

"I'm convinced. And, by the way, Louis reports that Uncle Leo says Grandmama has returned to the idea of Charles of Sweden for you."

"Louis wrote this?"

"Yes, in his letter from Tuesday. My dear intended dined with Uncle Leo and Aunt Helen at Claremont. I'm sorry I forgot to tell you—I've been preoccupied."

Ella looks at Victoria sadly, but her sister tosses her head. "You mustn't worry. I don't care," she says.

Victoria has received bad news. The leaders of the Darmstadt *Landtag* have decided that they cannot support their princess reducing herself from a Royal Highness to a Serene Highness. Should Victoria marry Louis of Battenberg, there will be no state dowry for her.

Papa fumes, sure that the Prussians—Bismarck himself most likely—orchestrated this snub. The chancellor must have pressured the Hessian deputies to oppose the match in some high-handed attempt to preserve the "purity" of German royalty. Papa resents the interference. He announces frequently, to anyone who will listen, that he rules in Darmstadt and no outsider will tell him whom his daughters might—or might not—marry.

"I agree with Papa; it's a horrid gesture," says Ella.

"With our limited funds we shall have to live in a small way," says Victoria blithely. "We may yet be happier for it."

"Is this what Louis thinks?"

"It's what we both think." And she smiles.

Ella hates that Louis and her sister are so shabbily treated. Would she ever accept such a cramped life? Ella can't say it appeals to her. Perhaps she just doesn't understand true love—and never will.

Chapter Three

The Return of the Grand Duke

Jagdschloss Wolfsgarten, April 1883

*E*lla finds it all rather head-spinning.

The Darmstadt assembly's insult has an extraordinary consequence: Grandmama now fully embraces Victoria's choice of husband. Louis is *such* a fine young man with, *thankfully*, a very English outlook, the queen writes. Although he lacks a fortune, riches don't make happiness, and she, Grandmama, joins dear Papa in taking great offense at the Prussian interference. Regarding people as if they are animals, insisting some have better blood than others, *it can go too far*!

When Victoria finishes reading this letter aloud to Ella, she remarks, "Next thing we know, Grandmama will be espousing republicanism."

Letters from Windsor come fast and furious. In the following one, addressed to Ella, Grandmama requests that she come over in May and remain in Britain for the summer. The queen's beloved Highland servant John Brown has died, leaving her bereft, and Ella's company will be such a comfort. Also, they need to discuss Ella's future.

Meanwhile, with spring advancing, Papa takes them to live at Wolfsgarten, a hunting lodge built around a grassy court, surrounded by woods and meadows twelve miles outside of Darmstadt. Designed at the time of Bach, Wolfsgarten reminds

Ella of his music—measured, elegant, and creating a single, harmonious whole out of diverse elements. The buildings stood empty for many years, but now their father has resolved to restore their former glory. Workmen are repointing the red stone of the elegant main house, called the Herrenhaus, plastering the two smaller residences that flank it and expanding the stables opposite.

After luncheon on Victoria's twentieth birthday, April 5, they are sitting outside in the sun, Ernie cranking the new barrel organ Papa bought for them, when a messenger crosses the grass and hands Papa an envelope.

He reads the note and he scowls. Ella worries: Is Madame de Kolemine beckoning him back to Darmstadt? Does he feel torn in his loyalties?

She's glad Victoria asks: "What's wrong, Papa? Bad news?"

"It's Cousin Serge. He finds himself in Frankfurt and proposes to ride out here tomorrow to visit us."

Ella is surprised. "When did he come to Germany?" she asks.

"I'm not sure. I worry he's here to see doctors or to take a cure. Perhaps his chest has weakened as his mother's did?" Papa shakes his head. "He says only he looks forward to seeing us and asks to stay several days."

Victoria, in the chair beside her, nudges Ella with her elbow.

Ella frowns, and whispers fiercely, "Stop! This may very well have nothing to do with me."

THE NEXT MORNING Ella stands at the window of her bedroom, watching Serge take the stairs of the Herrenhaus two at a time, and her heart gives a strange little leap. What if he *has* undertaken this long journey to see her? She lifts her chin and straightens her spine. Then her stomach flutters nervously.

A few minutes later—when she and Victoria join Papa and Serge—Serge meets her gaze meaningfully. He lifts her hand to

kiss, and his fingers hold hers for an extra moment. He says nothing beyond a polite greeting, yet she is convinced. He's acknowledging the tender, mutual sympathy that flowered between them
in November. She hasn't imagined it.

Victoria senses the same. "How vexed Grandmama would
be to know Serge has returned, and is so taken with you," she
says to Ella in a low voice as they walk into luncheon behind
the gentlemen.

"We needn't be in any hurry to tell her."

"Certainly not," Victoria agrees.

Once they've sat down, Serge declares his health strong. He
has returned out of a simple desire to repeat his very enjoyable
visit of last autumn and spend time with them here at beautiful
Wolfsgarten.

He says, "We barely touched on all there is to discuss about
Italy—isn't that true, Ella?"

She nods. "Very true."

"Ella has begun to study Italian," Alix pipes in. "After you
said it was a fine thing to do."

"Also, because I intend to return to Italy one day," Ella adds
quickly.

"I pray all my suggestions will be as well received," Serge
says, with a smile.

PROMPTLY AFTER THE meal, the skies open and rain comes
down in torrents. Victoria tactfully withdraws with the children, and Papa invites Serge and Ella to sit in the library with
him. Serge has brought the catalogue from the Städel Museum,
which he visited passing through Frankfurt. They examine it,
sitting side by side at the long oak table, while Papa, settled in
his favorite leather armchair, reads the *Darmstädter Zeitung*.

Soon, Serge excuses himself to retrieve something from his
room. The rain blows in wet gusts against the windows. A

log collapses in the hearth, sending a shower of sparks up the chimney. How snug and happy they are together inside, warm and dry.

When Serge returns and sets down a stack of three leather-bound volumes with gilded pages, she recognizes his edition of *The Divine Comedy.*

"As you now are a scholar of Italian, we must read together my favorite passage—the very last," he declares. He slides out the bottom book, flips to the back, and spreads open the pages so they both can read. He begins to recite, translating smoothly, *"As the geometer who sets himself to square the circle . . ."*

She follows as best she can until suddenly he halts. "You finish," he says, and places his finger at the spot on the page where he left off.

"I'm not able."

"You must try," he says, impatient.

She begins haltingly: *"Now my will . . . and my desire . . .* had come?"

"*Volgeva* is the imperfect, so here it means 'were turned' or 'were moved.'"

"Oh yes. *Now my will and my desire were turned as I like a perfect wheel . . ."*

"No, no, it's: *Now my will and my desire were turned like a wheel in perfect motion."*

She nods, hesitates—hoping he'll take over.

"Go on, my child," he says. "Final line now."

Very slowly she reads, *"By the love . . . that moves . . . the sun and the other stars."*

"Magnificent Dante," Serge says, sitting back in his chair, shaking his head. "Placing God at the heart of the entire mechanism of the universe; it's breathtaking—a stunning image."

He closes his eyes for a long minute. Gazing at him, Ella feels a welling up in her throat, a yearning to join him in spiritual communion with the poetry—to float above everyday existence, to be elevated, as he clearly is, by the beauty of the words.

THAT NIGHT THEY are six to dine: Ella and Victoria, Papa and Serge, and Madame de Kolemine with Prince Karl Isenburg, Papa's good friend, who has escorted her to Wolfsgarten.

Politics preoccupies the company. Serge is quizzed about conditions in his homeland since his father's assassination. Cousin Sasha has demanded that anarchists and nihilists across Russia be rounded up, and the Okhrana Guards, a special police force, are ferocious in their pursuit. Thousands have been arrested—expelled from Russia, or exiled to Siberia—on the mere suspicion of terrorist sympathies. Jews are targeted in particular. "Because they are so numerous in the ranks of the tsar's most committed enemies," Serge maintains.

As the conversation swirls and eddies around her, Ella is content to study Serge, in his elegantly tailored long black dinner jacket and his immaculate white linen waistcoat. The candlelight beautifully illuminates the sharp planes of his face—his long nose, his high, knobbed cheekbones, his square brow. Ella remembers from her book of English history the Plantagenet kings. Something about Serge's physiognomy recalls the portraits of those medieval crusaders. But her cousin's intensity—his arresting gaze—could any artist capture that in two dimensions? Or the limber gestures of his long, narrow hands, with slender fingers?

After a while, her own fingers itch for her sketchbook and pencils. She'd like to try and commit something of Serge to paper. Perhaps tomorrow she will have the opportunity.

"*Hoheit*, you find no fault with how your brother has answered terror with terror of his own?" Prince Isenburg asks Serge, breaking into Ella's musing.

"The tsar must introduce a constitution!" Victoria cuts in

before Serge can answer. "Your brother is only fueling the fire of dissent by delaying."

"To bend to the demands of murderers would be immoral," Serge replies calmly.

"Although it could be strategic," counters Isenburg. "No need for a radical document. In our German one, monarchial control is preserved in all crucial respects. The chancellor throws the socialists a few bones, keeping them docile . . . rules limiting working hours and such."

"We don't require a constitution. Autocracy has kept Russia strong for nearly three centuries," Serge answers.

"Autocracy's day is done, Serge!" Victoria declares.

"I fear, my dear cousin, you don't grasp how different Russia is," Serge says, smiling. "It's nothing like Germany, your newborn country of jealous little states corralled together by a military alliance of Herr Bismarck's devising. Nor is Russia anything like Britain, smug in its proclaimed liberalism, an avaricious society, where money is worshipped above all else."

"A very cynical view of our mother's homeland," Victoria grouses.

"To the contrary, an accurate one. Russia is a land apart, a civilization of its own, with a sacred tradition and unique history. It contains a multitude of tribes and requires a strong hand leading it, if it is not to fall to pieces."

"That sounds like a simple-minded excuse for repression," Victoria says.

Serge's eyes narrow, his mouth tightens, but his voice stays even. "Should the Russian people no longer regard the monarch as a paternal all-powerful lord, Russia will descend into chaos. The responsibility my brother now bears is staggering. A lesser man would be crushed by it."

"Heaven knows I am no advocate of liberalism, British liberalism or any other kind," Isenburg expounds. "Still, your brother's harsh reprisals haven't brought an end to the violence and political assassinations, have they? Ministers are still targeted. Wasn't the governor of Kharkov killed? And the governor of St. Petersburg too?"

"General Trepov was shot at close range, but he survived," Serge says.

Victoria rolls her eyes. "No need to worry, then?"

Serge frowns, picks up his wineglass, and examines its golden depths for a long moment before taking a sip.

The purring voice of Madame de Kolemine breaks the short silence. "For six years, Your Imperial Highness, I've lived here in Darmstadt, where the administration is quite benevolent," she says, bestowing upon Papa a fond smile. "I cannot claim to be current on matters in Russia. However, has the liberation of the serfs actually improved their lives? The peasantry remains terribly poor, does it not? And those unfortunates who move into the cities, abandoning the land, don't they live in a dire state?"

Serge nods. "Emancipation may have been my father's biggest mistake."

"Rubbish!" Victoria asserts. "It was a century or two overdue, and only half-done! The mass of people are justifiably dissatisfied with a mode of government entirely out of date!"

"What evidence can you muster for your view, Victoria?" Serge asks, twisting the gold ring he wears on the smallest finger of his left hand. "A society cannot be recast overnight—or not without tremendous bloodshed. Our people are not educated for participation in government. To grow and prosper, we require order. If tsardom collapses, Russia collapses. Thank God my brother resists the radicals and draws the reins of control in tightly. Thank God I am able to support him."

Papa leans forward. "Unlike my dogmatic eldest daughter, Serge, I won't question your beliefs, nor attempt to talk you out of them."

Serge nods again, curtly.

Papa continues. "I am aware that your faith in the regime is unwavering. And when has life in Russia ever been easy? My aunt Marie, your dear mother, learned that most painfully. However, the current situation strikes me as so very unpleasant. I hear from my brother-in-law, the Prince of Wales, that Anichkov Palace has been fortified with two ranks of trenches. Is it true? Sasha and Minnie imprisoned inside? Too terrified ever to venture beyond palace walls? Forced to take all their exercise in the walled garden?"

"The Prince of Wales is not up to date, Ludwig. Sasha and Minnie have moved. They reside at Gatchina now," says Serge. "It's a grand old palace outside of Petersburg, set in an enormous park, easy to guard, and far from troublemakers."

"Still, to feel constantly under threat from nihilists and revolutionaries?" Papa shakes his head. "It cannot be healthy."

Is Papa making this observation for a particular reason? For her benefit maybe? Ella wishes she knew. She also wishes they would discuss something other than the state of affairs in Russia.

Madame de Kolemine exclaims: "I've neglected to mention the news from this afternoon! Pablo de Sarasate has recovered and will give a concert in Darmstadt next week after all!"

Ella nearly laughs with relief. Trained as a diplomat's wife, this lady recognizes when a conversation needs redirecting. The talk turns to music, the candles burn down to stubs, and it is past midnight before they rise from the table.

AFTERWARD, UPSTAIRS, ELLA gets into bed, tired and oddly fretful, while Victoria sits down at the dressing table and begins plucking the pins out of her hair.

"You don't like Serge, then?" Ella asks abruptly. "You were so argumentative with him tonight."

Victoria laughs, shaking her head to loosen her thick blond

hair. "I like Serge very much. Clever, serious, and full of little
attentions to you."

"Why did you speak to him as you did—insulting his brother,
being rude about how things are run in Russia? Think how we'd
feel if he called Grandmama a sentimental old woman ruling
Britain according to her own whims?"

Victoria laughs again. "We would struggle to refute it!"

Ella scowls. Her sister is ignoring her point.

"You know I enjoy debate," Victoria says, graver now. "And
Serge is wrong. Russia can't continue in its current semifeudal
condition. Reform must come; it's just a matter of time."

"But he is our cousin, and our guest. You and Prince Isenburg
should have been much more courteous."

"Don't worry, Ellie. Serge is accustomed to defending his
brother's regime—and notice he has the confidence of a true
believer. The opinions of a minor German prince like Isenburg
can't shake him. And certainly none of mine will!"

Ella recalls Serge's face becoming taut and unsmiling in the
candlelight. Even if you know you are right, it can't be pleasant
to feel attacked.

Victoria turns down the lamp and climbs into her bed.

Addressing the dark, Ella says, shyly, "Should I ever end up
living in Russia . . ."

"If you choose to marry Serge, you will do him good. Soften
him, expose him to your very English outlook," says Victoria.

Ella giggles. "You mean like the one Grandmama claims
Louis has?"

"The very same," says Victoria.

THE FOLLOWING DAY, the weather turns sufficiently fine in the
afternoon to venture out. Serge proposes a ride, and Ella agrees.
Papa waves them off, promising to follow after he confers with
his gardeners.

The grassy court is so sodden, the grooms have put down wooden planks for people to walk on while crossing from the Herrenhaus to the stables opposite. Serge strides ahead. From behind, Ella admires his square shoulders, his tapering back, his narrow waist. He carries his impressive height with agile grace.

Once on horseback they find the sandy paths that cut through the woods have been sheltered by the trees, and only a few puddles remain. They travel a mile or so, saying nothing much at all. What does Serge intend for this excursion—of what will they speak? Not politics, she hopes.

Arriving on the banks of a narrow brook, Serge suggests they get down from the horses.

"Your sister Victoria is in such high spirits," he begins, stroking his mount idly.

"I'm sorry if she upset you last night," she says quickly. "She can be very disputatious and holds some radical views."

Serge shrugs. "People who have never been to Russia have difficulty properly understanding. Still . . ." He smiles at Ella. "I don't believe the opportunity to quarrel with me over dinner accounts for Victoria's great good humor."

Ella returns his smile, relieved. "While happy to see you, her real joy is to be soon marrying Louis—defying all those who say she mustn't do it."

"My sister Marie tells me even your redoubtable grandmother now endorses the match with Battenberg."

"She does," she says.

"Do you envy Victoria, free of doubts, excited about her future?"

"I envy Victoria soon to be free of responsibilities here, embarked on a new life. While I . . ."

"While you?"

"While I will remain here without her company. My brother

and sisters, although dear, don't offer the same quality of companionship."

"You admit to no desire to soon marry?" His tone is casual, but Ella flushes immediately. What is the proper answer to this?

He saves her by adding, "I have not felt certain, within myself, that I should marry, although it is expected of me."

"Why?"

"In the eyes of God, it is the most solemn and holy undertaking in any man's life."

She nods, without fully comprehending.

"I am by nature solitary—most at ease alone or with the men of my regiment. I don't crave female company, and I've never met a woman I thought worthy of marrying. Until . . ."

He glances down at the slow-moving stream.

"Until now," he says. His grave eyes rise to meet hers.

She feels her heart hammer, her blood surge. This is more than she expected, and so soon after his arrival. Overcome, she looks away.

"I have given it much thought since Paul and I visited here," he continues. "Now I feel I can be certain. And I would like to express to you what I believe." She hears a surprising note of appeal in Serge's voice and turns her eyes back to rest on his face.

"Russia is nothing like this," he says with a wide sweep of his hand. "Last night I tried to explain—it's a place apart, and to lead it, we all, all of us in my family, we must uphold something sacred. God gave us this destiny."

Regarding Serge, so resolute as he speaks of his righteous cause, she is reminded again of the crusading knights of old. "The responsibility can be isolating," he continues. "And to do it properly I believe one must walk a straight line. Not deviate, nor fall into temptation."

"I can't imagine you would ever—"

He quickly raises his hand to silence her.

"When I was here in the autumn, I saw how you, Ella, once a sweet, pretty little child, have become a great beauty. And with your sensitivity and your grace—well, it would be a waste to confine yourself to this pocket duchy. To live an insignificant, provincial life. To be *eine kleine deutsche Prinzessin* among so many others."

Isn't this exactly what she dares to believe of herself? Ella is both amazed and excited to hear Serge voice her secret ambitions aloud.

Face quite stern he says, "You should consider becoming my wife."

"Consider?" she replies, without thinking. Such a strange word to choose. She struggles to understand. Does he imagine a practical partnership? Something calculated? Not a love match?

"I cannot expect you to answer now. You don't know me well. And I have neglected first to speak with your father. But here, alone with you, I felt compelled to reveal how—"

He breaks off, a pained expression crosses his face, and he looks away. After a moment, he nods sharply, as if affirming something to himself, and turns back to her. "I am not as many other men are—who find it so easy to seek pleasure, considering one woman as good as another. It's a game to them."

He pauses again, as if to allow her to absorb his declaration, before adding: "And be assured, should you accept me, you will always be loved and you will tether me to the world. I will ever honor your innocence and your trust."

"Serge—"

His hand is up again, stopping her words. "If our lives on this earth require suffering, if we must tolerate calumny and witness sin, we can still live in accordance with our most sacred beliefs, and establish a home of order and piety, where corruption is banished and virtue honored."

Now she feels lost. What exactly is he talking about? Calumny? Corruption? General evil or something more specific? Apprehension sweeps over her. Her legs tremble. She is called upon to respond, but how?

"Ah, I see I have disturbed you," he says. "Inevitably, I think. But, Ella, I look at you and I see rare perfection."

The color mounts in her cheeks.

"Radiant, serene, chaste, you must never be sullied or reduced. And great opportunity awaits you. Come to Russia and you will enhance our society, and be, in turn, enhanced by it."

A splendid prospect, but is that what she desires? "My cherished aspirations are . . ." she begins, and then stops.

She changes tack. "My mother, you know, was such a good and high-minded person."

"I well remember. She was so very kind to me when I was a bashful boy."

"I think to honor her, I must live an exemplary life."

"Worthy of the goodness of your soul, and hers."

She nods, relieved that he understands.

"I will guide you!" he declares. "It will be my duty as husband, to direct and lead!" His vehement expression matches his words. His is a spirit of fire, naturally domineering. She admires this, and yet she feels herself drawing back. It's so much—maybe too much.

Apparently sensing her disquiet, he says encouragingly, "You will grow and learn. You are so young."

Still, her mind races. Serge sees only the outside of her now. Upon intimate acquaintance he may discover she lacks depth. She may not please him. He will not be generous in disappointment.

"Have no doubt, I will idolize you," he declares, unrestrained—his voice is loud. He drops the horse's bridle and steps toward her to cup her face with both his hands.

Looking into his striking green eyes, her nerves tingle, and her heart swoons in a dizzying way. Isn't it commendable to have earned his singular admiration? She senses the melting pleasure of surrender, the strong temptation to submit to his greater force, to be protected, cherished, and possessed by him.

But then a shadow crosses his face, the pained expression returns, and he drops his hands. "I entreat you: Please know this, please know me," he says. "I am capable of great devotion."

Now it is he who requires encouragement. "Yes," she answers.

"You agree to be my wife!" he exclaims.

Oh, he's misunderstood. She meant only to acknowledge the sincerity of his plea. She needs to consider his proposal further. Doesn't she? He said so himself. They should take more time to know each other better. Unsure whether to voice this, worried that her tentativeness reveals a weak will, unequal to his own, and bewildered—for she does respect him so—she stands silent, gazing up at him. His features soften, the mask of his steely control dissolves, and the eyes that meet hers widen and reveal a yearning soul. She cannot bear to correct him.

"Yes, I agree," she says.

VICTORIA CLAIMS TO be unsurprised. Papa is stunned.

"Ludwig, please excuse me," Serge says, standing in the library. "I meant to speak with you beforehand, but when I was out with Ella, I could not contain myself. I intended merely to raise the possibility with her, and instead . . ."

He stops here and turns to gaze at Ella standing a short distance away by the window.

"She accepted me. I am overjoyed," he finishes.

"This is all very sudden," Papa says, disgruntled.

"I'm not rash—you know me. I have thought constantly of Ella since my last visit."

Papa shakes his head. "I'm not giving my consent now. Nothing is to be said for the moment. On such a serious question we shouldn't be too hasty and also . . ." Now he addresses Ella. "You need to consider this very carefully, Ella. Serge does you a great honor, but you must think about how it will be to live in Russia, with all of its drawbacks, so very far from home."

She nods, attempting to look sober and obedient. But she feels rather light-headed—in the room but not.

Serge pleads. "Ludwig, please, can I not tell Paul in whom I have been confiding? And my sister Marie?" He turns to look at Ella. "Your future brother and sister endorse my choice wholeheartedly."

"*Ja*," Papa says. "You can tell those two, confidentially, but no one else outside my family here. I will not be rushed. Also, the marriage contract. Until I have something in my hand from Sasha, and I feel satisfied with all that's in it—only then can an engagement be announced."

Serge nods. "After his coronation, I will ask my brother for this. We will provide for Ella most generously. Of that you can hardly be in doubt, my dear Ludwig."

"And Ella will not change belief," Papa says sternly.

"She is not required to, no," Serge replies. He—all the Romanovs—are of the Orthodox faith.

Her father nods slowly. Is he warming to the idea? Ella can't tell.

THAT EVENING, SERGE appears euphoric—beaming, laughing, relishing the family's excitement.

"You will be the luckiest grand duke in the whole world if Ella is your wife," Alix tells him.

"Correct, my darling girl," he says, and he sweeps Alix up and perches her on the chimney piece.

"Put me down!" Alix says, shrieking with laughter.

"Serge is practically giddy, a word I never expected to apply to him," Victoria says later, as they get ready for bed.

Ella nods.

"You are completely happy too, dear Ellie?" her sister asks.

"Yes, although a bit dazed."

Victoria smiles. "I imagine. And think of Grandmama's shock, and displeasure."

Ella sighs. "Papa says he will write and tell her that an engagement is being contemplated. We can't have her hearing about it from Marie."

"Good thing," says Victoria. Everyone in the family knows the queen and her strident Russian daughter-in-law—married to her son Alfred, their uncle Affie—do not get on very well.

Ella lies awake for a long time. Serge's wife? Can she truly picture it? Perhaps the idea will feel more real tomorrow. When she closes her eyes, she sees again his elegant tapering back as he strides ahead of her, she hears his words of praise and summons up his handsome, noble face, vulnerable, for once, and longing for her.

THE NEXT MORNING Serge's demeanor has changed. He's retreated into a brooding silence. Is Ella already disappointing him? She fears so.

A final conversation between them, on the following afternoon, just before his departure, reveals more.

They stroll along the lane next to the kennels—the hounds bark frantically, bounding up against the mesh of their cages, eager to be released.

"Think how very eager they are to accompany us, rather than stay confined," Serge says with a smile.

"True, but they might streak off, never to return," she replies.

"And run into the forest and make it their own domain. Can you imagine it?"

She laughs. It's a sweet idea, the forest ruled by dogs.

The sound of barking fades behind them, and Serge, again somber, walks along wordlessly, his hands clasped behind his back. What is required of her? Some apt inquiry? Some worthwhile observation? All she manages to say is: "I will miss you when you've gone."

"I hope so," he replies. He does not look at her.

Finally, he sighs heavily. "I should confess something to you. My father did not behave well, in private, during the last years of his life. And this grieved me very much—I never condoned it."

So, this is what is preoccupying him? "Princess Yurievskaya?" she asks.

He gives her a brief, sharp look. "You know about her? What have you been told?"

"Papa said that while he was still married, your father had children with this lady."

"Yes, three. A most repugnant betrayal of our whole family," Serge says bitterly. "How Mama suffered, and nonetheless always remained loving and generous. She even allowed that wicked woman to move into the Winter Palace, afraid that my father might be targeted on his regular visits to her house on the English Quay. When Mama was lying on her deathbed, she could hear the lady's children running across the floor above. For all of this she forgave my father, but I never could."

"The princess no longer lives in Russia?"

"My brother gave her a fortune on the condition that she leave the country. She's taken her children to live in France."

She nods, waiting for more.

"That the father whom I worshipped could behave so despicably haunted my childhood, for Papa took up openly with this young woman, his ward, when Paul and I were still young. Mama urged me to pray for my father, to forgive him, and I did try. But after Mama died it was as if our family's guardian angel flew away. My father, corrupted by lust, married his concubine. We were all obligated to dance around her, simulate affection and respect. And then his dreadful murder—everything turned to ashes. Even as I mourned my father I raged at him for what he'd ruined and how he'd left us. I hated him even as I loved him, and I despaired of the barren future without him. For months I was overcome with this . . . this turmoil. I am calmer now. But I swore then, and I swear to you today, I will never harness a woman's life to mine and treat her in such a reprehensible manner as Papa did Mama."

He imagines she doesn't know this? "Serge, I—"

He cuts her off. "Also, I warn you, as soon as I leave here, people will rush to tell you what a mistake it would be to marry me."

"Are you thinking of my English grandmother? It's true, she will be anxious about my moving to Russia."

Serge shakes his head. "Others, too, will feel free to condemn me, condemn your choice."

"Are you aware I refused the man Grandmama and numerous others believed would be my ideal husband?" Ella asks.

"My sister mentioned this," he replies, flashing a brief smile. "I'm glad you didn't find a self-satisfied Prussian officer to your taste."

"The tedium might have killed me," she answers tartly.

She expects a laugh—or at least another smile—but Serge remains grim. "Many people believe me cold, arrogant, a reactionary with unacceptable views. Your own sister, even."

"Victoria is very fond of you. Haven't you noticed how pleased she is for us?"

"I suppose that's because she knows your heart well, and sees how you have generously carved out a place in it for me."

"Exactly," she answers, happy to be so recognized.

"Thus, I must trust you."

"Of course, you must!"

"All right then. I choose to trust you," he says quietly. "I choose to believe that you will rely on your own assessment of my character when others inevitably attack it."

"And I will," she answers stoutly.

He stops, faces her, and places his hands on her shoulders. He bends down to kiss her forehead. "God bless you, my child."

It's benediction—bestowed with a kiss.

AFTER SERGE LEAVES, Ella finds herself unmoored. The new tsar's coronation is to take place in a month's time, and afterward Serge will join Sasha and his wife, Minnie, on a long tour of Russia. Meanwhile, Ella will spend the summer in Britain.

As time carries her away from Serge—away from his tall figure, his intent expression, the force of him—doubts blossom in her mind. Are they well-suited? Didn't she initially agree to his proposal so as not to disappoint him? She admires his dignified demeanor—even the melancholy strain in his manner speaks of a profound soul. She's flattered to enjoy his high regard. She hasn't forgotten the swooning sensation she felt standing close to him on the afternoon of his proposal. But does she ever feel truly at ease with him? Isn't she always a bit on guard? And they never share jokes or tease one another as she sees Louis and Victoria doing constantly.

In her mind's eye she stands in front of a tall iron door, resembling the door of the Duomo in Florence, open to a mysterious, shadowy place that she can't properly make out, but it's something like an Aladdin's cave, lanterns glowing in secret reaches, agate and jasper and other precious jewels piled on the floor, stone walls veined with gold. This is Russia to her, dramatic and intriguing, although a bit dangerous too. And, it's undeniable, she is hesitant to cross the threshold. Perhaps anyone would be, contemplating such a big step. But Victoria seems to be rushing toward life with Louis as fast as she can, arms open wide. Shouldn't Ella feel likewise?

As for Papa, he acts oddly short with her. Is he still irritated she accepted Serge, at least provisionally, before the matter was appropriately raised with him? Would it help if she admitted she's still thinking things over? That she is in no great hurry to be formally engaged? Yet should she confess to any uncertainty, will Papa then decide for her? Insist on shutting the tall door? She's not sure she wants that either.

Papa goes into Darmstadt to attend to state business. Ella assumes he will also visit Madame de Kolemine. Perhaps his lady will improve Papa's mood.

On a subsequent sunny morning, Ella sits on the ledge of the fountain in front of the Herrenhaus, dragging her hand idly in the water, making glistening streaks on the surface. Lost in thought, she doesn't hear Papa approach, noticing him only when he sits down beside her. He has changed into his country clothes—a soft slouch hat and an ancient riding jacket patched at the elbows.

"Hullo, you're back!" she says.

"Hullo, my dear," he replies, very genial. "Are you feeling well?"

"Very well."

"Not pining?"

"Pining a bit. I might roust myself and go inside and write to Serge," she answers, smiling.

"Well, then, I have chosen an excellent moment for my little speech."

Ella tips her head, quizzical.

"*Ja*, I've been mulling things over." He pushes his hat back and knocks his forefinger against his forehead. "Often this brain must grind like a mill before I properly understand my own thoughts."

A brief pause, then he says: "I have known Serge for his whole life, you know that?"

"I do."

"Such a solemn, awkward lad! He wore high boots even as a small child. Your mother called him her favorite Puss in Boots, to make him smile. He adored her."

"I like to picture it," Ella says.

"When I see the two of you together, I noticed how he is so . . . how to say it . . . so entranced by you." Papa gives her a fond smile. "A Russian grand duke, son of one tsar, brother of another, Serge could have made a far more brilliant match—a lady from a ruling house. I'm sure the empress hoped he'd fancy one of your Prussian cousins—Moretta, perhaps."

Papa chuckles at the thought of Prussian ambition thwarted. "But, instead, Serge has chosen you, and that speaks very well of him."

He nods. She nods. What is Papa trying to say?

"And, *Liebes*, the splendor of that court, it has to be seen to be believed. The Romanov palaces make this place seem like a paltry holding." Papa scans his favorite property before turning frank eyes directly at her. "Should you marry Serge, you will become—at a stroke—a very wealthy woman."

She will, won't she? Able to buy all the gowns and hats she ever fancies. And, of course, do good. Once she is rich, she will also be extremely charitable.

"*Ach*, if only you might make this marvelous match and still never leave me," her father adds.

Her throat tightens. Poor Papa. Can she really move so far away from him?

"Impossible, of course," he goes on. "And if marrying Serge is truly what you desire, I will agree. However . . ."

He draws out of his pocket a silver cross threaded on a thin chain.

"That's Mama's, isn't it?" she asks, surprised to see it again after four years.

"Yes, I've carried it with me since she died, but now I've decided you must have it. Give me your hand."

She holds her right hand out, palm up, and carefully he feeds the rippling chain downward, making a small nest and resting the delicate cross on top. Then he closes up her fist and squeezes it.

"Thank you," she says, very touched.

"Do you remember your confirmation?" Papa asks now.

"Of course."

"And the confession of faith you made?"

"Yes."

"Recite it. Start with the rector's part."

"Pfarrer Sell asked: 'Do you, Elisabeth, as a member of the Evangelical Lutheran Church, intend to continue steadfast in the confession of this Church and suffer all, even death, rather than fall away from it?'"

"And your reply?"

"I answered: 'I do so intend, with the help of God.'"

"*Ja*," he says, squinting at her in the strong light. "Your mother would not have wanted you to break that promise. You must never forsake the faith of your fathers."

"But I don't mean to!"

"Promise me," he says.

"I promise."

For a moment Papa falls silent. "When my aunt Marie met Serge's father, she was fourteen, you know?" he asks.

"Yes."

"And only sixteen when she traveled to Russia to be married. Because her husband was to be tsar one day there was no question; she had to change beliefs. She was received into the Orthodox church a week before her wedding."

Why is Papa going over this? The fourth of five brothers, Serge was never likely to become tsar—and now Sasha has three sons of his own.

"Russia was difficult for my aunt for many reasons," her father continues. "And while she had no choice, the sacrifice of her religion was the start of a pattern—a pattern of submitting to the will of her husband. In the years that followed she continued to submit, even permitting him to move his mistress into her home."

He shakes his head, disgusted.

"Papa, Serge never condoned that attachment," Ella says. "He told me he hated how his father betrayed his mother—to say nothing of ignoring Christian teaching."

"Nevertheless, as I envision you going to Russia, marrying Serge, I find myself reflecting on my aunt's life."

"Serge is so honorable! He will never behave to me as his father did."

"*Ja*, that sort of bad behavior I doubt he will indulge in."

"What concerns you then?"

He pats her knee. "You are the most compassionate and empathetic of characters, *liebe* Ella. Married to Serge you will upon occasion need to answer his strength with your own. Will you be capable?"

"Serge won't compel me to do anything contemptible," she says.

"You are not hearing the question. Can you imagine disagreeing with him?"

"On what matters will we disagree?"

"Religious questions, political questions. In public, as his wife, it will be your duty to support him. But privately you must believe yourself free—your conscience your own—to voice your views, and most importantly to worship as you choose— whatever pressure is brought to bear. Do you understand?"

"I suppose."

Papa nods. "*Gut*. When you write to Serge next, please remind him that you will live and die in the Evangelical faith."

"Having promised this to you today, Papa, I won't break my promise," she says stiffly.

"If you are so resolved, Ella, what's the difficulty in writing it out?" And he pats her knee again. "I will wait to hear how he answers."

He stands and whistles for Tyrus.

"I am glad to have told you all this—it's been weighing on me," he adds, smiling, squashing down his hat to make it firm on his head. And he ambles off, his dog at his side, heading toward the green-painted doors of the stables, flung open on this lovely, sun-filled day.

Ella remains sitting by the fountain, disheartened and faintly indignant.

SHE DOES WHAT her father requests and has a reply from Serge a week later. He understands her commitment and respects it. Any children born to them, however, must be baptized Orthodox, and there will frequently be Orthodox services they will attend as a couple. But her personal belief remains her choice.

This letter, like Serge's two previous ones, is written in a spidery hard-to-decipher hand, in red-brown ink. He uses a formal French, requiring her to look up a few of the words. She rereads the letter from time to time, but she doesn't answer it. She tells herself preparations for her trip to Britain are keeping her too busy. She will write from Windsor, or from Balmoral in Scotland, where Grandmama plans to take her in June.

Papa moves them all back into town. Ella has daily fittings with the dressmaker. Frau Hoyer is sewing two new dresses for her and unpicking three from last summer to remake to follow fashion—bodices are even tighter this year; skirts are draped over underskirts garlanded with fringed-out flounces. Between fittings, she visits Zorn's shop in the Luizenplatz to buy small presents for the aunts and uncles and cousins she'll see in England.

On these rounds it occurs to her that should she in the future be going not west but east, to become Serge's wife, she won't be arriving in a familiar country where she speaks the language, is aware of the customs, and has dozens of relations. She'll instead travel to a place completely foreign, where she knows no one well, and where members of the ruling house live in some peril. Will she be equal to this? Since her conversation with Papa her misgivings have multiplied.

Victoria senses her state of mind. "You refused Fritz of Baden and he lived," she says to Ella on the evening before her departure, when they sit together on the terrace steps, in the rosy twilight, listening to the late birdsong.

"But I knew from the first I didn't want to marry Fritz." Ella is fingering the silver cross—Mama's cross—that she wears every day now.

"You can care for Serge and still not want him as your husband," Victoria says.

"Can I?" She is asking herself as much as her sister.

"Certainly! Take your time away to think things over in peace. Goodness, I forgot," Victoria says, and she laughs. "You will have to cope with Grandmama's objections. She will likely be bombarding you with new ones every day."

"I do hate contentiousness," Ella says.

"In this case it could be useful."

"Why? Because you believe I should give up the idea?"

"No. Not at all. I see how you admire Serge. But being obligated to defend something—or in this case, someone—isn't that a fine way to discover if he's worth defending?"

"Maybe for you. I prefer a quiet life," she says, wistful.

"You defied all the Prussians. Grandmama is only one person."

"True, although never someone easy to dismiss."

"You won't do that," Victoria says. "You will listen and think and come to the best decision—your own."

Chapter Four

The Queen Carries the Day

Windsor Castle, May 1883

Oh poor, poor Grandmama. Dressed in her usual coal-black, with her thinning hair pulled back into a tiny bun covered with a scrap of white lace, the queen looks haggard, her skin pasty and her shoulders oddly hunched. Ella has only ever known her in mourning—perpetually for Grandpapa, and then for Mama. Now, bereft of her favorite servant, John Brown, the queen appears not only sad but defeated.

Nor does Ella's arrival improve matters much.

"Just to see you brings back endless dear recollections. How like your mother you've become," Grandmama says, protuberant eyes swimming with tears. "Baby, I need a fresh handkerchief," she says to Aunt Beatrice, who immediately produces a folded, starched square. The queen's youngest child, Beatrice has the unenviable task of supporting her mother as both companion and secretary.

Ella attempts to divert her grandmother, during a half hour's conversation in the Green Drawing Room, by reporting on the ailments of everyone in Darmstadt: Irène's intermittent tooth pain, Papa's gout, the sad fate of Ernie's cocker bitch, Gracie, who recently went lame and had to be put down.

The queen seems brighter, until she tries—and fails—to rise from her chair.

"Wait, Mama," says Beatrice, and hurries over with two sticks. Grandmama recently tripped on the stairs and now her right foot is so swollen that she has trouble walking.

"I am a desolate old woman and my cup of sorrow overflows," she tells Ella before Beatrice helps her upstairs to an early bed.

Her aunt returns and shakes her head. "She found Brown's presence so soothing. Every day is hard now without him. Mama complains no one cares for her as tenderly as he did."

"Oh dear, how difficult for you, with all your kind efforts," Ella says.

"I will be content if only she would cheer up a bit," her aunt answers, with a brief smile. "I have high hopes for your visit, Ella! A fresh face, and one she's been longing to see."

Has Beatrice heard of Serge's proposal? If so, she makes no reference to it.

THE NEXT DAY is the queen's sixty-fourth birthday. On account of her low mood and painful foot, she decrees no celebration and no visitors, only to breakfast with Ella and Beatrice under the trees near the royal mausoleum at Frogmore, with a period of quiet contemplation beside Grandpapa's tomb to follow.

On this mild morning, the breeze is gentle and the sun peeks out from between downy clouds. They drive out of the castle and down the Long Walk in an open barouche, drawn by a pair of sleek matching grays. Ella marvels at the broad view, and at the great, unruffled peace of England. What a tidy, equable realm this is—everything in its proper place, fields neatly plowed and hedged, the people purposeful, the queen secure on her ancient throne.

Men, walking along the road, doff their hats at the sight of the sovereign. Under a green-fringed parasol, head settled into the folds of her neck, Grandmama stares straight ahead. She's thinking, Ella is certain, not of those loyal subjects within view but of the dear departed missing from her own circle.

Turning into the entrance of Frogmore House, the carriage proceeds in dappled light under a canopy of trees. The scent of flowers wafts over them—pungent lilac, musky azalea, sweet and spicy hawthorn. A white-clothed table, set under a large elm, awaits, and ten yards distant, behind tall bushes, is a flapped serving tent, out of which swish black-jacketed pages who ferry cups of coffee, plates of eggs and bacon, marmalade jars and racks of toast.

After the meal, Ella and Aunt Beatrice walk on either side of the queen as she stumps, very slowly, up the stairs, and into the large mausoleum she had built for Grandpapa, where she plans to join him someday.

They pass a half an hour inside, Grandmama sitting on a small bench, Ella strolling around the soaring interior in the shape of a cross and peering at the elaborate marble walls.

"I sense your admiration for this special place," the queen says, smiling up at Ella as they leave. "How proud dear Albert would have been of you, Ella. You share his deeply feeling nature, his artistic eye."

"If only I could have known him," she replies. Grandpapa died three years before her birth.

"My angel," Grandmama says, sighing.

Unfortunately, it has started to rain. A footman must carry the queen down the stairs and across the grass to the carriage. She scolds him for jostling her, tipping her this way and that, first carrying her too high and then too low.

"Poor man," whispers Beatrice. "His great crime is not to be Brown."

As he asked specially, and has always been a good friend to all of them in Darmstadt, Uncle Leo is permitted to call at teatime. He's eager to bring his new baby to meet Ella. Mama doted on Leo, her youngest brother—the cleverest member of the family she frequently stated. It's a great shame he has never enjoyed good health. If cut, Leo will bleed copiously, bruises appear on his skin after the slightest knock, and blood pools inside his joints. Sweet little Frittie, Ella's brother now gone, suffered from a similar ailment—his blood vessels lacked the correct adhesiveness, Mama explained.

On account of his malady Leo was for years forbidden by his mother the queen to take a wife. But last year he persuaded her to allow him to marry Princess Helen of Waldeck and Pyrmont, a nice young woman from a German principality not far from Darmstadt.

"We named the baby Alice after your mother, of course," he tells Ella as she sits beside him cuddling the tiny girl.

"Such a darling." Ella smooths the baby's white muslin dress. "And you look awfully well, dear Leo!"

Her uncle, in former times always pale and wan, frequently limping from swollen knees, today has good color and walks without a cane.

"Your favorite old uncle is not only a husband now, and a father, but a peer—Duke of Albany, with a seat in the Lords," he says, beaming. "Beaconsfield entreated Mama, and my brother Bertie too. I am grateful."

"Your new life clearly suits you."

He smiles broadly. "Also, Mama pays me a great compliment—asking for my help with the foreign questions on which her cabinet consults her. As Papa once did."

"You like that work?" says Ella.

"I do. Now, let's give Alice back to her nurse—I must speak seriously with you." He gestures to the white-aproned nursemaid in the corner, who comes and collects the baby from Ella.

"What is this that I hear about you and the notorious Grand Duke S.?" Leo asks.

She feels herself coloring.

"Ah, so it's true," says her uncle. "Well, I have not met the man. His sister Marie describes him as a sensitive, honorable man who is thoroughly misunderstood. She insists people mistake his reticent manner for cruel hauteur."

Uncle Leo raises his eyebrows, skeptical.

"Serge is quite reserved," Ella says.

"Although not retiring—none of the Romanovs are."

She gives him a puzzled look.

"I correspond from time to time with Sir Edward Thornton, who recently took over as our ambassador in St. Petersburg," Leo explains. "Thornton, like Lord Dufferin before him, is alarmed that the Russians continue to stir up trouble, threatening the peace, interfering in the Balkans. No appeal to the tsar, his ministers, or any one of his brothers is fruitful. The Romanovs are adamant—that area must remain exclusively a Russian sphere of influence." Leo shakes his head. "And at home the new tsar is reversing the welcome reforms undertaken by his father, exiling all his opponents and relentlessly persecuting the non-Orthodox. Meanwhile, Russia is changing rapidly— every year more factories, more railways, more mines. The tremendous gulf between the masses and the small, wealthy ruling class grows ever wider. This is not merely unjust, Ella— it's dangerous. Russia is like a colossal gas boiler, the pressure mounting inside. One day it will blow."

Leo looks at her sternly. She struggles to think. What should she say? What would Serge say? She recalls the contentious dinner at Wolfsgarten.

"I believe it's Serge's opinion," she begins, tentative, "that because Russia is a rather different sort of place, not as advanced as other countries in Europe, the Russian people aren't yet ready for the kind of government men like you would approve of."

"An argument both self-serving and tragically short-sighted," Leo says sharply.

"Possibly I am not stating it correctly."

"No, that's the gist of the Romanov view. You've parroted it obediently."

This remark stings.

"Dear girl, Mama dreadfully opposes this marriage. She's told you so?" her uncle asks.

Ella shakes her head.

"She will. And in other circumstances, I would urge you to ignore her." He smiles briefly and adds: "I did, and I am so happy for it."

They both, simultaneously, look across the room at Princess Helen—now Duchess of Albany, a dainty brunette with a turned-up nose—chatting with Beatrice and the queen.

"But have you any idea what you'd be getting into?" Leo says. "Russia is nothing like Britain. All of us in this family—Mama, Bertie, Affie, me—what we value above all else is the goodwill of our countrymen. In fact, we strive ever to *deserve* this goodwill. I fear the attitude of the Romanovs is completely opposite. They believe they are owed everything and their people are owed nothing. They insist they have a sacred right to rule. Their countrymen are of no real consequence to them. The lower orders must obey—only that."

Ella feels her stomach pinch. Why must Leo be so condemnatory?

"Is this the family you wish to join?" he continues. "Will you be comfortable raising your children amongst them? In that provocative, reactionary atmosphere?"

She can't think of any answer. Fortunately, just then Grand-mama calls out, sharply: "Leopold, come now, don't monopo-lize Ella."

He shoots an irritated look at his mother. Then he says to Ella, "I suppose we must join the others. But promise me you will consider what I've said?"

"Yes, certainly," she says, falsely bright.

"Won't you visit us at Claremont? Then we can talk together at length. You know, don't you, that Helen and I live in the loveliest house in England?"

"Papa mentioned something of the kind."

"A man with excellent taste, your father," he says, smiling now. "You're a sterling soul, my dear Ella, as kind and generous as you are beautiful. How proud your mother would be of you! I don't wonder Grand Duke Serge wishes you for his wife. And perhaps he can make you happy, but you mustn't be blind. Think carefully. See him—and crucially, see Russia, for what it is."

She nods and smiles, but inside she feels flattened.

GRANDMAMA GROWS IMPATIENT to leave Windsor and go north to Scotland. But before undertaking the arduous journey, she must, her physician Sir James Reid advises, spend a further fortnight living quietly and exercising only gently. Ella walks with her grandmother each afternoon around the Norman Tower, where cornflowers grow in the grassy banks, or through the gardens of Frogmore, where their outings always include a stop at the mausoleum. Her grandmother invariably talks about the past, when Grandpapa still lived, and all her nine children, including Ella's mother, were small.

One tranquil afternoon, as they slowly circle the Frogmore pond, the water shining silver in the sun, the queen says, "To have you to myself is such a great pleasure, Ella. I can't think of anyone's company I prefer."

"I had hoped to be of some comfort, and to enliven you a little," Ella answers, most sincerely.

"You have done both," her grandmother says with a small sigh, then falls quiet.

Ella holds her breath. Is this the moment? Every day she expects the queen to launch into a broadside against Serge. But her grandmother has not once uttered his name. They stroll along silently for a few minutes, before Grandmama begins to marvel at the day's heat.

Does her grandmother believe that if she simply ignores the topic, then she, Ella, will abandon any thought of marrying Serge? Or perhaps she is waiting for Ella to raise the matter, only to rain scorn and disapproval down upon her? Not a cheery prospect.

Life here at Windsor is so comfortable. Ella occupies her own capacious suite on the castle's second floor, and is often at leisure to walk along the hushed, red-carpeted corridors, studying the imposing landscapes and portraits hung on the walls. The air smells pleasantly of beeswax—used to polish the furniture and keep the miles of wood paneling gleaming. Her grandmother constantly praises her looks and her manners. "*Du bist wie eine Blume*, Ella," the queen says, quoting a favorite poem of Heine's, likening her to a flower.

But the unaddressed question of her possible marriage hangs in the air. Like a lonely gray cloud floating incongruously under a dome of bright-blue summer sky, it cannot be wished away.

PROMPTLY UPON THEIR arrival at Balmoral in the early evening, Grandmama asks Ella to accompany her to a special place on the grounds, where she plans to have a memorial statue erected in Brown's honor. It's no great distance, a mere ten yards beyond the far end of the parterre on the left. But Grandmama, weary from the long journey, her foot throbbing, has the pony trap brought around, and Ella drives them there.

The queen points to a large salmon-red plinth in place, clearly visible from the lane, on top of a small rise, awaiting the arrival of the statue. "It's made from the finest Aberdeenshire granite, the same as dear Albert's tomb. Let's climb down and see it properly."

Ella obediently drops the reins, steps out, and comes around the vehicle to help the queen out. Leaving the white pony to nose in the bushes, they walk along a narrow path, Grandmama's arm tucked in hers.

"I have lost the dearest friend I ever had," she says. "You remember how devoted we were to each other."

"I do. He was always so faithful, Grandmama."

"Isn't this a lovely spot?"

"Very lovely."

"Good Brown. For thirty-four years he served us, and for the last eighteen and a half he didn't leave me for a day. Anticipating my every wish. I miss him hourly."

Her grandmother drops Ella's arm and they stand side by side gazing up at the empty plinth.

"I can no longer be silent, darling Ella," she says. "The idea that you would marry a Russian grand duke and move to that dreadful country, it sends shivers up my spine."

Ella—not anticipating the swift pivot to this subject—is rendered momentarily speechless.

"I have felt quite unable to refer to it until now, it upsets me so, but here, where I feel close to beloved Brown, I have found the strength," the queen declares.

"I hate to add to your distress, Grandmama," Ella says anxiously.

The queen shifts her weight and groans softly—her foot must be bothering her.

"Wouldn't you be more comfortable indoors?" Ella asks. Light lingers in the midsummer sky, but the air is chill.

The queen ignores her. "Since your mother died, I have felt responsible for you—and for your brother and your sisters too."

"We are all forever grateful."

"In the past weeks I have felt your tender care for me in return, the dutiful love of a cherished child for her mother," the queen says, gazing up at her fondly. "You are always gracious and *posée*, as well as so very lovely—oh dear Ella, you mustn't walk into that lion's den."

Ella feels the instinct to answer, mollifyingly: *Don't worry, I won't marry him.* But a small voice of conscience holds her back. Didn't she promise Serge she would trust her own assessment of his character? Will she throw him over at the first airing of her grandmother's disapproval?

"Your mama always said she would never hear of it—would *never* hear of one of her girls going to Russia." The queen's voice quavers.

"Papa recalls she rather doted on Serge," Ella answers.

"Of course your mother was generous to your Russian relations!" Grandmama snaps. "That is neither here nor there. With your refined character I can see nothing worse than living in Russia, which is in such a disgraceful state. What's more, your health will never stand the Russian climate, which killed your poor great aunt Marie."

"I'm blessed with a strong constitution."

The queen looks up at her beadily. "So it must be your head has been turned by the Romanov riches."

"Not at all. I admire Serge. He's a serious, deeply religious soul. You would like him if you met him, I am quite sure."

"No, I would not like him. And I know that he—that *they*—simply want to procure you. For you are a most wonderful prize."

"I don't believe so, Grandmama. Serge thought it over for months before proposing to me."

"Perhaps he did! Which changes nothing. The ostentatious ways of the Romanov family are distasteful. And the Petersburg court is decadent, pernicious, and morally lax, worse even than Berlin—as stiff and ludicrous as the Prussians surely are."

The queen wrinkles her nose as if sniffing sour milk.

"Serge is not taken up with court doings. He has an important command," Ella says.

"Command?!" she replies scornfully. "The disordered state of things in that country is so bad that at any moment something frightful may occur. The last tsar was hunted like a hare, and the new one is not safe on his throne."

"But Serge isn't tsar."

"You believe that will protect him? That he'll never be an assassin's target? Don't be naïve! It was only a few years ago when criminals stuffed dynamite underneath the dining room of the palace in St. Petersburg, intending to blow up the entire family. Some unforeseen delay in serving the meal saved them all."

Ella's stomach is tightening, and her spirits sinking.

"You trust and admire your uncle Leopold. I saw him speaking with you. Didn't he tell you that Russia is diseased to the core?"

"He told me of his reservations and—"

"You would ignore Leo?" Grandmama interrupts. "You and Victoria used to follow him around like baby goslings! And let me be clear. I could *not* have a Russian grand duke around me, an arrogant fellow spouting his reactionary opinions. Your Serge imagines himself perfect, yes?"

"Oh, no, Grandmama, he doesn't. Not at all." Ella feels on solid ground for a brief moment.

The queen sighs and drops her eyes. "You will be quite lost to me," she says in a sad voice. "Another wrenching loss, after all the many I have suffered."

"I would remain devoted, Grandmama. Even if I marry Serge."

"Oh, Ella," she continues, shaking her head. "You are such a lovely, trusting young woman, it's agony to watch you be taken in."

"No, I don't want to be." Ella's voice is tremulous now.

Once more addressing the space above the plinth stone Brown will one day fill, Grandmama declares, her voice rising: "Because your mother was so cruelly taken from you, you are vulnerable. You can be lured into a country where no one of rank is safe. Who knows what dreadful fate awaits you!"

A wave of dread crashes over Ella—a sudden undammed flood of grief. She can't deny it. No wise maternal hand, sure but light, rests on her back, steering her forward. She must make the most important decision of her life without a mother's counsel. What will living in Russia with Serge be like? Will they be happy together? It's so difficult to know.

Her grandmother again fixes her beseeching eyes directly on her. "Ella, I am sure that when your dear mother was on her deathbed, she took comfort knowing *I* remained. She assumed I would protect and help all of you children. Should you wed this Serge, I will have failed in my task. Failed utterly."

It is true—Grandmama is the nearest thing she has to a mother. Can she really marry in defiance of her objections? Against Uncle Leo's advice?

"I suppose you are right," Ella says, shivering. She feels so cold standing out here. "I suppose I must refuse him."

"Certainly I am right."

"But he's such a good man, Grandmama, very noble." Her voice cracks, her eyes fill.

"There, there, dearest. You are young and have so little experience of the world. It's best to let me guide you."

"How disappointed he will be." And how feeble of her to have given in so readily. Tears roll down her cheeks.

"Better that than agreeing to an unfortunate marriage."

"Would it really have been that?"

"Most definitely."

Leaning heavily on her stick with one hand, her grandmother reaches out the other to stroke Ella's left arm. "You mustn't worry any more. Know how very proud I am of you, darling girl. I count you as one of my very own."

"I am happy for that," Ella says softly, wiping her tears away with her sleeve.

Despite herself, she begins to relax. The struggle is over and she is on the other side of a confrontation she has dreaded for weeks. She takes a deep breath and looks around her, at the wooded hills, and the pale sky above. In the west, the low, grayish clouds are streaked with yellow from the setting sun. She feels her feet on the ground beneath her, her sturdy legs holding her up. She will not collapse. She will turn away from the door Serge held open to her, but she will be able to walk past, to go forward toward another fate, whatever that might be.

THE NEXT FEW days are very wet, and on the third, although the drizzling rain continues, Grandmama is determined to proceed with her plan for an afternoon picnic in the Ballochbuie Forest, five miles from the castle.

Ella and Beatrice travel in an open carriage with the queen. A kitchen maid and a second driver follow in a wagon. When they all arrive at Grandmama's chosen spot, damp despite umbrellas, a board is placed across the wagon and Ella watches the young servant, looking wet, woebegone, and overawed, setting out the tea, her hands shaking.

"Let me see to this," Ella says to the girl. "Go stand under the big tree over there, where it will be drier."

The queen notices. "How very capable you are, my dear," she

says. "Don't you believe your first duty now is to remain with your father for a few years, until the children are older?"

"I do, Grandmama." Ella smiles and passes her grandmother the first cup.

"Irène is not quick." Grandmama sighs. "And Ernie so inattentive to his studies, most concerning given his future position."

"And there's Alicky, still quite small," says Ella. To avoid confusion with Aunt Alix, Uncle Bertie's wife, Grandmama always calls Ella's youngest sister Alicky, and the rest of the English family follows suit.

"Well, frankly, I worry least about Alicky," the queen says. "Such a bright and conscientious little girl, and quite beautiful, with those lovely light eyes and that shining mane of golden hair!"

"Yes." Ella smiles.

"I can confess to you now, dear Ella, that since your mother's death, I have feared your dear father might drift into an unfortunate misalliance."

Lucky thing Grandmama has not heard of Papa's attachment to Madame de Kolemine. And likely never will, as even in Darmstadt few are aware.

"One of the Württemberg princesses was recently widowed," Grandmama continues. "I thought perhaps Ludwig might—"

"Oh, I don't think Papa intends to marry again," Ella interjects, eager to halt her speculation.

"No? Ludwig strikes me as a man who doesn't like to be alone," says Grandmama, and swallows the last of her tea. "Of course, a widow with children and property brings complications. Better someone unencumbered."

The wheels of her grandmother's mind spin always toward making matches.

"For the time being, Grandmama, Papa can rely on me," Ella says.

IN THE MIDDLE of August, they depart Balmoral for Osborne House, by the sea, on the Isle of Wight. Three days later Ella receives a sad letter from Alix asking her why she has stayed away so long. Papa apparently complains aloud that Ella has forgotten about them altogether.

At luncheon Ella announces she must leave in two days' time. Her grandmother's face immediately falls into a forlorn expression.

"I'm dreadfully disappointed. It has occurred to me you haven't seen your cousin Eddy in an age. Yesterday I wrote to the dear boy asking if he might join us here next week. You'll find him much improved, Ella."

Her eldest Wales cousin improved? In what way? And why is her grandmother so eager to bring Eddy here? She notices, across the table, Aunt Beatrice smiling into her soup.

Ah, the single-minded queen has a new notion—that Ella might marry Eddy.

"I'm certain Eddy has become a nice young man; he was such a sweet boy," Ella says, fibbing. She remembers this cousin as rather a dolt. "Still, you said so yourself, dearest Grandmama, my duty is to support Papa, be *Landesmutter*, and help with the children. I begin to think that will be my life."

Her grandmother laughs. "Ella, you are far too lovely not to marry one day." Then a frown. "But never, ever to a Russian!"

BACK AT WOLFSGARTEN, Ella tackles the necessary task immediately, writing a short letter to Serge. After much thought, she tells him, she has concluded that she would not be happy living in Russia. Ella begs his pardon for any pain she has caused him, and she hopes their affectionate bond, as cousins, is not severed permanently by her decision.

Chapter Five

A Brother Takes Advice

Schloss Ehrenburg, Coburg, September 1883

Serge receives Ella's letter while staying in Coburg as a guest of the old duke, along with his sister Marie and her cloddish British husband, Affie.

Serge has heard nothing from Ella in nearly three months. He reads the letter, and for an hour afterward he sits alone in his room, sunk in despair. Ella sees through him. She has intuited somehow that he's defective. And she seemed like such a child! How did she manage it?

He will go home now. He'll have to, his hopes dashed.

There's a sharp, peremptory knock, and the door swings open. His sister, short, plump, and square-shouldered, sweeps in.

"We have the date fixed?" Marie demands.

It had been their intention, as soon as Ella returned from England, to travel to Darmstadt with the proposed marriage contract, and once Ludwig agreed to all it contained, formalize the engagement.

"There is no date. She will have nothing more to do with me," Serge says.

Marie's mouth drops open. "She breaks it off?"

"Yes."

Anger blazes across his sister's face. "This is the queen's doing!" Marie exclaims.

"Ella doesn't say that—only that she cannot be happy living in Russia." Serge offers up the single piece of paper. His sister bats it away.

"I've suspected the queen was adamantly set against the match," Marie declares. "She's always spewing poison about Russia and contends there are already too many Russians in her family. By which she means me!"

"Well, it doesn't matter. Ella has renounced the whole idea."

"Of course it matters. Now, promise me, don't be angry with the poor girl; she's not to blame. Pressure was applied."

"She has concluded she does not want me. It's over."

Marie laughs dismissively. "Having come so far, you'll let that mad old lady thwart you? With her nasty meddling?"

"I'm unwilling to go back on bended knee."

"Don't be silly! We cannot let her win! Remember how Papa loathed her? The queen?"

Serge smiles despite himself. "I can hear him still," he says. "Cursing her when the British sent their fleet to the Dardanelles in '77—'*That old madwoman, that tramp!*'"

His sister's expression is fierce. "Precisely. So take heart."

Serge pictures the lovely Ella, in her brown riding costume, on the afternoon they told Ludwig their intentions. Her cheeks pink, her expression radiant. Possibly a bit apprehensive too? He can't properly recall. What struck him then was her fine purity, how it moved him—this impossibly delicate creature, with ivory skin and slender limbs, almost too good for the world. If he really is to marry, then no one could be more ideal.

"You believe Ella isn't acting on her own volition? Only to please the queen?" he asks Marie.

"What else? Ludwig told me Ella admires you exceedingly, as

she should. Nothing has changed but she has spent weeks and weeks in the company of her deplorable grandmother, listening to lies." She shakes her finger in an admonitory way. "It would be the sign of a very weak spirit to give up."

He's often thought Marie—dauntless, opinionated, invincibly stubborn—the feminine replica of their father.

But doubts still nag. "Who wants a bride who shies from the altar?"

"She's so young, you admit this yourself, and soft. The queen leaned on her and she gave way."

"I present myself once more? Press my suit?"

"Yes, we'll telegraph Ludwig immediately," Marie replies. "We will explain that you must speak to Ella in person and inform him we will travel to Darmstadt in two days' time."

"If he allows it."

"Of course he'll allow it. Our dear cousin? I imagine he's more than a bit irritated with his daughter's changeable nature."

"But the matter was never settled. She was to think on it. Ludwig himself had reservations."

"Nonsense, you were encouraged in every way. I will send the wire now. If this marriage is going to fall through, Ella needs to tell you to your face."

Marie moves purposefully toward the door. On the threshold she turns. "You are a prince amongst princes, my dearest brother; she cannot do better."

Serge grimaces.

"None of that now," Marie scolds. "Remember, a young woman doesn't want to be advised in love by her old granny—even if that granny is the Queen of England."

"You're certain?"

Marie ignores his question and poses her own. "Volkov has

the gifts under his watch? We'll tell Ella this is but a fraction of what's to come. Those Hesse girls have never had much."

He nods.

"And start thinking over exactly what you will say!"

With that, Marie exits, her heels tapping emphatically along the stone passageway.

Chapter Six

The Queen Is Defied

Jagdschloss Wolfsgarten, September 1883

How strange, Ella thinks, that Alix is the person most disappointed she has decided not to marry Serge. Papa is gratified Ella will not move far away from him. Victoria, while liking Serge personally, regards the Romanovs as a band of callous oligarchs. Faithful Orchie takes Ella aside to confess how much she wept at the thought of Ella living in "dreadful Petersburg." Now her nurse thanks God hourly that Ella will never settle in that menacing place.

But her youngest sister, crestfallen, follows her around every corner, badgering her with questions.

"You don't love Cousin Serge?"

"I respect him very much. But I am reluctant to leave Papa and the rest of you children."

"We can visit you," Alix insists.

"Russia is a world away, dearest. Much farther than England. And the climate terrible."

"But Cousin Serge is such a fine man. He seems stern, but underneath, he is good and kind," Alix persists, eyes fixed on Ella. "Also, I like how he looks, tall and dignified and sharp like a knife."

Ella smiles at this.

"And he's always gazing admiringly at you! I don't believe he admires just anyone," Alix says.

Ella laughs.

"You don't want to marry some ugly and squat little man," Alix says.

"Certainly not." Who is her sister thinking of?

"I discussed this with Madame de Kolemine," Alix adds.

Ella frowns. "When exactly?"

"While you were gone, I heard Papa tell Prince Isenburg that things weren't settled, and then that lady whispered in my ear how you certainly wouldn't forgo the chance to marry the tsar's brother. The two of us agreed: who would?"

"I would. I know what's best for me."

"Is it because Grandmama spoke so strongly against Serge?"

How does Alix learn these things? Likely her long habit of lurking in doorways. "She said only to think very carefully," Ella answers.

"And have you?"

"Yes."

"Perhaps you need to think some more."

"Aren't you doing lessons today, Sunny? Off you go," Ella says, pointing at the door. Her sister gives her a final, petulant look and leaves.

THE NEXT AFTERNOON, Ella and Victoria return from a walk to find Papa standing on the Herrenhaus steps.

"Serge has sent a wire, asking if he might visit here, Ella. I don't like to refuse him as he is our cousin, but I will, if you so desire."

Ella feels her heart leap.

Both her father and her sister regard her with worried eyes. "Perhaps it would be best if he doesn't come exactly now," Victoria says.

Papa nods. "We can allow more time to pass before you must see him."

Ella shakes her head and smiles. "I am capable of welcoming Serge."

Her father raises his eyebrows. "You're certain?"

"I am."

"His sister is coming too. Marie and he would like to arrive the day after tomorrow."

"Fine."

Once they are alone together again Victoria asks: "You aren't worried about unpleasant scenes? Serge's such a proud character, he must be offended."

"Certainly he is proud. But if he were so very offended, he would not come."

Victoria wrinkles her forehead. "You believe so?"

"He's hardly going to berate me, is he? That would not change my mind, would it? He obviously feels bold enough to come and make his case once again."

"You're willing to hear it?"

"Why not? I've already said no once. To refuse him a second time won't be half as hard. And I quite like that . . ."

"You like that he's persisting," Victoria hazards.

"I do. I find it valiant. Not every man would act as he is acting."

Victoria laughs. "Maybe not. Still, it's you who surprises me."

"Why? Serge has shown me something about him, so I can show him something about me. That I need not quail. Or feel myself weak. I listened politely to all that Grandmama and Uncle Leo were so very anxious to tell me—about Russia, where they have never been, and about Serge, whom they have never met!"

She hadn't realized quite how much she resented this lecturing.

"And so?" Victoria asks.

"And so, if Serge is undaunted, impatient to try to persuade me differently, I will listen to him too."

"And people call you the compliant one!"

"It is you who always insists I decide for myself," Ella replies. "Here I am following your direction!"

"I can hardly object to that," Victoria says, with a laugh.

DESPITE HER BOLD words, and the exhilaration she feels knowing that Serge refused to abandon his suit without a second effort, Ella has trouble sleeping that night. She turns over and over in bed with her heart beating very fast. Can she remain composed, in full possession of herself, when speaking again with Serge?

Inspecting her face in the glass on the morning Serge is due, she's glad to see good color in her cheeks, and her skin clear of blemish. Only her eyebrows displease her. Madame de Kolemine has admirably delicate, arched brows. Ella's are too heavy and straight. She spends some time pushing up the middle of each brow with her finger, plucking out hairs, and using water to smooth them into a better, finer shape.

When she casts eyes on Serge again, walking up the Herrenhaus steps, beside his sister, their pigeon-busted aunt Marie, she feels a surge of excitement. Serge gazes at her in a way she finds wordlessly expressive, and heart-touchingly tender.

At luncheon the sensation of being watched so attentively, admired and responded to, thrills her. Conversation remains happy and easy at the table, and afterward Papa proposes a walk around the park. The afternoon is warm and still. She and Serge, Papa, Victoria, and Marie embark together—followed at a short distance by the thickset detective with a ruddy face and small, hard eyes, who has accompanied Serge and Marie to Wolfsgarten.

Papa says, "Call off your man, Serge. Tell him the property is fenced and I ordered the gates locked."

Serge drops back to speak to the detective in Russian.

"My brother would happily do without Volkov," says Marie brightly. "But it's best that he be guarded whenever he's traveling, even incognito."

Serge catches this as he approaches. He frowns. "It will not become my habit, Marie. I agreed to use a detective in this instance, given all that I am carrying."

What is he carrying? Ella has no idea.

Marie smiles. "As you wish, dear brother."

"Shall we go along there, Ella?" he says, a touch impatiently, and points to the white pebbled drive that leads from the houses to the front gate of the estate.

Ella nods. She and Serge set off—while the others immediately fall behind, giving them privacy.

As they gain the drive Ella feels as if the curtain is about to rise on a play in which she has the leading role, although she doesn't know what lines she'll speak, nor how the drama will unfold. The drive runs for a half mile, lined on either side by tall oaks—a silent audience for the action commencing below.

"How is it possible?" says Serge softly. "If anything, Ella, I find you more beautiful than before."

She smiles, casting her eyes demurely down.

"My purpose in returning to Wolfsgarten must be obvious to you," Serge says. "I will not extol—rather I am not comfortable extolling—my own virtues. I must pretend to be someone else, your advocate, and confine myself to presenting in a disinterested way all the reasons it benefits you to change your mind, and to marry me."

"I see, and how will you do that?" she asks, laughing lightly.

"I will remind you of your own words," he says. "In April,

you spoke about yourself, about the principled aspirations you have for your life."

"Silly, girlish notions, possibly," she responds, although not in earnest.

"Not at all," he answers gravely. "I know you are a unique young woman, who requires an extraordinary position. I can provide this. I long to provide it."

"Careful, advocate, you are straying from detachment," she warns in a teasing voice, and smiles up at him. She's surprised to find Serge's brow lowered, his gaze straight front, his mouth tight.

"I am flawed, as we all are," he continues. "But by the grace of God I can offer you so much. As my wife you will join a family that is looked up to by millions of people. And St. Petersburg society has too few virtuous women gifted with your innocence and grace. There you will be the focus of much interest—no doubt at times envious interest, but you are more than equal to this." His voice trembles as he speaks the last bit.

He must be nervous too. Perhaps her previous joking tone was too cavalier?

"I am honored by your view of me," she says quietly.

He tuts impatiently. "Ella, you deserve to be praised. No one who encounters you could be in doubt. What I speak of is how . . . more than the outward admiration you attract so easily, Ella . . . is how you should be necessary."

"Necessary?" she asks.

"Necessary to me. Haven't you understood this? Didn't I make this clear?"

A jagged stab of remorse cuts into her chest. She recalls the expression on his face when she first accepted him, yearning unmasked. He is such a strong and gallant man, and yet susceptible to desire—desire for her. For a moment she teeters—

should she just fold away objections, cast aside doubts, dispose of all possible reservations?

No, she rebukes herself. The most composed thing to do is to air the matter fully.

"What of all the trouble in Russia? Doesn't it frighten you? Shouldn't it frighten me?" Ella asks.

He sighs. "Yes, my father's murder changed things, and has required harsh measures. Still, for the tsar to yield to demands for reform would be to sound the death knell of the empire. And don't tell me you care much for the dirty business of governing. Are you really worried about how the police are instructed and how they act?"

"I've been told it would be imprudent to ignore the dangers."

"As my wife no violence would intrude upon your days. You will be well protected."

She absorbs that for a long moment. "And the religious difference? You assure me you have accepted this. But I cannot believe it is easy for you."

He draws in breath. "No, I don't find it at all easy."

"Is it wise, then, to marry with this impediment?"

He exclaims: "I am making this sacrifice for you! Because if I love you, and I do love you, I must not interfere with your conscience!"

Never before has Serge said he loves her. That and the vehemence of his declaration unsettle her further. Has she let others distort her thinking? Influence her unduly? Yes, he is a Romanov, a grand duke of wealth and rank, a public figure, but here, now, with her, he is also himself, a reserved man with a deeply spiritual temperament and carefully guarded pride.

She needs to ask him the most important question. "Did you feel I betrayed you, with my decision? By refusing you?"

"No. I believe . . ." He stops for a moment. "I can say simply this: If you should refuse me a second time, I will renounce my hope of making you my wife without rancor. But you must assure me this is your decision and no one else's. You must say you have pleased yourself by saying no."

"It never pleased me to say no," she admits.

"I forgive you then," he says, a bit stiffly.

She gazes ahead at the high iron gate in clear view now. "I can't really picture life in Russia," she says. "Papa has told me Petersburg is magnificent."

"I find it so, naturally," he says. "I like even better Moscow, and my favorite place in the world is Ilinskoe, my estate on the banks of the Moskva. At Ilinskoe you feel the real Russia."

They have only a few yards more to walk to reach the gate.

"Ella, we can live well, we can live close to God, we can read and walk and look at pictures. You and I, we have the same taste for things. And I am convinced that the woman you are meant to be is exactly this—my wife, my consort, my support, held up before all as the most beautiful and most commendable of grand duchesses."

He halts, so she does too.

He turns to her, and leans down to kiss her. Her lips quiver against his, her legs shake, but her soul soars.

"Join me there in Russia, Ella," he says, his voice low and fervent.

"You see me and I see you," she replies, and she smiles. She doesn't know where these words come from, but as she speaks them, she feels their truth. "And, yes, I will," she adds simply.

His face lights up, with pleasure and with awe. "Ah, my dear, you have made me happier than you can ever imagine," he says, gazing down at her reverently for a long minute. He picks up her right hand, kisses it, tucks it into his elbow, and they turn back toward the house.

They walk along for a short while silently, both contemplating, Ella feels, the weight of what they've committed to, the prospect of all that lies ahead.

"Do you know," he asks, "I chose our route deliberately? I noted it was some distance to the gate, but not so very far. If I could not persuade you by the time we reached the gate, I thought I might rattle the bars in frustration, but then I intended to get a hold of myself, return to join the others, exchange pleasantries, eat a few meals, admire Ludwig's hunters, and depart, never to mention the subject again. I could picture it so well, all hope gone. I had a harder time imagining the alternative, however, now . . ."

She glances up and sees his shy smile, her true and most noble knight. To follow and to obey a man as fine and as upright as Serge is a worthy purpose. No doubt it won't always be easy; he doesn't have a relaxed temperament. But she will be giving herself to someone deserving of the gift, and that, she realizes, is what she has longed for all along.

AT BREAKFAST THE next morning, Serge announces he wishes the family to gather in the Saal. He doesn't explain further, nor does Papa, although together they direct the servants.

The Saal was once the grandest room at Wolfsgarten, and is now the one they enter least often. Their forefather Landgrave Ernst Ludwig built this elegant concert room to entice famous musicians—on their way to bigger, more important locales—to stop here for a night and perform. He had the walls painted with gold leaf and hung two large chandeliers from the lofty ceiling. Because Papa lacks the funds to properly restore the Saal, the walls are cracked and peeling, and the large chandeliers are shrouded in canvas sacks. Yet even in disrepair, the room retains a stately golden aura.

Ella waits with Victoria and the children outside as Serge's detective, along with a footman ferry a number of chests up the staircase and into the Herrenhaus. A gardener struggles with a large old-fashioned wooden armchair from the estate office. Papa, holding open the door, encourages the man. "Two more steps—you're nearly there."

Ella asks Marie, "What is happening?"

"Oh, I couldn't say," she replies with a small, knowing smile.

Papa comes to the head of the stairs and summons them inside. The armchair sits in the middle of the floor. The room is otherwise empty of furniture, except a piano and a harpsichord in the corner, covered in heavy sheets, and a dozen or so shabby gilt Chiavari chairs, stacked in another corner. Dust motes spin in the beams of morning sun streaming through the windows. Serge directs Ella to sit in the armchair, and for everyone else to range themselves behind him as he faces her. Papa is grinning now—what happy surprise does he anticipate?

"I have a few things to present to you, my dear Ella," Serge declares, and he gestures to the detective, who brings forward a black leather chest. Serge turns the key in the lock, flips the lid open, and from inside he draws out a large gold bracelet.

"Your left arm, please," he says to Ella, and when she extends it, he slips the bracelet onto her wrist. "A precious family artifact—my father gave this to your great-aunt Marie, at the time of their engagement here in Darmstadt."

The wide band is set with an oblong ruby, and starred all around with diamonds, forming a complex pattern of interlocking circles. Nothing she owns, that Mama ever owned, is as lavish as this. She lifts her arm and the diamonds catch the sun, throwing coins of light across the far wall.

"Ooh, look," exclaims Alix. "Shake it some more, Ella."

"No, give your attention to Sasha and Minnie's gift now," Serge says, and lifts out a brooch—an enormous, cushion-shaped sapphire, rimmed with diamonds, with a single large pearl drop hanging off it. He carefully pins it high on her right chest. He takes a step back and rocks his head back and forth, assessing: "Yes, I like. A touch matronly for a young woman, it could be said, but you will wear it for years."

The brooch tips forward a bit, her gray cotton day dress is not dense enough to support the weight. This piece properly belongs on an evening gown of stiff silk or brocade.

Serge takes another peek into the chest and turns to her with a confiding smile. "You have heard of Carl Fabergé—master goldsmith and jeweler?"

She shakes her head. Should she know this name?

Serge laughs. "You will become very familiar with his work. He is the greatest craftsman in Russia, perhaps all of Europe. Earlier this year I asked him to design a parure in aquamarine and diamonds, with the hopes that I would bestow it upon you as my affianced wife."

Marie steps close, to whisper in Ella's ear: "A parure is a set of matching jewels, to wear all together or one at a time."

Serge announces, "Here is the tiara," and holds it before her eyes long enough for her to examine the exquisite scrollwork, a delicate motif of festoons and bows, studded with square-cut diamonds and surmounted by five large pear-shaped aquamarines. Then he gently places it on her head. To Ella's surprise, the tiara is quite light—it feels rather like wearing a halo.

"And the matching necklace," Serge says. He drapes around her neck a long chain of dozens and dozens of square-cut diamonds separated by tiny, delicate openwork gold flowers. Ella feels breathless—the extravagance of this necklace is overwhelming.

"And now the bracelet." Matching the necklace, it has the same pattern of diamonds and flowers.

"The earrings." Ella sees these are sizable, teardrop aquamarines. Serge passes them to his sister, and Marie attaches one to each of Ella's ears. Their weight pulls down on her earlobes.

"Monsieur Fabergé is still completing the stomacher. It will be awaiting you in Petersburg." Serge rubs his palms together with great satisfaction. "I am delighted with this set and how well these pieces suit you."

"Now we are ready for the other chest," he says, and instructs Volkov in Russian. More? Ella is astonished.

Serge announces: "So, pearls. My mother loved pearls, and wore them constantly, sometimes woven in her hair, sometimes sewn into the neckline of her gowns, but always around her neck."

"I recall this," Ella says. In the hazy reaches of her memory Serge's mother sits in a rocking chair at Heiligenberg—a thin lady with large eyes set in a waxen face, wearing heavy pearl necklaces.

"Here are my favorites from her collection," he says, and begins to drape rope after rope of milky pearls around her neck. A few are long enough to be doubled, or tripled. The thick cascade of stones falls down to her waist. She runs the pearls through her fingers—some creamier, others pinker, still others almost silver in hue.

"*Bella, bella,*" says Serge in Italian, beaming at her.

She should say something—but she's speechless.

"And I felt you needed some emeralds, so I had an old piece of my grandmother's reset in the new style." He produces a triple-rowed choker—which Marie fastens on carefully.

"And rubies go so well with pearls." He draws out a necklace with a heavy fringe of red stones, and hangs it around Ella's neck.

"Also, a diamond pendant." This is a large lozenge-shaped gem set in a silver backing.

"Now, diamond brooches." He takes out two and pins them above her heart, with some help from Marie, since the clasp of the second, in the shape of a rose, is tiny.

"And a diamond hatpin," he says. He stops to consider for a moment. "We will put this in your hair. Alix, might you?"

Her little sister is happy to oblige, carefully pushing the long pin into Ella's back bun.

"Now, stand up, my child," says Serge. "Let us all see you in your finery."

Very slowly Ella rises to her feet, determined to keep the tiara balanced on her head. Under the weight of the numerous heavy necklaces, she sways slightly before getting fully upright.

"You look like a Christmas tree, Ella," shouts Ernie.

She can't help but giggle.

Victoria shakes her head, amazed.

Papa stands back to get a full view. His eyes gleam, as if mirroring the wealth of jewels that Serge has showered upon her.

"It's so romantic," says Alix, gazing up at her. "You are so lucky, Ella!"

"I did not forget you, Alix, nor you, Irène." Serge signals to Volkov to retrieve a third chest. He takes from it two coral bead necklaces, one for each girl. They thank him with happy smiles.

"And for the future Princess Louis of Battenberg, soon to be a proud sailor's wife, I commissioned a special piece." Serge bows to Victoria and then carefully lifts out of the chest an object wrapped in gray velvet. He unfolds the soft fabric to reveal to them all a large diamond brooch in the shape of an anchor. Victoria looks astonished. For a moment Ella worries her sister will reject the gift, telling Serge that she doesn't approve of such excess.

"Oh, Serge," her sister says. "You . . . I . . . well, it's lovely. I will wear it for my wedding."

"I must sit now," Ella says, and collapses into the chair.

Marie remarks, "You think you are weighed down now? Wait until the important state occasions—you'll be obligated to wear the traditional kokoshnik headdress decorated in diamonds and emeralds the size of duck eggs! And stand for hours!"

"Marie," Serge says, pretending to be stern, "I've only yesterday persuaded Ella to become my wife. Don't scare her off by mentioning burdensome duties that await her."

Everyone laughs.

Now it's time to put the jewels away. Marie and Victoria have quite a time taking pieces off of Ella—searching for the brooch clasps and untangling all the necklaces.

"Might I wear Aunt Marie's engagement bracelet for the rest of the day?" Ella asks, admiring once again the play of the light on the diamonds.

Serge smiles and lightly strokes the side of her cheek with two fingers. "My child, all these jewels are yours now. Wear them whenever you wish."

Hers? That's difficult to take in.

THE DAY AFTER Serge and Marie leave, her older sister reports that Grandmama has learned of Serge's return and written Victoria a frantic letter.

"She prays you have remained firm in your refusal," her elder sister says, looking rueful. "For it will be your ruin should you marry him, she is convinced."

Ella sighs.

"I must reply—keeping her hanging any longer is cruel," says Victoria.

"No, it should be me who writes," Ella says.

The next morning, before breakfast, before she has even changed out of her nightdress, Ella goes down the passageway and sits down at the schoolroom table. She picks up a pen and begins:

Dearest Grandmama, I am afraid this letter will not give you as much pleasure as I should wish.

Chapter Seven

An Ambassador Investigates

Saltykov House, St. Petersburg, January 1884

$\mathscr{S}$ir Edward Thornton doesn't, as a rule, revisit his decisions. He so rarely feels the need. And men who fret and wring their hands over matters they've already put in motion do little but waste valuable time. Nonetheless, sitting alone in his office, in the rapidly diminishing light of an abbreviated winter afternoon, waiting for John Baddeley, Thornton wonders if he's chosen correctly in this instance.

Open on the desk in front of him is the letter he received from Sir Henry Ponsonby, the queen's private secretary, just after Christmas. Distasteful rumors have reached the ears of the sovereign and her son Prince Leopold. The Grand Duke Serge Alexandrovich apparently enjoys too-close intimacy with a number of officers under his command. As he is poised to marry the queen's granddaughter—the young and beautiful Ella, Princess Elisabeth of Hesse—her English family is naturally concerned. Can Thornton investigate? Should certain facts come to light, there's still time to call off the couple's engagement.

It would not be fitting for Thornton, Her Majesty's ambassador, to circulate in the Russian capital, making pointed inquiries about the private life of a member of the imperial family. Which is why he has enlisted Baddeley for this very delicate task. Handsome and well-schooled—a Wellington man—Baddeley has cultivated a vast network of connections as Petersburg correspondent for *The Standard*, and he's such engaging company that Thornton and his wife frequently invite him to dine.

Undertaking the work as a service to the crown, the journalist promised to report back within a fortnight. Now Thornton expects him at any moment. What will he have discovered? The ambassador gets up from behind his desk to stand in front of the large window overlooking Millionnaya Street. The gas lamps below are already lit, blurring the frosty mist.

Thornton can appreciate that the queen wishes to know if the man her beloved granddaughter plans to marry is sound. Having met Grand Duke Serge on various occasions, Thornton knows him to be nothing like his eldest brother the tsar, that bearded, lumbering giant, famous for shouting tyrannical orders and bending pokers as a party trick. Nor does Grand Duke Serge share the blustery good humor of his other brothers, Vladimir, Alexis, and Paul. He is a solemn, dignified, rather stiff man—far from niminy-piminy. As for what lies beneath, who knows? Attempting to pin down the intimate desires of a royal person strikes Thornton as the diplomatic equivalent of putting an ear up against a bedroom door.

Thornton sighs. Stuck with this scurrilous assignment, what other option did he have? Baddeley was the ticket, is the ticket. "The only ticket," he announces aloud, to no one but himself.

A minute later, his secretary, Evans, opens the door and announces, "Mr. Baddeley, sir." And in the man comes—purposeful, with candid eyes and thick blond hair swept off his forehead, in the style of Lord Byron. There's nothing shifty about Baddeley, thank God, and in this he stands apart from others of his ilk.

"Good evening, Your Excellency," he says with a bow.

"No ceremony, not tonight, John, here amongst ourselves," Thornton says.

Baddeley smiles. "Good evening, Edward."

"Please." The ambassador gestures at the brown Chesterfield sofa and sits in the armchair alongside. "What can you tell me, my good man?"

Baddeley reaches into his jacket pocket. "You don't mind if I smoke?"

"Not at all."

He lights a cigarette and inhales luxuriantly. "Not exactly as I expected," Baddeley says, exhaling.

"The rumors are complete nonsense?"

"The rumors are rampant, but devilishly hard to prove."

"This is no surprise," says Thornton gloomily.

"Among the ranks of the Preobrazhensky Life Guards, Grand Duke Serge's regiment, it's said their commander selects adjutants who share his alleged predilections. For a long time, his favorite was a man called Konstantin Balyasany, who has recently married and now has a child. Another, Alexander Martynov, is rumored to be living with the grand duke currently. I dug up an address for him in Gorokhovaya Street, and when I went round it was Martynov's widowed mother who greeted me."

"I assume you didn't interrogate her?"

"No, but she offered me tea, and I got her chatting. She told me all about her wonderful son, resident with her in the apartment, without once mentioning the grand duke."

Thornton shakes his head. "So nothing there."

"No," Baddeley says, tapping ash into a small glass saucer on the side table. "Next I decided to call on Count Pyotr Shuvalov, as he knows the whole Romanov family well."

"Shuvalov! Hasn't the old devil retired to his estate in Latvia?"

"He still comes to Petersburg on occasion. The new tsar likes to confer with him, but he's prevented from restoring Shuvalov to office—thought to be too pro-British, you know."

"I do. He saved the day after the Turkish War. Kept the peace between us."

"The count received me at his palace on the Fontanka Embankment."

"Did your questions offend him?"

"No," Baddeley says, with a short laugh. "He immediately presumed, correctly, who had sent me. He was happy to help as long as none of his comments are attributed to him."

"Of course."

"The count has been acquainted with Grand Duke Serge since he was a boy."

"Likes him?"

"Not particularly—Shuvalov describes an austere character, very rigid. The count wonders if the grand duke's early life—his mother's poor health, his father's dalliances, his education supervised by that reactionary Pobedonostsev—accounts for a certain grimness of outlook. That he is devoted to the officers of his regiment, entertains them frequently, and likes to drink with the handsomest and most aristocratic among their number—this has been true for many years, according to the count."

"The grand duke hasn't enjoyed any liaisons with ballerinas or actresses?"

"Beyond his sister, Marie, the Duchess of Edinburgh, and also his sister-in-law, the Empress Maria Feodorovna, it seems the grand duke is not close to any women."

"While his brothers and his cousins pick up and drop mistresses regularly. Isn't that so?"

"Not the tsar, a faithful husband, but the rest, yes. And as you are aware there's no more scandal-mongering society in the world than Petersburg's."

"Undoubtedly. I've heard matters discussed openly at dinner tables here which would bring blushes to the face of any hostess in London—let alone Washington."

"In the beau monde where love affairs are commonplace, and malicious tittle-tattle constant, everyone presumes if a handsome, wealthy grand duke is not taking a woman to bed, he must have opposite vices," expounds Baddeley.

"I see."

"Add to that there's a certain amount of animosity within the family. Grand Duke Serge is the tsar's favorite brother. And especially close to the young heir, Nicholas Alexandrovich, Shuvalov says."

"So other members of the imperial family encourage the rumors about him?"

"Likely."

"What a backstabbing lot the Romanovs are!"

"But here's the extraordinary thing, Edward," Baddeley says, stubbing out his cigarette and leaning forward. "Gossip about Grand Duke Serge has spread to Berlin. Prince William apparently told Count Kapnist, the Russian ambassador there, that he knows the grand duke bug—"

Thornton puts up his hand—he won't have crude talk. He asks, irritably: "Prince William? The crown princess's son? Whatever does he know about it? When was he last in Petersburg?"

"He hasn't any direct knowledge—he maligns the grand duke deliberately."

"For what possible reason?"

"Shuvalov couldn't explain it. So, I contacted a man I know, an attaché at the Prussian legation, cousin of the Duke of Saxe-Meiningen, married to Prince William's sister. We shared a beer, and he told me this story. Princess Elisabeth of Hesse was apparently Prince William's first love. Do you remember that one Hesse prince died of a bleeding disorder, like Prince Leopold's own?"

"I thought the Princess Alice and several of her children died of diphtheria," Thornton says. "Anyway, why is this relevant?"

"Apparently, the Crown Princess Victoria, his mother, having consulted with doctors in Berlin, became concerned that a woman whose own brother suffered from uncontrolled bleeding could be a risk to the Hohenzollern dynasty. She persuaded her son to give up Princess Elisabeth and choose a different bride. But now Prince William detests that his beautiful cousin is marrying someone else."

"Thus, he slanders the man?" Thornton stares at the journalist. "This sounds farfetched."

Baddeley shrugs. "Hell hath no fury . . ."

"The prince wasn't scorned, nor is he a woman."

"Choose a different aphorism, then."

"Contemptible, really—if true."

"I'm quite certain it is."

"Which leaves me in a wretched position. What precisely to report?"

"I'd say your duty is clear." Baddeley looks at him earnestly.

"You do? How? I inform Ponsonby that while it's possible the grand duke has unnatural inclinations, what's certain is that the queen's own grandson lays siege to his reputation?"

"No, no." Baddeley shakes his head. "You should report that while rumors, likely mean-spirited, swirl around the grand duke, you have no proof confirming their veracity."

"Only that?"

"Yes. Without evidence, how can you add one straw's weight to the adverse side of the balance in Her Majesty's mind? It wouldn't be honorable."

Thornton nods slowly. "So leave out mention of the Prussian prince?"

"Do antagonisms amidst the queen's family fall within your remit?"

"No—but I've not been convinced any of this does."

"It seems royal families are like all other families," Baddeley says with a wry smile.

"I can't agree."

"No? You don't recognize the acrimonies and the jealousies? The irresistible desire to gossip about each other, and compete?"

"Certainly. But the stakes are raised when it comes to royalty. *How* they are still matters—especially here in Russia."

Baddeley nods. "I don't dispute it. Still, if there's nothing else . . ."—he hoists himself to his feet—"I should get on with reporting stories I can actually publish."

Thornton does have a final question. "Tell me, do you feel sorry for Princess Elisabeth?"

"About to marry one of the richest men in the world? Hardly."

"Yet with a husband who is perhaps . . . ?"

"The grand duke is said to adore her, and the match pleases the tsar." Baddeley cocks his head, considering further. "It won't be pleasant for her, should she become aware of the insinuations. But once the couple is settled, produce a few children, the vicious talk will fade away."

Thornton rises to shake the man's hand. "Thank you, John, for your work and your good counsel. I appreciate both."

Chapter Eight

※※※※※※※※※※※※※※※※※※※※※※※※※※※※※※※※

The Gift of a Brooch (Soon Returned)

To Peterhof, June 1884

There's been the most tremendous upset, and it's all the fault of Madame de Kolemine, who somehow persuaded Papa to marry her. They had a wedding in secret—on the very same day as Victoria!—but as soon as Grandmama and Uncle Bertie heard they said absolutely no. The wicked woman was "sent packing," Ernie tells Alix, although not before Papa was obligated to pay her a large sum of money not to be his wife anymore.

This last part seems quite ridiculous, so Alix asks Ella to explain. Her sister turns pink and tells Alix sternly that no one may discuss the matter further—"Least said, soonest mended." And she adds: "Papa knows it's for the best that Madame de Kolemine has gone."

Does he though? Alix has studied Papa's face often enough to recognize the angry look—brows low, eyes like steel coins, his mouth an upside-down U. He's rarely home and when he returns, he stomps up the stairs, unwilling to stop and chat, even when Alix waits for him in the entrance hall. She's eager to discuss their trip to St. Petersburg, which for so long has hovered tantalizingly all the way on the other side of Victoria's wedding, and now is only a few weeks off. She secretly worries that Papa is so irate he won't want to go, and she and Ernie and

Irène will be made to stay behind with him. And that would be terrible, to miss traveling to Russia, and not to see Ella and Cousin Serge get married.

On the day of Alix's twelfth birthday, Victoria and Louis come back from England, and her eldest sister says that they will indeed depart Darmstadt, all of them, the next day as scheduled. Alix has imagined a ceremony at the Hauptbahnhof—Papa and the prime minister making speeches, a band playing, garlands and flags hanging from the rafters, some in the crowd wiping away a tear at the sight of lovely young Princess Elisabeth leaving her homeland forever. But no, the family will leave quietly from a small junction north of the city.

As they drive to Wixhausen, through the twilight, in a caravan of carriages, Alix, Ernie, and Irène in the second with Miss Jackson, Alix points out it really isn't right that Ella is deprived of a proper send-off. The governess shakes her head. "People here are aggrieved with their grand duke," she says. "Discretion and a period of contrition on your father's part is required."

Thank goodness Papa isn't there to hear this—he wouldn't like it. True, his marriage was a scandal, but Alix will never reprove dear Papa. He can always count on her love and loyalty, even if Darmstädters are fickle, and Grandmama and Uncle Bertie order him about, and Miss Jackson feels free to prescribe contrition.

At the junction a special private train stands waiting for them. Cousin Serge arranged it, Victoria explains, and the sleek red-brown cars, all through-going, are the most modern ones in the world. They were made by a company in Belgium, which is why the words *Compagnie Internationale des Wagons-Lit* stretch out above the windows of the four cars—two sleeping cars, a car in the rear for the baggage, and, most amazingly, a restaurant car. Always before when Alix has traveled on a train, they ate from a basket brought along, or stopped for meals at stations en route. Alix sidles over to her father as they stand on the short platform, hoping he'll share her excitement. "Don't you think it will be marvelous, Papa? Eating in a restaurant on the train?" she asks.

"*Ja*," he replies. Though still he glowers.

THE NEXT MORNING, waking in her berth above Irène's, Alix nudges open the blind to watch fields, tidy pastures, and green-and-golden patchwork hills glide past, regularly interrupted by small towns, like toy towns, with sloping red tile roofs and cobbled streets. It's Brötchen with sliced cheese, ham, and boiled eggs for breakfast. They stop briefly in Berlin—Westerweller barely has time to nip out for the papers—and afterward the waiter in a white peaked hat serves delicious spaetzle soup for luncheon. In the afternoon, the landscape out the window changes, it's broader and flatter with stretches of grassy marshes, tracts of wild heather, and acres of brown, furrowed farmland. She and Ernie play cards with Victoria and Louis. Aunt Julie, Louis's mother, organizes a jolly game of charades. They push the chairs and the tables in the restaurant car to the side to make room. But sitting in the corner, behind the wall of his newspaper, Papa doesn't utter a word. Not until supper does he speak properly to the rest of them.

"Now, it's an early start tomorrow," he announces. "Cousin Serge has told me at the Russian frontier there will be an official welcome, and there we will change onto one of the imperial trains."

"But I adore this train!" Alix says. "Why must we change?"

Everyone smiles, even Papa. "*Mein Schatz*, in Russia everything is different," he begins. "The railway track in the German Empire, as in the rest of Europe, has a fifty-six-and-one-half-inch gauge." He raises and separates his hands to demonstrate.

"For reasons of their own the Russians decided on bigger—sixty and a half inches." He pops both hands a bit farther apart.

"I wager a Romanov imperial train will be even grander than this one, don't you, Ellie?" says Victoria.

Ella is gazing out the window. Lost in a dream of love, Alix thinks. Her wedding is only nine days away.

"Ellie?" Victoria presses.

"Excuse me, did you ask me something?" Ella asks, startled.

"We are discussing our Russian train," Victoria says.

Ella nods absently. "I was wondering, white lawn or pink barège tomorrow?"

"Definitely white lawn, as it will be rather a formal occasion," Alix puts in, and turns to her father. "Papa, don't you agree? Ella must wear the lawn?"

"On such matters, I always defer to young ladies," he says benignly. There, she got him to smile again.

SOMETIME LATE IN the night Alix is jolted awake. Men shout and an engine passes by. A juddering shunt forward and another back, a loud clank of metal, and then silence—the train has halted. She rolls over and goes back to sleep, but soon enough Orchie is shaking her shoulder. "Get up and get ready now," she says. Draped over her arm are two freshly ironed frocks, yellow for Alix and blue for Irène. She hangs both on the peg behind the door and pulls the door shut with a sharp click.

"Much too early for this," complains Irène, still lying in her bunk.

But Alix rises, dresses quickly, and pulls up the blind to take a first look at Russia. A few high, wavy trees, a crude plank bridge over a small stream, a wire fence stretching across a scrubby meadow—not very impressive. Still, they have arrived at last.

Everyone gathers in the restaurant car. From the windows Alix can see a collection of perhaps a hundred people standing in front of a shabby stone stationhouse. Among them, a group of soldiers, wearing red jackets crisscrossed with bands of gold cartridges, cylindrical black hats, and wide baggy blue trousers with a red stripe down one side. "Cossacks," says Ernie, pointing. Most of the other people waiting look like country folk—the women in aprons, the men in blouse-type shirts. One woman, very tall, is more smartly dressed than the others, in a beige coat and matching bonnet.

First Papa and Ella climb down to be greeted by a rotund little man wearing a white, blue, and red striped banner across his chest.

"That must be the mayor," surmises Miss Jackson.

"What's this place anyway?" asks Irène.

"The border town of Verzhbolova," Miss Jackson answers.

Presently the rest of them file out of the car, off the train, to array themselves on either side of Ella and Papa. Ella has indeed chosen her white lawn frock, along with two long ropes of pearls Serge gave her, and a sweet straw hat, brim turned up at the back. The mayor begins speaking in Russian, with an occasional flourish of his arm. Ella and Papa nod politely, although Alix can tell from their faces they don't understand much.

The stationhouse door squeaks open and a man in a brown suit carrying a heap of white lilies steps carefully out. The crowd parts and the man passes through to bring the flowers to the mayor, who, with a quick swivel, thrusts them at Ella. Her sister requires both arms to cradle them. How awkward— Alix is irked on her behalf. But her sister thanks him—the Russian sounds like *oh-grom-no-ya spa-see-bo*. With no free hand to wave, she bobs her head sweetly in various directions to acknowledge everyone.

The lady in the beige coat brings forward a flock of small children, who begin to sing somber tunes—the lady waves a finger in the air to keep them in time.

When a third Russian song begins, Ernie nudges Alix with his elbow and whispers, "How much longer can this possibly go on?"

She frowns and whispers back: "Remain quiet and dignified!"

He laughs quietly. "Don't tell me you're enjoying this, Little Miss Fuss."

In fact, Alix's new shoes pinch her feet, it's hot on the exposed platform, and she's hungry for breakfast. Out of the corner of her eye she sees Orchie helping the other servants unload cases and trunks from the baggage car, aided by the two Belgian conductors in flat caps.

Irène, standing on Alix's other side, says in a low voice, "Where is the train that will take us on?"

Alix wonders the same. And her stomach growls. *Please don't let us be stranded too long here in Verzhbolova, where there is possibly nothing nice to eat.*

The children sing out a final note, the lady's finger waves no more, and silence descends. No one claps. The mayor's eyes dart about nervously. Just then, the loud blare of the train whistle shakes the air. With a lazy, grinding screech of wheels, the red-brown cars slowly roll in reverse out of the station, past the wire fence, and disappear around a bend in the track, leaving them abandoned, along with an enormous pile of their luggage.

In the stillness, the horde gawks at them standing in their row. The mayor looks a bit panicked, and the schoolteacher—for she must be that—orders her charges into pairs and leads them away, down the dusty lane toward the plank bridge.

What a shambles. Never in Darmstadt would a ceremony peter out like this. At least Papa seems unperturbed—he's chatting quietly to Louis's father, Uncle Alexander. Ella stands perfectly still, looking patient and holding her heap of flowers.

A few Cossacks begin talking loudly, jostling one another. One yells some incomprehensible remark at the two Prussian border guards, wearing black-belted coats, who stand, watching, from the other side the fence. Another Cossack points at the Darmstadt party, jabbing a finger in the air, saying something else unintelligible in Russian. Is he taunting them? Does he not feel happy to greet the German princess soon to be married to the tsar's brother?

Perhaps they never should have come. Alix notices how, standing on the far side of Irène, Victoria and Louis look worried. Louis is tightly gripping her sister's upper arm with a white-gloved hand. What is making him nervous?

"See there!" shouts Ernie, and he's pointing at the sky above the trees on the left, where a small puff of gray-violet smoke is now visible. A moment more and the prow of a black engine looms into view, and the Cossacks swarm down the platform—past them, past a wooden gate on the rails that is the terminus of the European tracks—to stand at attention at the long, far end.

The massive engine curves toward them, pulling a half dozen shiny cars painted royal blue—a large yellow coat of arms emblazoned on the side of each. The train slides to a stop.

Papa grins. "*Ach so*, the imperial train. Shall we board?"

He leads the way with Ella; the rest of them follow. Several porters in blue double-breasted jackets pushing wooden hand carts race in the opposite direction to retrieve the baggage. The mayor of Verzhbolova stands forlorn in the crosscurrent, sad, Alix imagines, that his moment of glory is over.

"Notice the fearsome eagles sticking out their tongues at us," Ernie jokes, pointing at the coat of arms.

"That's the Romanov family crest," Miss Jackson says, turning sharply to instruct them. "It's a *single* black eagle, double-headed. The two heads represent the tsar's two jobs—sovereign over the state, sovereign over the church."

As they follow the governess's bustled backside up the steps into the car, Ernie mutters, "Miss Jackson's name should properly be Baedeker."

Alix giggles. Her excitement for their trip is fully restored.

While the first train was sleek and clean, this one is opulent and exotic. The air smells like cinnamon and orange peel mixed. The corridors are paneled in shiny mahogany, which sets off bright gold window frames and doorknobs. Each compartment is an elegant, carpeted little parlor furnished with an oblong wooden table, inset mirrors, and a green bench seat that pulls out into a bed. A washroom adjoins. One car seems to be just for games, with a square table and four matching chairs perfect for cards; also a wide desk, several deep armchairs, a chessboard flanked by two stools, and a glass-fronted cabinet storing bottles of drink. Red leather, embossed with tiny double-headed eagles, has been stretched over the walls. "It's like standing in the palm of a giant wearing very fine gloves," Ernie says, stroking a patch.

The far door opens, and Papa is there. "*Kinder*, why are you dawdling? Come now, come see the marvelous salon car."

Papa looks merry, restored to his best self, and Alix skips ahead of Ernie. In this car, three crystal chandeliers hang in a line from the ceiling, a broad Turkish rug covers the floor, and each wide window has an ivory-colored shade with a scalloped bottom edge and dangling gold tassel. The walls are upholstered like furniture, in light-blue silk, with squares of dark-blue enamel below. There are several velvet chairs, and Uncle Alexander and Aunt Julia have sat down on the matching rolled-arm sofa. And in every corner, behind every piece of furniture, flanking the doors on either end, are masses of flowers—all white—gardenias, carnations, roses, freesia, and lily of the valley.

Ella stands in the middle of the car, gazing around with wide, shining eyes. She's cast aside the lilies, which lie—limp, already wilting—on the seat of a chair.

"How do you like my flowers, Sunny dear?" she asks.

"These are all for you too? Where did they come from? Not that silly mayor?"

She laughs. "Serge sent them."

"The train brought a message from our cousin," Papa says, smiling. "He decreed that Ella must enter her new country surrounded by beautiful, sweet-smelling flowers—white of course, as befits a bride."

Such a lovely husband Serge will be.

WHILE THE OTHERS play games, Alix sits in her compartment to watch Russia go by. Towns are infrequent now—it's mostly woods upon woods, and more woods. Sometimes the train passes a field fenced with rough-hewn wooden boards, confining a few head of cattle, or a clearing with a small cottage and an even smaller barn. The afternoon grows misty, and the train crosses a lake on a long spit of land that splits the water into two pewter-colored halves. The farther east they travel, the more mysterious it seems. In Germany, farms and lanes, towns and streets, are out in the open, known and mapped. Here the forests keep so much hidden. If Russia is the vastest country on earth, and Miss Jackson says it is, must it inevitably be, also, the most secretive? What magical wonders unfold in the enormous, murky, remote stretches of land?

Of course, they won't be staying anywhere wild and nameless. Papa says their home for the trip will be Peterhof, the seaside palace of the Romanovs, built by a tsar called Peter the Great. A bit like Osborne, Alix imagines, but with onion domes.

Late that evening, long after supper, they disembark at the Peterhof station, a lofty stone structure like a small church. Serge is there, flanked by an honor guard. He embraces Papa, kisses Ella on each cheek, and when he reaches Alix, he takes both her hands in his. "Welcome, dear girl, to my homeland," he says, his voice joyous, his face beaming. "I trust you will love it."

They travel in two open-topped charabancs, with rows of benches to accommodate them all. It's past ten o'clock but oddly bright. "The Russians call these June weeks the *Beliye Nochi*—the 'White Nights,'" Miss Jackson says, as soon as they settle in their seats. "The sun will never properly set, children, you shall see. The sky will merely turn dark gray for two hours after midnight."

No one would guess their governess is also making her first visit to Russia.

They drive along a straight road and then up a steep hill— from there they can see iron-blue water on the left. "The Gulf of Finland," Miss Jackson intones. "Peter the Great visited Versailles and desired the same for himself—by the sea. So he chose this bluff, only a hundred yards from the shore."

They pass between high gates—golden, double-headed eagles topping the rails—and into astonishing grounds, so much grander than Osborne. Grandmama's house has a single fountain, set on the pebbled parterre, above a smooth skirt of lawn. Here, the royal residence announces itself with tiers of fountains, shooting water high in the air, separated by broad waterfalls, studded with gold statues of classical figures and bordered by intricately patterned flowerbeds and rows of conical pines. The Grand Palace itself is massive. Alix's mouth drops open as they drive along the white-and-yellow facade to the entrance, a distance that must be twice, three times as long as the entire Neues Palais. Rows and rows of fretted windows are arrayed under a broad roof crowned by four cupolas and an enormous vase of dense, gleaming gold.

Under the strangely luminous sky, this palace seems to radiate pride, as if conscious of its rarity, as if a bold, living heart beats somewhere deep in the cold stone.

Alix hears Victoria, on the bench in front of her, say quietly to Louis: "All this, in a country where millions toil for pennies a day? Disgraceful!"

Alix frowns. How rude to cast aspersions when you are the

guest, and how disrespectful to scorn such high-reaching grandeur. At least Irène feels as she does. "It's like we've stepped into some beautiful dream," she whispers to Alix.

Clambering down, Alix feels the cool breeze off the sea and tastes salty freshness in the air. They have come such a long way, and at journey's end, distant Darmstadt, although dear, seems suddenly so dull and ordinary as to be almost pitiful compared with the magnificence of Peterhof.

THE NEXT MORNING, when they are to meet the tsar and his wife—Uncle Sasha and Aunt Minnie—Alix is anxious. It can't be right, she thinks, as Orchie braids her hair, to appear in plaits today. But her nurse, in a fluster about the unpacking, won't like complaints, so Alix lingers behind as everyone else heads downstairs. With nimble fingers she takes out the braids, gives her hair a few strokes with the brush, and pins the front bits high on the crown of her head. Peering into the looking glass, she fluffs her fringe, pulls out her coral beads from under the collar of her dress, and nods at her reflection. Much better.

Downstairs, a surprise. Next to a set of double doors, flung open to the jetting fountains and the sea beyond, an older boy waits. Neat and compact, like a toy soldier, he is wearing a pressed navy uniform jacket, gray trousers, and leather boots that shine with polish.

He gazes at her with steady curiosity as she crosses the shiny tile floor. And then he smiles. "You are Alix," he says in English. "Uncle Gega told us you are a darling."

Alix feels herself flush.

"Are you Nicky or Georgy?" she asks. The two eldest of the tsar's five children are sons—sixteen and thirteen.

"You don't know?"

The way he says it tells her the answer. "You are Nicky." The elder, the heir, the tsarevich.

He smiles again. His large blue eyes are velvety, like a rabbit's. He bows briefly from the waist. "Georgy is outside with your brother. We are going to the mast. Say hello to the others, and then come along. It will be fun."

The tsar, barrel-chested, has broad shoulders and huge hands. He smiles kindly at Alix when Papa presents her. His wife is small, with an oval face, big brown eyes, and dark hair. Her straw bonnet is decorated with red cherries, and a wide red ribbon is knotted in a big bow at the side of her chin, right below her ear. Yes, Alix sees the resemblance to her sister who lives in England—Aunt Alix, the wife of Uncle Bertie—but this lady has more sparkle.

"Ludwig, your baby isn't a baby," Aunt Minnie coos in German.

Papa nods. "Still my special pet," he says, and bends to kiss the top of Alix's head.

Cousin Serge smiles at her from the far side of the terrace. So many other Russians stand about, all the men in uniform, and there's an excited whir of chat amongst the adults. No one objects as she and Ernie go off down the steps with Nicky and his brother Georgy, a gangly boy with a sleek round head.

Walking along a gravel path, Alix suddenly feels shy. What does she have to say to these Russian boys? Of course Ernie is already joking. "We thought we'd never get here. There was a gruesome welcome thing at the border and then hours and hours in the train."

"What did you expect? Russia is not a puny place like your Hessenland," Nicky answers.

"The German Empire compares well with the Russian Empire," Ernie counters.

"In military might maybe, but not size."

"In any case, the Germans and Russians are properly friends and allies," Ernie says.

"And all of us here, fond cousins," Nicky adds, smiling at Alix. She manages to smile bashfully back.

The mast turns out to be exactly that: a tall ship's mast stood up in a small field some distance behind the palace. Iron rungs poke out of either side, and a fine-meshed net has been suspended around it, about five feet off the ground. The Russian boys remove their tall boots and tell Alix and Ernie to take off their shoes. Nicky holds down the edge of the net while Georgy demonstrates how to swing up in one smooth motion. Alix's swing is more like an awkward scramble, and she worries her skirt is riding up. But once on the net, she finds it taut but not too taut, perfect for bouncing. With the others she's soon sailing high, the air delightfully cool under her stockinged feet—it's like bouncing on the bed with May long ago. No, she mustn't think about poor May just now and spoil the happy moment. She's practically weightless. Her soles touch the net for only a second before she's aloft again. Stretching out her arms, she flutters her fingers as she flies.

A shrill little voice calls: "Wait for me!"

A small girl, running down the path toward them, is barefoot, wearing a blue sailor dress.

"That's our sister Xenia," says Nicky. "She's nine and she's very lively. Too lively, Mama says."

Xenia's dark, curly hair is falling loose from its pins. Her arms and legs are almost too long for her small body. One effortless swing, and she's up on the net. She comes directly over to bounce next to Alix, staring at her with eager brown eyes.

"You are very pretty," she announces. "Like a princess in a fairy tale. If only I had golden hair like yours."

How to answer this extremely flattering remark?

Nicky laughs. "Don't embarrass our guest, Xenia. Look, you've made her blush."

Ernie says: "Sunny is forever blushing. Every time Papa tells her to play the piano for his guests, her face turns red as a beet-root."

Why must her brother mention this? She shoots him a hurt look.

"I too dislike people staring at me," says Nicky kindly. "Do your family call you Sunny?"

"Sometimes. My mother called me that."

"You prefer Alix?"

"That's my proper name," she says. "Why do you call our cousin Serge Uncle Gega?"

"Because I couldn't say his name correctly when I was small."

"Does he mind?"

"'Course not—he's our dear uncle and he often stays with us. Mama and Papa are happy he's finally getting married."

"Cousin Serge is extremely lucky that Ella will be his wife."

Nicky looks surprised. Has she offended him?

"She is lucky too," Alix adds, hurriedly.

Now he laughs. "I'm to be a best man. I'm looking forward to it, but I warn you our weddings last a long time. Cousin Konstantin was married in April and I almost toppled over in exhaustion. Luckily, we have days and days till then."

"A little over a week," Alix says.

"Days and days," he corrects cheerfully.

Xenia wants to hold hands with Alix as they bounce. *"Ring around the rosy, a pocket full of posies, a tissue a tissue, we all fall down,"* the girl sings, and the two of them collapse for a minute, before Xenia pulls Alix up to do it again.

"Rather a baby game, but I enjoy it," announces Xenia.

Uncle Sasha and Aunt Minnie spoke in German, but these Russian children speak English like they are English.

"Do you have an English nurse?" Alix asks the little girl.

"She's Nana, Mrs. Franklin. Now she mostly takes care of our little brother Misha, and our baby Olga. There's also Mr. Heath, my brothers' English tutor."

Xenia pulls her face into a frown, raises her forefinger, and says in a plummy voice, "Aristocrats are born, but gentlemen are made." Then she laughs. "He's very pompous—poor man, he can't help himself."

The boys begin to climb the rungs. Alix hopes none of them will slip. At the top of the mast, Ernie touches a hand to his forehead to shade his eyes and scans the horizon. "I can see right out to sea, Sunny!" he calls. The three wave and hoot for several minutes before climbing back down.

"Have we had enough of the mast?" Nicky asks.

"Yes," Georgy answers immediately. "Hoops now."

Xenia insists on holding Alix's hand as they walk across the springy grass, down a path between high laurel hedges that smell faintly bitter, out onto another lawn, bordered on both sides by beds of roses. Two dozen hoops are laid out in what appears to be a wide figure eight. Georgy explains: the game is rather like tag but players run through the hoops. The chaser can go in and out, but everyone else must remain within the hoop path, although it's permissible to reverse direction to avoid being caught. Nicky, as eldest, will be first chaser.

Everyone is faster than Alix—Ernie and Georgy because they are boys, and Xenia because she's so little she doesn't have to stoop to go through the hoops. Also she tucks up the sides of her skirt into her waistband to run at speed. It's shocking to see the girl's exposed brown legs churning. But Alix gamely tries to keep up.

She's gone only a short distance before she feels Nicky's arms slide around her waist, and his breath on her neck. "I've got you now," he says. His embrace isn't rough; she likes it, how he holds her for a moment. Then he tickles her under the arms, and she can't help giggling.

"I'm going to let you off," Nicky confides.

Xenia comes up, panting, and is caught by surprise when Nicky whirls around, grabbing her by the shoulders, and says: "You are chaser now, Xenia."

"Not fair!" shouts Xenia, but Nicky has already taken off, Alix running right behind him.

THERE SEEMS NO end to the ways the Russian children romp. After the hoops Nicky and Georgy want to show them something they call the turning machine.

"It's in the garden of the cottage," Nicky explains as they walk by the rose beds and onto a long, straight carriageway. Lined with manicured lime trees, this road is flat and stretches a long way in front of them and behind. They pass by a huge stone fountain on the right, and then a smaller gold one on the left.

"We're going to a children's cottage?" asks Alix, thinking of the Swiss Cottage at Osborne that Grandmama built as a playhouse.

Nicky looks puzzled. "For children? No. The Cottage Palace is where we live here at Peterhof. The Grand Palace, where you are staying—Mama hates it, she calls it a drafty old barn."

Alix is surprised. She likes the white rooms they've been assigned, with immensely high windows. And how can the tsar of Russia live in a cottage?

Ah, but it isn't that. They turn into a pebbled lane, and Nicky points—"There"—at a large, steep-roofed yellow-stone house, with pretty white gingerbread trim, bay windows, and wrought-iron balconies. Ivy climbs the walls and a dense exuberance of blooms—hollyhocks, poppies, sweet peas, and more—surround the house.

"How lovely," Alix says.

"My great-grandfather, the tsar Nicholas, for whom I am named, built it as a present for his wife, Alexandra."

"Did Nicholas and his Alexandra go back and forth?" she asks. "From the pretty house to the splendid palace?"

Nicky laughs. "I suppose so. Mama's choice would be to stay here in the Cottage Palace forever, but now Papa has become tsar, he's been persuaded that he needs something more imposing."

"Yes, I can see why," she says earnestly.

He laughs again. "How funny you are, Alix."

She feels a bit hurt.

"Funny and sweet," he adds with a smile. "For our new residence they are expanding the Lower Dacha. It's right down by the sea. I will take you to see it later."

Now he leads them past laburnum trees and fragrant lilac into the back garden, where there's a round iron platform, rather like a small merry-go-round without horses or chariots, only a curved bar for pushing against. They take it in turns to shove the bar—jumping on and off the spinning platform.

After a while, Xenia begs Nicky to push her in the swing hanging from a tree limb nearby. Alix stands alongside as Xenia cries, "Higher, higher!"

Nicky, his face red with effort, already has his arms stretched over his head as he pushes hard on the wooden seat.

Suddenly Georgy—on the turning machine with Ernie—yelps. Alix turns to see a man spraying him with a hose. The tsar! Uncle Sasha has changed out of his uniform and wears a long cotton blouse that hangs below his belt, and baggy trousers tucked into the top of his boots.

"It's time for luncheon! Better move fast, all of you, or you'll get soaked," he shouts.

Nicky grabs Alix by the hand and they run around the side of the house, under an arbor draped in giant purple wisteria, and through a glass door. Inside, the Cottage Palace is buzzing with people. In the drawing room Papa stands in the center of a large group talking, while Serge and Ella sit beside each other on a small sofa. A bell rings for luncheon, and everyone takes a seat at a long table, the young people seated at the foot. During the meal Ernie and Georgy and Nicky pelt one another with bits of rolled-up bread, which alarms Alix. And she silently disapproves when Xenia grabs an apple out of a bowl and takes a big bite. At home, a knife and fork are always used to eat fruit at the table.

From his thronelike solid-backed wooden chair at the head of the table, the tsar, she notices, frequently has his eyes on them. Pudding is vanilla cake with strawberry fondant, and then the children are allowed to get down. As they file from the room, Uncle Sasha grabs Nicky's arm, shakes it, and says something sharp to him in Russian.

"What was your father telling you?" she asks, once out of doors.

Nicky looks a bit downcast. "That I am too old for these silly games. Only because I am entertaining you and your brother is it allowed."

A grown man who sprays his children with a hose accuses his son of childishness? That seems unjust. But Nicky is soon smiling again. "Back to the swing?" he asks. "I'll push you if you promise not to screech the way Xenia does."

THANK GOODNESS MISS JACKSON immediately gives up on lessons. "Each evening we shall meet for an hour and you will recount what you have observed of Russian customs," she tells Ernie and Alix.

Even that resolution comes to nothing. Their governess joins the daily sightseeing party going into St. Petersburg—some combination of Victoria, Louis, Papa, Irène, Uncle Alexander, and Aunt Julie. Miss Jackson arrives home so worn out they never see her after supper.

Ella is occupied preparing for her wedding with a gray-bearded priest clad all in black, who wears a black headdress shaped like a hatbox. This small man has a grand name, the Metropolitan of St. Petersburg. When she's not with the priest, Ella spends all her time at fittings, having new gowns for Russia made under Aunt Minnie's direction.

Alix and Ernie are free to range all over Peterhof with the Russian children. They run along the narrow *allees* of clipped trees, paddle in the fountains, and visit the tropical greenhouses. When, on the third day, Nicky proposes a mushroom hunt in the back woods, Alix is forced to confess she is too scared of spiders to join in. But Nicky finds her a fallen branch, quite thick, and shows her how to swing it in front of her, to clear away any webs. Properly armed, branch in her right hand, basket dangling off her left wrist, Alix happily pokes and prods in the damp, bosky reaches. Back at the Cottage Palace, they deposit their harvest in the kitchen, and for supper eat the mushrooms, crisply fried in butter, doused with sour cream. Heavenly.

One afternoon, workmen arrive in the fragrant back garden of the Cottage Palace and proceed to erect a maypole with dozens and dozens of trailing ribbons attached.

"I'm planning to host a children's party," Aunt Minnie explains. "After the wedding, on the day before the Darmstadt family must return home."

"Mama better pray it doesn't rain before her party," Nicky says to Alix in a low voice. "Those ribbons will be ruined."

He needn't have worried. The sun continues to shine—day after dazzling day.

"TELL ME A secret," Nicky says. They've come to the Lower Dacha, the future summer home of the imperial family, now being remodeled. Nicky and Alix sit on a bench on the unfinished glass porch, where new windows are framed by bare timber boards and the air smells of sawdust.

"What kind of secret?" she answers.

"Something you don't tell most people."

"You will laugh."

"I won't." His velvety eyes look at her expectantly.

"Sometimes in my mother's room," Alix begins, "I can close my eyes and float, and then I am right beside Mama."

He gazes at her steadily, absorbing this.

"Perhaps we are in heaven or maybe somewhere between heaven and the earth. But my mother is there," she says.

"Do you converse?"

"Not really, but on occasion I hear her speak a few words."

"This is pleasant?" he asks.

"Yes!"

"Do you remember her in life?"

"Not her face precisely, nor her voice, but how she was. There's a picture still hanging in Mama's room. By a painter called Raphael of the mother of Jesus. Mama resembled her." Alix says this firmly, even as she worries that to draw this particular comparison is a touch blasphemous.

Still, Nicky doesn't laugh. He looks interested.

"Also I recall my little sister, May, who loved to play. She died a short time before Mama."

"I saw my grandfather die," Nicky remarks, quite matter-of-fact.

"Directly in front of you?"

"Oh yes. My mother and I, we were with my cousin Sandro on that afternoon, and we had just left the Anichkov to go skating when we heard a big explosion from near the Winter Palace." He raises his arms, stretching them wide. "Mama directed the coachman to take us to the rear of that palace and we ran in, our skates bouncing against our shoulders. When we reached the main hall we could see large drops of black blood on the marble floor, and following these drops we went up the stairs and into my grandfather's study. There he was, lying on a sofa where they had put him down. Criminals had thrown a bomb and one of his legs was blown away, and his face was cut up and covered in blood. My father saw me, and he took my hand and brought me forward. 'Papa,' he said, 'look, your favorite boy is here.' But my grandfather only had one eye remaining, and it wasn't seeing anything anymore, although it was wide open, like this." With two fingers Nicky spreads open his lids, exposing the white of his right eye all around the iris.

Alix gasps.

"Soon after, the doctor felt Grandfather's throat and announced he was dead. Mama and the other women began to wail," Nicky says.

"How horrible."

He shrugs. "Papa says we shouldn't dwell on what happened."

But how can they forget it?

"You see," Nicky goes on, "I was born on May 6, the feast day of Job the sufferer, which means I'm destined to be very unlucky in life."

Kind-hearted Nicky ill-fated? "Oh, I hope not," Alix says.

"It may well be God's wish," he says with another shrug.

Golden sun spills in through the west windows. She hears the thwack of a tennis racket hitting a ball—Ernie and Georgy are playing on the court below. All is peace and beauty, and in spite of that they are talking about death and dying.

"Today, I'm very lucky," Nicky says, breaking into her thoughts. "Lucky to be here with you, dear Alix. I want to cut our names in one of the new windows."

She looks at him questioningly.

"Side by side. As we love each other—don't we?" he asks, smiling.

She's so startled, she has to look down at the floor.

"Don't we?" he asks again.

"Yes," she says softly. How happy this makes her.

"Good. Then our names should be together forever." She sees him look around. "I think that one," he says, pointing at a window in the right corner.

"What can we use? A sharp rock? Or maybe a nail?" She scans the stone floor for something suitable. But there are only wood shavings left behind by the builders.

"This," Nicky says, and he reaches into his pocket. He waves his clenched fist under her eyes momentarily before slowly opening his fingers. There lying in his palm is a silver disc with a diamond at the center, a brooch.

"This is yours?" she asks, confused.

He smiles. "I obtained it—but it is for you."

She pulls back a bit, she's so surprised.

"You don't like it?" he asks.

"I do."

"Fine then. First, we'll use it to scratch our names, and then you will have the brooch to keep."

She stares at him and feels her cheeks redden. Can she really accept?

"It's just a brooch," he says mildly. "Come now, let's write our names."

Standing by the window, Alix watches as he carefully scratches N-I-C-K-Y in square letters.

"Now you, right below me," he says, passing her the brooch.

Her A comes out a bit too large, then the L, the I, and the X smaller. A lopsided, slanting result. Not very good. She looks at him anxiously.

"Perfect," he says. "Now whenever I'm in this house, I can come and see our names together."

He takes a small blue velvet pouch out of his pocket. "For the brooch." He slips it inside, pulls the drawstring tight, and holds out the pouch. "I hope you will wear it often."

Oh no, what to do? She can't bear to reject the gift, but she is almost certain taking it is improper. Still, she stretches out her hand. "Thank you," she says softly.

He smiles and presses the pouch into her palm.

UNCLE BERTIE ARRIVES on the HMS *Osborne*—dropping anchor right off Peterhof. But he has left Aunt Alix and their five Wales cousins at home.

"Grandmama insisted—she considers Russia too dangerous to visit," Victoria explains.

"Why dangerous?" Alix asks.

"Because of revolutionaries, like the ones who killed the old tsar," she says. "But we are safe here. Notice the soldiers all around? Peterhof is extremely well guarded. Don't worry."

Alix isn't worried exactly, although it is disquieting to think that somewhere, out there in the mysterious vastness of Russia, evil men may be lurking. Might a whole group of them storm lovely Peterhof? Once in Windsor, she and Ernie went up into the old Norman tower and saw the open slots in the thick stone walls where archers in medieval times could shoot down on raiders coming to attack the royal fastness. But that was centuries ago. England is completely peaceful, and Darmstadt too. Citizens might feel aggrieved at Papa, but she can't imagine they'd ever hurt him. When he walks in town men and women smile and bow and greet him so cheerily. "*Guten Morgen, Hoheit!*" Occasionally a bold person will ask Papa for help with some problem. Alix has been with him when he stops to listen, stroking his beard and nodding before giving advice.

Perhaps because Russia is so big and so rich it could never be the same as in Darmstadt or even England.

Not everyone English in their family is afraid of Russia, because Uncle Affie, another of Mama's brothers, has arrived. He has brought his wife, stout Aunt Marie, who is Cousin Serge's sister, and their little daughters, Missy and Ducky.

A formal banquet will be held at the Grand Palace to welcome the new arrivals. But at luncheon Aunt Minnie says Alix, Ernie, Nicky, and Georgy are excused—she is ordering up a picnic supper for them to eat on the rocky shoreline in front of the Lower Dacha instead. Xenia will stay back to play with Missy and Ducky.

Xenia stamps her foot and shouts. "I won't be left behind with those little babies!" Missy is nine, the same age as Xenia, and Ducky, whose real name is Victoria, is only a year younger—so hardly babies. Still, Aunt Minnie relents and Xenia is allowed to join Alix and the boys for the picnic.

TWO SERVANTS COME to lay out the cold meal and clear away the remnants before leaving them alone except, Alix notices, for a pair of gray-coated soldiers, rifles slung over their shoulders, watching from twenty yards distant. After eating, they jump between boulders on the water's edge—Nicky holding her hand for daring leaps. They take off their shoes and stockings to wade in the cool shallows and lift up rocks and watch little brown crabs skittering away—indignant, Alix imagines, to be so disturbed.

The sky gradually fades from bright blue to soft lavender, and presently she finds a smooth rock and sits down. The sea has a soft, metallic sheen on this still evening. Hugging her knees, she watches the boys lob stones into the water, competing to hurl one the farthest. Xenia demands turns too. The cool air smells of salt and pine both, and in the quiet Alix feels a momentousness in the atmosphere, as she did in the train, that curious sense Russia gives you of grandeur and scale, of secretive possibilities hovering close, just beyond what you can see with your eyes.

Alix is thinking, happily, that the adults have forgotten all about them and they will stay out here for hours, past midnight even, when she hears her sister call: "Ernie! Alix!"

Victoria is standing beside Louis at the edge of the rocky beach. In the evening light, the trees behind them appear as a single dense mass of branches.

She's sorry to say good night, but Nicky grins. "See you tomorrow."

As they walk toward the carriage, following Ernie and Louis, Victoria says, "I can tell you are having such a nice time here. You like those boys?"

"Very much," she says. "And Xenia is very sweet."

"Although she often looks like a ragamuffin."

Alix giggles. She remembers something that's preoccupied her. "Victoria, do you believe the day you are born on matters?"

"What do you mean?"

"Does your birthday determine something about your fate?"

Victoria smiles. "Don't you remember? I was born on Easter Sunday."

"That's right," Alix says, suddenly recalling.

"Those born on Easter are said to be able to see fairies and find hidden treasure, neither of which I have ever managed," she says with a light laugh. "Why do you ask?"

"No particular reason," Alix says hurriedly. To Ella, she might reveal what Nicky said, but Victoria is bound to scoff.

"These notions about birthdays, which days are better than others to be born on, and what the dates portend—it's like telling fortunes with cards, or tea leaves," Victoria says. "Harmless, but fundamentally nonsense."

There she goes, scoffing.

Alix is taken by surprise when Victoria's voice softens. "I have come to believe, ever since Uncle Leo died, that one's health is really what determines one's fate."

"Dear uncle. So very sad," Alix says. A month before Victoria's wedding, their uncle Leo, always delicate, slipped on the stairs in a house in France, hit his head, and died.

"I think how lucky Leo was—born a prince, grown to be a clever and able man," Victoria continues, sadly. "Married to a woman he adored and living at beautiful Claremont. Yet he wasn't granted the most vital gift of all—a healthy body."

Her elder sister sniffs. Is she weeping?

Alix looks up, but can't read Victoria's face in the low light. She's prompted to confess: "I thought of little May the other day, but I pushed it away because . . ."

Alix doesn't know how to finish her sentence. She hopes her sister won't think her heartless.

Victoria reaches out and strokes the back of her head lightly. "Dear girl, you are right not to be melancholy, here, now. We must enjoy being all together, with the magnificent celebration still to come!"

RUSSIAN ROYAL BRIDES, by custom, enter the capital city on the day before their wedding. Papa explains they will accompany Ella by train, spend the night in town at the Winter Palace, and the next day *both* weddings—her father says this with special emphasis—will take place, the Orthodox one followed by the German one.

Outside the city station, a line of old-fashioned gold coaches, with elaborately carved crowns perched on their roofs, awaits them. The first one, the largest, is for Aunt Minnie and Ella, and after they get in, it swings away—drawn by six white horses with red plumes attached to their bobbing heads. A large troop of soldiers on horseback, each man in a white jacket and what looks like a double-sided gold turtle shell, march behind. Rank after rank pass by, horses with shining flanks and rippling manes, their riders forming a river of gold, the strong sun glinting on the bright chest plates and backplates.

Ernie, speaking loudly over the tramping of horses' hooves, tells her: "They're cuirassiers, because what they're wearing is called a cuirass. In our armory at home we have some, but dull and iron, nothing as impressive as these."

Cousin Serge, Cousin Paul, Nicky, and Georgy take the second coach, while Papa is directed to the third. Ernie slides in beside him; Irène and Alix sit with their backs to the driver. The bench seats, covered in red velvet, are surprisingly narrow and hard. Alix squirms around trying to get a comfortable perch as the coach bumps along. Papa laughs. "No proper springs in Catherine the Great's time, so not easy on the bottom. Distract yourself with the view."

St. Petersburg is a wide place—the broad boulevards lined with large, pillared buildings, mostly stone, painted in light colors, yellow, pink, and pastel green, trimmed in white. They recall the square marzipan French cakes, with hard sugar icing, sold at the bakery in the Luisenplatz in Darmstadt. Plenty of people stand on the pavements, gazing at the procession, but not all cheer and wave. "Do you think, Papa," she asks, "that Russian don't love their rulers, the way Darmstädters love you, and Londoners love Grandmama?"

"Here in Russia the citizens consider the tsar and his family rather like gods." He chuckles. "Which of course they are not. But the Romanovs inspire as much awe as they do affection, you are correct."

The carriage rattles over a stone bridge and then turns onto a street that runs along the bank of a river. "The Neva," Papa says, pointing. "We are close to the Winter Palace now."

From her seat, looking left Alix has a fine view of the river, the slate-colored surface ruffled by the breeze. She likes the delicate iron railings, with oval and square cut-out shapes, topping the stone embankment. Only when they halt and alight from the gold coach can she see the palace properly, craning her neck to take it all in. Stretching wide in both directions, four stories tall, the building is painted creamy butter yellow, with elaborate details—columns, bas-reliefs, and decorative balustrade—caramel brown. She recalls her grandmother's London home: that sooty, gray edifice with small windows. "It is just as well Grandmama hasn't come, Papa," she says to him. "She would be so envious—this Winter Palace is much, much prettier than Buckingham Palace."

"Don't let's ever tell her that," he says, laughing. "I can't imagine she'd be pleased." And he squeezes her shoulder with his hand.

THE NEXT MORNING Alix—along with Victoria and Irène—waits outside a pair of tall, gold-and-black doors, behind which Ella is donning her gown and having her hair arranged. Even if Ella's own mother were alive and here, Aunt Minnie would still be in charge, Victoria reports.

"Not right at all," Alix grumbles.

"It's traditional for the women of the imperial family—Aunt Minnie as empress is the most senior—to welcome a new bride by dressing her for the wedding," her sister explains.

"So, you and me and Irène, and even poor Orchie"—Alix points at their nurse, who, white-faced and anxious, stands a short distance down the hall—"can't help? We can't even see Ella? Speak to her?"

"Aunt Minnie and Aunt Marie promise that at the appropriate moment we will be allowed in," Victoria says, her voice strained. Her eldest sister clearly isn't happy either.

She and Irène, in the matching white muslin frocks they

wore to Victoria's wedding, have wreaths of pink roses on their heads. Victoria is in a blue gown trimmed with silver, her anchor brooch from Serge pinned above her heart. They've been ready for more than an hour. How much longer will Ella's preparation take?

Finally, the left-hand door opens, and Aunt Marie is there beckoning them in. "We are nearly done."

The room inside is gigantic, with bright-green stone walls and four round pillars of the same stone holding up the ceiling. Alix gapes. "Admiring the malachite, dear?" Aunt Marie says with a proud smile. "The world's largest mass of it was discovered in our Urals earlier this century."

Alix nods politely; the green stone is impressive, but she can't imagine why this huge hall was chosen as the dressing room.

"Stop here," their aunt commands. Victoria, Irène, and Alix must halt, still a good ten yards behind Ella, who is standing in front of a huge mirror, wearing her gown, which looks to be made out of heavily embroidered silver cloth. Ten or so women mill around the bride, chatting to one another.

"We were kept out while these others—these who-knows-who ladies were admitted just to hang about?" Alix whispers to Victoria.

"We're in now. Smile and look grateful," her sister says.

The only man in the room is a very small, elfin person, wearing a yellow waistcoat, white shirt, striped trousers, and no jacket. He's up on a stool, his hands busy twisting Ella's hair. Beside him stands Aunt Minnie, holding out pins to him.

"By tradition the empress must 'coif' the royal bride herself," Victoria says in a low voice. "Which I suppose means helping the hairdresser do it."

The little man affixes the last strands of Ella's light-brown hair to the back of her head, and calls out: *"Les boucles, les boucles!"*

Curls, what curls?

A young woman in a gray uniform scurries out of a corner, holding high two long ringlets of hair, one in each hand. Alix thinks suddenly, incongruously, of sausages—as if this maid is about to drop sausages into a hot frying pan. Instead, she comes to stand motionless, arms raised, next to the hairdresser as he, rapidly plucking pins from Minnie's outstretched palm, attaches first one curl and then the other so they lie softly on either side of Ella's bare neck.

"*C'est fini!*" he declares.

"Now we'll go?" Alix asks Victoria.

"Still the jewels to come," her sister warns.

Aunt Minnie begins winding wire around Ella's ears, from which she eventually hangs large diamond earrings, triangle-shaped. Aunt Marie carries over a red pillow with something glittering on top. Aunt Minnie lifts up off the pillow a huge diamond necklace rather like a baby's bib. "These diamonds are the Russian Crown Jewels, they belonged to Catherine the Great," Victoria tells Alix. "Every grand duchess wears them on her wedding day."

From another velvet pillow, held out by a different Romanov lady, Aunt Minnie picks up a diamond tiara and gently places it on Ella's head, careful not to muss her hair.

There's a pause while Aunt Minnie, Aunt Marie, and two other ladies cross the room and come back with a heavy, crimson velvet mantle trimmed with ermine. They tie it to Ella's shoulders. The four of them then drape a white lace veil over the top of her. The hairdresser returns, steps up on his stool, and places a gold crown on Ella's head.

Her sister is regarding herself in the mirror. Is she amazed? Happy? Overwhelmed? Alix refuses to wait any longer to find out. Running forward, she comes up on Ella's left side and meets her sister's eyes in the glass. "We've been watching, Ella! And I think you are . . ."

What is the right word? Ella's gentle, winsome self looks a bit lost under all the regalia—the crown, the veil, the tiara, the stiff silver dress, the two sausage curls, the heavy earrings, the bib necklace.

But she mustn't say *that*. Instead Alix declares: "Glorious. You look glorious."

"Thank you, dearest. I do hope Serge will still recognize me," Ella says with a small laugh, still studying her reflection.

THREE HOURS! THE Orthodox service goes on and on, the congregation standing throughout, and Alix, her feet sore and her legs aching, must shift her weight about, and pick up first one foot and then the other, to shake it and relieve the strain.

She notices Nicky, on the other side of the aisle, watching her. Once he even winks at her. She did smile back, although she probably shouldn't have.

The ceremony appears less like a wedding—the quick and simple exchange of vows that Victoria and Louis had—and more like a crowning. Flanked by two black-robed priests, wearing hatbox-like headpieces, the Metropolitan in his elaborate gold cape spends endless minutes passing crowns over the heads of the bride and groom. And then all the several best men—including Nicky—do the same.

Ella and Serge hold tapers, the small flames flickering brightly in the low light of the church, illuminating their serious faces from below. The priests chant long prayers while clouds of incense waft over all onlookers. A small choir sings slow, rather mournful hymns.

This church within the palace, while astonishingly ornate—the tall white marble walls are encrusted in gold—isn't huge. And, packed with so many people, it's awfully stuffy. Alix begins to feel rather faint. What a great relief when the formalities are over.

Following the bride and groom, everyone files out of the church and troops through a gallery into a lofty blue-and-white room. At least this next service is quite brief. Amidst the Russian grandeur Pfarrer Sell, come from Darmstadt to preside, looks a plain little mouse—bareheaded, in his black cassock and white surplice. And, naturally, there's no incense and no chanting at a German wedding.

Next, they are directed upstairs. Such a din of rattling metal as everyone climbs the steps—nearly all the men are wearing swords. In an immense hall painted pink with gold trim, long tables have been pushed together to form an enormous T, set with gold plates, with towering green and white flower arrangements as big as small trees for centerpieces. Ernie and Alix find their seats on the right arm of the T, the rest of the bride's family seated with them, except there's no place for Louis. He and Victoria go off to inquire, and her sister comes back alone. Victoria sits down next to Papa and begins whispering to him vehemently. Alix rises to scan the hall. She sees a stream of red-and-gold liveried waiters entering the room, bearing enormous covered trays, but where is Louis? With his very black beard her brother-in-law is never hard to spot. Oh, there he is—sitting at a place far away, quite near the door.

Alix throws Victoria a questioning look, which Papa catches instead. "Sit down now and pay attention, *Kleine*," he says with a stern point.

One of the waiters is sliding in front of her a bowl of hot soup. She picks up the paper menu on the right-hand side of her place.

"Consommé," she says aloud.

"Delicious," says Ernie, who is already spooning it into his mouth.

Nine courses follow, with a lengthy wait between each one. A fish called sterlets, beef in tomato sauce, partridge, lobster, chicken. The last and best is hot cherry pudding and ice cream. Alix wishes she had pen and paper with her to make sketches of some of the beautiful gowns she sees on the lady guests. Instead, she has to sit, empty-handed, through the meal and several long speeches afterward. They are finally able to get up and walk down the hallway to what Papa says is called the Concert Hall, where there will be not a concert but a ball. In other circumstances Alix would feel excited: She's never been to a ball. But her feet are still sore from all the standing and it's wearisome to be surrounded by so many people for such a long period of time. While Ernie goes off to explore the palace with Nicky and Georgy, Alix is content to sit in a quiet corner and watch the dancing. Ella does something called the polonaise with Serge—it's more like a march than a dance. No longer with her veil or her crown, Ella is still wearing the glittering diamonds—tiara, necklace, and earrings. Her sister looks beautiful, but very pale. She must be tired too.

After an hour or so Ernie returns, and soon afterward Miss Jackson appears in front of them—wearing a dark-purple gown trimmed with jet beads, quite the fanciest thing Alix has ever seen her in. A small jet-fringed reticule hangs from her wrist. "Your sister and her husband will depart shortly for their new home, the Sergievsky Palace. There the tsar and tsarina will welcome them with bread and salt, a Russian tradition," she says. "These gifts signify luck, plenty, and happiness. Presenting them is properly the job of the groom's parents, but as the grand duke Serge's father and mother are no longer with us . . ."

Miss Jackson trails off. Is she picturing the bloody demise of Serge's father?

After a pause, the governess resumes instructing. Papa and Irène, Victoria and Louis, along with Uncle Bertie, Uncle Affie, Aunt Marie, and the rest of the Romanovs, will accompany

Ella and Serge to the Sergievsky Palace and stay for a light supper. "But you two children have had enough," Miss Jackson announces.

At first Alix wants to protest—why should she and Ernie miss anything?—yet once they follow their governess out of the hall, walk down the corridor, beautifully cool after the crowded Concert Hall, and descend the enormous, red-carpeted main staircase, she's glad to be departing. It's been a long day.

EVEN ERNIE LOOKS droopy at breakfast the next morning. Papa comes downstairs to eat before announcing he's going back to bed. He and the others returned to Peterhof a mere three hours earlier.

Cousin Paul reports that Nicky and Georgy and Xenia will not come to play, because they stayed in town at the Anichkov Palace. And he, Paul, can certainly not play.

"I feel a hundred years old," he says, using a long spoon to stir some strange milky concoction in a tall glass. "I need to settle my insides," he explains, and quickly gulps down the whole thing.

Victoria is still angry about the banquet seating. "I intend to take this up directly with Uncle Bertie," she announces.

They sit together in the conservatory off the dining room, where Ernie and Alix enjoy the sweets—flat cream caramels and lozenge-shaped fruit drops wrapped in white paper—left in a bowl on the low center table.

At noontime their British uncle strolls into the room.

"Good morning, if it's still morning," he says amiably. "I trust everyone slept well."

"Uncle, I barely slept!" exclaims Victoria. "I have been waiting to speak with you."

"Ah," replies Uncle Bertie, with a brief, ironical smile.

He sits down in a wicker chair, pulls a cigar out of his pocket, asks Cousin Paul for a match, lights the cigar, draws deeply on it, and tips his head back, blowing smoke up at the ceiling.

Only then does he wave his cigar at Victoria, inviting her to speak.

"Louis was placed miles away from me at the table!" she explains. "Given a seat below the salt and near the door."

Uncle Bertie nods.

"And when I objected, one of Uncle Sasha's factotums told me off. Louis could not sit beside me, this man claimed, because he is not my equal. So please, Uncle, will you ask the British ambassador—what's his name, Thornton?—to lodge a complaint? It's terrible that a member of our family should be treated so shabbily!"

"Ridiculous, I agree," Uncle Bertie replies, raising his brows. "But, my dear, I've already investigated, having noticed the seating arrangements myself. It seems the emperor of Germany, a valuable Russian ally, requested that the German royals be placed at the table according to their blood rank. Which is why, you may have noticed, your in-laws Prince Alexander and Princess Julia were also seated at a distance from the rest of us. Sasha put your dear husband with the officers of the *Osborne*, where, he felt, Louis would enjoy the company best."

"So, Uncle Sasha does whatever the German emperor asks?"

"When it costs him nothing."

"It has cost him my ire!" Victoria exclaims.

"That's next to nothing, I fear," Uncle Bertie says.

Victoria scowls. "You are not outraged?"

"Is Louis outraged? Where is he, by the way?" Uncle Bertie looks around the room.

"He's gone out for a sail with some men from the *Osborne*," Victoria says.

"His new friends! Aren't their heads too sore to be out in the sun? Mine certainly is," Uncle Bertie says, rubbing his temples.

Her elder sister continues to glare at their uncle.

"My dear Victoria—please," he says. "Your sister has only yesterday been very grandly married. Ella is now one of the most important ladies in this somewhat backward country. We must do all we can to help her smoothly launch into her new life, and that includes not making a fuss over what is essentially a petty matter."

"Petty to you maybe, but to me—" Victoria begins.

"You will desist now, Victoria," Uncle Bertie cuts in, looking stern.

Why exactly is Russia backward? Alix longs to ask—but senses her inquiry will not be welcome. Victoria, red in the face, begins to examine her fingernails.

Uncle Bertie continues, more gently: "Once our duty to Ella is done, we can be on our way—together. Your father and I have conferred. You will join us on the *Osborne* when we depart the day after tomorrow. At Kiel, Ludwig will disembark with Ernie, Irène, and Alicky, and you and Louis will continue on to Portsmouth, where your husband can get back to work."

"I will be extremely happy to leave here," Victoria says hotly.

Not me, Alix thinks. *I will be sorry.*

SHOULD SHE WEAR the brooch Nicky gave her to Aunt Minnie's party, or not? She turns this question over and over in her mind. It's possibly too ornate for the occasion. But Nicky might expect to see her wearing it? And will be pleased? Yes, that seems more probable. Her white muslin frock, the one she wore for the wedding, is her smartest and will set off the brooch best. Alix asks Orchie to iron it so she might wear it again.

"Mind you don't spill punch down the front," her nurse clucks.

Honestly, she might be a child of six the way Orchie treats her. After she's dressed, her nurse says, "Where's that come from?" and points at the brooch Alix has pinned under her right collarbone.

"From Nicky."

Orchie frowns and leaves the room. Alix is brushing her hair when Victoria appears.

"What is this I hear? You've taken a brooch from Nicky?"

"I haven't taken it—he gave it to me." She cups her hand over the brooch protectively.

"Yes, yes, of course," says Victoria, impatient. "But I don't like how high-handed these Romanovs are. Come into the light, so I can see properly."

By the window her sister stoops to take a closer look. "That's a sizable diamond."

Alix nods. "I did wonder—"

"What?"

"I did wonder whether it was correct to accept such an expensive gift?"

Victoria gazes down at her, although not, Alix is surprised to see, in a stern way.

"Yes, perhaps it would have been better not. Although no one could blame you. It's quite spectacular." Her sister laughs lightly.

"So, should I return it?"

"Hmm . . . having already accepted it? . . . I'm not sure."

"If you believe I should return it, I will."

Now Victoria smiles. "I think you should decide this for yourself."

Very unlike her eldest sister not to pronounce a verdict. At the bedroom door, Victoria glances back and says, "Enjoy yourself, dear Sunny, you look very pretty."

HOW SAD, ALIX thinks, to be going this way for the last time. She and Ernie walk out of the back of the Grand Palace, down

the terrace steps, across the field where the mast stands, between the laurel hedges, alongside the lawn with the hoops, to
reach the smooth carriageway. From there, it's a short distance
to the point where they turn into the pebbled lane that leads to
the Cottage Palace.

From amidst a clutch of children in front of the house, Xenia
comes tearing toward them and throws her arms around Alix's
waist.

"I've been waiting for you! I hate that you are leaving tomorrow."

Xenia tows Alix by the hand over to Aunt Minnie, on the
doorstep, greeting guests.

"Hello dears," the empress calls out.

Ernie bows, Alix bobs a curtsy, and she watches Aunt Minnie's smile change to a frown. The empress seems to be staring
at the brooch on her chest. Does the sight displease her? Will
she ask Alix how she came by it?

But Aunt Minnie only purses her mouth and says: "Nicky
and Georgy are in the back and will be delighted to know
you've arrived."

"Come on," says Xenia, pulling again on her hand.

In the rear are a vast number of children, the smallest around
four, the oldest Nicky's age. "Quite the horde!" exclaims Ernie.

"Most are cousins," says Nicky. "We are a large family. My
great-grandfather had seven children and my grandfather had
eight. So that makes for a crowd. Also, Mama has invited some
children of her friends. The Vorontsovs are our best chums; I'll
introduce you."

"First, you must have a jelly tart before they're all eaten up,"
Georgy urges. When the boys head toward the laden trestle
table, Alix deliberately falls behind.

She can wait no longer. Aunt Minnie has wordlessly convinced her—she mustn't keep Nicky's gift. She finds a quiet spot next to one of the large lilac bushes and unpins the brooch. If only she had thought to bring the velvet pouch.

Winding her way through the boisterous children, she finds Nicky, and pulls on his sleeve. He turns, sees it's her, and smiles gaily. "Do you have more secrets to tell me?" he asks.

"I am giving you back the brooch," she says.

"What? Why?" he asks, a bit petulant.

"I can't . . . it's not proper to take . . . I've decided I must return it," she concludes, blushing.

He shakes his head. "Don't worry about this."

"Please understand," she says, near tears. "Here." She presses it into his hand.

Now he looks annoyed. "I certainly wouldn't want to compel you to keep something you prefer not to have." He scans the throng. "Xenia," he calls.

His little sister gallops over. "What?"

"I have this for you." And he carefully pins the brooch on her dress.

"Thank you," she says cheerily, glancing down and giving it a pat. "Very pretty. I've never had a brooch before. The maypole dance is about to begin."

Xenia runs off again.

"Are you planning to take part?" Nicky asks Alix, in a slightly mocking tone.

Oh, she's ruined it. Their special bond. Now he'll believe he was mistaken about her. She's not sweet and lovable but prim and prissy—the sort of girl who doesn't like nice things like gifts and parties and playing games.

"Yes," she answers, smiling, attempting to appear merry, but her spirits are dashed.

"Good," he says, and walks away, hands thrust in his pockets. There's such a crush around the maypole, with so much screeching and yelling that in the end Alix watches from the side as children weave the ribbons in a complicated braid around the pole in time to music from a small band. Nicky and Georgy and Ernie all dance—somehow Ernie managed to grab two ribbons for himself.

A SMALL OPEN carriage, a *droshkey*, the Russians call it, has been sent for them—one of a line waiting outside the cottage at the end of the afternoon. Ernie stands next to the vehicle, joking with Nicky and Georgy, while Alix is alone a few feet behind them. How miserable to be going away having completely failed to explain herself, to feel sad and self-conscious and silly. After everything—after they jumped on the net, ran through the hoops, hunted mushrooms, picnicked on the beautiful rocky beach. After Nicky declared she and he loved each other! Oh, the pain of her failure feels like the point of a knife being slowly dragged across her insides.

Finally, Ernie steps up into the *droshkey*, and Nicky turns and extends his smooth, warm hand to help Alix. When she whispers, "Thank you," she feels him squeeze her fingers. Once in her seat, she looks down, into his velvety eyes. His expression is fond, if a little teasing. Maybe it's not ruined. Maybe he still loves her.

"I wish I could stay longer," she says quietly.

He grins, and just then the *droshkey* springs forward. Nicky runs alongside until they reach the turn into the white carriageway. He stops at the short stone gatepost and sings out: "See you again one day, dear Alix."

She keeps looking back, anxious to hold him in sight, until he raises his hand high in the air in final farewell, and the carriage lurches to the left and she can see him no more.

Chapter Nine

A Bride Makes Discoveries

Russia, summer 1884

*E*lla sits next to Serge on the wide, gold-canopied bed in their suite in the Sergievsky Palace—her new home. *Forevermore I will live here*, she thinks. What a peculiar notion. And how peculiarly they are dressed—Serge in the heavy silver dressing gown and turban-like headdress that's traditional for Romanov bridegrooms on their wedding night; she in a loose pink peignoir and lace pink cap.

At the start of the day, she felt excited but nervous. While being extravagantly dressed for the wedding, she worried all the fuss would keep her from feeling what a bride should. A woman married in a simple wooden chapel has little to distract her from the meaning of the ceremony. And yet when Ella spotted Serge's lean figure waiting at the church door, poised to be hers, irreversibly, everything else fell away. A large congregation waited within, but at the altar, she was aware only of Serge and the Metropolitan of St. Petersburg. She had been instructed how, in Orthodox belief, marriage is a kind of martyrdom—husband and wife become one single flesh. As she breathed in the heady scent of incense, listened to the prelate's whispered instructions—*clasp this candle, repeat the vow, hold out your finger to receive the ring*—along with a stream of Slavonic incantations, she gladly surrendered. Looking up at Serge, his color high, his face reverent, she knew he felt this moment as deeply as she did—perhaps more so.

But the sacredness of the occasion dwindled quickly, afterward, as they trudged from one cavernous room to another. The heavy earrings wired around her ears began to pull painfully. Her feet, squeezed into narrow shoes, with a ten-ruble coin inserted at the toe of the right one for luck, throbbed. Hours of smiling have left her mouth aching. Her temples pound and her neck is stiff. She rolls her head, front to back, side to side, trying to ease the tightness.

Serge reaches out, picks up her hand, and brings it to his dry lips to kiss, and she notices how pale he is.

"No one failed to remark on your poise and your beauty, Ella," he says. "And while at supper you barely spoke a word, I appreciated that by then you were exhausted."

Ella nods sadly. "The room had begun to spin."

"You must rest, we both must. Tomorrow we will greet the entire diplomatic corps here," he says with a small smile.

He rises to his feet. "Come, my child."

She's trembling inwardly as she stands. What will happen next? How should she behave? She doesn't know. All she can do is follow Serge's lead. He folds back the bedclothes; she slips into bed. He goes to extinguish the lamps and climbs in on the other side. The bed is so firm and wide that the springs barely sag under his weight.

"Good night, Ella. All the years of our life together stretch out ahead of us now."

She appreciates he wants to spare her more novel experiences tonight. And it's true they have plenty of time to achieve physical union. Still, she's surprised. She may be unclear on the mechanics of the act, but she's quite sure consummation is the goal of a wedding night. She feels a sharp, unexpected stab of distress, and then nothing—nothing but sweet relief. What she desires most now is merely to sleep.

IN RUSSIA, SERGE has explained, newlyweds don't rush off on honeymoon, to indulge in a tedious, extended tête-à-tête. Instead they begin their new life joyfully, by welcoming friends and family to their new home. Because of Serge's position, he and she will receive not only people they know, but dignitaries of all sorts.

Minnie, having faced the same prolonged period of official receiving when she married Sasha, oversaw the creation of a formal wardrobe for Ella. And while Ella is glad that Papa was spared the expense—he paid only for a basic trousseau of underclothes, nightgowns, and a few day dresses—she doesn't much like the gowns Minnie commissioned. The empress is always boldly and brightly turned out, and loves elaborate details—beading, ribbons, contrasting trims. She appears most often in yellow or gold, cherry-red, bright emerald green, and a constant favorite: milky-coffee-colored brown trimmed with black. These all flatter her glossy dark hair and large, shiny brown eyes, and reflect her vivacious personality. Naturally enough, Minnie has selected fabrics and styles for Ella that she might have chosen for herself. But Ella has fairer coloring and prefers to wear white, or her favorite pastels—blue-gray, soft apricot, clear pink. Ella also likes simplicity in tailoring.

Yet, in those busy days at Peterhof before the wedding, Ella didn't protest as the imperial dressmakers fitted the gowns on her. How could she—the newcomer, the bride, a nineteen-year-old German princess—object to what the empress desired?

Now on this first morning as a married lady, Ella sits at her dressing table and studies her reflection. Wearing a garish watered silk gown, chartreuse in color, with gold buttons, and trimmed with cascades of creamy lace—she looks wrong and false, as if she's dressed up for a theatrical pageant. Playing a rich merchant's wife perhaps—someone born poor who imagines this is what elegance looks like. What will Serge think when he sees her?

It was rather crushing to find herself alone in bed when she woke an hour ago. Was her new husband in such a hurry to get away from her?

Masha, her unsmiling Russian maid, who has strange, lashless eyes, begins brushing out her hair. In the mirror, Ella sees the door behind her open. Serge comes in looking elegant in the white uniform of the Chevalier-Gardes.

"Good morning," he says. "Stand, please."

She does, still facing forward. He shakes his head, contemptuous. "Beautifully constructed bodice, emphasizing a slim waist, yet I deplore the overall effect."

Ella sits back down and meets his eye in the glass. "Minnie declared it a lovely springtime color for a new bride."

"Not this new bride." He leans down and kisses her cheek. Ella is surprised—such an intimate gesture in front of Masha, who tactfully backs away.

"Minnie has been very generous," Ella says, still talking to him via the glass.

"Just the same, can we not agree her taste is . . ." He pauses for a minute. "*Un peu vulgaire?*"

She laughs. "We can."

He beams back at her, pleasingly conspiratorial. "You'll wear what she's chosen for this short period, but never again. For the winter season we will have a superb new wardrobe created for you. I've always thought your eye excellent, Ella—even when you had limited monies to spend."

"Have you forgotten a certain felt hat? With a feather? Which you found disappointing?"

He looks puzzled. "I recall no such hat."

"Never mind," she says, smiling again.

"Meanwhile, our first callers are due at ten," he says, stern once more.

"I will be ready," she answers.

ALL THAT WEEK Ella and Serge receive guests, acknowledge congratulations, take tea, eat meals. Serge leads small parties through the picture gallery on the first floor, where he has hung on crimson-covered walls Romanov family portraits as well as his collection of Boucher, Fragonard, Watteau, and Titian. Her husband—will the term ever trip off her tongue?—enjoys explaining the paintings to all, and also showing off his collection of eighteenth-century snuff boxes and precious Chinese porcelain. In the evenings they dine with selected visitors and members of Serge's family, her own family having departed on HMS *Osborne*.

She tries to push away the painful last glimpse of Papa, eyes clouded, repeatedly blowing his nose. Ernie joked to keep spirits high, but her sisters were solemn, Victoria chewing on her lip. Who knows when they will meet again?

How fortunate, really, that her mind is crammed with new names and new faces. Each morning, her toilette complete, Serge reels off a list of those they will entertain that day. It's pleasing how people seem so eager to meet her! Her apologies for her scanty Russian are waved away. Every guest speaks French, and most have good English or German. One stout, bejeweled matron, a Princess Drubetskoy, tells her, "None of the best people in St. Petersburg speak Russian, and if they do, they try to forget it."

When Ella repeats this remark to Serge, he snorts. "Such contemptuous creatures make me long to shun society forever!"

At night, they always go upstairs together and change into their nightclothes in their respective dressing rooms. In their bedroom, he tugs back the covers and directs her to get into the bed first, and he arranges the blankets around her. He perches on the edge of the bed, as Ella used to do, when singing lullabies to Alix. But Serge doesn't sing, he reviews their day. What a terrible vaunter that Prince Orrusov is—avoid him whenever possible. And the French ambassador Couchmaillo? An under-handed character, although Sir Edward Thornton, the British ambassador, is pleasant enough. A great mistake of Ella's to laugh at his uncle Nikolasha's jokes—that old campaigner needs no such encouragement. And why did Ella spend time chatting to Countess Sumarokova? Really, such a trivial woman. Ella mustn't make a friend of *her*.

Tired as she is after a day of conversing with strangers, Ella marvels at Serge's focus, his bold opinions, his bracing energy. Although his rebukes do sting. Does he not sense how hard she is trying to please him?

After a quarter of an hour or so of this, he gets to his feet, extinguishes the lights, climbs into the bed on the other side— and does not touch her.

SERGE MAKES IT a habit to rise before Ella, so she's surprised to find one morning, when she wakes and rolls over, his head still resting on the pillow beside hers. His closely cropped hair re-sembles soft moss. She'd like to reach out and touch it, to see if it's as soft as it looks. But fear stops her hand. Perhaps he would not welcome this caress?

Serge stirs, and she closes her eyes again, feigning sleep. Through half-cracked lids she watches him get out of bed, pick up his robe from the side chair, yank it on over his nightshirt, and stride into his dressing room, shutting the door. She waits for a good while before rising and ringing for Masha to draw her a bath. Afterward, she puts on her underthings and summons Masha back.

Serge reappears, as usual, after she has her gown on and is at her dressing table.

"One of Minnie's *most* unfortunate efforts," he says, scowling at the orange and gold striped satin dress she's selected. "The lavender silk from yesterday was adequate; change into that. We are seeing a different group today."

Ella suppresses a smile. Would any of their guests suspect that stern Grand Duke Serge frets over his wife's toilette? But she doesn't mind. She's always eager for the moment when, completely ready for the day, she stands, faces him, and watches his assessing gaze range over her—her face, her neck, her bosom, and her waist. The bright glint in his eyes excites her, the way he invariably admires what he sees, although he might request a different necklace or an adjustment to her hair. This is the moment when she feels most loved.

In other ways, he is not demonstrative. Which troubles her. He might guide her by the elbow in to dinner, or put a hand on her shoulder, or an arm around her waist when they are speaking to a guest—public gestures of possession. But never when they lie in their bed, where no one can see, does he reach for her, embrace her, stroke and kiss her. And if he never approaches her, how can he plant his seed inside her? The first time will certainly be awkward, and maybe painful, but until they accomplish that, will they truly be married?

TEN DAYS AFTER the wedding, they travel back to Peterhof. Serge's wish is that they recover here from their exertions in the capital for a fortnight, then travel to Moscow and on to the monastery in Radonezh, before spending the balance of the summer at Ilinskoe, his beloved country estate.

Ella feels a sharp pang, riding through the Peterhof gates, remembering that the last time she arrived here she was with her family. The post is so slow. Beyond a telegram from Papa to say they have arrived safely home in Darmstadt, she has heard nothing from any of them yet.

They will stay at the Farm Palace, once a favorite Peterhof residence of Serge's mother. A modest residence, Serge promised. Maybe by Romanov standards—the neo-Gothic house with wrought-iron balconies is as large as the Neues Palais.

Sasha and Minnie come to dine the first night, bringing their eldest son. When she sees Nicky enter the room, Ella pats the sofa cushion beside her.

"My dear Tetinka," Nicky says, kissing her hand before sitting down. "I am delighted to see you looking so well."

It is already a great joke between them, how he calls her "my little aunt." At sixteen, he's only three years her junior.

"And you, darling nephew," Ella teases back. "I hope life is kind to you."

This good-humored boy has inherited Minnie's large eyes and open expression. Also, her short stature. Ella does hope Nicky will grow a bit still, otherwise Sasha is bound to be disappointed. The tsar and all his brothers, including Serge, stand over six feet tall.

"I am well, but I miss my boon companion Ernie and your little sister . . ." Nicky stops and sighs, dramatically. "Oh, how we loved each other."

Ella laughs. "You were very generous to Alix. She's usually so shy with strangers, and yet you had her talking and laughing constantly. Victoria and I agreed—we've rarely seen her as happy."

"It was a great pleasure," he says, grinning. "But what of you, Tetinka? Are you content in your new home? Is Uncle Gega a satisfactory husband?"

Her stomach twists. Does Nicky have reason to suspect Serge might not be? But she banters back: "Oh yes, we sailed through our obligations in town, Serge taking pains over every detail, and being a most wonderful guide for me."

"What's that you're saying about me?" Serge asks, sharply, from across the room.

"How wonderful you were, Serge, introducing me into society," she says.

"Ella coped superbly with the multitudes, a beatific smile for every guest, and was, of course, splendidly attired," Serge adds, with a nod to his sister-in-law.

Minnie beams, unaware that Serge regularly derides the gowns she chose. "For the winter season I can direct again," she says. "Or take Ella with me on a lightning trip to Worth in Paris."

Ella looks at Serge, silently alarmed.

He smiles mildly. If Ella didn't know better, she would think her husband amenable to Minnie's suggestions. "We shall see," he says.

At the table, Sasha and Serge drink a great deal of wine and begin speaking Russian. Minnie, sitting beside Ella, explains the men are making plans to take Nicky for a day to the army's summer training camp, held at nearby Krasnoye Selo.

"Let me tell you an amusing tale about your sister Alix," Minnie says confidingly. "Did you know she turned up for the children's party at the cottage wearing a diamond brooch?"

"Alix possesses no such brooch," Ella says immediately.

"Well, for a short while, she did. I recognized it—last I saw it, my dear friend the countess Apraksine, my chief maid of honor, was wearing it."

"How on earth? Why would Alix have this?"

"I was most perplexed," says Minnie, smiling. "Until I spoke with Aprak directly. She recounted how Nicky told her he needed a gift for a very special person, and pointed to the brooch she had on. 'Something resembling that,' he said. She took it off and gave it to him! Aprak so dotes on Nicky."

Now Minnie laughs.

"My goodness," Ella says. She had imagined Alix, of the two, more likely to be the adoring party, as Nicky is older and so good-looking. But it seems the tsarevich really lost his heart to her little sister. Perhaps one day? She hardly dares hope it. Might Sunny join her here in Russia as the wife of the heir?

"I was so startled to see Aprak's brooch on Alix I said nothing," Minnie continues. "Still, the girl must have felt some compunctions about keeping this treasure because two hours later I spotted Xenia wearing it! Her brother had given the brooch to her during the party."

"So now it belongs to Xenia?"

"Yes. Aprak is content for her to keep it, but I've put it away until she's older."

"Did you reprimand Nicky?" Ella asks, anxious.

"How could I? The dear, sweet boy—he was likely hurt his gift was rejected." Minnie smiles indulgently. "Although I do wish he'd asked me for a token rather than taken something off my lady."

The tsar calls out: "You two wives, with your heads together, what are you gossiping about?"

"Nothing vital, Sasha, children, mostly," says Minnie.

"Children are vital!" he bellows. Then the tsar smiles directly at Ella. "Can I tell you, my dear, how worried I was that my brother here would never choose a wife? He's so damned picky. I should have known. He was waiting for a paragon of grace, with a loving heart, and quite breathtaking good looks."

Ella blushes. The wine is making the tsar expansive.

"And now I wait impatiently," Sasha continues. "For your union to be blessed with children."

"Yes! To the future children of Tetinka and Uncle Gega," proclaims Nicky, raising his glass.

Serge's face stiffens—no gracious acknowledgment or even mild smile like previously. This toast pains him, but why?

She watches him hesitate before he raises his glass along with the rest of them. Then he drains it. He signals the footman to fill it with wine again. Her husband's face only relaxes as the conversation moves on to the rebuilding of the Lower Dacha—a project Sasha and Minnie fervently hope will soon be completed.

SUPPER OVER, AND their guests gone, Serge's cheeks are flushed, and his eyes glassy—he has drunk far more than usual. On the way up the stairs, he stumbles twice, clutching the railing to avoid falling.

Ella goes to wash and to change into her nightdress, and returns to find Serge already in bed, turned away from her, his shoulders bare—he is apparently not wearing his nightshirt. His clothes have been thrown haphazardly on the side chair. Is he still awake? She guesses yes, but she isn't sure.

Turning down the lights, slipping in between the sheets, her heart thumps in her chest. Is this the moment? Away from the formality of their city palace, no more dignitaries to receive, no longer on display, having enjoyed a warm family supper—now will he approach her, embrace and caress her?

In the dark, he does turn and bring his face inches from hers. She smells the wine on his breath. "Our children, Ella," he says, his voice thick. "Do you hope to meet our children?"

"Yes, of course, my love."

"Well, then, we must perform."

He begins by pulling up her nightdress, clumsily, until it is bunched beneath her armpits. Before she can protest that she prefers to take it off altogether, he rolls on top of her, pushing her onto her back. A shock to feel his weight pressing down, his warm, naked body against hers, skin to skin. She tries to relax under him, but in order to breathe she must shift her body sideways, freeing the top part of her chest. His head rests below her left shoulder, cushioned by her upper arm and left breast. His face looks strange—he's wincing, eyes closed, mouth slightly open. For a long moment he just lies on her, breathing through his mouth, overcome, it seems, by the effort of getting this far. Is he waiting for her to encourage him in some way? To position herself so he can move that most private part of him into her? Should she open her legs wider? Pull her knees up? Touch him in a particular way? If only he would tell her what to do.

He rolls off her again.

"Not tonight, too drunk tonight," he says.

It's a relief to take a few calming, full breaths, but she's very disturbed. He's made an effort, and that's heartening. Although discouraging to think that he obviously needed the wine to spur him on. And how mortifying to discover that people are like horses, males mounting females. She imagined the act more like dancing, something they would do lying on their sides, face-to-face. But most of all she hates that she and he have not achieved union. He must long for it too. She can't imagine he is happy they are still not truly intimate with each other. And whatever distaste she feels—and thus far the act seems quite unappealing—surpassing her squeamishness is her yearning to feel herself fully and properly wed, to know Serge and she share a physical bond, and, of course, to have the possibility of conceiving a child.

THE NEXT MORNING, Serge says nothing about what passed between them. If anything he is brusquer, sharper, more commanding than usual. She feels quite shy of looking at him, as if by meeting his eye she might remind him of their failure. His failure.

Over breakfast he complains the Farm Palace's flower beds look overgrown; he must speak sternly with the gardeners. She nods along, smiles frequently, responds when responses are called for. She's careful to appear serene, to convey with her composed manner that she has complete confidence in him. But when he announces that he will be away all day, taking Nicky to Krasnoye Selo, she feels a surge of relief. Indeed, after Serge rises, bids her goodbye, and leaves the room, she slumps back in her chair, limp from the taxing effort of pretending nothing is wrong.

Later, upstairs in the salon Serge's mother decorated with pretty lilac-and-green floral wallpaper, she sits and considers matters further.

Perhaps the two of them simply need more time. It's still quite recently they were married. They have only just arrived here in pastoral Peterhof. She must be patient with her tense, high-strung husband. Every day she learns more about Serge's perfectionism, his need for order. He insists on punctuality, he hates untidiness, he requires cleanliness in all things—he spilled a tiny drop of wine on his white cuff at one of their Petersburg receptions, and he immediately excused himself to go upstairs and change his shirt. The physical act might be difficult for such a fastidious person to undertake. She understands this, as she feels some similar reticence herself. And perhaps he has experienced marrying her—the change from being a single man to a husband—as deeply disruptive. He may need time to become more accustomed to having a wife before he can take the required initiative in their bed.

But maybe—and this thought causes a shudder; she rises from the armchair to pull shut the window—maybe the fault is hers. Perhaps something about her is distasteful. Which would explain why he couldn't bring himself to embrace her without being drunk. Of course, in all other settings, he seems to admire her. She pictures again his hard, bright eyes raking over her figure each morning in Petersburg, and the thrill this gave her, a thrill that he must share, as it became their daily ritual.

No, it is unlikely to be aversion as such. But it might be, she worries, that her very innocence discourages him. Over the last few years, Ella has frequently seen Madame de Kolemine preen and flirt and tip her head in fetching ways while speaking with Papa. The two never touched in front of the family, but Ella noticed how all the playful teasing on that lady's part would tantalize Papa. The enraptured look on his face—it bordered on contemptible.

Ella can't imagine acting the coquette—flashing her eyes, throwing arch, knowing remarks in Serge's direction. But maybe this is required to engage a man? At least some small bit of it? Even with someone as grave and serious as her husband is?

She feels ashamed suddenly. Is she so lacking? Alone here in Russia she has no one to ask. Not Serge himself—nothing in their relations with each other would allow for such an indelicate inquiry. Minnie? Never. Not only is the empress not her friend, Ella and Serge's marriage is a dynastic one. To cast any doubt over the inevitable arrival of offspring would be most unwise.

If she and Victoria still saw each other every day, might Ella, somehow, find a way to allude to her situation? Her sister, always full of good sense, could well have something useful to suggest, especially now that she's a wife too. Ella remembers how Victoria and Louis, once engaged, would come back from a walk in the garden, their clothes a bit mussed, her sister's cheeks flushed red. Kissing and spooning, Ella had assumed then, with a tolerant smile. Of course, Serge never wanted to spoon; he was too decorous. And she respected that, rather welcomed it, as she would not have been comfortable acting as Victoria did when merely engaged. But should Ella have recognized Serge's restraint as a telltale sign? Evidence of some essential incompatibility between them? Or a lack of deep desire on his part?

Ella puts her face in her hands, cut to the quick. How humiliating to think your husband does not find you sufficiently appealing. And could she, really, even with Victoria, bring herself to discuss this most intimate concern? It strikes her as so immodest as to be obscene.

If only her mother still lived. Mama, she could tell. Her mother always took a most practical, no-nonsense approach to what she called "the good body." When Ella first bled, she gave her the special napkins and laundry sacks and—Ella remembers it so clearly—she said: "Don't be ashamed or disgusted; this is your good body doing what it needs to do to grow a baby one day."

Now sitting in the Farm Palace, a thousand miles from Mama's tomb, nearly six years after her death, Ella is gripped with a vicious, agonizing grief, the like of which she cannot remember feeling. She lacks a mother, and a mother is what she needs now, more than anything or anyone else.

When Serge returns that evening, they eat a polite supper together. He recounts the maneuvers he and Sasha and Nicky watched at camp. She and he go to bed as usual and lie side by side, and she feels the three feet of space between them—that stretch of smooth, white linen—like a chasm. Perhaps it will never be bridged.

THOUGHTS OF HER family and scenes of her old life in Darmstadt begin to run continually through Ella's head, and every day she is beset by a nervous upset that constricts her throat, sickens her stomach, weighs heavily on her arms and legs. She walks around woodenly. This fearful sadness prevents her from sitting down to paint or to play the piano. When she does manage to converse or eat or smile, she has an odd sense of playacting. It's a life-size, obedient doll doing these things, not the real woman, because the actual Ella is stiff with dread.

Upon waking in the morning, Ella feels at first restored—muscles relaxed, stomach untroubled—as if all the days in Russia have never happened. She's learned to be careful, when opening her eyes, to savor this ease. She trains her gaze on the curvaceous floral inlay decoration of the rosewood table beside the bed. So pretty. But once she rolls over, to see Serge's head beside her, or, more frequently, the concave imprint where his head lay on the pillow, the sick feeling descends.

She frequently scolds herself: *Don't feel so unhappy and nervous, it isn't practical.* Her life can never be as it was before she married Serge, before she walked through the door he held open. And if life here isn't exactly the wonderous Aladdin's cave she imagined so childishly, she lives amidst luxury, and her new family is pleased to accept her. Always admiring of Serge's elegant figure, chiseled face, piercing gaze, Ella is also proud of what she senses is the unique sympathy she offers Serge. She appreciates qualities in her husband that others are put off by—his vigor and his high standards. His stern sense of duty to family, regiment, and country always appeals to her.

Not that she is spared the lash of his sharp tongue. He reproves her when he sees her spreading butter on a second piece of bread at meals. "You mustn't spoil your figure." She has thrice-weekly Russian lessons with Madame Catherine Schneider, the niece of the court doctor. One afternoon when she is practicing with Serge, he snaps, in French: "Your French is marred by an ugly German accent, and now it seems you can only speak Russian with an English one."

"*Mais, Serge, je ne suis qu'une débutante.*" She enunciates every word as precisely as she can. She is a beginner, *une débutante*, with Russian. How can he expect her to be perfect?

"True," he says, waving his hand impatiently. "I suppose you will improve eventually."

"Most certainly I will," she answers with a trace of asperity.

His ears turn red, a sign, she's come to recognize, of his irritation. He nods curtly and says: "You have no choice, my child."

If she were braver she would ask him to choose another endearment. She doesn't like "my child." Not one bit.

PETERSBURG, ACCORDING TO Serge, is infected with a cosmopolitan European decadence, while in Moscow people live more simply, closer to God. "The saying here is that there are *sorok sorokov*—forty times forty—churches in Moscow. We can't visit them all, but I will take you to my favorites," he tells her on the first morning they spend in the city.

Looking at the magnificent frescoes and murals, countless icons and artifacts, Ella is ever conscious of her Protestant sensibilities. The sloe-eyed Madonnas and the fierce faces of the prophets—exotic, alien, nearly pagan—resemble nothing she encountered in the plain churches of her German girlhood, or even in England, at St. George's Chapel in Windsor, or the Chapel Royal, St. James's. And she feels awkward when Serge falls to his knees in front of the most holy of the icons. Unsure what to do, she settles for a very low curtsy, which seems appropriately respectful. But if a priest holds out a cross to her, she will kiss it, as Serge always does. It seems only polite.

From Moscow they travel nearly fifty miles north to the holiest and most revered monastery in all of Russia, founded by Saint Sergius of Radonezh, Serge's patron saint. In 1422, after Sergius's death, construction began on the Trinity Cathedral, over his burial place. Now the monastery complex includes small chapels, shrines, and simple lodging for pilgrims. She and Serge are assigned a small cell, barely room enough for a bed, with whitewashed walls hung with a few simple icons.

Pious contemplation suits her husband. Serge's face takes on a most devout appearance; his eyes are soft, his voice low and gentle. He's calmer and more patient with her and with everyone. Perhaps, Ella thinks, he finds so much about the world not to his liking—corrupt, sinful, unethical—that it's a relief for him to be here, communing with the sacred and the pure. Ella is surprised to find herself likewise soothed by this holy setting, the scent of pine in the air, the chanting of the monks, the soft rustle of the congregants moving quietly, reverently up the path to the church. Standing for the long service, Ella closes her eyes and prays, for the health of all her family and also for whatever impediment prevents their marriage's consummation to be removed.

At night, lying in bed in their cell, Serge sleeping beside her, she looks out the small square window, at the stars spilled like sugary candy over the immensity of the night sky, and appeals silently to God again. *You married us. You must be confident we can live together in faith and love. Please show us the way.*

APPROACHED VIA A winding drive through large evergreens, Serge's house at Ilinskoe is a wide wooden structure, two stories tall, with a single squat tower sitting at the center of the roof.

Now *this*, Ella says to herself with a hidden smile, is actually a modest residence, scarcely larger than the Herrenhaus at Wolfsgarten, and occupying such an appealing position, high on the banks of the wide Moskva River. The furniture—glazed black-walnut cabinets, finial-topped chairs, stiff-backed sofas with lion's paw feet—looks funereal and dated. A spacious covered veranda running along the whole length of the back side of the upper floor—at treetop level—affords broad views of the river below and the meadowland on the opposite bank. A long table is set up for meals, the heavy canvas awning overhead filters the strong sun, and standing at the railing Ella feels a gentle breeze off the water.

Serge, beside her, points. "That's the footpath down to the landing," he says. "And do you see the variety of boats tied up? We have great fun on the river. People come and stay for weeks at a time. Paul writes that he will arrive on Sunday, you don't mind?"

"Not at all."

"I imagine you find the rooms gloomy. Things have been left very much as my mother had them," Serge says. "But I hope you will redecorate the interior to your taste."

She smiles—this is a project she will enjoy. "Thank you. Let me get a sense of the house and the setting and then I will embark."

In the mornings, before the heat rises, they row across the river and walk in the meadows where wild strawberries, tiny and sweet, grow in patches. After Ella confesses that she has never learned to swim properly, Serge has one of the stablemen fix up an enormous, inflated rubber ring suspended by straps that she wears over her shoulders. She loves to bob in the cool water, the skirt of her swimming costume billowing around her, while he swims up and down, getting his daily exercise.

Serge generally doesn't enjoy hunting, but here at Ilinskoe he makes a habit of wandering out in the evening with a gun looking for crows. When he fires at them, the sound of the shots shatters the evening stillness. Ella secretly hates this.

"Why do you bother with them?" she asks him.

"They are so ugly and cunning and predatory. I want them all banished," he explains.

After they have been in residence a week, Serge reports proudly: "The crows stay away now. I hear them cawing still, but only from a distance."

He has a satisfied gleam in his eyes that Ella finds rather unnerving. But now at least the evenings are no longer disturbed with the noise of his shots.

Serge and Ella share a bed but they do not touch. His reticence remains a puzzle. Cousin Paul arrives. At least twice a week Serge's friends the Prince Felix and Princess Zinaida Yusupova come to dine. Their estate, Arkhangelskoye, is only a few miles away. Ella immediately warms to Princess Zinaida, a willowy woman with raven hair smoothly drawn back, an olive complexion, and bright-blue eyes. She is supremely well dressed—not surprising, as she is one of the richest women in Russia, Serge reports. But money alone doesn't buy excellent taste, and Ella finds great pleasure in their discussions of art, and in working together to arrange wildflowers in vases for the house.

Many mornings, the nervous dread wells up again inside her, but now she reminds herself firmly of what she concluded at the monastery: God will show them the way. Waiting for divine direction—and with the sun, the river, and the country landscape to savor—she usually feels restored by the afternoon.

IN LATE AUGUST, she receives a letter from Victoria.

I've suspected for most of the summer, her sister writes. *After a certain thing stopped and then for four or five weeks, I felt constantly ill. Now I am a good deal better and the doctor confirms. The baby will be born in early spring.*

Ella folds up the letter without finishing it and tosses it on a side table. She rises to her feet and goes to look out the window. She feels Victoria's news like a punch to her middle. Her own courses come exactly twenty-eight days apart—three times since her wedding, each time like a rebuke.

She can see Serge below, standing, teetering a bit to balance himself, in a small boat, tied fast still. On the landing Princess Zinaida stands next to her father, Prince Nicholas. Serge is holding out his hand to the elderly gentleman, trying, it seems, to convince him to step down into the boat. After a few minutes, he's managed it, settling the old prince in the prow. Serge unties the lines, takes his seat on the center board, an oar in each hand, and rows them out into the river. The princess remains on the landing, waving gaily. She must be grateful to Serge for giving her father—a bent-over, infirm-looking man—the treat of a boat ride.

That night Ella takes heart. As soon as Serge has extinguished the lights, when they lie side by side, she shifts carefully, inching closer—close enough to stroke his head.

His back is to her, and he starts at her touch.

"What, what?" he says, alarmed, and immediately rolls over to face her.

"I saw you helping Prince Nicholas into the boat. You were so kind to take him out."

"Yes," he says, tone clipped.

"You looked so gallant, handsome and tall," she says, and lays her hand softly on his arm.

"I would, wouldn't I? Next to that stooped old gentleman."

"Always I find you remarkably striking." She's talking in the most coaxing way she can manage.

"Why are you prattling on?" he demands, and he jerks his arm away.

She'd like to stop, but if she doesn't keep going, she may never reach her object. "I want to tell you how much I love you. I am your wife and I long to be properly so." Only in the dark would she dare utter these words.

"What do you mean?" he asks scornfully.

She's certain he knows what she means, but in his pride he's pretending otherwise.

"I can do or be whatever you want," she says, timid now. Never has it been so hard to speak.

He rolls over and presents his back to her once more. "You are fine."

"Serge, please, can we not . . ."

"Enough. I cannot stand to listen to more of this."

Denied and humiliated, she lies on her back, staring at the ceiling. Tears run down the sides of her face and gutter in her ears.

SERGE IS GONE in the morning—who knows where. She breakfasts alone, sits on the veranda and tries to read a book, but the words dance in front of her eyes.

Finally, he appears on the veranda an hour before luncheon, sweaty, harried-looking, and wearing his riding clothes.

"Come, walk out with me," he commands.

He leads her out the front door and down a lane through the woods that makes a large loop from one side of the estate to the other, past four small wooden houses where guests are lodged.

"I don't like women to be desirous, it is ill-becoming," he announces without preamble.

She feels her cheeks go hot with shame.

"And base impulses distort life," he adds.

In her embarrassment and hurt, a part of her silently resists. How can it be, when they enjoy the most sacred state of marriage, that the marital relation is base? But his condemnation has frozen her tongue.

"I am aware that it is my duty as a husband to—" He breaks off.

Then he sighs a heavy sigh. "Perhaps I am selfish. At the moment as I cherish your companionship, I want to preserve your unadulterated beauty."

She forces herself to lift her eyes, to acknowledge this compliment. His face is stony and he does not look at her.

"You know so little of the world," he says. "But I have seen how women after they become mothers are never as lovely. Their faces swell along with their figures; they endure the strain of delivering and feeding a child. It sullies and coarsens them. Too many lose their bloom."

She attempts a mild protest. "Did this happen to Minnie? And what about Zinaida Yusupova? You so admire her, and she has borne two sons," she asks.

"Both retain great charm," he replies impatiently. "Although Minnie is getting a bit plump."

"Sasha's love appears undiminished," Ella answers quietly.

"The thing is, those women are not mine. You are mine and I want you to exist in your lovely state for as long as possible. Don't you understand?"

There's a pliant, almost boyish note of appeal in his voice. Can she really ignore this? If this is what Serge truly desires? Doesn't she intend always to be a good and sympathetic wife?

With a surge of empathy, she answers, "I can certainly try to understand if that's what you ask of me."

"Thank you, my child. We will go on as we have been for now," he says firmly.

Her eyes fill. She fumbles in the pocket of her dress for her handkerchief. While she feels noble, answering his plea, it pains her that he does not feel as she does—how, as long as they are not intimate, they are not properly married. She blots her eyes.

Unexpectedly he says, quite tenderly: "I know you hope for more, and bless you for that."

Her heart unclenches a bit.

He adds: "Also, I sense how difficult it has been for you since our wedding. You miss everyone in Darmstadt."

"Yes. Most keenly." She thought she'd hidden her homesickness successfully.

"Aren't you feeling a little better here in lovely Ilinskoe?"

She nods.

"No one can arrange the feelings of another," he says. "But I ask that you trust me when I say that you will come to love life in Russia, as you claim you do me."

She nods again. Why does he doubt her declaration of love?

He goes on, and his voice sounds boosterish now, cheerful even: "Of course, you are in regular touch with them all. I noticed you've had a letter from your sister Victoria—I saw it on the table in the salon yesterday. What's the news? How do she and Louis fare back in England?"

She stops. He stops. She turns to face him. She folds her arms in front of her chest, hugging her elbows for comfort. "Victoria expects a child," she says.

"Ah," answers Serge, the curt edge returning to his voice. "Ah, I see."

She can almost hear his mind racing, making connections and suppositions as they stand there together ten yards from the end of the lane.

"This morning I found the farm in great disorder; I must return there now and sort things out. Don't wait for me for luncheon," he says sharply.

Without a wave, or a final acknowledging look, he veers off toward the stables—eager, it seems, to be immediately out of her company.

Chapter Ten

$\mathbb{K}$

A Wife Is Resolved

St. Petersburg, winter 1885

*E*lla did not anticipate the effect she might have just entering a crowded drawing room. How quickly clamorous talk can shift lower, and how a fashionably dressed assembly turning as one sounds like wind blowing through dry leaves. Nor did she realize that, when you are the focus of all eyes, the air vibrates slightly. Or seems to.

This attention feels wondrous. Also, like a spell she casts without trying. She is the new wife of the tsar's brother, appearing in St. Petersburg society for her first winter season. Her clothes are magnificent, her jewels unrivaled. Her favorite ball gown—apricot silk trimmed with sable—earns its own article in the illustrated paper *Gala*. She's a phenomenon, a person of note, a *rara avis*.

She's also a beautiful, slender woman, just twenty, and enthralling to men. Having worried that she lacked Madame de Kolemine's fluency, she discovers her own power to captivate—by simply presenting herself, exquisitely turned out, with a smile and a gracious word for everyone.

Arousing fascination is one thing. What repels her is the expression of wolfish desire that overtakes some men's faces, especially after they have had a few drinks. How they lean in too close or presume to lay a hot hand on her arm. Are they imagining what she looks like without her fine clothes on? She disdains such boorishness and quickly moves away. That she is married to a man who is never coarse nor vulgar gladdens her heart, as does Serge's delight in the rapturous way society receives her.

During the season's last big ball, hosted by Serge's brother Vladimir and his wife, Miechen, Ella escapes the stuffy ballroom for a moment. She leans against a stone wall in the conservatory, partly hidden by a large potted palm. She overhears one officer say to another in French: "The most gorgeous woman here tonight is Grand Duchess Elisabeth Feodorovna."

"No quibble there," the second man says. "And why the surprise? That husband of hers has spent a fortune on paintings and *objets précieux*, and now he's acquired a beautiful little wife. He drapes her in silks and jewels and exhibits her for us to venerate, like the pagans of old worshipped their goddesses."

"Do you assume otherwise he keeps her on a high shelf?"

"I think, yes, as he prefers Greek love. Always has. Look at the way he runs his outfit."

They both laugh heartily.

Ella retreats back into the ballroom before they can spot her.

These two officers are obviously envious of Serge's wealth and position. But what is Greek love? How has it to do with being a commander? Devotion to one's men? Then why the rather lewd tone? She can't ask Serge. He always hates her to repeat gossip, admonishing her that nasty chat is beneath them both. And this subject is not one he would ever want raised, she is sure of that much.

She's left puzzled, and from time to time returns to the incident, holding up the memory in her mind, examining it from all angles.

AT THE END of the ten-week-long season Ella has had enough of going out every night, mixing with hordes of people, eating and drinking too much. Even admiration has grown stale.

She's pleased when Serge decides they will pass Lent with Sasha and Minnie and the children at the Gatchina palace. Ella will never confess this to him, but she feels more relaxed in this sprawling medieval fortress with its towers and battlements than she ever does in the coolly elegant Sergievsky Palace. Sasha and Minnie keep the formal rooms practically empty. They live on the cozy mezzanine level, once the servants' quarters, where the rooms are small and narrow like ships' cabins, the ceiling so low that Sasha and Serge must duck their heads to walk through the doorways. Meals are served in the vaulted Arsenal Hall on the ground floor, where a billiards table sits alongside the carved mahogany dining table, the baby carriage little Olga uses for her dolls stands next to the door, and tennis rackets and boat oars are propped up against the walls. Sasha's sheepdogs Kamchatka and Sakhalin lope in and out. The tsar's study, reached by a small staircase in the hall's far corner, is the only room off-limits to children and dogs at Gatchina.

They've been in residence only a few days when a telegram comes from Louis. Her sister Victoria has given birth to a girl—Victoria Alice Elizabeth Julia. Named for her great-grandmother, her two grandmothers, and her aunt Ella, she will be known in the family as Alice. A letter that Ella receives the next week provides longed-for details. Victoria asks Ella to be a godmother to the new baby. She then describes how, at Grandmama's insistence, she traveled from Portsmouth to Windsor for the lying-in and was installed in the very same small chamber off the Tapestry Room that Mama had for Victoria's own birth twenty-two years ago. Painful labor lasted twenty hours, but baby Alice is a darling.

I hope you will think her pretty. She is rather more like Louis than like me, but she has nice big gray eyes, a sweet little nose, and a mouth which she opens like a fish. When angry she turns as red as an old turkey cock.

Ella laughs. Gray eyes! Sweet nose! A mouth like a fish!

Then she bursts into tears. Is it joy or sorrow? She hardly knows. If only she didn't live so far away. If only she could fly through the air and land at her sister's side. If only she could hold the baby with a mouth like a fish. If only she could have her own baby.

That afternoon she avoids everyone—Serge, Sasha, Minnie, even Nicky, whose company always lifts her spirits. Wearing her heaviest cloak and fur-lined boots, she goes out into the bitter cold. The packed, icy snow squeaks under her feet. She's alone in the wintery stillness of the vast park but for two red-coated Cossack guards, on horseback, far in the distance. She sobs. She shouldn't grieve so, she tells herself. She can travel to visit Victoria and the baby soon. Yet still she weeps.

After two hours, heading back indoors, her inner voice is admonitory. She must compose herself. No one in the family can know how desolate and homesick she feels today.

Before supper, she carefully washes her face, then puts a little powder on her nose, and a touch of geranium petal on her cheeks. At the table she shares the happy news that she's to be one of Alice's godmothers. Sasha and Minnie are full of warm congratulations. She senses Serge's appraising eyes on her, but she is determined to appear cheerful. All five children have joined them this evening. Ella amuses Misha, age six, by counting the buttons on his double-breasted jacket and singing an English nursery rhyme: *"Will you be a captain, a colonel, a cowboy, or a thief?"*

"As a son of the tsar, Misha is unlikely to become a cowboy," Georgy points out.

"Or a thief," adds Nicky.

"One can only hope," remarks Serge gravely. Which makes them all laugh.

THE NEXT DAY Sasha and Minnie depart early for Petersburg for investitures, and after breakfast Ella sits alone in Minnie's pink-and-silver sitting room, looking through some knitting patterns, trying to decide on something to knit for baby Alice.

Serge comes in, carefully closing the door behind him. Ella is surprised. During the week he most often rides over to the regimental barracks or summons officers to meet with him here at Gatchina.

A quick glance, and she notices his face looks oddly strained, his thin lips closed in a tight line. What has upset him? The past days have been peaceful and pleasant, except for her distress, which was private.

He takes the armchair directly across from her. "Are you well, Serge?" she asks.

"Well enough," he answers testily.

She resumes sorting through the patterns, instructing herself to remain patient. She knows him. When he has something to say, he doesn't like to be prodded, or condescended to by her solicitousness. Whatever is bothering him, he will express it when and how he wishes. She does hope he won't speak too harshly. She still feels rather fragile from yesterday.

The ormolu clock on the chimney piece ticks loudly in the silence. "You deserve better," he says abruptly.

She looks up. "Better?"

"A better husband," he says in a choked voice, and stares straight at her, stricken.

She gazes at him intently. What is this he's saying? What is the look in his eyes? She reads guilt there, and hurt. Yes, he has been hurt, but not by her, by someone or something that he can hardly bear to speak of.

"I am happy with my husband," she says in a hurried voice, trying to soothe him.

"By law you have the right to end it."

"End what?" She is confused.

Now he looks away, into the corner of the room, beyond her left shoulder, and he's shifting his jaw in an odd, nervous way.

She's frightened. "Serge, please, what has come over you?"

"Once our marriage is annulled you could leave me." He almost spits the words out.

"Leave? You want me to leave you?" Her throat tightens in panic.

"Never." His voice is like a moan.

"Yes, never. Please, dear Serge, tell me what is wrong. Are you ill?" Perhaps he is going mad. Is this what madness looks like?

"No." He's still looking away from her, working his jaw nervously.

"Then speak no further like this," she says, almost shrill.

He dashes his hand against his right cheek. He's weeping.

"I thought when I married you . . ." he says, and he stops, drawing in a ragged breath. "I thought with you I might be capable. But I am not."

His chest heaves with silent sobs; it's appalling. She should comfort him, but she is frozen in place by the shock of the unutterable spoken aloud.

A minute or two passes. He stands up and leaves the room.

The disciplined clock ticks on as if nothing has happened. But to her, the world is suddenly swaying precariously on its foundations.

In her incredulity and her horror, she clings to a small bit of comfort. Now she can be certain he, too, grieves over their failure. It's not something that he doesn't care about. The aversion he claimed to have to pregnancy and what it does to a woman's face and figure was just an excuse. In desiring their physical union, she hasn't been deplorable or unseemly.

She's relieved he blames himself, not her.

But deepest fears assuaged, she still struggles to gather her wits. How hideous to watch proud Serge driven to this, to declare himself lacking. She knows her husband, his stern temperament, his fastidiousness, his extreme dignity. As her mind spins around his words, trying to absorb them, she flashes back to those officers at the ball—their nasty comments, their insinuating laughter. Does Serge know how people speak of him behind his back? That it's a Greek kind of love he's said to prefer? Which must be something smutty, mustn't it? She's offended and enraged. How abhorrent that a proud and upright man is slandered by despicable individuals not anywhere near as worthy as Serge.

Her thoughts lurch again. Is Serge's incapacity permanent? Never to be overcome? Perhaps with patience and care she could help him surmount it? She so longs to have a child.

She tromps on this idea immediately. At this moment, she mustn't think of her own needs but of Serge's. While she hated hearing his confession, she can only imagine the agony he felt in making it. She must convey to him how she admires his courage, but, most important, how her love and loyalty remain unaffected. She refuses to regard him as deficient. She knows him to be good, to the very depths of his soul.

She remains in the sitting room until luncheon, seeking equilibrium. She doesn't want to appear agitated in any way. She checks her face in the glass as she exits the room, to assure herself she looks calm. She prays that when she sees Serge she can do and say exactly what will best reassure him.

But in the hall, the table is set for only one—her. A footman explains. "The young grand dukes are eating upstairs with Mr. Heath, the other children in the nursery."

"And Grand Duke Serge?"

"He left for Petersburg, Your Imperial Highness."

She understands immediately. Her husband needs more time before he can face her again. Later, a note comes from the steward at the Sergievsky Palace—business detains her husband in town for the night.

Only on the following evening, when Sasha and Minnie have arrived back, does Serge reappear, entering the hall just in time for them all to sit down and dine together. Ella requires only a minute or two in Serge's company—a glance at his guarded expression, the hint of something imperceptibly remote in his manner toward her—to know what is wanted. The two of them are to go on as if nothing has happened. He is not angry nor is he unsteady, but he does wait to see if she will receive his wordless command.

Yes, she has. Yes, she can comply. This is the Serge she recognizes and loves. She smiles at him, serene and composed. The unruffled surface of their existence can be restored, smooth and intact.

DAYS PASS AND the horror and confusion she felt upon hearing Serge's confession fades somewhat. The resumption of their normal communications reassures her. She has no desire to revisit the subject—she senses they are allies in this. Instead, she begins to think anxiously about their upcoming trip to Darmstadt.

She longs to see home again after nearly a year away and little Alice's christening is fixed for April 25 at the Neues Palais. But she worries: Are people in the family wondering if Ella expects a baby? Her wedding to Serge took place only six weeks after Victoria and Louis's. Perhaps everyone anticipates she will have happy news to share when she arrives? But when they cast eyes on her—slender as ever, even a bit more so, since she follows Serge's example and never overindulges at the table—and she has nothing to announce, will they speculate about the state of her marriage? Will anyone guess the truth?

No, she prays fervently, they must not. Ella will be sure to convey, in word and actions, how very happy she and Serge are together. She'll describe her triumphant season, talk about the plans they have for the redecoration of Ilinskoe, pass along good wishes from Sasha and Minnie.

In any case, Ella thinks, plenty of brides don't give birth during their first year of marriage.

Of course, Mama did, and Grandmama did, and Aunt Vicky did and now Victoria has.

Her grandmother's reaction concerns her most. When does the queen ever restrain herself? She may ask directly about a possible baby. And if so, Ella must parry the query adroitly. Having defied Grandmama to marry Serge, Ella will never, ever, allow her grandmother to have any of her doubts about her husband confirmed.

HOW DEAR, HOW quaint, how *gemütlich* Darmstadt appears, as she and Serge drive along the quiet avenues lined with chestnut trees and neat white houses. At the Neues Palais, she is flooded with a sense of well-being, to be back in the familiar rooms, surrounded by those she loves best. Baby Alice is a darling and everyone is overjoyed to see Ella.

Aunt Beatrice and Grandmama arrive the next day. Never has Ella seen her aunt so animated and smiley. After much argument, the queen has agreed to allow Beatrice to marry Liko, Prince Henry of Battenberg, Louis's younger brother, whom Beatrice met at Victoria's wedding.

When, after tea, Ella draws her aunt away to hear about plans for the wedding, Grandmama immediately joins them.

"You look very pale, dear Ella. Does Russia really suit you?" the queen asks.

The dreaded inquisition has begun.

"I'm still recovering from our long journey," Ella replies, as serenely as possible.

Grandmama frowns. "You look very thin, practically a skeleton. Don't you agree, Baby?"

"Ella is exquisitely beautiful, Mama."

Ella shoots Beatrice a grateful look. "I am nearly the same weight as when I married, and my clothes don't hang on me," she says, pulling at the tight waist of her fawn bombazine dress.

"Have you hopes?" her grandmother asks.

Hopes—hopes for a baby. "Not currently, Grandmama."

"Perhaps you never will! If you are too slender, your body won't function as it should!"

"No, it functions. My . . ." Ella blushes and looks at the floor. It's too embarrassing to announce that her courses are regular.

Grandmama taps Ella's right wrist urgently with her forefinger. "Yes, these matters are indelicate, but as you are without a mother I must act as such. If you tell me all is regular, then you need to be very careful with yourself. Give up riding."

Ella nods. She rarely rides.

"Quinine will strengthen you. Discuss this with Dr. Eigenbrodt while you are here, so he can prescribe the right dose."

She nods again, to appease her grandmother.

"And don't keep late hours."

Now she laughs. "When we are not in Petersburg, we live a very dull life."

Her grandmother scowls. "I understand from Marie—" The queen pauses and purses her mouth, such is her dislike of Serge's sister. "I understand you are the belle of every ball you attend."

"Not true. There are so many beautiful and accomplished women in St. Petersburg. As a new arrival, naturally I garnered extra interest this past winter."

The queen points at the diamond bracelet Ella is wearing on her left wrist. "That is hardly appropriate for the daytime."

Ella looks down at it fondly. "Serge loves to see me wearing this. It was his mother's—a first gift from his father at the time of their engagement here in Darmstadt."

The queen snorts. "You've clearly been infected with the Romanov ostentatious style of life."

Ella counters: "I strive to be as simple in manners and as good as Mama would have wished."

"But are you happy?" Grandmama looks at her beadily.

"Oh, Mama, one glance and you can tell she is," says Aunt Beatrice. Bless her.

"Let Ella answer."

"Perfectly happy," Ella says. "Serge is a person the more you know him the more you love him."

"Where is your husband? I desire to speak with him," Grandmama demands.

Ella waves Serge over, and he bows low. Her husband met her grandmother for the first time at Victoria's wedding. Serge knows her anti-Russian prejudices, but naturally acts as if nothing could delight him more than an audience with this most venerable matriarch.

Ella steps back to allow them to converse. Observing Serge with that oh-so-familiar figure—tiny, black-clad, and domineering—Ella feels a flare of enmity. How vile of Grandmama to poke and prod, airing her suspicions and her biases. How smug her grandmother would be, to be proven right, even if that would mean Ella suffers in her new life. What a mean-spirited impulse—to be eager for confirmation that you knew best all along.

Perhaps it is just as well Ella and the queen now live at such great distance from one another, and will rarely meet. Her grandmother is no longer someone she can love as she once did. In fact, Ella rather dislikes her now.

Part II

Chapter Eleven

A Summons to Osborne

Osborne House, July 1888

Alix is sure Grandmama will not like Ernie's hair—it looks greasy from all the pomade he has applied.

"Why don't you pop down to one of the state-rooms?" she suggests, tipping her head toward the stairs belowdecks. They have, minutes before, cast off from Gosport on the *Victoria & Albert*, the last leg of their long journey from Darmstadt. "Rinse your head in the washbowl; comb the hair wet back into place. Then it will look neat and natural."

"No need," Ernie replies, grinning. They are standing side by side at the ship's railing. "Grandmama won't concern herself with my appearance—she'll hardly notice me at all. On this occasion you are the object of her keenest interest, sister dear!"

Alix frowns.

Ernie laughs. "You doubt it? Pretend all you like, silly goose, but this visit is a tour of inspection—to take your measure now you're a proper young lady aged sixteen. To discover if you are worthy."

"Worthy," Alix scoffs.

"Of the greatest position there is!" says Ernie, finishing on an up note.

Grandmama has told Papa that she dreams of "darling Alicky" becoming the bride of Uncle Bertie's elder son, Eddy.

Should she pass muster, Grandmama will desire to slide her into place like a piece on a chessboard. No complaining, no objecting; what sensible princess would balk at the prospect of becoming Queen of England one day?

Perhaps Alix just isn't very sensible. Nor does she relish being shipped over from Darmstadt like a parcel, to be opened and the contents examined—as if she were a *something* rather than a *someone*.

"Do you think there's a chance she will lose interest in this?" she asks her brother.

"Unlikely. And remember what Papa said before we left," Ernie says.

"How he'd miss me."

Ernie smirks. "How you should feel grateful. Alone among all the granddaughters you've been singled out for special attention. Irène says Moretta and Margaret are green with envy—they've received no invitations to come and stay with precious Grandmama for two months, on their own."

"I'm not on my own, you're with me."

"Only for the first few weeks."

"Anyway, Moretta and Margaret are still in mourning for their father. They couldn't visit now."

"Poor things," says Ernie, somber for a moment.

Uncle Fritz was crowned German kaiser in March and died of a cancer in his throat in June. Cousin Willy is the kaiser now, and full of glee, he travels around, showing himself off, pleased as punch to have ascended at age twenty-nine. Papa says it's sick-making.

Alix sighs. "I do feel terribly sorry for them, losing their father. And it's always nice to visit England, especially Osborne, but I dread . . ."

"Dread what? Being found wanting?"

"More how Grandmama will treat me like breeding stock.

Can't you just hear it? How she'll ask the whole company: 'What do we think of this girl? Her posture? Her way of walking? Does she look strong enough to get healthy children?'"

Ernie laughs. "Quite possibly."

"I'll hate that, and anyway, I'm too young to take any decision about marrying."

"Sixteen is nothing! She had Aunt Vicky engaged at fifteen!" Ernie laughs.

"Look how that turned out," Alix counters.

Which isn't strictly fair. Grandmama couldn't keep Uncle Fritz from falling ill, dying young, mute, and in terrible pain.

"She's trying to avoid a repeat of what happened with Irène," Ernie says. "How she read in the newspapers about a possible engagement before anyone told her Irène and Henry were serious."

Their sister married Aunt Vicky's second son, Henry, in May, three weeks before Uncle Fritz's death.

"Yes, but Grandmama never had a grand plan for Irène the way she seems to have for me."

"She did! You've forgotten. Irène was designated to stay home with Papa. Then the ungrateful girl went out and snagged herself a prince of Prussia!"

"Irène was absolutely right to do as she wished. And Henry is so kind."

"If a bit dull."

"Don't be cruel."

"Admit it; you think the same."

"I'm glad she's happy, married to the man she chose," says Alix stoutly. "And I will do the same, if I marry at all!"

"Listen to you, making pronouncements."

"It wouldn't be nice to be dragged to the altar."

"Don't state this aloud to Grandmama."

"Why not? She'd be spared the trouble."

Ernie gives her a forbearing look. "I know you'd prefer to run away and hide in a corner, but remember Grandmama wants the best for you—"

"What *she* believes is best," Alix cuts in.

"You need to keep an open mind about Eddy." Ernie's face is uncharacteristically grave.

"And what if I refuse?" she asks, suddenly fierce.

Ernie shakes his head. "It doesn't do to be childish, Alix. Having been asked specially for a lovely stay in Grandmama's lovely houses, you must listen to what she has to say. And if she arranges a meeting with Eddy, be pleasant, not petulant."

"You imagine I don't know how to conduct myself?"

"It's your pigheadedness that worries me. And remember, should Grandmama start grieving aloud over Irène's marriage or Ella's, don't contradict, don't tell her she's mistaken, and don't announce how you, too, will make your own choice. That would be rude."

"You're very commanding today."

"Not like me, I agree," Ernie says with a quick smile. "But you are my darling little sister and I must look out for you."

"And issue me orders?"

"The vital ones," he says with a serious look.

"Just wait until she tries to arrange *your* life, telling you who to marry, and so on. You'll see it's not pleasant!" she exclaims.

"My turn may well come, but meanwhile—"

"Meanwhile, what about washing that awful stuff out of your hair?"

Ernie smiles. "Having discharged my fraternal duty, I can relax now and take a look around," he says, and he strolls away down the deck.

HOW IMPOSSIBLE HE is! Alix turns to rest her arms on the rail and gaze across the sun-spangled Solent. Her sisters, too, are quick to direct her these days. Last month Victoria came from England to host a meeting of the charity Mama founded, the Alice Frauenvereine. When they were entering the crowded hall together, her sister whispered: "Big smile now, Alix, otherwise the fine ladies of Darmstadt will imagine you're looking down on them."

It's true she's shy, and now she's out mixing in society, there is always the danger of being thought dull or glum—or worse, haughty. Why is it that young women are expected to be gay, and act that way, even when they might not feel gay? And why do people like receptions and parties? She never has a happy time unless she's with Ernie or dear Toni Becker, her best friend since they met in dancing class when they were nine.

Papa teases: "Whatever serious matter are you mulling over now, *mein Schatz*?" But he's so doting. He listens closely to all her ideas about God, about people in the family, about books she is reading. He declares nothing lifts his mood at the end of the day more than her company and hearing her sing or play the piano. With him she never feels deficient or unequal to the expectations other people have for her. Perhaps that's what indulgent fathers do—they convince you you're perfect as you are. And who is to say she isn't just as God intended? For a moment, she raises her chin, acting not as if she were alone on a boat deck but instead in a ballroom, answering prying, critical eyes with a defiant gesture of her own.

But it's no use. It's silly to imagine that how you are at home, at ease with those you love, is the person strangers will take you to be. And as Papa's daughter, and Grandmama's granddaughter, she gets far more attention than Toni or any other young lady in Darmstadt. When she thinks about it—about strangers gossiping, about newspapers speculating, and about the people around her, however well-meaning, compelled to tell her how to act—she does feel the urge to run and hide, just as Ernie said.

And this scheme of Grandmama's makes her particularly anxious. Perhaps one day, years from now, she might marry. She has lovely memories of Nicky, and the days they spent together at Peterhof, but they've never met again. Marrying Eddy? Alix can't imagine it. This cousin is eight years older than she, and rather peculiar-looking she noticed last year when they both attended Grandmama's Jubilee. During that celebration she overheard her sisters joking about how slow Eddy is in conversation, constantly asked: "What's that you say?"

Which means the object of all the examining and assessing she's about to endure is for Grandmama to push her into the arms of a man she's sure she won't ever want. And then what? In years past Victoria and Ella often complained about their grandmother's meddlesome ways. But to Alix the queen has always been rather like Santa Claus—sending gifts, writing loving letters, and showering her with praise. No one else in the family has enjoyed such unstinting approval: her sister Victoria told off for being argumentative, Irène considered slow, Ernie chided for lack of seriousness, and Ella—well, their grandmother has been perpetually disenchanted with Ella ever since she married Serge. As for poor Papa, he had no choice but to give up Madame de Kolemine completely to stay in Grandmama's good graces. And Alix knows he misses that lady still—another reason why she has difficulty imagining marrying and leaving home. Her father would be so lonely.

She sighs. She will be polite and respectful—Ernie is wrong to imagine otherwise—but eventually she will have to tell Grandmama she can't accept Eddy. Will she then be cast aside? Receive no more effusive notes? Never again be asked to stay? How sad. Dear Mama is such a distant memory. Alix has enjoyed basking in Grandmama's favor, knowing that the queen considers her "my very own child."

The white lighthouse at Cowes, with its cap of black roof,

passes in front of her eyes, and the boat begins to slow. Soon they will disembark. Her lady companion, Gretchen von Fabrice, must be below, out of the wind. And wherever has Ernie got to? She looks around. Ah, there he is, chatting with one of the seamen near the prow.

At least he's here. She never feels truly anxious with Ernie nearby.

DEAR LIKO IS pacing the landing stage at East Cowes, waiting for them. His full mustache makes this Battenberg cousin look like an affectionate walrus—and Alix has been especially fond of him since she was a bridesmaid at his wedding to Aunt Beatrice three years ago.

Today Liko, usually so cheerful, seems dispirited. During the quick ride up to the house, he warns them it's very dull at Osborne. Grandmama has invited no one else to stay this week, vowing that she intends to devote herself to Alix.

At this, Ernie elbows her.

"Please stop," she whispers urgently.

Liko continues, speaking German, "We must go out, Ernie, make some expeditions to do some shooting. I get so tired of having no companion to speak with properly."

In order to marry Aunt Beatrice, Liko had to promise to leave behind his home in Darmstadt and his regiment, the Rhenish Hussars, to live forever more with Grandmama in England. Rather hard, everyone in the family agrees.

"How are the children?" Alix asks. "I long to meet the baby."

"*Sehr gut,*" he replies. "I am teaching Drino to ride."

Liko and Beatrice have two children: two-year-old Alexander, known as Drino, and baby Victoria Eugenie, called Ena, ten months.

They turn through the gates and drive along a curving avenue flanked by silver blue conifers that leads to the carriage ring in front of the house. Inside they find Aunt Beatrice and Grandmama are drinking coffee in the drawing room.

"There you are, Ernie dear, and Alicky! Quite the most beautiful of all my granddaughters," the queen proclaims.

In turn, brother and sister kiss the downy cheek.

"We have insufficient cups and saucers," the queen says sharply, pulling the bell rope.

Ernie whispers, "Remember, be grateful."

THAT DAY, AND the next, are fine and warm. The house, with its cool, plant-lined corridors, lavishly furnished rooms, and marvelous outlook offering broad views of the sea, is cozily familiar. Alix walks beside Grandmama on the grounds, past the hedges full of sweet-smelling honeysuckle; Aunt Beatrice pushing sweet baby Ena, with her shock of white-blond hair, on the queen's far side. Grandmama asks about Alix's progress with lessons. They go from English to German to French and back again—her grandmother assessing her fluency in all three languages, she suspects. And the queen is generally very praising.

On the second evening, Baron Halsbury, the Lord Chancellor, comes to dine, and Alix is alarmed to find herself placed to his right. A heavy-faced older gentleman, with a large, curved nose like a parrot and a forbidding demeanor—what on earth does she have to say to him? It's fortunate that Mary Ponsonby, wife of Grandmama's private secretary, is seated on the man's left, and conducts a lively debate with him over whether nonbelievers should sit in the House of Commons—or some such. Alix can eat in peace, murmuring occasionally in German to Liko, who sits on her right side.

But the next morning Grandmama scolds, "Alicky! Your duty is to amuse your neighbors at table. You said hardly a word to Halsbury last night."

"I did not like to interrupt Lady Ponsonby."

The queen frowns. "Very rude to burden another person with all the effort of entertaining!"

Alix nods obediently, although she's quite sure their guest enjoyed Lady Ponsonby's clever chat far more than what she could have offered.

"Nothing is more hopeless than a princess who never opens her mouth. This afternoon, we will practice conversation, *en cercle*," Grandmama announces.

Chairs of various sorts are arranged in a circle in the Council Room, and the queen directs the exercise. She will call out the names and brief descriptions of guests expected to dine at Osborne during the next fortnight—represented by the chairs— and Alix and Aunt Beatrice will make imaginary conversation.

"Lady Constance Stanley, once a bridesmaid for your aunt Vicky, now married to the new governor general of Canada."

"When will you be going out to Canada, Lady Stanley?" says Alix to a spoon-backed chair.

"Do you worry you will catch your death?" puts in Beatrice.

"Baby, you wouldn't say that!" exclaims the queen.

Aunt Beatrice flashes a merry smile at Alix.

"Next, the new home secretary, Mr. Henry Matthews, a very intelligent man and a lawyer," declares Grandmama.

Alix, at a loss, turns panicked eyes to Beatrice.

"Mr. Matthews, is it true that legislation is being proposed for the better treatment of prisoners?" her aunt inquires of a chintz armchair.

"*Is* that true?" asks Alix, amazed her aunt would know such a thing.

"Could be. And if not, Mr. Matthews will be glad to tell me why not. Politicians love holding forth." She smiles and rolls her eyes.

"And now Lord Lathom, the Lord Chamberlain—he arranged the Jubilee celebration and he and his wife, the former Lady Alice Villiers, have nine children," says Grandmama.

"Lord Lathom, the Jubilee was splendid . . ." Alix begins, but staring at the gilt chair with the red damask seat all sensible thought flies out of her head.

"Is there a part of the celebration you will plan differently next time?" prompts Beatrice.

"Unlikely to be a next time," the queen interjects.

"Don't say that, Mama! Imagine it, your Diamond Jubilee will be in the year 1897! Something to look forward to."

Grandmama snorts, disbelieving.

They rattle through several more august persons, and Alix gains confidence, asking chairs about sporting pursuits, the new London plays, the climate in various corners of the British Isles. After she inquires of Lady Emily Revelstoke—wife of the director of the Bank of England, represented by a plush green chair with a lace antimacassar, "Do you often journey abroad during the summer?"—the queen announces: "Good, that's enough."

Beatrice goes up to the nursery, and Grandmama takes Alix out for a stroll on the parterre. The air is heavy with the aroma of jasmine and of roses in full bloom.

"Now, I recognize, dear Alicky, how gravity of deportment is your habit," her grandmother begins. "But this is a deficiency you *must* overcome. You should strive to be poised, amiable, and whenever required produce that radiant smile of yours."

Alix thinks of the electric lights Papa has had recently installed at the Neues Palais. She should learn to switch herself on like a light?

"Darmstadt hasn't offered you enough opportunity to blossom as you should," her grandmother insists.

Alix nods, although an ungoverned inner voice counters, *Says who?*

"And my dream is that you settle in England." Now Grand-mama beams up at her. "Loving you as I do and having acted a mother's part to you since you were a little girl."

Alix nods again.

"I suspect your dear father prefers you stay in Germany, with him, but my heart is set on having you here," her grandmother continues. "I ask you to make no judgments, form no opinions beforehand, but at the end of next month we travel to Bal-moral, and I have invited your cousin Eddy to meet us there. See if you don't like him, such a good and affectionate boy."

"I will, Grandmama, but I do prefer to wait for a few years before I think of marrying."

"No need to rush to form a close attachment! Just get to know him better." Then the queen adds, most earnestly: "Eddy is not stupid."

Goodness, isn't this an admission that many people find him so?

"Of course not, Grandmama," she replies.

"I could not bear to lose you as I have lost Ella." Her grand-mother's voice trembles. "I grieve over that unfortunate marriage as much as ever."

Despite Ernie's caution, Alix's urge to object is too strong. "But Ella is very happy with Serge—she always says so."

"This constant speaking of her happiness I do not like! If people are happy, they don't feel the need to announce it! And notice, Ella has no children, although she's been married four years."

Quite ungenerous of Grandmama to point this out. "Aren't some women not able?" Alix asks.

Grandmama sniffs. "The women in our family are very fe-cund."

What a strange word. Does it mean having many children?

Her grandmother continues: "For Ella to live in such a terribly corrupt country where the politics are so antagonistic to one's own views, is so distressing! Not only for me—but for your uncle Bertie, your aunt Vicky, for all your aunts and uncles. And look how seldom Ella comes away from that exile to visit Darmstadt or England. Serge dares not release her from his fierce grip!"

"Ella and Serge are going on a pilgrimage to Jerusalem quite soon. She is looking forward to this very much; she wrote and told me so," Alix says.

"Yes, yes." Grandmama waves a plump hand in the air. "Your sister will be forever describing her perfect contentment, the many glories of her life. But she lives like a bird in a cage in Petersburg. I hear from your aunt Alix, Bertie's wife, that even the empress, who is her sister and has many more reasons than Ella to be happy—the mother of five children, a husband passionately devoted to her—even *she* weeps when she must go back to her Russian prison. Minnie *dreads* returning to a place where violence lurks around every corner, where there's constant menace in the air, and criminality continues despite all the terribly *brutal* measures her husband takes. That throne is very unsafe!"

Grandmama looks up at her, expression vehement.

Oh dear, what can she say? She mustn't contradict; on the other hand Grandmama doesn't seem to know how it is, really, in Russia. "When we were at Petersburg," Alix says, "I saw Aunt Minnie very much at ease and happy, directing everything, Ella's wedding and her wardrobe, and all of her children. Also hosting numerous parties. She took such good care of her many guests."

To her surprise that raises a smile. "You are very observant, my sweet Alicky. Dear Minnie possesses great skill with people—enviable skill."

Grandmama's clear implication is that she, Alix, does not possess such a talent. Ignoring that, she offers, "And Aunt Minnie and Ella are good friends."

"Yes, Ella enjoys that consolation at least." Her grandmother sighs, and for a short while the crunch of pebbles under their feet is the only sound. Alix thinks for a moment of glorious Peterhof, those sunny days of romping, and dear Nicky. Surely all the Russian children are safe and happy and kept well protected from whatever violent upheavals might be taking place beyond the palace gates?

Without warning, Grandmama jumps to a new subject. "Tell me, dear, how are you managing all the responsibilities at home, now Irène has cruelly abandoned you and your poor father?"

LONG DAYS OF walks, picnics, and bathing in the sea follow. On the Monday of the third week of August, Ernie is departing after breakfast. He will take up university studies in Leipzig for the autumn term.

Alix and he stand outside the front door as a coachman drives a curricle up under the portico.

Ernie says, "Now, it hasn't been so bad, has it?"

"No." She smiles at him. "It's been pleasant. I find even Grandmama's lectures tolerable."

"I told you so," he says, smug.

"Of course, the worst is yet to come! Eddy at Balmoral!"

"He won't bite. Be kind to him. Nothing else is required."

"I wish I could believe that," she says, worried once more.

"Grandmama loves playing cupid, but she can't compel her arrows to land where she desires," he says with a fond smile. "And the Wales girls are coming to Scotland, too, and they are amusing."

"I do hope Grandmama hasn't told *them* what she has in mind."

"You'll soon find out, won't you?" he says, then kisses her cheek and climbs in. The coachman chirrups, Ernie waves, and they are away.

As Alix watches the vehicle round the curve in the drive,

she's surprised to find she has no longing to be sitting next to him, heading to Darmstadt. Papa has gone on a long trip to Poland for the hunting. She would be alone if she went home now. The trip north on the royal train with Aunt Beatrice, Liko, and the babies will likely be jolly. Her three Wales girl cousins are often boisterous and loud, but good company. And given Grandmama's dearest wish, she can't avoid forever being thrust together with Eddy, can she?

No, she thinks, she cannot, and she sighs.

THE CASTLE, WHEN they arrive, smells as always of damp log fires and cool stone. They take up a routine quite similar to that at Osborne, plenty of walks and picnics, with less sun but pleasantly cool temperatures. "Balmoral has the finest air in the world," Grandmama announces regularly.

On the afternoon Eddy is expected, the weather is very blowy. With her grandmother, Alix is crossing the great lawn, her hand atop her boater hat to keep it on her head, when she spots a carriage pulling up under the portico. Two men climb down—the taller most certainly Eddy, the other, shorter and stockier, unknown to her. The dreaded moment has arrived. Her stomach cramps nervously.

Eddy stands in front of the huge fireplace in the entrance hall. Dark-haired, slope-shouldered, he wears a smart Hussars uniform—gold-frogged blue tunic and blue trousers. His clothes are the handsomest thing about him. He has a narrow head sitting atop an overstretched neck, his heavy-lidded brown eyes make him look drowsy, and his absurd little cavalry mustache, waxed to turn up at the ends, might have been glued on.

He introduces his companion as Major Miles.

Grandmama kisses Eddy and coos, "How extremely tall you are, my boy." She inquires about the journey, acknowledges Miles's bow with a nod, and turns to her. "Now, Alicky, I leave you to entertain these gentlemen. I must rest, we expect Lord and Lady Campbell to dine."

As her grandmother stumps away, Alix looks up at Eddy, mute and self-conscious. *Imagine him a chair—ask him a question.*

Eddy saves her the trouble.

"I say, Alicky, why hasn't Ernie traveled here with you?" Without waiting for an answer, he says to Miles: "My Darmstadt cousin is a fine fellow, very humorous, and an excellent shot."

"Ernie has gone to Leipzig to continue his studies," Alix says softly.

"A great shame," Eddy says, appearing truly cast down. He addresses Miles again: "I went to university, don't you know. Cambridge. Didn't like it much—rather a bore."

Alix is astonished. Has Grandmama said nothing to Eddy of her intentions? Not even a hint? Apparently not; otherwise her cousin wouldn't so offhandedly reveal that Alix's company is less desirable to him than Ernie's. For a moment she feels like laughing in relief. Then new worries take shape and gallop through her mind. When exactly will their grandmother reveal her plans? Will she spring them on Eddy at the table, in front of everyone: "You two must get to know each other better"? Eddy will look confused, struggle to understand, and no doubt ask—"What's that you say?" And Alix will be forced to watch him take on board their grandmother's directive to woo her—a girl who minutes before he considered just another one of his many cousins. How completely mortifying. Alix's heart sinks.

"Miles, we must track down the gamekeeper," Eddy announces, oblivious to her silent fears. "We need to find out what he's seen, what might be about to shoot."

"Jolly good," says Miles, whose florid face and hearty manner strike Alix as comically English.

"Alicky, see you later," Eddy adds, fluttering his fingers in her direction nonchalantly as he walks toward the door.

Chapter Twelve

Theatricals

Balmoral Castle, September 1888

It's one thing to be organized by Grandmama, summoned for a visit, obligated to be charming at her table, accompany her on drives, et cetera, et cetera. She's the queen.

But to be told what to do by his three younger sisters—this Eddy hates.

And for days now Louise, Toria, and Maud have been ordering him about, making him dress up in ridiculous outfits, laughing at him.

Toria says they have no choice. Grandmama demands theatricals, so theatricals they must produce.

Their grandmother is convinced that Liko, due to turn thirty on the fifth of October, would enjoy having his birthday celebrated with a performance. But Eddy knows the man won't care a penny's weight for such bosh. Liko would vastly prefer to mark the day with a yachting trip, or with sport. Always quite deadly with the stags, Liko is.

When Grandmama wrote to say she expected Eddy to visit her in Balmoral and stay at least a fortnight, he'd imagined he'd be out every morning with Miles and Liko stalking.

But for reasons best known to herself, his grandmother announced to him that no, most days he can't hunt. "Keep us company—both Alicky and me."

His cousin from Darmstadt is a pretty girl, but shy; she barely utters a word to him. She doesn't know whist; instead they've played numerous games of Halma in virtual silence. He had waited impatiently for his younger sisters to turn up—the three of them are like a gaggle of geese, never calm, constantly squawking—but more than capable of amusing Alicky.

Yet, gallingly, as soon as Louise, Toria, and Maud arrived, Grandmama ordered up this show. Over breakfast! Having sent Liko out to the stables on some made-up errand.

"I'd like to see all the letters of dear Liko's name spelled out," Grandmama explained.

"How, exactly?" Eddy asked her.

"In *tableau vivant*, of course," his grandmother said, looking at him sternly.

"L-I-K-O—that won't take long," said Eddy.

"You mean his full name, isn't that right, Grandmama?" puts in Toria.

"Yes, Henry Maurice."

"Quite an undertaking," Maud said.

"Eddy, you must take the leading parts," Louise demanded.

"That's right," said Toria. "We have plenty of women staying here at the moment, not many men. You can't skulk off."

"I wouldn't." Of course he would, if he could.

"Eddy always looks very well on the stage," Grandmama said, and, beaming at everyone around the table, added: "I do love theatricals."

Eddy managed to glance sidelong at Miles—and roll his eyes. Alicky caught this look too. He saw her suppress a smile. He thought then, and he still believes, she shares his disdain for this whole ludicrous palaver.

Louise, the eldest of his sisters, is idiotic. As usual, Toria has taken charge.

"Eddy, you will appear in at least four *tableaux*; not only are we short on men, Grandmama will expect it," she orders.

He will feature in H for harvest, as a farmer, naturally enough, and R for royalties, as Charlemagne (not bad, that), and M for military, clad in the uniform of the Scots Guards—scarlet jacket, blue collar facings embroidered with thistles. Miles and he look bloody good dressed this way. But Eddy attempts to draw the line at acting the groom in the Hessian wedding scene planned for U, union.

"But you *must*, Eddy, and Alicky will be the bride," Maud says, tittering.

"I've already agreed to do N, as the novice nun, that's all I can act," Alicky says, sounding rather frantic. "I'm also taking charge of the costumes."

The girl has turned bright red. He will rescue her. "Leave Alicky alone. If you insist on my doing groom, then one of you"—and Eddy waves his finger at his sisters—"must be bride."

The three leave the room for a private conference, Alicky scuttles off who knows where, and Eddy takes the opportunity to go out for a smoke with Miles.

After a quarter of an hour Louise comes to find them in the garden. "It will be me, and you'd better look properly devoted when we are acting the scene," she admonishes. "We need to start rehearsing this afternoon."

A TROOP OF men in shirtsleeves comes to hammer together boards to make a large stage in the ballroom. Miss Robson, his sister's former governess, now their chaperone, designs the scenery assisted by that German lady-in-waiting of Alicky's who is as stumm as she is. Louise and Toria do most of the painting—along with Lady Jane Churchill and several others of Grandmama's suite. Even the queen takes a turn with the brush. Alicky and Maud scour the attics for costumes.

Eddy hates the lederhosen he's told to wear as the farmer, but far worse are the cream-colored trousers and matching vest dug up for him to wear as the groom. He can barely button the front of the trousers, and they feel tight through the seat.

"There's nothing else?" he appeals to Alicky when first he tries them on.

"Nothing that looks like what a young man would wear at a Hessian wedding," she says, biting her lip nervously. "These must be Grandpapa's, brought from Coburg, years ago."

"Our grandfather was clearly a diminutive man."

"Don't be so fussy, Eddy," says Toria scornfully. "You'll be wearing them for all of ten minutes."

A LARGE GROUP of staff and many neighbors have been invited for the performance. Sixty people in all it must be. And things start very well, with Liko seated in the front row, next to Grandmama, putting on a fine show of looking surprised and happy to be so honored, while bouncing little Drino on his knee.

Eddy acts out H for harvest with Maud—he's the sturdy farmer with a scythe and she's a demure little farmer's wife holding a basket of straw.

He's pleased, as Charlemagne, in R for royalty, to strike a thoughtful pose, chin in hand, leaning on the arm of his dining-chair throne. For his kingly robes, he's wearing one of the crimson drapes that used to hang in the library, fastened with a paste brooch of Lady Ely's.

And sword in air, alongside Miles, he feels suitably martial in M for military.

But as the curtains part for U as in union, when he has his sister Louise on his arm, she whispers, "What are you doing, Eddy? You are too far forward." He takes a step back and there's a loud ripping sound. His trousers have split open in the rear.

Great bursts of laughter ensue—even Grandmama begins to giggle, her shaking shoulders up near her ears.

"You didn't need to step back *that* far!" whispers Louise. "Now you've ruined everything."

He retreats from the stage, awkwardly sidestepping crab-wise, because he doesn't want to present his exposed bottom to the audience.

He finds refuge in the cloakroom off the ballroom, designated as the changing area. Costumes for earlier scenes, along with proper clothes, are piled on chairs. Out from under one mountain of garments he pulls his shirt, trousers, and jacket, and quickly changes.

Someone knocks. It had better not be that damn Louise. He won't tolerate any more jibes from her.

"Come."

Oh, it's Alicky—looking miserable. "Might I see the trousers?" his cousin asks in a barely audible voice.

He hands her the offending pair.

She looks them over carefully, inside and out. "I'm very sorry. I see now the center seam at the back was quite frayed. I should have re-stitched it."

"I should never have agreed to wear them."

"They do resemble traditional Hessian dress."

"Still, there are limits." He's running his eyes around the floor, searching for his shoes.

"Eddy, you were kind to carry so much of the burden of performing," she says quietly. "What would we have done without you?"

He glances over at his cousin, rather touched. "Oh, well, yes, my duty to Grandmama, don't you know?"

She nods, eyes down, blushing, from the looks of it.

"Also, I have had plenty of practice," he continues. "Being onstage, in public, I mean. I opened a bridge the other day."

"Did you?"

"Yes, in Hammersmith. Huge crowds of people. I felt a bit like a goldfish in a crystal bowl."

"I can imagine." Now she has tilted her face up and is gazing at him with an earnest expression on her face. She's wearing the gauzy white dress she wore to play a novice nun. With her thick blonde hair rippling loose down her back, and her big, solemn blue eyes, the role suited her to a tee. She's certainly going to be a beauty one day. A face like a Grecian statue, and that milky complexion. But never one for smiling.

He tries to joke. "Goes with my lofty position; I must endure."

Alicky remains grave.

Toria careens through the doorway, breathless. "I've been looking for you two. Come on, now we've reached the end, everyone must take a bow."

HIS SISTERS DEPART for Sandringham with Miss Robson. The next day, Alicky and her German lady-in-waiting—what's her name, Greta?—also leave. Grandmama insists Eddy stay on.

A great relief when Motherdear wires and asks please can't Eddy come back to London in time to greet his father, who will return on the twentieth from a most taxing trip to the Continent.

The queen relents. But she asks to speak privately to Eddy, at breakfast, on the morning of his departure.

"Isn't Alicky lovely and kind?" his grandmother says.

"She is."

"Don't you think perhaps, Eddy, dear, she might be perfect for you?"

"For me?"

"As your wife?"

"She's so young." This suggestion surprises him very much.

"Already sixteen, and I fear you mustn't wait too long."

"Why?"

"She might be snapped up. By a Russian!"

"Oh, could she be? As her sister was?"

"Exactly."

"Alicky does not seem ready—" Eddy hesitates. Is it unseemly to refer to a young virginal girl as "not ready" for romance?

"Oh, she is very shy, which is a worry. Of course your mother was very shy to start, when she first came from Denmark. She had yet to win the nation's heart. But now! The lovely Princess of Wales is celebrated for her beauty and her grace, admired by peers and paupers alike!"

Paupers? Do paupers spend much time thinking about Motherdear? Eddy rather doubts it.

"Alicky said hardly a word to me," he tells Grandmama.

"Toria told me you enjoyed a tête-à-tête after the performance."

"She was commiserating with me after my drat costume ripped."

"Those trousers were a bit small," Grandmama says, stirring her tea. "Dear Eddy, you know your choices are not infinite, and I believe that Alicky will be a wife you could both love and admire."

Goodness, his grandmother is quite attached to this idea. "Well, if you think she seriously would be interested . . ."

"Of course she would."

"But she seemed so distant."

"I know Alicky and I know you," the queen insists. "She wouldn't turn down the chance to marry such a good and steady husband and join our united, happy family. To say nothing of assuming a position second to none in the world!"

At the moment Eddy finds bachelor life most agreeable. In London he is beset by flattering women, eager to entertain him. A few he "sees" regularly. But he must get married—eventually. He concedes this.

But he must get married, eventually, he knows this.

ON THE TRAIN journey to London, idle for hours, Eddy reflects on next week's plans—a trip to Aldershot for polo, a shooting party in Gloucestershire, and Alicky. Her lovely face certainly goes well with her serene and gentle aura. She's never shrill nor hoydenish like his sisters.

Yes, his Darmstadt cousin is very refined, and he likes that.

He still finds it difficult to believe the girl is well disposed toward him. He appreciates how she felt sorry for him over the ripped trousers and praised his contributions to the theatricals. Is that solid evidence of something? Was she signaling her affectionate regard? Hard to know. She seemed very reticent in general. Maybe a bit intimidated? He's the heir, after all, next in line after Papa for the throne. That's got to overawe a princess from obscure little Darmstadt.

Come to think of it, shy girls likely make the most tenderhearted wives. He must remember that. Brassy, confident women such as the ones he meets around town—you definitely shouldn't marry one of them even if you could, and as an heir presumptive he definitely can't. There is the type of women you step out with—actresses and the like—and then there's the other sort. And for him, that second category, the marrying kind, is narrowed further by his duty to keep up the blood royal.

Home at Marlborough House, before retiring for the night, Eddy reaches into his desk drawer for some letter paper to write to his brother George, at sea with the navy.

He briefly describes his stay at Balmoral, makes a few complaints about Grandmama's craze for theatricals, and then imparts his main point: their cousin Alicky has grown up.

He ends thus: *I've got my eye on her now and you know what that means.*

Chapter Thirteen

<hr>

A Prayer from a Distance

Jerusalem, September 1888

*W*hen Ella and Serge stand in front of the Church of Mary Magdalene for the first time, Ella hears her husband catch his breath in awe at the sight.

They have traveled here to the Holy Land to be present at the consecration of this new church, which the tsar, together with his four brothers, had erected to honor their late mother, once a princess of Hesse, later the most truly believing Maria Alexandrovna, Empress of Russia. Serge supervised the construction from afar, paying close attention to every aspect of the design.

Occupying a prominent spot on the western slope of the Mount of Olives, the location in Russian belief of the Garden of Gethsemane, the church is of white sandstone, polished to look like marble, and built in the grand Muscovite style with seven gold onion domes, crowned with golden Orthodox crosses.

Ella reaches out her hand to squeeze Serge's, to tell him wordlessly that she, too, marvels at the magnificent outcome.

In truth, she finds *everything* about Jerusalem miraculous. While smaller and more compact than she envisioned, this city of golden stone invites at every turn the most profound contemplation. Here, where the Lord suffered so that man might be redeemed through His blood, she senses as never before how no human person nor human grief is beneath Christ's compassion.

On their first day she and Serge walk the Via Dolorosa, stopping at each Station of the Cross, and, at the Church of the Holy Sepulcher, find intense comfort praying side by side.

Surrounded by fellow pilgrims of differing denominations—Roman Catholics, Anglicans, Lutherans, Methodists, Greek Orthodox—Ella senses how the paths to Christ are various, but all lead to the same place. Perhaps, out in the greater world, beyond this sacred capital, Christians make too much of the divisions amongst themselves?

WHILE SHE MUSES on this question and rejoices to see in life holy places she has pictured since childhood days, one earthly worry pulls her away from her exalted surroundings: Alix. Is her sister in Scotland being persuaded to think seriously of Eddy?

Ella thinks of her sister in the Highlands, accompanying Grandmama on drives to Corriemulzie, Dantzig Shiel, Glen Gelder—all the beauty spots Ella remembers from her own solo visit to Balmoral in '83. Grandmama will be showering Alix with attention and affection—complimenting and coaching, petting and stroking. Alix is a stubborn little thing, not likely to agree to a marriage on anyone else's say-so. But mightn't she find the queen's blandishments flattering? Won't she be tempted by the vision of a future in that lovely country—as a most important member of the ruling family? How can such a glittering prospect fail to captivate a sixteen-year-old girl who must wonder what her beauty and her rank will gain her in life?

But Ella considers the idea of Alix marrying Eddy quite dreadful. As soon as she heard from Papa that Grandmama had extended a special invitation to Alix to spend two months in Britain, Ella was in no doubt of her grandmother's intentions. She wrote immediately to her sister Victoria listing her concerns. Marriages between first cousins are best avoided—isn't that the latest thinking? Eddy looks stupid and none too strong—didn't they agree when they met him again last year at the Queen's Jubilee? Why should Alix take on someone so dreary? Might it not be dangerous? Married to Eddy, pretty, clever Alix could very well turn into a flirt.

Victoria replied promptly. Yes, Grandmama is set on securing Alix for Eddy—she's requested Victoria's help in encouraging the match. Yes, the young man is definitely no great shakes. And yes, their sister might feel dissatisfied as the wife of a man as insipid as Eddy. Although Alix a committed flirt? Victoria can't picture it. More probably Alix would just become gloomy and miserable.

Still, Victoria asked pointedly, doesn't Ella oppose Alix's marriage to Eddy because she has a scheme of her own for the girl? Hasn't she cherished the hope that Alix might one day be Nicky's bride? Ever since the young man was charmed by their sister at Peterhof, at the time of Ella's wedding to Serge?

She does dream this, Ella conceded by return of post. Nicky is such a sweet, affectionate, and generous-hearted young man. A tendency to passivity may be his only fault. Sasha, so domineering, has rather squashed his son. Nicky will need to act decisively and remain resolute in his future role—and with this Alix can help him. She's reserved, yes, but never weak-willed. And what a handsome couple they would make! Also, to have her sister here in Russia would be such a joy for Ella. Despite her loyal husband and numerous new friends, she feels isolated. Of course, there is the religious question. Alix would be obligated to convert to marry the future tsar, and Papa might object at first. Although couldn't their father be won over, envisioning the splendid life Alix would enjoy as Nicky's wife?

Ella added a postscript: *How improbable that we should be*

debating whether our little Sunny might be best suited to be Queen of England or Empress of Russia!

She pictures Victoria laughing merrily over that.

DURING THE CONSECRATION service at the church, standing beside Serge amidst the clouds of incense, she remembers how, before they departed Petersburg, Minnie took her aside to ask, quite solemnly: "Dear Ella, are you aware that prayers offered up as a church is consecrated are always granted by God?"

"Truly?"

"Yes, so pray for your most cherished desire," the empress instructed.

Her sister-in-law must believe that Ella intends to pray for a child—to fall pregnant, finally, after four years of marriage. But Ella has a different appeal in mind.

Listening to the sacred music and the solemn liturgy, she silently prays: *Please, Holy Father, bless both dear Nicky and darling Alix, and bring them together in love for one another.*

ELLA WILL NEVER have children. She's convinced of this now. After the day at Gatchina when Serge revealed he could not consummate their marriage, they have dropped the subject entirely. Without exchanging a further word, it was established between them that they would still share a bed, but nothing more.

Do all marriages involve unspoken agreements of one sort or another? Ella imagines so. Although she suspects few couples are compelled to leave as much undiscussed as she and Serge do. Ella is no longer the naïve girl enjoying her first season in Petersburg. She's aware those odious officers she overheard slandering Serge were not completely mistaken; she understands, now, what they were saying. Her husband has an affinity for other men.

She can't pinpoint the exact moment when she determined this. Watching him walk to the Farm Palace stables with his arm flung over the shoulders of his adjutant? Or that evening she saw him, chatting with a few fellow officers, throw his head back in an ecstatic, unrestrained way? Or did the particular glad yelp he emitted when a handsome young ensign turned up unexpectedly at Ilinskoe give him away?

What Ella will never know—nor does she care to—is if in his youth Serge behaved indecently. Her husband, with his deep religious faith, must have always battled against profane desires. And as a married man he has, she is sure, refrained from acting upon them—a sinful betrayal of her would not suit his self-image. But because his sensual urges are not aroused by Ella, he is deprived of the gratification and release that other men find in their relations with their wives. He's naturally left frustrated, which, to her mind, helps explain his frequent irascibility and his short temper.

For all this, Ella pities him. And in pitying him, she is determined to protect him. She will never betray any dissatisfaction with him in public or private. She's proud to provide Serge with the devotion he deserves—to uphold him and the Romanov dynasty. When she hears others describe her husband as cold, she marvels: Is his intensity lost on them? The convictions that burn inside of him—don't people sense how they burn with a pure flame? And, for her part, she's never aspired to drift idly through the world and make personal happiness her goal. She learned that much from Mama's life.

If Serge cannot help but snap complaints, make testy remarks, raise a scornful eyebrow when she expresses her opinions at the table, she has grown accustomed to it. She rather welcomes the challenge of always keeping her temper, even when he's out of his. She relishes the sense of self-sacrifice that life with Serge gives her. She finds fulfilling the exacting task of behaving irreproachably. Perhaps no one else could ever understand this. But she is not like most other women—she can acknowledge that—just as he is not like most other men.

ON THE LAST day they spend in Jerusalem, they return to the new church for a final time so Serge can confer with the architect on a few last unfinished details of the construction.

For a quarter of an hour Ella stands on the stone stairs, in the sun, staring at the walled city. She has found the Holy Land overall shockingly barren and derelict—the ruling Turks have neglected it for centuries. But the radiance of Jerusalem, the particular glow of the stone, entrances her. She feasts her eyes on the sight, and goes inside only because she feels drawn to take a last look at the icon of Virgin Mary, hanging on the church's iconostasis, separating the nave and the sanctuary. Dating from the sixteenth century and having survived a fire where it hung previously in a church in Lebanon, this icon is said to have cured hundreds of people who have come seeking miraculous intervention.

As she gazes at the solemn, pious face, the slender hand gesturing at the Christ child, she feels a jolt. Is she, herself, not in need of intervention?

Ella suffers from no dread disease, that's true. But in Russia loneliness dogs her, and on occasion she allows herself to regret, wistfully, the children she will never bear. Perhaps this explains a sudden ache of emptiness in her chest, and a compulsion to kneel on the floor. There, she finds herself mimicking, for the first time, a gesture she has seen Serge make a thousand times. With pursed fingers she touches her forehead, then her breast, right shoulder and then left.

In the sacred quiet of the church, she is conscious of herself floating in time and space. She's the Grand Duchess Elisabeth Feodorovna, a woman of noble birth, a member of three august families, but in truth merely a forlorn, pitiful creature, like all of God's creatures. She will now leave behind here in Jerusalem the profound gladness of worshipping with Serge in harmony.

Her husband always acts studiously neutral about her choice of belief, but she knows it grieves him. To be separated in this fundamental way—when they are deprived of so much else that married couples share—seems particularly cruel.

She prays. *Dear Lord, most joys in life are transitory; the only eternal joy is serving You. How can I serve You more profoundly?*

She hears an inner voice. Her own? God's? *Become Orthodox.*

She nearly gasps out loud. She asked for guidance, and having received it, she feels a shocking, pulsing excitement. She rises to her feet with difficulty, her legs shaking beneath her.

And why not? Shouldn't she take this step if it will lead to a more profound belief? Unite her and Serge truly? Choosing a new faith would be the culmination of her journey from girlhood to womanhood. And perhaps this is why God guided her to the life she has—so as to grant her this opportunity to follow Him more closely.

Still, as she walks slowly toward the door of the church, where Serge stands speaking with two workmen, she's cast into turmoil. What will people think? Will they believe her shallow? So indifferent to the Lutheran church she was born into that she could throw it off? And what of her German and English families? She hates to imagine how Papa will react, should she break her vow to him never to convert. Although wasn't her father worried that she would change belief under pressure from Serge? And her husband has never pressed her, not once.

Serge turns as she approaches. Their eyes meet. She feels an urge to declare herself. But she's gripped with a strange agitation. She worries she is suffering from a kind of hysteria. Perhaps this high pitch of emotion is brought on by being in

Jerusalem? She'll leave and her former calm certitude in her faith will wash over her again? She rather hopes so.

He seems to read something in her face. He asks: "My child, do you feel faint?"

She shakes her head, forces herself to smile. "I am well. I am just trying to imprint on my memory the great beauty of this place."

JOURNEYING HOME, THEY depart Constantinople in the evening on the frigate *Kostrama*. The crossing is rough—a night and a day and a second night on the bucking seas—before they sail into the harbor at Odessa on a rainy, fog-bound morning.

It's like Scotland here today, Ella thinks, walking down the gangway behind Serge. Thoughts of Alix have occupied her mind during the sea voyage, alongside meditations on her strange experience in the church.

Once settled on the train north, Ella says to Serge, "While I can't be sure, I've heard nothing from anyone, I do hope Alix has not fallen in with Grandmama's plan."

"The plan to make her the wife of your cousin Eddy, he of the deplorable soft chin and half-mast eyes?"

"Yes, that plan," she says with a small laugh.

"Poor fellow. When we were in London, I thought he looked like a cow struck on the head with a mallet," Serge says. "Hard to imagine him king of anything."

"How terrible for my sister to be shackled to him!"

Serge shrugs. "Think of the compensations."

"Serge, you cannot be serious. Is that what you want for Alix?"

"Such is my disdain for the anti-Russia claque among the British ruling class, I would be gratified to see a close relation of ours become their queen." He grins, looking for an instant like a mischievous little boy.

She frowns at him and shakes her head. "No, she mustn't sacrifice herself in that way. And we should counteract Grandmama's efforts directly. Let's issue our own invitation to Alix—to travel to Petersburg with Papa and Ernie for the upcoming winter season."

Now Serge laughs. "Everyone will immediately assume you are trying to promote the match between your sister and the tsarevich."

"Not everyone," she says defensively. And, in truth, Ella has no idea how Nicky feels about Alix, beyond fond memories of a fortnight spent together when her sister was a child of twelve.

Serge gives Ella a forbearing look. "You imagine the newspapers won't notice? You think St. Petersburg society will shrug? Your sister's arrival in the capital will be spoken of in every drawing room with heavy innuendo. As soon as Nicky and Alix are spotted dancing together, they will be as good as engaged in many minds."

"We cannot live our lives in accordance to what will or will not create gossip."

"No. But dear Minnie knows Alix is slated to marry her sister's son. She'll sense your purpose and won't be pleased."

"My purpose? I miss them, all of them, and since our marriage we have not once had them to stay with us in Russia."

"If you are prepared for the consequences . . ." he says with a skeptical shake of his head.

"I am."

"Then write to your father inviting them, once we are at home."

Within the month Papa has accepted.

It's late October, and the days are rapidly closing in.

Late in the afternoon, a time when Ella is most susceptible to homesickness, she often seeks solace in the music room. Today, the aquamarine curtains are drawn against the early dark; the air smells of the freesias she's arranged in a dark-pink Orletz vase and placed on the sideboard. Ella is at the piano, stumbling a bit through Bach's French Suite, fingers stiff, when the door flies open and Serge strides in still wearing his black cloak, a footman hurrying in his wake.

"I have most shocking news," he tells her.

He turns his shoulders to the servant, who lifts the cloak off him. Serge is breathing heavily; he must have run up the stairs.

"Sasha and Minnie and the children were traveling on the imperial train south of Kursk when the cars went off the rails and overturned. They were together eating breakfast. Little Olga was thrown clear but the rest of them became trapped under rubble, Sasha himself pinned down by the collapsed roof of the dining car. My brother, colossus that he is, managed to push off this heavy weight and then pull the others out of the wreckage."

Serge puts his hands over his eyes, and she watches him praying silently for a minute. "They might all have died. Minnie's favorite Cossack guard was killed, among two dozen other people. And, so sad—Sasha's lovely Kamchatka was crushed. You remember that beautiful dog?"

"Yes," says Ella, struggling to take in his account.

"At first everyone believed it was a bomb, but it seems to have been an accident—the train, traveling fast, jumped the tracks. They will return to Petersburg on Saturday," Serge says.

"God be praised, for His mercy," she says.

Out of the pocket of his waistcoat, Serge pulls a yellow telegram. "Sasha's message to me is not to worry, and can you imagine Miechen's disappointment?"

Now he laughs.

"Oh, don't joke," Ella says. "This escape was too close."

Had Sasha along with his three sons—Nicky, Georgy, and

Misha—all died in the accident, Miechen's husband, Grand Duke Vladimir, would become tsar and her son, Kirill, tsarevich. Ella can't imagine life in Russia under those circumstances. Bereft of Minnie and Sasha, darling Nicky, and the other children? Unthinkable. She gazes at the white flowers, imagining her horrible bereavement.

"Masses of Thanksgiving for the tsar's deliverance are to be said throughout the land, the largest here at the Kazan Cathedral, tomorrow afternoon. You and I will go, with the rest of the family," Serge says.

THE ENTIRE IMPERIAL family gathers again on the platform of the Nikolaevsky Station to welcome Sasha and Minnie and the children back to Petersburg on Saturday after their ordeal. Ella finds no opportunity to speak with Nicky alone, so she sends him a note on Monday morning, inviting him for afternoon tea.

So eager is she to see him, she waits in the porter's room off the palace's entrance hall. At the sound of a quick step and a soft jingle of spurs, she rushes out to clasp Nicky in a long embrace.

Once she leads him upstairs to her sitting room, and is pouring tea from the samovar, she asks for details of the accident.

"One big bump and then a much stronger bump and everything started to crash and we were thrown out of our chairs; the table flew over my head and disappeared," he says, taking the cup and saucer she offers. "I shut my eyes and I expected to die."

"Oh my goodness."

"Do you have any more of those delicious English biscuits?" Nicky asks.

"Yes, in a moment, but first, finish the story."

"There's not much more to it. Everything was dark and dusty for a short time and then I thought I saw a light, so I began to scramble forward and found I could climb out. Papa had wrenched open a hole somehow."

"And not one of you badly injured?"

"Xenia and Georgy have cuts on their arms from the flying glass, and didn't you notice Mama's left hand in a sling? It was trapped until she wiggled it free, and it bled all over her yellow silk dress, one of her favorites, from Worth. And then for hours Mama and Papa and the rest of us were helping with the wounded. Dead bodies all around, people screaming and moaning. It began to rain. It was hours before another train came to rescue us."

Ella stares at him, trying to picture the ghastly scene.

"Biscuits?" he repeats.

Trembling, she stands, crosses to the glass cabinet, opens it, and reaches for the flat, round tin containing brown-sugar biscuits.

She takes a deep breath and instructs herself to banish her nerves. God is indeed merciful. The whole family saved. Nicky alive to meet Alix again. She can't ignore God's hand in this. He is pointing her the way. She turns to walk back to the handsome boy, tin in hand, a smile on her face.

She says cheerily, "So, Serge and I have decided something— to invite Papa and Ernie and Alix to visit. They will come for the winter season. Won't that be grand?"

Chapter Fourteen

≼≼≼≼≼≼≼≼≼≼≼≼≼≼≼≼≼≼≼≼≼≼≼≼≼≼≼≼≼

One Winter Season

St. Petersburg, January 1889

To Sandra he is always Nicholas Alexandrovich, never Your Imperial Highness.

When he was seven and she was six, he asked: "Sandra, would you like never to part?" And she answered (allegedly; she has no memory of this exchange), "What a good idea! I will marry Paul Shuvalov and you will appoint him your equerry: that way we will never part."

The tsar enjoys telling the story of how the eldest Vorontsov girl palmed off the heir's proposal, preferring an officer of the Fifth Horse Guards Battery instead.

"Let's hope Nicky has better luck with the next woman he asks," the tsar laughs.

Never could Sandra imagine marrying Nicholas Alexandrovich. Brought up together, they have been the fondest of playmates. He is like another brother. Their mothers are best friends, and Sandra's father, Count Illarion Ivanovich Vorontsov, is chief minister of the imperial court.

On Sundays, in former times, Sandra, along with her younger sisters, Sofka and Maya, and her older brother, Vanya, would travel in a special carriage attached to the 9:30 train to play at Gatchina with Nicholas Alexandrovich, his sister Xenia Alexandrovna, and his brother George Alexandrovich.

The vast park, with its forests and its lakes, was their kingdom. In the autumn they built fires and roasted apples and nuts. In winter they made snow houses and tobogganed along the steep and narrow-channeled runs designed by the tsar himself. After the spring thaw they rowed on the largest lake—the water so clear stones lying at the bottom forty feet below were perfectly visible. They formed a secret club, which they called the Potato Society, after the time Sofka hid for hours, lying prone in a just-seeded potato field during a game of hare and hounds. The empress instructed Fabergé to fashion a little golden potato, hung on a golden chain, for each of them to wear around their neck. And when Nicholas Alexandrovich came of age, he gave them all gold badges with his initials on the front and the inscription *Gatchina 1880–1886* on the back.

The other legacy of those happy childhood days is this: Nicholas Alexandrovich confides his private thoughts in her, and Sandra tells him some of her own.

AS IS THE custom, two days after Epiphany, three thousand guests are invited to the Nicholas Ball at the Winter Palace. With her parents and her sisters, Sandra climbs the magnificent marble Jordan staircase, processes down the cavernous hallway pillared with purple-red stone, to wait in the Concert Hall, where, at precisely nine o'clock, the grand master of ceremony strikes the floor three times with his ivory-tipped ebony rod and announces, "Their Imperial Majesties."

The tsar, in crimson dress uniform, his chest laden with medals, heavy sword bouncing against his leg, looks uncomfortable (he hates to be out of his patched tunics and baggy trousers) escorting the beaming tsarina, who wears a magnificent white-and-silver brocade gown, open in the front to reveal a diamond-encrusted silk underskirt. The sapphires of her tiara are the size of eyes, and across her bodice lies the blue ribbon of the Order of Saint Andrew. The empress loves to be on show.

Nicholas Alexandrovich follows behind. He winks at Sandra, and a few minutes later, as the polonaise begins, they sneak away for a chat.

Count Paul Pavlovich Shuvalov, still the man Sandra hopes to marry, left Petersburg two months ago for a year's service in Poland—not ready to formally propose. She's vowed to wait for him, although her mother calls her a fool. Princess Alix of Hesse, whom Nicholas Alexandrovich admired as a child, is coming next week to stay with her sister the Grand Duchess Elisabeth Feodorovna. The tsarevich has concerns.

"What if she is not as pretty as I remember?" he asks Sandra.

"Why wouldn't she be?"

"She was just twelve when I last saw her; she's nearly seventeen now—a lot can change."

"I think once pretty always pretty."

"On his desk Uncle Gega has a photo of Alix and Aunt Ella taken at the Queen's Jubilee in London. Alix looks a little stern."

"She had to keep still for the camera."

"Mama says Queen Victoria plans to marry her to my cousin Eddy."

Sandra laughs. "So, if you *do* like her, there's going to be trouble?"

"Mama seems annoyed she's coming. But if Alix is beautiful, I will pursue her."

"And if she isn't?" Sandra teases.

"If she isn't, she will just be my dear cousin."

"Simple enough." Sandra laughs.

"Aren't you dancing the quadrille with me? Come on, let's not miss that," he says, and grabs her hand to pull her to the ballroom.

YES, SANDRA'S MOTHER confirms, the empress is not fond of Princess Alix of Hesse and is unhappy she is coming to Petersburg now.

"Don't repeat this, Sandra, Minnie told me in confidence."

"What exactly about her does the empress dislike?" Sandra asks.

"Apparently the girl's a bit odd."

Sandra feels very curious to meet this odd princess, who may or may not be pretty.

She gets her chance, when, a few days later, they are introduced at a large luncheon party at the Anichkov Palace.

Slim and tall—the princess stands an inch taller than Nicholas Alexandrovich himself, and she holds herself regally. Truly glorious hair—thick and a deep shade of golden red. Large light eyes, pink-and-white complexion, and nicely arranged features, although, if you were looking to find fault (and Sandra finds she is), you'd say the mouth is rather small, the chin a bit foreshortened, and the nose a touch too sharp. And such a morose expression! It will require effort to get this girl to laugh.

Xenia Alexandrovna introduces them: "Alix, here is dear Sandra, one of our gang."

The princess produces a tight smile. Sandra and she converse briefly about the schedule of the season—without any great pleasure, it would seem, on the part of Alix of Hesse, who has a strange way of hardly moving her lips when she speaks.

A very German type, Sandra concludes, or maybe English. Not Russian, in any case.

But Nicholas Alexandrovich is enchanted. After his sister guides the princess away to speak to other people, the tsarevich slips over and whispers in Sandra's ear: "I went down with Papa to the Warsaw Station to meet the party from Darmstadt and I immediately saw how much she's grown—and how she's become even better-looking."

"She has a lovely face and figure."

"And you will like her when you get to know her. She enjoys skating."

"Will you take her to the Jardin de la Tauride?" says Sandra. That's society's favorite skating spot.

"Less fuss if we stay here. Papa has ordered the back lawn flooded and an ice hill built for sliding. Come tomorrow. At two o'clock, for a little party."

"Your mother is happy for you to host skating parties?"

He shrugged. "Mama is being uncharitable about Alix. Telling me I mustn't spend too much time with her. But Xenia is under no such restriction, so if asked, she'll say she has invited Alix, and I just happened by."

Nicholas Alexandrovich smiles, nudges her playfully with his elbow, and turns to go, weaving between guests.

Watching him Sandra recalls Paul saying once, "I can't picture that boy as tsar. Too slight, for one thing. Not the substantial man our sovereign is, appropriately forceful and impressive."

"Nicholas Alexandrovich won't shy from the responsibilities of office when his turn comes," Sandra replied.

"And in the meantime? What keeps him busy? Drinking with his brother officers, playing billiards, cards, and skittles, slipping off to the midnight clubs to hear the bawdy ladies sing?"

"His father is still young. Why shouldn't he enjoy himself?"

"If for no other reason than living in a serious way is the duty of a man of rank," Paul said, with a disparaging click of his tongue.

Her beloved left off his studies to join the army when war was declared against the Turks. Now, a decade later, Paul is still doing his duty, having been pressed to take up a taxing command in Warsaw. Does he envy Nicholas Alexandrovich, allowed such a carefree existence? Or is he contemptuous of the heir's immaturity?

A bit of both, Sandra must admit.

THE TSAR IS there the following afternoon, wearing an ancient greatcoat, standing on a patch of sand at the edge of the ice. He never skates. He prefers to look on and make fun of everyone else and how they skate. Or throw tennis balls at them to hit with long hooked sticks.

"Thank God you have arrived, Vorontsovs!" he shouts. "The tone here is becoming entirely too rowdy."

Amongst the skaters are a half dozen of the tsarevich's fellow Preobrazhensky officers, and the "Mikhailovichi"—three sons of the Grand Duke Mikhail Nikolaevich, the tsar's uncle. Brawny and handsome, they are good friends of Nicholas Alexandrovich, especially the eldest, Alexander, known as Sandro. The dark Montenegrin princess Melitza is skating alongside her fiancé, the tsar's cousin the Grand Duke Peter Nikolaevich. How satisfying to see Melitza, a beauty with a noxious, preening attitude, wobbling on her skates, her ankles buckling.

The army officers move in a pack, joking and guffawing. Sandro and his brothers noisily compete for Xenia's attention, racing from one end of the ice to the other. Presently Princess Alix arrives with her sister Elisabeth Feodorovna, and her brother-in-law.

The Hesse sisters wear elegant, fur-lined coats and matching tall fur hats, and they both skate well—as well as any Russian. At one point, Princess Alix skates backward, in front of Nicholas Alexandrovich, her body swaying gracefully. The princess holds out her hands to him, which he eagerly clasps, and they spin in a circle. Sandra is impressed—that's not easy.

The Grand Duke Serge stands on the ice next to his brother

the tsar, conversing, his arms folded in front of his chest. With his pointed beard and hard, narrow-pupiled eyes, he always looks faintly menacing to Sandra. What a strange pair they make—the grand duke and his wife—as if Mephistopheles persuaded an angel to marry him.

After an hour, Nicholas Alexandrovich leads the way to the ice hill, waving them all to follow. They go down on wooden boards in pairs—the tsarevich with Princess Alix, Sandra with Maya, Xenia with Sofka. The Mikhailovichi slide down on their bellies, whooping. Such a comical sight! She can't help laughing uproariously along with everyone else.

ON THE EVENING of the lavish supper party Father and Mother host every year, the empress arrives wearing a magnificent floor-length sable cloak, so dark as to be almost black, and before even taking it off demands to visit Sandra's little brother Sasha up in the nursery, as he is too young to appear.

Sandra, at her mother's direction, follows their honored guest up the stairs in a cloud of the hyacinth scent the empress favors.

"*Bonne nuit, mon petit*," the royal lady croons, rocking the pudgy six-year-old in her lap. "Next year you will certainly be allowed to join in."

She kisses the boy and, taking Sandra's arm as they exit, says confidingly: "All you children are as dear to me as my own nieces and nephews."

Downstairs, the rooms are filling, and pages, arms heaped with cloaks, run back and forth, hardly able to keep up with the crush at the door. Sandra spies the family from Darmstadt speaking with Mother and Father.

The Grand Duke Ludwig is a gruff German army man with a beard and a paunch, and his son Prince Ernst a handsome and square-jawed young officer. Princess Alix's face is flushed, her eyes cast down, lips pressed together. So tense! Father, smiling benignly, has his head bent forward slightly as he speaks to her, in a solicitous manner, as if eager to catch every soft word she might utter. Despite his high office, he's not intimidating—her friends envy her such a kindly, thoughtful parent. And yet he has clearly not succeeded in relaxing Princess Alix.

It's the princess's mediocre French that surprises Mother. "Imagine Queen Victoria's granddaughter conversing so poorly!" she exclaims at the breakfast table. "Minnie is safe; this girl won't do—so *gauche*. I can't imagine her leading society as an empress must."

"I hear Nicholas Alexandrovich speaking English with her."

Mother shrugs. "French is the language of the court."

"What did you think?" Sandra asks Father.

"A reticent young lady—awkward in manner," Father says. "Even so, very conscious of her rank. Does she imagine she's not obligated to make an effort? Or is she unable to extend herself naturally and thus feels inadequate? An interesting question."

"It's no question at all! That girl considers herself superior, although she's from practically nowhere! A speck on the map!" Mother says.

Father raises his brows, unwilling, Sandra can tell, to concede the point.

With a sniff, Mother leaves the room, and Father, eye twinkling, smiles at Sandra before picking up his newspaper.

FOR THE SO-CALLED English Ball at the Winter Palace, the emperor and empress invite only the aristocrats they like. Invitations are already out when grave news arrives from Vienna. The Crown Prince Rudolf has shot his teenage mistress and himself.

Royal etiquette dictates the ball be canceled. But the empress, recalling herself condescended to by Rudolf during a state visit to Austria some years ago, has decided to take a modicum of revenge, Mother reports. The empress reissues the invitations, to what is now a *"bal noir."* Married ladies are required to appear in black. Unmarried ones can wear white.

Sandra, unwilling in Paul's absence to be too available to bold young officers, arranges with the tsarevich beforehand that she will be his partner for several dances, including the final mazurka, the culmination of the evening.

But twice Nicholas Alexandrovich begs her pardon. Due to a mistake, Princess Alix has no partner for the second waltz—might he be permitted to rescue her?

"Go ahead, my gallant friend," she tells him, laughing.

And just before the mazurka, the tsarevich brings over his cousin Alexander Mikhailovich.

"I've asked Sandro to take my place because Alix doesn't know the mazurka and I want to teach it to her."

Sandra doesn't mind. Sandro's a strong partner, and the mazurka is not an easy dance.

On the way home, Mother scolds. "Why did you sit out for the second waltz, Sandra? And then dance the mazurka with Alexander Mikhailovich?"

"Those were Nicholas Alexandrovich's wishes."

Mother scoffs. "I saw Princess Alix stumbling through the mazurka."

"She's still learning." Sandra feels an unexpected surge of sympathy for stiff Alix of Hesse, stranger in a strange court; Mother and all the other ladies close to the empress act like crows, circling, eager to peck at her.

"I thought the princess looked stunning tonight, in white, with lily of the valley in her hair and diamonds around her neck," says Sofka.

"Those are her sister's diamonds," Mother points out, waspishly.

"They suit her," puts in Maya.

Mother owns several spectacular diamond necklaces—and never shares them.

Closing her eyes that night, Sandra finds her head full of scenes from the ball. Twirling pairs, ranks of preening officers, clutches of black-clad matrons conferring in the corners. She recalls watching Princess Alix's face as she danced with the tsarevich: her smile guileless, her eyes sparkling, her sharp features softened by the glow of inner happiness, like a light shining up from underneath ice.

EVERY AFTERNOON SANDRA, Sofka, and Maya go to skate in the garden of the Anichkov Palace and find Princess Alix there, and frequently Nicholas Alexandrovich too. Xenia Alexandrovna invites them all to come up to her suite for tea afterward. Xenia loves to act as hostess. Pouring tea for them all in her drawing room, chatting away, her eyes dance in her darling elfin face. Sandra and her mother agree on this at least—both the empress and her daughter possess enormous charm.

Sandra doubts the empress knows how often the tsarevich is meeting Alix under the palace roof, but it's not her place to tattle. And Sandra recognizes the princess's clumsy efforts at friendship. Would Sandra like to play piano together—there are some four-hand compositions by Bach they might try? With a short laugh Sandra tells Alix she's never learned piano. Next the princess asks if there is a sewing circle she might join here in Petersburg? Apparently in Darmstadt, in the winter, nice young ladies meet regularly to make clothes for the poor. No, we have nothing like that, Sandra explains, as there is so little free time during the busy social season.

One fateful day, after they have skated and trooped upstairs, they drink tea for ten minutes before the tsarevich announces he must return to the barracks. He waves, promising to see them all the next day. In the doorway he collides with his mother. Why the empress has chosen this moment to visit her daughter's suite, Sandra has no idea. But she senses immediately the empress is both surprised and angry.

"We were also just leaving," announces Sandra. "Princess, shall we go down together and wait for the carriages?"

Alix looks confused that the afternoon is ending abruptly, but agrees. Sandra, Sofka, and Maya curtsy to the empress and kiss her hand on the way out.

When they bid Xenia Alexandrovna goodbye, the poor girl whispers, "I'm in for it now."

Within an hour, word comes from the palace that the empress would like to see Mother. When she returns she goes directly into Father's study, and Sandra and her sisters are soon summoned to follow.

Her father looks amused, sitting behind his desk, while her mother, standing at his side, is furious.

He addresses the three of them. "Was everything as usual today at the Anichkov?"

They nod, but Mother cuts in, "Do you know that Princess Alix takes tea with you all without Their Majesties' knowledge or permission?"

Sofka and Maya look at Sandra nervously. "Yes, we know this," says Sandra.

"How could you have participated in such a vile deception? All of you! Sandra, as eldest you are most culpable."

Sofka begins to cry; Maya too. But Sandra won't have it. "Mother, you've always said that we are privileged to be intimates at the court and that we must never abuse the family's trust."

"Don't make excuses!" Mother snaps.

"Excuses? You've told us this a thousand times. Never ever can we reveal private court matters."

"Which is not the case here."

"The tea parties are private," Sandra counters.

"Don't try to justify yourselves! Minnie is so upset!" Her mother's voice is shrill.

Sandra looks to her father in wordless appeal.

Father nods. "What Sandra says is not unreasonable, Lili."

"There you go, favoring Sandra, as ever," Mother wails.

"When the imperial family is at odds with one another, it is best not to get involved," Father explains. "I know this from experience."

"Minnie does not like to be duped," Mother says.

"Yes, I quite understand. And the girls should write and apologize. But in general they cannot take sides. What now? No more skating at the Anichkov?"

"Minnie desires that you three continue to skate there as usual, but she does not want the princess coming in for tea. Not ever again."

"So we are to tell Princess Alix this directly?" asks Sandra. "Yes, we will announce, we are having tea with Xenia Alexandrovna, such a shame you're excluded!"

Mother waves dismissively. "Sort it out—you think yourselves so clever."

SANDRA AND HER sisters arrive early the next day, hoping to catch Xenia Alexandrovna alone before Princess Alix turns up.

She's in the garden, sitting on the bench, lacing up her skates. "I'm to tell Alix I can't host any more tea parties, as it interferes with my music practice," she says.

Sandra nods. "We heard of this."

"But you three will still come?"

Sandra and her sisters nod.

It's a great relief when Alix swallows the story without question.

To further the deception, Sandra, Sofka, and Maya go with the princess after skating to wait under the palace portico for the carriages. When hers appears, they wave her off, allowing her to believe they expect their own conveyance promptly. Instead, they go upstairs for tea.

"Do you think she has any idea?" Xenia asks nervously.

"None. Where is your brother? Does he know all?"

"Yes, Mama took him to task. Vehemently. But Nicky says he has other ways to see Alix."

"How, exactly?"

"Her sister has strung up a badminton net in the back hall of the Sergievsky Palace. My brother is developing a passion for badminton."

"Badminton if it's with Princess Alix," puts in Sofka.

And they all laugh.

DAYS PASS, THE sun gains strength and warms the air. The snow-banks begin to melt, and water drips from all the roofs. Porters scrape ice off the pavements and sand them. Carnival begins. In the Mars field, showmen set out their stalls with their puppets and their dancing bears. Peddlers hawk toy balloons—pink, blue, orange, violet, and red—tied with tails of thick twine. The Samoyeds come from Finland to give reindeer rides on the frozen Neva. Everywhere there's the delicious aroma of baking gingerbread.

Sandra and her mother are strolling down Millionnaya Street one February afternoon when they notice the Grand Duchess Elisabeth Feodorovna, with her brother Prince Ernst, walking toward them. They move aside to bow and smile, but the grand duchess and the prince hurry quickly by, tossing out a cursory greeting. Another couple follow on their heels, heads down, chins nuzzled into scarves—a young man with a cap pulled low, a young woman with a heavy shawl over her hair.

"Was that the tsarevich?" Mother asks, amazed.

"It may have been," Sandra says.

"Trying not to be noticed!"

"We can assume."

"And surely Princess Alix with him!" Her mother looks irate. "I will go to the Anichkov immediately to tell Minnie."

"Oh, Mother, must you?"

"I won't let her down," her mother says, lips pursed. "Not the way you girls did."

"Consult Father first."

Her father agrees with Sandra. "Don't throw fuel on the fire, Lili. You may have been mistaken—"

"I was not!"

"Nonetheless, allow the boy to have his fun. How much longer can it last? Isn't the Darmstadt family leaving when Lent starts?"

"Yes, good riddance," says her mother bitterly. She turns to Sandra. "Your friend is fooling himself if he thinks he can marry a woman his mother doesn't like!"

Sandra wants to argue, or laugh at Mother, but she doesn't have the heart. Why does the tsarevich's attachment to Princess Alix make her uneasy? She's not jealous. She believes Nicholas Alexandrovich should have his choice. The princess has much to commend her—fine-boned beauty, queenly bearing, royal blood. If she and the tsarevich marry one day they will produce very handsome children. Numerous tall sons, if God smiles on them.

Perhaps, though, the tsarevich should look around more. Meet some other princesses. Maybe there's one he'd like who possesses an easier temperament.

She recounts recent events to Paul in a letter. His reply is gloomy. Every week in Warsaw violence breaks out. Morale among the troops is low. His officers are weary of enforcing tyrannical dictates no one in Poland will ever accept. He writes:

Petersburg, and all society there, seems so impossibly distant as to be fantastical. One hears about it, but one doesn't really believe it.

Chapter Fifteen

‗‗

A Father Feels Affronted

St. Petersburg, March 1889

How dramatic Russia is in wintertime—every morning inky black until after breakfast, a brief interlude of daylight to savor, before the curtain of darkness descends again at three. Ella warned them of the constant chill, the stinging winds, the relentless overcast of the Russian capital during this season. But never did she mention how, on occasion, after a snowfall, the vault of heaven clears. Then the frosty furrows of sledge cuts along the wide avenues glisten, bright powdery white edges every windowpane, and the shiny roofs and the gold cupolas stand sharp in silhouette against an ice-blue sky.

Walking briskly beside Nicky, Alix never minds when the air nips at her nose, or the cold strikes up through the soles of her boots. She's snug in the fur-trimmed wool coat and high fur hat Ella had made for her. And her companion from Peterhof, that fondly remembered youth, is now a handsome officer—not tall, yet broad in the shoulders, with a spring in his step. Alix isn't acquainted with so many young men, but she met enough to deplore the numerous slack-jawed and spotty ones among them. Nicky is neither. And his beaming eyes and his wide, happy smile betray his admiration for her with every glance.

She and he while away the afternoons in the large garden of the Anichkov—skating, sliding, chasing each other between the lumpy forms of the towering marble statues shrouded against the cold in straw and tawny brown canvas. When Xenia serves tea in her suite afterward, Alix learns to drink it Russian-style, with a spoonful of strawberry jam stirred in. In the evenings Nicky is with them at the ballet or the opera, or at the same ball or supper party—the St. Petersburg season is a parade of constant entertainments, as her sister promised.

If they have a long night ahead, Ella instructs Alix to rest upstairs for an hour late in the day. Rather than lie on her bed the entire time, she often takes many minutes to stare at her face in the glass. To see what Nicky sees. Since she came out last year, she's known she counts as a young woman, no longer a girl. But only here, now, can she see it. Nicky's regard has unlocked the sight for her—the full and vivid and definite person she's become, there in the mirror. Coloring pretty, features elegant—yes—but most pleasing is the serious cast of her face, reflecting a deep soul. She looks appealingly like someone who ponders the important things, who has known grief but is still fresh, who is set apart by delicate solemnity. How befitting for someone in her position. She thinks of her Wales cousins— Louise, Toria, and Maud—those princesses are high-spirited but plain, she noticed at Balmoral in the autumn, and worse, there's a certain lax emptiness about their faces. Here in St. Petersburg, Xenia looks dear, with lively dark eyes, but her manner is too excitable. Nicky has such affection for the Countess Vorontsova, and Alix supposes Sandra's broad cheekbones, black eyes, and strong features might appeal to some men, but they lack subtlety. And Sandra's usual expression—assessing, ironical—is, to Alix's mind, insufficiently feminine.

No, God has gifted her with a face that is not merely beauti-

ful but one she can be proud of, and while certainly unlucky
in other regards—deprived of a mother and beastly shy—she is
fortunate, at least, in this regard.

ELLA HAS A badminton net set up in an empty gallery in the
back of the palace. They compete in two teams: Germany
(Ernie and herself) against Russia (Ella and Nicky). Alix chases
after the shuttlecock vigorously and is always willing to smash
it over the net, or argue over points.

"And why not?" she asks a surprised Nicky.

Ernie laughs. "I tell her sometimes—that she should have
been a man."

"Can't you see my invisible trousers?" she teases Nicky.

"Alix!" Ella exclaims.

"How is that improper? They're invisible!"

Her sister shakes her head, even as she smiles.

Alix feels far less confident with chess. When she and Nicky
face off, either side of the intricately carved set in Serge's study,
she hesitates too long when it's her turn, her hand wavering
between pieces.

Nicky says: "I'll tell you exactly what you should do."

"No, no you mustn't," she says hastily, pressing both hands
against her ears.

He mouths something at her.

"All right, let me hear your suggestion." She drops her hands.

"Too late. You missed out, such a shame," he says, and lets
out a low, swooping whistle of mock regret.

At that she picks up a piece and places it down, defiantly, on
a new square. He invariably shakes his head. "An unfortunate
choice."

"Don't say that!"

He just laughs—he has a delightful, playful laugh. And in

truth, he isn't any better at chess than she. Sometimes he wins; sometimes she does.

Nicky finds it amusing to stroll through Petersburg, where everyone knows him, and remain unrecognized under a workman's wool cap pulled down to his eyebrows—so they take long walks with Ernie and Ella. Or go out in a troika, drawn by three horses, strung with bells, driven by a coachman in a padded overcoat and low-crowned top hat, all of them cozy under a pile of bear skins. One afternoon they travel along the slippery, snowy streets to the Mikhailovsky Palace to see the bicycle Grand Duke Michael recently acquired in London—a newfangled type with two wheels of equal size. Nicky and Ernie persuade Alix to try it—flanking her, they run alongside, hands holding her steady on the high seat. Ernie shouts, "Let her go!" and for a moment she's pedaling down the vast marble corridor under her own power, and it's astonishing, heart-stoppingly exhilarating. But in a clutch of terror at the speed she has reached, she jerks the handles slightly to the left, throwing herself off-balance. She barely has time to put her feet down before the bike topples sideways underneath her.

"You did well," says Nicky. "Try again."

"I dare not," she says. She's shaking despite—or maybe because of—her excitement.

"Next time then."

But their glorious days in Petersburg run out before there's an opportunity to return to the Mikhailovsky Palace.

ON THE AFTERNOON of their departure the air is frigid, the sun pale and shrunken in a parchment-gray sky. As they drive toward the Warsaw station, Alix senses herself deflating, as if she had been blown up like a toy balloon and now the air is seeping out, and she's floating back down to earth again—

back into a life where all the days have numbers and the weeks follow a quiet, set routine.

The imperial family is there to see them off. On the platform, in the hazy light filtered through the dirty, glass-paned roof, she feels Nicky's eyes fixed on her face, taking in what he can before she leaves. The scrutiny makes her self-conscious, with so many others looking on. But she knows later she'll call up this sensation of his intense gaze, to savor when alone. Xenia stands next to her, her arm encircling her waist, her head resting on Alix's shoulder.

Papa is jolly, clapping Uncle Sasha on the back, recalling their bear hunt. Her father speaks fondly with Aunt Minnie and jokes back and forth with Serge, their breath coming out in visible clouds. But her father ignores Ella. Which is odd. At home in Darmstadt, Papa mourns Ella's absence, and here in Petersburg Alix has seen them absorbed in frequent, private conversations. Is Papa angry with Ella? For what reason? She'd like to ask Ella, but her sister wears a proud, dignified smile. Living with Ella again, Alix has been reminded of her steady, unruffled demeanor, her dislike of acrimony. Nor will her sister descend into weepiness here at the station—not willing to set upon this wonderful visit a capstone of lamenting.

A loud whistle blows and the heaving engine emits a rush of white smoke.

"Even I cannot hold this train longer," says Uncle Sasha. "Up you go." He kisses Alix, then Aunt Minnie does, then Xenia, and finally she feels Nicky's lips graze her cheek. She longs to reach out and squeeze his hand. To thank him for all he's given her. She understands now why people call it *falling* in love— heedlessness is necessary. Their sojourn in Petersburg has been a suspension of time. Never could she live permanently in Russia, this wondrous but fearsome place—exiled from home, from

Papa, and all her nearest and dearest. She feels for Ella in her isolation. And yet, how terrible it would have been to have died without ever feeling what she's felt here, with Nicky. When they were children, he playfully declared they loved each other. And now, older, something beautiful and true has grown up between them, and she'd like to acknowledge it, but her tongue sticks to the roof of her mouth; she can't say words. She turns away, praying he senses even a fraction of what's in her heart.

Papa and Ernie follow behind. The iron stairs clang under their feet. In the car vestibule, Alix takes one last look back at the group on the platform. Ella's eyes are shiny and wet now, her lips pressed tight. But catching Alix's gaze, she slips her gloved hand out of her ermine muff and blows a kiss. *Dearest Ella*, she thinks, *I hope you won't feel too lonely left behind.*

DARKNESS FALLS QUICKLY as the train glides through the silent, snow-bound countryside outside of Petersburg. Alix puts her night case in her compartment and unpacks her toiletries. She unpins her hair and brushes it out to wear loose down her back. She meets her brother and her father in the salon car.

Papa's face is stony. All the bonhomie he exuded at the station has vanished. He is definitely in a foul temper.

As soon as she sits, he says to them both: "I received yesterday, via the British legation, an urgent message from your grandmother."

Alix is surprised—Grandmama has upset Papa?

"Apparently, last week, *Berliner Post* reported that your engagement to Nicky is to be announced imminently."

"But that's nonsense," Alix says.

Ernie laughs dismissively. "They believe they know more about this than we do?"

"I thought Grandmama knows to ignore what's written in the newspapers," adds Alix.

"She is furious—remembering Irène's secretive behavior," says Papa.

"How will you reply?" Alix asks, wary now.

"I sent her a telegram this morning," he says. "Two words only: *Keine Sorge.*"

No worries? Despite herself, she feels a swift kick to her spirit over the curt definitiveness of Papa's message.

"She needed prompt reassurance that we aren't pursuing some counterplan against her wishes," her father says.

"Of course," Alix answers automatically.

Ernie looks sharply at her from across the table. Her brother is aware that since she's returned from Balmoral, she's received a few short letters from their cousin Eddy. Most perfunctory. The last read: *Dear Alicky, I hope you are well. I've been on maneuvers. Next week is a fox hunt. Fond regards, Eddy.*

Alix says nervously, "Papa, you don't believe that I acted in any way improperly, encouraging—"

He cuts her off with a wave of his hand. "Of course not. I observed you and the boy frolicking about, playing games; I was happy to see you enjoying yourself so, *mein Schatz.*" He smiles at her fondly.

She smiles back. Although Nicky, a boy? He's nearly twenty-one.

"I don't understand, Papa," Ernie says. "You're angry about the newspaper article itself? Or Grandmama's rebuke?"

"Neither!" he says, ire rising once more. "It's your sister."

"Ella?" asks Ernie.

"Of course Ella!"

Alix and Ernie exchange an alarmed look.

"Yesterday evening when you two were off—where was it?"

"In Tsarskoye Selo, for a tea dance, the last of the season," says Alix. She had such fun, and ate so many blinis Nicky teased her that the waist seam of her gown would certainly burst.

"Yes," says Papa. "When you were out, and I informed your sister about your grandmother's upset, she took the opportunity to lecture me on how I make too much of the difference between the beliefs. When Serge and she were in Jerusalem, she had some kind of revelation—"

Here he throws his hands up in the air, irate. "Imagine! A religious revelation that Orthodox belief and the Lutheran faith are not really far apart. That to see a great divide is nonsense."

"Oh, Papa, she would never call it nonsense," Alix exclaims.

"She did! In so many words! She went on proselytizing to me, how she's discovered that God is indifferent to however we choose to approach Him. And how He opens His arms to all who seek Him."

"Why would she say this?" Alix asks.

Ernie rounds his eyes at her, trying to convey some message, which she doesn't understand.

"Because to Ella's thinking, should you and that boy desire to marry, then the religious difference need not stand in the way!"

Papa looks at her with such vehemence—both offended and enraged—that Alix feels frightened. And it tears at her heart to realize that her feelings for Nicky, so private and tender, and his for her, so generous, are already being dragged out for public dissection, speculated about by strangers in Berlin and discussed and debated within the family. In truth, she arrived in Petersburg very curious to see him—although slightly worried their little childhood romance could make things awkward between them, should Nicky recognize immediately he'd outgrown her. Instead, their mutual sympathy deepened, which is their secret joy and only that. She's not even seventeen yet. She's not setting her cap for Nicky. If only she might be left alone, not the subject of conjecture or gossip, free instead to remember how she felt being with Nicky, joking, playing, dancing—all of it—without imagining what it might imply. Is this wish naïve? Perhaps they could never have met again without ensuing talk. In Petersburg Aunt Minnie often looked at her sternly and spoke to her in a faintly patronizing tone. It occurs to Alix now, sitting in the swaying car, that Nicky's mother was trying to tell her something. That she shouldn't get her hopes up. That his parents have other plans for the tsarevich. That the heir to the Russian empire will not be marrying awkward, solemn, bashful little *her*.

Papa booms: "Are you aware that nothing good could come from a marriage based on sin? That it would be a sin for you to abandon the belief you have been brought up in?"

"Of course, Papa," she says hurriedly. "And I never will."

Her father nods, still angry. "I am glad to hear it, although I suspected as much. I told Ella you are no weak-willed, craven little fortune-hunter! Your head won't be turned by that boy's attentions."

"Do you refer to His Imperial Highness the Grand Duke Nicholas Alexandrovich, our cousin?" asks Ernie with a small smile.

"The very one," growls their father.

Alix's mind races. Why would Ella court their father's rage? Is she already convinced that Alix should marry Nicky? An upsetting thought. Will Ella push the notion on Nicky? Give him false hopes and make the empress angry? Will Minnie believe Alix a sly hussy? All of this would be terrible.

"Isn't it possible, Papa," Ernie begins again, "that living in Petersburg, Ella naturally strives to see what her own faith and that of her beloved husband have in common?"

"*Mein Jugend*, when I permitted Ella's marriage to Serge, I made a single condition—a single one!—that she would never change her belief."

"Yes. I remember," says Ernie.

"And you saw her, how she's a grand lady now, adored by all Romanovs, living in opulence. Perhaps she thinks her faithful old father doesn't count for much. Ella suggested that choice of belief is a minor matter—a difference in *approach*. She implied I am some kind of narrow-minded ignoramus not to immediately agree with this."

"Oh, she could never think that of you, dearest Papa," Alix says.

"No? Then why did she speak so disrespectfully to me?" he declares, face thunderous. "Wars were fought, hundreds of thousands died, especially in Germany, to defend the Lutheran religion."

Both Alix and Ernie nod.

"Nonetheless she assumes that the lure of an important position for you will tempt me to adjust my conscience? Forsake my beliefs? She believes me that kind of man?"

"No, Papa, she knows you to be the opposite kind. Please, Papa, don't speak this way about Ella—all alone in Russia, without any of us." Tears spill out of Alix's eyes. It's miserable to see him so upset, and condemning of her lovely sister.

"All right, then. We need not discuss further tonight. But do not, please, encourage Ella in any way to think you could be enticed to change your belief! Whosoever comes courting you!"

FOR THE BALANCE of the long journey Papa falls into a gloom and says little to either Alix or Ernie. She feels so anxious for his mood that she asks her brother if she shouldn't reassure him again, on the religious question.

"No, leave him be, Sunny," Ernie advises. "Poor Papa; I watch him vacillate between pride in Victoria, Ella, and Irène—boasting about how all three have married well, far better than Aunt Vicky's daughters, or the Wales girls, who are still unclaimed—and his resentment over their lack of attention to him. Those three rarely come to visit, they never offer to help, and they don't seek his advice on their lives."

Now her brother assumes their father's gravelly voice: "How is it that I, a sad and lonely widower, forbidden to marry the woman I loved, must cope with my onerous duties with scant support from my oldest daughters, for whom I sacrificed so much!"

Alix can't help but smile. Ernie is a fine mimic, and this unhappy refrain of their father's is familiar to her. "Of course, Victoria does return to Darmstadt on occasion," Alix points out. "To look after Mama's charities."

"Yes, but when she's home, she always stays with Louis's parents."

"Aunt Julie is such a fond grandmother—Victoria has her help with Alice."

Ernie shrugs. "Maybe so, but still Papa is offended. As for Ella and Irène, they hardly ever write or come to see him, and never seek his counsel. And now Ella thinks she can instruct him on religion!"

"Yes, she shouldn't have done that. And why? I didn't ask her to. I'll never marry Nicky and move to Russia!"

Ernie tips his head. "Never? You are certain?"

"Of course! Can you imagine me doing that to Papa? It would kill him."

Her brother looks downcast. "I do like him so much, our dear cousin Nicky."

"As do I."

"And he's so completely smitten!" Her brother laughs.

She frowns at him. "Don't be indecorous. No one must mention this, even you."

He smiles. "Dear girl, you can require my silence, but I won't forget what I witnessed."

Chapter Sixteen

━━━━━━━━━━━━━━━━━━━━━━━━━━━━━━━━━━━━━━━

The Tsarevich Declares Himself

Aboard the Tsarevna, *May 1889*

In Nicky's earliest memory, he rides on the train of Mama's gown. He sits atop crimson silk, clinging to the lacy edges, as she glides down the halls of the Anichkov, sweeping over the glossy parquet floors, darker and lighter gold in turn. Unlike his father's face, so high as to be on top of a mountain, Mama's face is rarely far from Nicky's even when she's standing. And she's constantly bending down to kiss his cheek. Or he's in her lap, his head nuzzled under her chin. Her scent is sweet, her white hands are smooth, the swell of her breasts pillowy soft. He wants to claim her body for his own, although he's aware his father has a definite hold on it. A hold Nicky could never challenge, because his father is a *bogatyr*—a warrior of immense strength and courage, the bravest of the brave, the hero of every epic poem written at the time of Vladimir of Kiev.

Nicky, to his shame, is not a *bogatyr*, and although he grows up to look like his mother, he lacks her wiliness. She wheedles and charms his father to get what she desires, even if she must fib to obtain it. Nicky can't do that. Papa reads his soul in his face. He knows Nicky's inadequacies, and they sadden him.

Since last autumn, when Nicky joined the Preobrazhensky Guards, relations with his father have improved by a small degree. Nicky is away from the palace more, out of his father's sight. Also, an officer's life suits Nicky—as it once did Papa, before the murder of his own father made him tsar. Nicky likes the comradeship, the order, the study of arms. He saves the funniest stories from the mess to repeat to Papa—and is proud when his father roars with laughter, slaps him on the back, appears to relish his company.

Still, Nicky is shocked when Papa announces his intention of taking him on a state visit to Finland to mark his twenty-first birthday—without Mama, without any of the uncles. Nicky can hardly believe his father wishes to spend days with him alone, and he thinks he must be bold and use the opportunity well. He will ask his father for permission to propose to Alix.

THEY SET SAIL on the imperial yacht *Tsarevna* on a cool, rainy afternoon in May. Nicky watches from the deck as the glorious pale facades of the capital retreat into the misty distance.

Such a shame that Polovtsov, the state secretary, has joined them, at the last minute, to discuss a crisis in Moscow. From the main salon, Nicky can hear Papa's occasional shouts—and the murmured replies of Alexander Alexandrovich. Nicky hopes whatever they are discussing won't poison Papa's mood.

To Nicky's relief, Polovtsov disembarks at Kronstadt. They sail on without him, and Nicky and his father dine alone in the tsar's state-room.

Papa looks tired, but not angry. Is this a good moment to bring up Alix? Perhaps, yes, if first he can cheer his father. Unarmed with regimental gossip, he looks around for inspiration.

"Weren't those slippers a gift from Uncle Bertie?" Nicky points at the red velvet slippers with paisley embroidery his father wears—most incongruous with the baggy private's uniform he's got on, his preferred attire.

"Ridiculous, I know, suitable for some dandified gentleman, at ease in his London club," his father replies. "I'd never wear them except I find by the evenings all the boots I own are too narrow."

"Your feet swell from standing during the day?"

"It's some slowness of my kidneys, according to Koronkov," Papa says, naming the imperial doctor. "In the accident, the roof of that train car struck me exactly here, on the small of my back." Papa pats the spot with his hand. "Alexander Mikhailovich says give up whiskey and stop working so much, especially late in the day. I'm unwilling to do the first, and unable to do the second. Does he think Russia runs itself?"

For a moment Papa glares at Nicky, as if he is Koronkov, with his contemptible advice. But then his face softens into a smile. "So the slippers are the price I pay."

Here together, alone, they talk like comrades, and Nicky, building on the feeling, asks: "Were you as happy as I was to see the back of Polovtsov?"

"Good Christ, yes! The state secretary was at his most irritating today."

"Why?" Nicky asks.

"There's a trial going on in Moscow—four university students who planted explosives in a post office, and blew up the back of it," Papa says. "No one was killed, thankfully. But one of the students, a woman, slapped the court gendarme yesterday."

Nicky looks at his father with distaste. "A woman did this?"

"She did! So I've ordered her flogged—the penalty for disrespect of the court. Polovtsov worries she won't survive a hundred lashes. Such nonsense. If the law is not applied equally and consistently, we shall have no order!"

Since the assassination of his grandfather Nicky has appreciated that order must be enforced in Russia. "You told Polovtsov so?"

"Naturally."

Nicky is glad to hear it. They eat their potato stew contentedly. Without Mama along, Papa will order the peasant dishes both he and Nicky prefer.

"Listen, my boy, I'm looking forward to our jaunt, but first I need to discuss something with you."

Nicky, instantly on guard, worries: Does this concern Alix?

"One day when I am gone," his father says, "you will have enormous responsibilities. And tremendous power. Ministers like Polovtsov may offer their advice. But they will never deny your will. They cannot."

Nicky nods, still nervous.

"Now, when you are still a very young man, unseasoned and unknowing, it is my duty and your mother's to guide you, and to deny you some of what you think you want."

Nicky's heart sinks. This *is* about Alix.

"You believe yourself in love, yes?" Papa asks.

"Yes," Nicky admits, and forces himself to meet his father's eye.

"You fancy yourself ready to propose?"

Nicky nods sharply, like the proud officer he is.

Papa surprises him by leaning forward and saying in a confiding voice, "When I was your age, exactly, I fell in love with my mother's lady-in-waiting, Princess Maria Elimovna Meshcherskaya."

Nicky stares at his father in astonishment—who?

"Such a beauty—wonderfully built, with a comely face, and some inexplicable sadness in her eyes," Papa says. "M.E., I called her, and she possessed a mesmerizing charm. When I gazed at her I could feel her reading my thoughts. She understood me like no other person ever has."

He sighs and shakes his head.

Nicky has never heard his father express admiration for any woman other than his wife. When Mama is gone for any length of time, Papa is invariably in a bad temper, and snaps peevishly at the rest of them.

"I declared to my parents I was prepared to give up my rights of succession in order to marry M.E.," Papa says.

"How did they answer?"

"Within a week, my father compelled her aunt, the Princess Chernysheva, to take her to Paris. She never returned to Petersburg. She eventually married Pavel Demidov, a pleasant enough fellow, and very rich, but a nonentity. She died giving birth to her first child."

Papa looks very sad.

"I'm sorry for that," Nicky says. Meanwhile, his mind is racing. Could he leave Georgy to be tsarevich and marry Alix and live in the south of France? It's supposed to be superb there. But he would miss everyone in Russia—his brothers, his sisters, his cousins, his brother officers. And he'd feel a bit of a fool, and a wastrel. To become tsar is his fate—although please, God, a very distant one! Papa will surely live thirty more years. And by that time Nicky himself will be fifty, old enough to cope. Yes, if he were to ascend in the inconceivably distant year of 1918, he will feel ready.

"I cannot allow you to marry Alix," Papa declares, breaking into his thoughts.

A surge of will courses through him—Nicky has a powerful retort. "But she is no mere lady-in-waiting. She's a princess of Hesse, the same house your own mother came from!"

"That's true," Papa says, and he looks thoughtful for a moment. Nicky congratulates himself.

"But the needs of Russia are different today. Our ambitions must be wider, as our challenges are greater."

"I am certain I can be happy with Alix," Nicky insists.

"I'm extremely happy with your mother, and she was my father's choice, not mine."

"Do you have a choice for me?" He hates even uttering the words.

"The obvious one is the kaiser's sister, Margaret. A familial alliance with Prussia would be sound policy."

Nicky's heart sinks. He's met the youngest Prussian princess in Berlin—so plain!

"Don't look like that! You haven't gotten to know her yet," says Papa with a smile.

"Papa, I can't conceive of it."

"Recently I've been thinking," he says, ignoring Nicky's misery. "The new kaiser is so ridiculous and unreliable. Will he respect the bonds of kinship? We are strengthening our ties with France, as a check on German ambitions. So, if you don't like Margaret, I'll wager there's a French princess you'll fancy! And your mother loves this idea."

His father looks at him, a happy glint in his eye.

"Papa, my heart tells me I can love no one as much as I love Alix."

"She's from a minor house, not suitable for you," his father says briskly.

"Uncle Gega married Ella."

"My brother is not the tsarevich, and notice Ella has never converted. Those Hesse girls are pious. Which rules out your Alix to start with—she will refuse to become Orthodox."

"I have thought this over carefully," Nicky says, straining to keep any hint of childish pleading out of his voice. "I believe if I write to Alix and tell her how much I love her—how I long for her to be my wife—then she will at least *consider* changing faiths."

Papa looks uncomprehending. "Aren't you listening? You are not permitted to write any such thing. She cannot be your bride."

"You forbid it?"

"I do."

Nicky feels like weeping. But he mustn't. He won't. He takes a deep breath. "Papa, I have such grave responsibilities ahead of me—"

"I'm not dead yet!" his father says, derisively.

"But one day when I will find myself in that formidable position, your position, I know that to be successful I must have by my side a wife I can both love and trust."

"Don't bother speechifying on this," says his father. "We have more interesting things to talk about. The new Kruger rifle, to name just one."

"But—"

"And I think you need to learn a thing or two about women before you marry," Papa interrupts. "We'll find an actress or a ballerina for you. How does that sound?"

His father grins at him. When has he ever treated Nicky so benevolently? Still, he cannot give up. "For me, Alix is the loveliest—"

Papa interrupts again. "Don't tell your mother I proposed that—about dancers and all."

"Will you at least invite the Darmstadt family back to Peterhof this summer?" It's Nicky's last desperate request—and now his father looks annoyed.

"Understand something, my boy," he says, jabbing his forefinger at Nicky. "You need a wife who can shine like a star, talk to a blank wall, and keep you on the jump. Someone energetic, with the stamina for the job. Alix is good-looking, I'll say that for her, but wooden—she appears to have swallowed a yardstick. Also she's . . . what's the right word? . . . overwrought. Rather brittle. No, definitely not the right choice."

Nicky is crushed.

Papa gives him a sharp look. "No moping! There are many,

many women in this world. In any case, I understand the English queen intends to marry your Alix off to Eddy of Wales. Now, there's a man who will struggle to meet his formidable responsibilities."

And the *bogatyr* roars with laughter.

Chapter Seventeen

A Sister Sees the Path Ahead

Sergievsky Palace, St. Petersburg, June 1889

Nicky makes a face. "I couldn't say this to Papa, but I will tell you, Tetinka. I'll become a monk before I marry that horse-faced Prussian princess."

Ella laughs. "Margaret's actually a sweet girl. But, yes, quite homely, poor thing."

"He also said something strange—he and Mama are looking into some French princesses."

"French? That *is* odd. For political reasons?" She gazes questioningly at Nicky, perched on the edge of the drawing-room sofa next to her, too agitated to sit back properly.

"I imagine. But I am interested in no one but Alix."

The dear boy has called at the palace—he explained to Ella—to confess exactly this, and to lament his father's immediate opposition to the match.

"Papa insists your sister is going to marry someone else," he says.

"Eddy?"

"Yes."

"Never."

"Really? Papa seems quite certain."

"My sister cannot love him," Ella replies. "She mentions him rarely, and never with praise."

Nicky's face lights up. "Eddy's nice, a perfectly pleasant chap. We've been on holiday in Denmark together. But he's not good enough for Alix."

"I agree."

"Tetinka, you must help me. Mama has to be brought round, it's the only way to get Papa to reconsider. And Mama is so fond of you. Won't you speak with her? Persuade her that Alix is the best choice for me?"

Nicky is clearly unaware that last month, Minnie summoned Ella to her private sitting room at the Anichkov to deliver a lecture. The empress very much resents what she calls Ella's interference—parading Alix in front of the tsarevich just as his parents are beginning to consider his future. Minnie's sister, their Aunt Alix, Eddy's mother, is also most displeased.

"As long as Nicky remains unmarried, your sister Alix will not be welcome again in Petersburg," Minnie pronounced.

Looking into the young man's imploring eyes, Ella replies, "Let me mull things over, and decide how best to proceed."

"Papa also says Alix will never convert, as you never have, and I wasn't sure how to answer that. Might you speak with your sister? Is the question of religion truly an unbridgeable gulf? I believe our feelings are mutual. Does Alix desire this obstacle to remain?"

Ella smiles. "I will write and tell her how you recall with great pleasure her visit this winter. How you send her your fondest greetings. And I will think of how to broach that other subject."

Nicky still looks dispirited.

"Can I confess something to you, dear boy? To answer all that you have confided to me?" Ella says.

"What's that?"

"Do you remember when Serge and I went to Jerusalem last year for the consecration of the new church?"

He nods. "Just before our accident."

"I was told that if one prayed deeply in a church as it was being consecrated, God would hear these prayers. I chose to pray for you and Alix. I wasn't certain of your feelings then, nonetheless I prayed that the two of you would be brought together in love for one another."

"God is already at work," he says, face brighter.

"Faith and love go very far, and if you have both—for God and for each other—all will turn out well."

Ten minutes later he takes his leave, feeling, he tells her, "a small bit of hope."

ELLA REMAINS IN the drawing room, alone, by turns gnawingly anxious and quietly jubilant.

Her fervent prayer in Jerusalem has been answered, in part.

Watching Alix and Nicky together she suspected the truth, but to have Nicky come today and announce he loves Alix and wishes to marry her—this makes her supremely happy.

But a glorious outcome, the fulfillment of his love with their eventual marriage, *that* is in considerable doubt.

Minnie's opposition Ella anticipated. But Ella had hoped the tsar felt more favorably toward Alix. Now she knows otherwise.

She stands and walks over to the window to admire the scene below—traffic crossing over the Fontanka River in both directions, the magnificent bronze statues of rearing stallions at each corner of the bridge. On this June evening, so like the first ones she spent in Russia, the light has a bright, silvery cast and carries the promise of lasting hours more, fading into a pearlescent glow but never entirely vanishing from the sky.

If Nicky is to be granted his dearest wish, and Alix united with an ideal husband, Ella must play her part. Hasn't she always, especially since Mama died, tried to care tenderly for her younger sister? Shouldn't she welcome the opportunity God gives her now to benefit Alix? Especially as that impulse coincides with what she secretly yearns for, for herself?

There's no longer any need to quaver, or fall back, or postpone further. She can commit to Russia unreservedly. She will embark on the serious study of Orthodoxy, change religions, and in doing so demonstrate to Alix that embracing this new belief is not a sacrifice but an enrichment.

How ingenious are the ways of the Lord, divinely choreographing this confluence of her desires!

She is still standing at the window, happy and at peace, when the door opens and Serge comes into the room.

She turns to smile at her husband. He says immediately, "What's happened? You look so pleased. Some good news?"

"The best," she says. "Sit, let me tell you."

From the sofa, he regards her expectantly.

"Nicky came to see me this afternoon. To declare how he loves Alix and wants to marry her."

Serge laughs. "That telltale, besotted look on his face—I noticed it frequently when your sister was here. But he's quite certain? They've passed only a few weeks together."

Should she point out that she and he spent mere days together before Serge declared himself? Perhaps not. "Nicky is in no doubt," she says. "He's already asked Sasha for permission to propose."

"Which my brother granted?" Serge looks surprised.

"No."

"Why are you so glad then?"

"Because it makes everything clear."

"Clear?"

She takes a deep breath. "I lacked the strength and the certainty to tell you at the time, but when we were in Jerusalem, on the final day, in your mama's church, I sensed the truth. Which is that I must join you in your faith."

Now he appears stunned.

"I have been beset with worries and doubts, so dreading what people will say," Ella goes on. "How they will scream about my lack of loyalty, how I will hurt people in the family. Papa's pain will be extreme."

Serge nods grimly.

"But it is cowardly to lie before God!" she exclaims. "I cannot continue in outward forms and before the world as if I were still Protestant when in my soul I know otherwise. I'm sorry I haven't told you until now. I was weak and could not manage better. Can you understand?"

"I suppose I can," he says, with an expression faintly troubled.

"Will you speak to me about your church and what it teaches and how I can find my place within it? Please, Serge, I need your help."

For a long moment he gazes at her. "I have prayed for so long that this moment might come, and now it has I can hardly believe it," he says.

"Since our wedding?"

"Most earnestly since the days we spent together at the monastery at Radonezh. Do you remember that sacred place? I was in despair. You were beside me day and night and I longed to feel close to you, but you stood apart from my belief, which is the foundation of my being. Still, I felt honor-bound to say nothing. I couldn't make any comment, any suggestion. Then or ever."

"I see now you've been a real angel of kindness."

He drops his eyes, as if her acknowledging of this sacrifice overwhelms him.

"Perhaps I would have hurried to make you happy if you had complained," Ella continues. "But you never did. How noble you were, leaving it all to my conscience."

"Is it for Alix's sake you do this now?" His tone is sharper; his eyes lift to meet hers.

"I admit it. I hope my example will inspire her, should she choose to return Nicky's love. But for many months I have been praying to God to show me the right way, to confirm my intimation that only in your religion could I find the true and strong faith one must possess to be a good Christian. I have that direction now. I can embrace the cherished desire of my soul, knowing that by following my own conscience I can also help my sister."

He nods slowly.

"Before I tell anyone else of my intentions, I must understand the belief thoroughly. Who can be a better teacher for me than you?" she asks.

"We will read together, yes, and discuss. It will be the greatest of pleasures," he says in a gentle voice, one she has rarely heard before.

She beams at him, taking in the moment, relishing this deep mutual understanding. They have run a tricky course and reached the finish. She notices that tears stand in his eyes. His spirit is hovering close to hers and she senses him yielding to something that he's resisted for a long time, all the time they've been married. The knowledge that Ella loves him deeply, and more, that he is truly deserving of her love.

He doesn't have to declare this aloud. They have no need for words. She knows him fully, and feels his most profound gratitude sweep over her like a soft caress.

Chapter Eighteen

A Brother Intercedes

Balmoral Castle, September 1889

*L*ast summer, when Ernie urged Alix to take her time, close no doors, see what Grandmama proposed, he was thinking practically. To one day be Queen of England? Not an opportunity to dismiss without careful consideration.

Since then, they have spent six weeks in St. Petersburg, and he's of a different mind.

Amazing to watch his sister, always reluctant to leave Darmstadt and as a rule wary of strangers, flourish in the tsarevich's company. Her face relaxed, her step quickened, and her smiles were constant. She came into full flower—there, in that very foreign place!

Yes, Nicky is the man Alix should wed, if only it were possible. But even if she could be convinced to move to Russia, Papa will never allow the marriage.

Nor has Grandmama surrendered the field. Alix, their grandmother declared, must return to Scotland to meet Eddy again. His sister begged to be let off, but their father insisted the queen's invitation could not be refused. Papa did permit Ernie to accompany Alix to Balmoral. And on this, their first morning at the castle, Grandmama requested Ernie drive her out to visit the lodge at Glas-allt-Shiel and—Ernie suspects—to enlist him in her cause.

He stands beside the queen on the edge of Loch Muick, the stone house, the fir trees, and the hunchbacked hills behind them.

"I know you and Alicky are close the way motherless children often are," Grandmama begins.

"Poor thing; she's stuck with me, our other sisters having fled," Ernie says lightly.

"Be serious, Ernst. You mustn't shirk your duty here." She looks up at him sternly. The top of the queen's head doesn't reach his shoulder, but her whole being radiates command. "Persuade Alicky that, married to Eddy and living in England, she will have such a pleasant home and an unrivaled position."

"Yes," answers Ernie, out of courtesy.

"Maidenly reticence is natural but shouldn't prevent her from grasping this chance."

"Perhaps not."

"As Eddy won't ascend for decades, there will be ample time for Alicky, with my help, and the support of her whole English family, to conquer her shyness and become, eventually, a beloved queen. Don't you wish exactly that for her?"

"I wish her to be happy and comfortable," he says.

"Comfortable!" the queen exclaims, scornfully. "We all live in the lap of luxury. This is about destiny. I look at Alicky and I see a beautiful young woman, of impeccable royal lineage, endowed with natural dignity and her mother's strength of mind. By good fortune, she has the opportunity to assume a public role worthy of her gifts."

"Last winter, Alix refused to open the Darmstadt Christmas Bazaar because it required making a brief speech," Ernie points out.

"Pshaw, she just hasn't been properly instructed yet!" his grandmother exclaims. "Your father should ask more of her. And meanwhile, Ella and that dreadful Serge are encouraging a different, most unsuitable match. Minnie is very offended!"

"Aunt Minnie was so cordial to us when we were in Petersburg."

The queen looks irate. "Don't imagine, Ernie, that I am unaware of precisely what is going on! Ella is attempting to compensate for her own poor choice by enticing her sister to join her in Russia. Most selfish and malevolent of her, for I can think of no worse environment for our sensitive little Alicky than that backbiting court."

Ernie should protest—Ella is kindness itself. Instead he remarks: "Aunt Minnie seems to manage."

"Yes! So amiable, so vivacious—Minnie can shine even amidst the dastardly Romanovs. But it wouldn't do for your sister."

Alicky would flourish in England but suffer in Russia, in a similar role? Isn't that contradictory? Not that it matters. "I thought you knew," Ernie says. "Alix has assured Papa she will never change beliefs, which rules out Nicky."

"Then tell your sister Ella to stop her scheming!" exclaims the queen.

"Strange to say, none of my sisters take direction from me," he replies, smiling.

Grandmama just scowls. Jokes don't help, but he can't resist.

"In two days' time," the queen continues, "Eddy will arrive, and he plans to propose immediately—he is as anxious as I am to have the question settled."

Ernie's heart sinks. Convinced by the queen that Alix is his perfect bride, his apathetic cousin likely fancies himself deeply in love. How else to account for this alacrity? Ernie recalls Eddy and his father on a hunting trip with them at Seeheim two winters ago. The Prince of Wales kept shouting: "Look alive, man!" at his son—and Papa kept muttering under his breath to Ernie, "A lost cause, that."

"Are you listening, Ernie?" Grandmama breaks in. "Dismiss *any* fears Alicky might have about leaving your father behind.

She can't waste her life languishing in Darmstadt. Do your duty and ensure that she says yes!"

His grandmother's single-mindedness is impressive, but she's quite blind. Ernie has his retort on the tip of his tongue. Were he a more candid person, or Grandmama a more curious and empathetic one, he would speak it aloud. He would explain that nothing he might say or do will convince his headstrong sister to marry Eddy. Nor does he, Ernie, think the marriage a good idea. And because he's her only brother, and they share a grievous loss—the death of their mother so young—Ernie is determined to always protect her. *Thus it is, Grandmama*, he would announce, *despite your forceful words, your small but dominating presence, the habit we are all in of bowing to your wishes—I refuse outright. I refuse to beseech my sister to marry a man she doesn't love.*

Instead of speaking the truth, Ernie smiles. And then he lies, shamelessly.

"Grandmama, I am ever at your service."

AT DINNER THE next night their grandmother says: "Dear Eddy will be arriving tomorrow before luncheon."

Ernie sees Alix's face fall.

Later, he finds her upstairs in her room, sitting on the bed, in tears.

"It will be so dreadful," she moans.

"Alix, just say no, it's as simple as that. I'm sure you can manage."

She gasps, as if in pain. "No, I can't. I hate it. I want the ground to swallow me up." Burying her face in her hands she begins to sob.

He sits down on a cane chair near the foot of the bed. The sound of his sister's anguish unnerves him. What should he do? "Perhaps," he says slowly, "perhaps I might intercept Eddy?"

She lifts her face, splotchy, red, and wet with tears. "How do you mean?"

"Tomorrow first thing, why don't you offer to take Grandmama for a drive in the carriage? With luck the weather will be fair, and even if there are some little showers, she's always amenable to taking the air. Keep her out for three hours."

"And in the meantime?" Alix says, swiftly wiping her eyes with the heels of her hands, like a child.

"In the meantime I'll wait in the front hall, and as soon as Eddy comes in, I will attempt to dissuade him from proposing—tell him you don't desire it."

She widens her eyes. "Might he accept this?"

Ernie laughs. "He might—he's so feeble."

"Tell him I am crippled with anxiety at the mere thought of discussing the matter," she says, animated at the prospect of her rescue."

"What a pathetic conversation to have to have," Ernie says ruefully.

"But soon enough he will forget me, don't you think? It's all Grandmama's idea. Eddy's just being led into it like a cow taken to pasture."

"True," Ernie says. "There has always been a touch of the bovine about Eddy."

"It's a mercy to release him from his hopes swiftly. Thank you, my dearest, dearest brother." Alix jumps up and rushes over, embracing him with such force she nearly knocks him and the cane chair over.

WAITING FOR EDDY the next day, Ernie reflects. Imagine you're the heir apparent, flattered at every turn, and still the girl you claim to love won't even listen to an offer from you? And why is it that God granted Eddy, the most unprepossessing fellow imaginable, the highest of positions?

Hard to picture, really, Eddy, a *dummkopf*, ascending the English throne. Ernie has grown weary of hearing Papa rage against Cousin Willy—but William is certainly cleverer than Eddy. And as kaiser, very energetic. Of course, parliamentary government is so advanced here in England, the talents of the monarch aren't as consequential as they are in Germany, or, God help us, Russia. Grandmama may be contemptuous of him, but Uncle Sasha is a giant man equal to a giant task.

And then Ernie sighs. His own future duties as Grand Duke of Hesse are likely to be dull but not overly onerous. He wouldn't want to be Nicky, forced to follow in his father's footsteps eventually. Nor can it be pleasant to be Eddy, inadequate in every way. Ernie feels sorry for his English cousin—never more than on this mild morning.

The castle's massive red-brown oak door is propped open by a heavy curling stone. Ernie sees a carriage draw up and a red-coated footman springs forward to unlatch the door, to allow Eddy to alight. His cousin wears a handsome pair of striped doe trousers, with braid along the outside seams, and a somewhat bewildered expression.

Ernie jumps up. "Hello, old fellow, you're well?"

"I am," Eddy says, smiling now and looking around. "Good to see you, Ernie, old chap. So quiet—where is everyone?"

"As the weather is fine, my sister drove Grandmama over to Invergelder to see the wild roses still blooming."

"Grandmama going out in the morning? That's unusual."

"Yes, and once Alix persuaded her, the rest of the party decided to go along too."

"Leaving only you?"

"Yes, only me," says Ernie cheerfully. "Shall we enjoy a smoke in the garden?"

They stroll out the back door, and Ernie leads them to a stone bench bathed in the cool, bright sun. They sit. Ernie asks

Eddy for one of those fat Turkish cigarettes he always carries and scratches a match on the side of the bench to light it.

"Listen, my dear cousin," Ernie begins, flashing a smile. "I have the idea that perhaps you may speak to Alix here."

"Yes," Eddy says, looking relieved. "I am impatient to reveal my feelings."

"Better to *know* rather than to feel, in such matters, don't you think?"

Eddy appears confused. "Eh?"

"Our grandmother's opinions can be so overpowering—out of eagerness to please one might come to feel persuaded of something one doesn't really believe."

"Of this I am certain," Eddy says.

Damn, he'll have to be more direct. "You should not speak of marriage to Alix," Ernie says.

Eddy looks very surprised. "She is not ready yet to consider it?"

"She would not welcome such a discussion."

"She wants me to wait? For some future time, when we are more private? I'm not sure that such an opportunity will present itself."

"No," says Ernie, his voice lowering. "She will never welcome a proposal from you."

A sharp intake of breath from Eddy. "How have I offended her? Please tell me exactly how."

"No, it's nothing like that."

"But then what?" Eddy looks incredulous, and, after a minute, angry. "She hates it, doesn't she? She hates that it's all been arranged, that we are pushed together, as if we have no choice in the matter? But it's not like that for me! Ernie, you must understand this."

"I understand Alix's wishes."

"I long to tell her exactly how I feel!" Eddy says, speaking at the top of his voice. "My admiration for Alicky, my high regard, has nothing to do with any of them, not Grandmama, not anyone." He grips Ernie's arm urgently. "I love her. For herself."

Who knew Eddy could be so passionate? "My dear fellow, say nothing; forget all about it. She'll always care for you as a cousin, but she knows you two can't make each other happy."

"Why would she think that?"

"She cannot love you as you deserve."

"I will persuade her. To have her is *better* than I deserve."

Ah, Eddy's not a complete idiot—still, he must be firmly managed. "You need to leave her be, Eddy!"

"Why shouldn't I try? Make a most sincere offer. Is it forbidden to me?"

"Of course not. Nothing of the kind," Ernie replies, lowering his tone, attempting to soothe. "But my dear chap, imagine how it is for Alix. Grandmama like a vulture, well, like a hawk, never taking her eyes off the poor girl. And to be put on the spot—the painful prospect of having to turn down a proposal, from a cousin she does care for—she dreads it."

"I don't understand," Eddy says, looking truly confused. "Everyone expects me to propose. I desire to do exactly that. If Alicky hears directly from me how much I love her, she might be stirred. It is not in her nature to be cruel."

"Cruel? It would be cruel of you, old man, to insist on speaking of your feelings when you are now aware that she does not want to hear of them."

"She doesn't? Not the least bit?"

"No, she doesn't."

"You really believe this?" Eddy looks disheartened.

"I do, otherwise I would not intercede."

"I would never want to hurt her. Or offend her."

Good, he's rolling over. "I know this—that's the true impulse of *your* nature," says Ernie.

"Ah, she is such an angel," Eddy adds, with a sigh.

"So, can I trust you to say nothing? Forget the whole idea?" Ernie asks.

Eddy looks down at his shoes. He shuffles his feet. "If you tell me that it would distress her, then I suppose I can't go ahead."

"Exactly right. There's a good chap," Ernie says, and slaps his cousin on the back enthusiastically. "We shall still have a pleasant time here, though, won't we? Stalking tomorrow, I hear."

Part III

Chapter Nineteen

═══════════════════════════════════════

A Bird of Ill Fortune

Neues Palais, Darmstadt, spring 1892

On March 4—a dismal day, of low, scudding clouds and damp wind—Alix and her father are alone at luncheon, as Ernie is in Nice, recovering from a severe case of bronchitis. It's been a miserable winter, Ernie so ill and Cousin Eddy, without warning, carried off by pneumonia in the last days of January. Papa had intended to take Alix to the funeral at Windsor, but he's suffered from an enlarged heart and shortness of breath in recent months, and Dr. Eigenbrodt advised against the long journey.

Now her father waits impatiently for the arrival of spring.

After the meal, she and he stroll out onto the terrace. Papa, wearing a jaunty green Tyrolean hat, has filled his pipe but not yet lit it. He expounds on plans for the garden while Alix, preoccupied—at what time did the singing instructor agree to come?—only half listens. Her father, pipe in hand, right forefinger crooked around the bowl, throws his arm wide, speaking ardently about new varieties of rhododendrons, and his face goes blank. He stumbles backward against the parapet and crumples to the ground.

"Papa! *Was ist los?*" she asks him urgently as she crouches beside him.

No answer. His face is so gray, the blood must have drained from it in a rush, and his mouth lolls open in a grotesque way.

Please, please, please, let it be nothing, just a faint, people faint.

She grasps him by the shoulders. In her panic, she has a mad desire to shake him, as if she could shake out what's wrong and he will be fine—and speak to her.

No, don't shake him; check his breathing.

With trembling fingers, she unbuttons the top of his jacket and slides her hand under the collar. The flesh beneath is warm. Is his chest rising and falling? She can't properly tell. She feels dizzy with fear. Time has snapped. Everything that happened before this moment has broken off and left her uncomprehending, uncertain what to do.

Get help.

Yes, she must send for the doctor. Can she leave Papa? Out here alone? She needs to.

Oh please, Papa, don't die. I cannot bear it if you die.

"*Ich komm zurück,*" she cries, and then springs up to run inside.

BY THE TIME Dr. Eigenbrodt arrives, Gunther and a gardener have carried Papa in and laid him on the sofa, with his hat off, boots removed, jacket undone. The left side of his face droops, but his right eye is open and he appears conscious.

The physician requires only a minute to make his diagnosis: a stroke.

At first Papa gabbles occasionally, attempting words. He follows Alix with his one good eye. She sits by his bedside. She sings. She helps two nurses bathe and feed him; she smiles when she wipes his mouth. She chats about the garden, resuming their conversation from the terrace. She's pushed down her panic and her dread. She will betray nothing of it. Papa must believe that she believes he can recover. And he can! She will pull him back into health. It will probably take weeks, but before long the weather will be warm; they can live at Wolfsgarten, where Papa will sit out of doors, gradually gain strength, talk and walk again. She imagines it all.

At night, when she leaves him to go to bed, she kisses the top of his head and tells him he will be better in the morning.

On the fifth day, he falls into a coma. He makes no more sounds, and nothing rouses him. Ernie, Victoria, and Irène arrive, and then, at last, her sister from Russia.

"*Ella ist hier, Papa,*" Alix says before surrendering the chair closest to his head. Ella sits, picks up his limp hand, and puts it against her cheek. She speaks quietly to him, telling him of the journey, of how she's missed him, of Serge's well-wishes.

Her sister seems calm, serene even. Alix feels a surge of resentment. Ella has caused Papa so much heartache in the last year by changing her religion. And now she acts as if nothing has happened.

Presently, Dr. Eigenbrodt comes in to examine Papa. He shakes his head and tells them their father's pulse is weak.

The five of them—Victoria, Ella, Irène, Ernie, and Alix—listen in silence to the sound of his rough, uneven breathing for a half hour. Papa seems to shudder, gasp, and then nothing more. He's totally still. Tears pour out of Alix's eyes. She doesn't wipe them away because she's frozen.

"Papa waited," Victoria says. "He couldn't go until we were all assembled a final time."

PAPA LIES IN state at the Old Palace—dressed in his favorite red *Leibgarde* uniform, his sword between his hands, the blue Order of the Garter from Grandmama across his chest. Citizens shuffle by the open coffin. Alix scatters fresh violets on the black-draped bier, but she avoids looking at his body. She senses herself hewn in two. A small part of her acknowledges Papa no longer lives, but the much larger part refuses to believe it.

At the mausoleum on the Rosenhöhe, watching Papa being

entombed next to Mama and little May, the ground beneath her feet seems to heave—rising and falling as if she's standing on a ship's deck during a storm. She feels her knees begin to buckle, the way a doe's do after she's been shot in the flank. She leans against the stone wall to steady herself. All those childish imaginings of hers—floating up to meet Mama in heaven, hearing her speak—how pathetic and ridiculous. The dead are beyond reach. Papa is gone, and for the rest of her life she will walk through the world without him. The whole of her knows this now. And worse, she knows she is a *Pechvogel*—a bird who attracts bad luck, bringing ill-fortune to those she loves. How else to explain the early deaths of her mother, her sister, and now her father, only fifty-two?

IRÈNE RETURNS HOME to Kiel, to her husband, Henry, and her little son. But Victoria and Ella linger at the Neues Palais, reluctant, Alix senses, to leave her and Ernie alone. In the mornings, Alix stares at the walls and longs to go back to bed. She can't summon the energy to draw, or sing, or read. When she sits motionless at the piano, Victoria's two little daughters, Alice and Louise, pull on her hands resting in her lap. "Come out and play, Auntie." She obediently follows them into the garden, where she stands, listless, as they race about.

The bright-yellow daffodils are springing up—how Papa loved them. She resolves to go inside for the shears and cut a few bunches to arrange for the table. Maybe they will cheer her. But once indoors, in vases, the flowers quickly droop, top-heavy, and are brown-edged on the second day. She should have left them in peace in the earth.

Her sisters lob questions at her. Shall we go for a walk? What might you like for dinner? Perhaps we'll invite Toni to tea? If only they would go away. Particularly Ella, who speaks much of God's will and the peace of the world to come. On the day before Ella is due to return to Moscow—where she lives now in the Kremlin, as Serge has been appointed the city's governor-general—she tracks Alix to the old schoolroom, a place Alix goes deliberately to be by herself.

Ella says in a galling, soft voice, "I know how you suffer, dearest."

It's all Alix can do not to snap at her.

"Do you remember, years ago when the rest of you were ill with diphtheria, I stayed at the Wilhelminenstrasse with Gross-mutter, away from the contagion?"

Alix nods. Why is her sister bringing this up now?

"Mama sent me a note to tell me May had died," Ella continues. "And she also wrote that while shaken by pain beyond words, she was beginning to understand what God in His goodness hoped to teach her. How death is a dark lattice letting in the bright light of eternal life. Can't you find comfort in this, dearest girl, as our mama did? Try, won't you?"

Alix nods again, while secretly she seethes. Ella opines on faith, smug in her piety, and still never acknowledges how terribly she made Papa suffer. That his daughter would renounce the confession made to God at her confirmation and break a promise to him—Papa told Alix the news felt like a blow to his head. He had trouble sleeping. One morning at the breakfast table, her father, hollow-eyed, having clearly drunk too much the night before, asked Alix to vow never to follow Ella's example. "I couldn't bear to lose two daughters to a foreign faith," he said.

On no account would she ever do likewise, she assured him.

Does her sister not recognize her cruelty? The anguish she caused Papa? Has it not occurred to Ella—as it has to Alix—that Papa's anguish weakened his health in his last months? Perhaps contributed to his fatal stroke? Is Ella too pleased with herself to see this?

Alix grips the arms of the chair to restrain herself. She

mustn't hurl accusations at her sister. She loves Ella. She tells herself that. But oh how she hates her too.

Ella, sensing her turmoil, without understanding its reason, stoops to embrace her.

Alix holds herself rigid within Ella's arms.

ELLA DEPARTS, AND two days later Victoria and her daughters return to England. It's a relief to have only Ernie for company. Although Alix is plagued by constant pain in her back and down her legs—sciatica, Dr. Eigenbrodt says, aggravated by grief and nervous exhaustion. Now Alix has an excuse to spend her days in bed.

In the last week of April, Grandmama travels out to Darmstadt, to impart to Ernie some advice about reigning.

On the first afternoon the queen sits next to Alix in her bedroom. The presence of her grandmother—unchanged, unchanging—is oddly comforting. She's old and tiny, but also sturdy and definite, wearing her familiar lemony verbena scent. Her pale blue eyes gaze mournfully at Alix.

"My dearest child, you must strive to put your grief behind you, although I know how difficult that can be," Grandmama says. "When we drew into the station today, I ached for Ludwig. He always bounded into the carriage, welcoming me so affectionately."

Alix nods. She'd watched her father do that a dozen times.

"And this cruel blow, after losing Eddy! Dead mere days after his twenty-eighth birthday! Have you ever heard of anything so sad, so tragic?"

Alix feels a spasm of guilt. Poor Eddy. She should have been kinder to him. After Ernie blocked him from proposing, Alix avoided speaking to Eddy altogether. He'd gaze dolefully at her from across the room, like a child who can't understand why his favorite toy has been snatched away.

Grandmama apparently follows her thoughts. "I was most unhappy about it at the time," the queen says. "But you showed such strength and rectitude, Alicky, refusing the greatest position there is because you did not love the man sufficiently."

Rather astonishing to hear this particular praise from the queen. Maybe Alix is strong—in mind, if not body.

Grandmama takes only a moment to move on. "Now, dear George is an altogether different character. Might you consider him, dearest? Come to Scotland in the summer and spend time together?"

Cousin George, Uncle Bertie's second son, is heir apparent now, and, as Victoria has already reported, his father and his grandmother are impatient for him to marry and have babies. Should anything happen to George, his sister, the brainless Louise, would be next in line for the throne. A most inauspicious prospect.

"Oh, Grandmama, I can't imagine going anywhere or seeing anyone for months."

"Perhaps not," the old lady replies, wringing her handkerchief in her hands.

"And when my health improves, I must try to be of help to Ernie," she continues.

"Our darling boy, only twenty-three and burdened now with weighty responsibilities." Grandmama shakes her head. "I pity him. Let me tell you, Alicky, there is no harder craft than the craft of ruling."

Chapter Twenty

━━━━━━━━━━━━━━━━━━━━━━━━━━━━━━━

A Brother Consoles

Bad Schwalbach, the Grand Duchy of Hesse, June 1892

Ernie lies on a swinging hammock in the garden of the rest house where he and Alix are staying, a straw hat resting over his face to shade it. The orchestra in the neighboring tearoom plays a cheerful waltz. It's the middle of the afternoon and very warm.

Alix complains about the expense of staying in this spa town, and wishes to go home, but Ernie likes it here. The food is tasty. He's met some amusing people, played a good game of lawn tennis nearly every day. And he's glad to be gone from the Neues Palais—away from all the dignitaries and the politicians who come to call, silent questions in their eyes: *Are you up to it? Can you do the job? Will you be better than your father, or worse?* He's been Grand Duke of Hesse and by Rhine for three months and he's still getting used to the idea.

He hears a rustling skirt, pushes aside his hat, and opens his eyes. His sister. Standing with her back to the sun, her outline is hazy, her face in shadow. But he recognizes the mauve dress she is wearing from last summer.

"Hello, are you well? Did you go with Gretchen to the springs?"

"I did."

"Shall we walk next door and eat some pastries? Enjoy the

music?" He sits up and gives her a happy smile. Which she does not return.

"So noisy there," she says.

Goodness, she resists even small pleasures. "All right, I'll ask the landlady to serve us coffee here."

Brother and sister sit down at the small iron table shaded by a tall oak.

"You look better today," Ernie tells her. "And I'm glad to see you out of black."

"My legs are less painful today."

"Marvelous."

She's pressing her lips together and looks fretful. "Darling Ernie, I must talk to you about something that's been preoccupying me," she says after a moment.

"Worries are *verboten*, the doctor says," he jokes.

"Are you going to mind?" Alix asks solemnly.

"Mind what?"

"Mind me at home. It would be wrong of me to hold you back. I imagine you hosting soirees, putting on theatricals, mounting art shows—all that sort of thing. There I will be, your sad little sister, hanging about, turning up like a bad penny at the table. Won't you prefer I live elsewhere, perhaps with Irène in Kiel? Or with Aunt Vicky?"

Ernie laughs. "Leaving me to cope alone? You care so little for me?"

"But do you truly want me?"

"I truly do. Goose."

"I might be of use, with the charities and such," she says doubtfully.

"Feel no obligation. Everyone in Darmstadt loves their *kleine Prinzessin*. She's free to do what she likes when she likes."

"Thank you, dearest."

"I suspect I will be managing some things differently from Papa—you can tell me what you think."

"I always have views."

"And never leave anyone in doubt of them, *Gott sei Dank*!" he teases.

She thwacks his arm with her napkin. "What a rascal you are."

He laughs and she smiles, and for a short while they sit together in contented silence.

"I hope you will live at home with me forever," Ernie says. "But mightn't you eventually want a home of your own? And children?"

She shakes her head. "I can't see myself marrying."

"Not even to—" He stops. Is it wise to raise the vexatious subject of the tsarevich?

"I can never marry Nicky, even if he were to ask me," she says.

"Poor man. Ella's convinced he wants no one else as his wife. When he refused to court Margaret, Uncle Sasha apparently shouted at him for days, calling him irresponsible and feckless. Imagine. That would topple me right over."

Alix frowns. "Don't be like Ella."

"I resemble her not one bit."

"Don't try to coax me along. I know what she's thinking—with Papa gone now I can be persuaded to forget my vow to him and do something horrid."

"Horrid?" One faith is likely as good as the next, Ernie thinks, as long as you remain a Christian believer. Not that pious Alix would ever agree.

"Yes! Papa told me all about it," she says, her voice louder. "At the service when one becomes Orthodox, one has to spit three times to demonstrate contempt! It's an *Abschwören*—the formal renunciation of the previous faith by declaring it evil heresy! I could never." She appears to shiver with dread.

"Yes, I understand," he says soothingly.

"Not Ella, though!" Alix exclaims. "Every week she sends me the same letter. First, she inquires how I am, how you are, and how the weather is here. She writes a short description of their new apartments in the Kremlin, and her plans for the décor. Then she fills three or four pages extolling her new belief and how much more fulfilling she finds it than her old."

Alix looks across the grass to where the landlady's little boy is kicking his ball, and sighs. "She imagines I can be easily moved—it's insulting."

"I'm confident she doesn't mean to insult you," Ernie says. "She's just eager to describe her happiness. Haven't we always worried about her, living in Russia so far from the rest of us? And sadly still without children? At Papa's funeral, she described to me the joy she finds in sharing her new faith with Serge, and how she's become a better Christian because of it."

"Yes, yes," his sister says impatiently. "For *her* it does this. But I am myself, someone completely separate."

"Of course."

"She treats me like a simple-minded girl—her baby sister in need of instruction. *Fall into line and do as I do.* That's what she's saying."

"You're misinterpreting."

"Am I? Why then does she never acknowledge that my feelings could be different? Why does she never commend me for my loyalty to dear Papa?"

Alix begins to cry.

"Don't, please, dearest, I was wrong to broach this painful topic," he begs. But it does no good.

"Ella must believe me a very poor creature. Weak and changeable," she continues, weeping.

"No one believes you a poor creature."

"Only Papa loved me as I am! For myself!" Her voice rises to a high note of distress.

"You are silly. All of us admire and dote upon you."

He pulls his chair closer and puts his arm around Alix. Her shoulders shake with sobs. He should have taken more care; she's still so fragile.

"I feel all alone," she says in a choked voice.

"But I am here," he replies.

After a few minutes, to his relief, she calms, and begins to wipe away tears with her handkerchief. He can sit back in his chair.

"Think, Alix," he jokes. "Even Grandmama is in awe of you now, since you refused to go along with her own cherished plan to marry you to Eddy."

Her face still wet, she shoots him a reproving look. "I acted very ungenerously toward Eddy. Remaining aloof even after you spoke with him."

"Forget all that now," says Ernie. "Your task is to get strong and find pleasure in life again. Attend to this, not the past, or what you imagine other people do or do not think about you— Ella included."

"Perhaps I shan't recover my health. I fear I will be a cripple all my life."

"Nonsense, you are not well because you are not happy. We will follow the doctor's advice and stay here a full month. And then, perhaps we'll take a trip. Didn't we always say we'd like to see Florence and Venice?"

She frowns, as if to mention such a treat in the current circumstances is inappropriate.

"Meanwhile, there's tonight." He smiles. "What do you say, shall we dine again at Wertheim's?"

IN AUGUST, WHEN Ernie and Alix live at Wolfsgarten, he hears regularly from Ella. It's Ernie's duty, this sister insists, to bring up Nicky with Alix whenever possible, to remind her what a perfect creature the tsarevich is, affectionate and loyal. The dear boy may be obedient—on the question of his marriage, he isn't going to compromise. And why should he? Meanwhile, how wonderful that their cousin Margaret has found someone else! That young man everyone calls Fischy—Prince Friedrich of Hesse Kassel. The two will probably announce their engagement soon. Which will mean a big family wedding in Berlin, where Alix can meet Nicky again. He's so longing to see her!

Ernie ignores Ella's exhortations. He's never tempted to mention Nicky to Alix. She has finally had some relief from her back and leg pain, and she's less tearful than she was at Bad Schwalbach. Her friend Toni Becker—an amiable young lady, quite in Alix's thrall, happy to follow her lead in all activities— has come to stay, and together the three of them are enjoying the hot, buzzy weeks of summer.

Ernie acquires two new horses for Alix, Kingbell and Tristan. Even after the rain, Alix enjoys driving, flying like mad through the rutted cart tracks, getting shockingly splashed. Over supper she and Toni join Ernie in imagining improvements at Wolfsgarten. Wouldn't it be wonderful to have somewhere beside the muddy pond to bathe? Should he put in a bathing pool on the grounds, if he can find the funds?

After eating, they sit out in the grassy court devouring sweets—the stickjaws Alix loves so much—and watch the stars come out.

THE BIRTH OF sister Victoria's third child, Prince George Louis Victor Henry Serge of Battenberg, on November 6 at Heiligenburg is a cause of great rejoicing, the first good news in the family for many months.

On a chilly day in mid-December Victoria drives over from Heiligenburg, bringing along Alice and Louise but leaving baby George with his nurse. Victoria hasn't been back in her old home since Papa's funeral. She's very admiring of Ernie's redecoration of the reception rooms—he has removed some of the furniture and had the walls painted a light *eau de Nil* trimmed with cream.

"This drawing room appears totally transformed," Victoria marvels, standing with him near the tall windows.

"And I spent next to nothing," Ernie replies. "Just disposed of what wasn't necessary. I always thought Papa kept too many pieces."

"Maybe so," Victoria says. "And your deft rearrangement makes everything look fresh."

"Give that to me! I want it!" Little Alice's shrill voice carries from the other side of the room, where Alix, sitting on the carpet, is letting the little girls try on some old hats and shawls of hers. Although hard of hearing, Alice is an assertive child. Age seven, she reads lips and speaks both English and German, and insists on directing four-year-old Louise.

"Sunny, dear, be sure Alice shares," Victoria calls out. Alix smiles back, unperturbed.

"Alix seems so improved, contented and relaxed," Victoria says quietly. "How did you manage *that*?"

"I let her alone. I never ask too much of her. She doesn't enjoy crowds. Although, when it's only our friends here to dine, she's happy to appear, and she's very convivial. But no one must mention Papa—she always weeps."

"Hers was the cruelest loss," Victoria says with a sigh.

"I'm afraid so, and she entertains terrible fears that somehow in adoring him as she did, she hastened his death. That she's bad luck to people."

Victoria shakes her head. "Such morbid thinking never helps anyone in the battles of life." She pauses. "I need to ask you in confidence—do you believe Alix would listen to an offer from Nicky?"

"Is he going to make one? His parents will allow it?"

"I had a letter from Ella yesterday," Victoria says. "Minnie's dream of Nicky marrying Princess Hélène of Orleans has come to naught."

"Hélène resisted trading glamorous Paris for remote Petersburg?" Ernie asks.

"No, the Vatican forbade her from converting."

"Ah, the pope shattered Minnie's fondest hopes."

"Apparently so, and now Uncle Sasha has put his foot down. Nicky will be twenty-five in the spring; he must marry someone; the dynasty needs heirs. So if it is Alix he wants . . ."

Ernie smiles. "Funny how steadfast Nicky is in his devotion, although he hasn't seen Alix for what—three years?"

"Nearly four. But Nicky will be at Margaret's wedding, so they can get reacquainted there. How will she answer, should he propose?"

Ernie sighs. Their cousin Margaret is to marry Prince Friedrich of Hesse Kassel in Berlin on January 25—he's surprised that Alix has even agreed to attend this event. He watches Alix drape a yellow silk fringed shawl over Louise's small shoulders.

"I wager she will say no," he says. "You know how obstinate she can be, and she resents the very suggestion that she would ever break her promise to Papa."

"It's a dilemma," says Victoria thoughtfully. "I've always worried that Russia would be too much for Alix, burdened with public duties as Nicky's wife, and subject to so much scrutiny. But staying here in Darmstadt, she's at risk of becoming a lonely, gloomy old maid."

"She'll always have me," Ernie says.

"One day you will marry."

"I must do, unless you fancy your baby George my heir, the next Grand Duke of Hesse and by Rhine?"

"Louis envisions a naval career for Georgie, so no; acquire some sons of your own."

"Aye-aye," he replies. They both laugh.

"Perhaps I'm mistaken," Ernie says, after a moment. "Perhaps if Alix sees Nicky again in the flesh, and they speak privately together, take up their happy relations once more, she would change her mind. I'm doubtful, but still . . ."

"Love might conquer all?" Victoria jokes.

"It's been known to happen," Ernie says. And he smiles.

Chapter Twenty-One

A Dancer Waits Most Anxiously

St. Petersburg, January 1893

On that unforgettable evening when the tsar brought his son to the Imperial Ballet School, for the graduation performance, Matilda danced a pas-de-deux from *La Fille mal Gardée*, in a peacock-blue silk costume, with a belled skirt and a tight bodice, the décolletage showing off her round bosom to perfection.

In the wings beforehand, Matilda felt a strange conviction—how her whole life depended on this night. And that, also, she would not fail. She desired greatness too much to falter.

Afterward, presented to the emperor, she sank into a curtsy with head bowed, her arms curving out in front of her, going so low her back knee grazed the floor.

"What a debut, little Kschessinska, you astonished us all," the tsar declared. A hearty man, humorous and rugged. Beside him stood Grand Duke Nicholas Alexandrovich, shorter, but with the same square face as his father. And what a tender expression in his eyes! She knew instantly. The tsar may be made of granite, but the heir is still soft clay, and has the soul of a romantic. She thanked God for it.

The tsar sat Matilda next to him at dinner, with the tsarevich on her other side. He kept busy speaking to other guests, leaving Matilda to converse with his son.

She started by teasing. "Do you like these plain glasses and china? Aren't you accustomed to far better?"

"We don't often use gold plate," he said. "My parents prefer simple things at home."

"And you, are you simple?"

He looked confused. She whispered: "I'm asking: Do you like the simple pleasures?"

He reddened and dropped his eyes.

She laughed. "I love easy country days, rising at dawn to pick mushrooms, climbing the trees in the orchards to eat the fruit, running barefoot through the meadows."

"You love this more than dancing?"

"No, I love nothing more than the ballet," she answered.

He entered the joking spirit. "I prefer folk dances to ballet; perhaps I'm uncouth?"

"Perhaps you are, a bit."

"Can you do folk dances?"

"I can do any dance. All I need is to be shown the steps— once, by a good partner." She eyed him suggestively.

He tittered and looked embarrassed, but also pleased.

As they got up from the table, the tsar smiled and wagged his finger at them. "I saw you two flirting! Watch out, people will talk!"

SOON AFTERWARD HE went on a tour of the world, which Matilda followed closely by reading the newspaper accounts. When he returned, he sought her out. At first, they went out with other dancers, other officers. But during the army training camp last summer, when Matilda performed at the Krasnoye Selo theater for a month, they snatched opportunities to be alone together, and began talking about becoming serious.

Matilda could not, would not, share a bed with him while she was still living at home with her parents. The tsarevich offered to rent a house for her and pay the wages for two servants.

"Don't imagine he'll ever marry you!" Matilda's father warned, when she told him of the plan.

"I will be content if he loves me as long as he is able."

The tsarevich expressed impatience for everything to be ready, but now on this January evening, when they are finally alone at Number 18, English Prospekt, her darling is sitting not next to her but in a chair in a far corner. He seems uncertain—when usually he is so eager.

"Come here," she says, patting the place on the sofa next to her.

He obediently crosses the room and sits.

She cuddles up against him. "Do you remember," she asks, "that magical night when you abducted me, carried me to your troika, and swept us through Krasnoye Selo town out on the plain so we could be alone under the stars?"

"How could I forget?"

"And the supper party at Cubats, when you threw the bowl of caviar in the face of the prefect of police? Defending my honor?"

He laughs. "That was unwise."

"But so gallant," she says.

"Perhaps," he replies, and now, finally, he leans in for a kiss. She presses her hand against the back of his neck to prolong it.

"I am your *dushka*?" she asks when they break apart.

"You are."

"But not properly." She reaches for both his hands and places them on her chest, where they've happily explored before.

He laughs nervously, pulls his hands back, and returns to the faraway chair.

"What is it, Nikolinka? Why are you hesitating?"

"I've been thinking; I cannot be your first."

She's puzzled. "You want me to love someone else?"

"No."

"Then stop speaking nonsense. Haven't we imagined so often the bliss of love that will be ours?"

"I will be tormented all my life to be your first, only to abandon you."

"You're planning on abandoning me?" she says, smiling.

"Eventually I will have to."

"Let the future take care of itself! We are here together now."

"No, I cannot." He stands, thrusts his open palm in her direction as if to ward her off, and hurries from the room.

HER NIKOLINKA IS not being honest. Matilda knows this, and it makes her very anxious. What is his true reason for holding back? Has he taken up with a different woman? This seems unlikely. What, then?

It occurs to her that Grand Duke Sergei Mikhailovich, the tsarevich's cousin, might know. He comes regularly to sit in the imperial box, looking at Matilda with desperate longing. He resembles a lapdog, grateful for the briefest petting, panting after her, even though he knows she's completely loyal to her Nikolinka. On an evening when the tsarevich fails to turn up for her performance, Matilda invites Grand Duke Sergei and two other officers to her house on the English Prospekt for midnight supper with her and her sister, Julia.

They play the piano, they sing, they share wine, and before long she's ferreted out the truth. At a family dinner ten days ago, the emperor and empress told their son that if he is still interested in Princess Alix of Hesse, he can begin to find out about her.

Matilda's heart sinks. All the Romanovs know—so plenty of

ballerinas know too—that when the tsarevich met this princess in the winter of '89, he believed himself in love. But his mother blocked the match—in her opinion, Alix of Hesse lacks the glittering personality required of an empress.

Such a shame the job can never be mine, Matilda has often thought. She would be perfect.

"Find out what exactly?" Matilda asks the grand duke.

"If she is willing to convert to Orthodoxy," he says. "Apparently, she's a serious Lutheran."

"She's coming here? To Petersburg? So the tsarevich can ask her this religious question? And should she agree, then . . ." She looks at the grand duke with alarm.

"No, no, little K. The princess is not coming here." Sergei Mikhailovich laughs. "We will be spared her lugubrious presence. There's a royal wedding in Berlin later in the month. Nicky will see her there."

"Will he ask her to become his wife?"

"Who knows? Why he's attracted to her is a mystery. She is nothing like you. She lacks all gaiety and spirit. It's true, she's tall. But insufficiently endowed up top, if you know what I mean." Laughing, he thumps his chest.

Matilda manages a semblance of a smile to acknowledge the grand duke's boorish remark, but inwardly she's distraught. Only this, loyalty and enduring affection for his youthful love, would keep Nikolinka from her bed. And now, imminently, Matilda may lose him forever.

It's hideous—she's in torment. But Matilda betrays nothing. No jealous scene or angry outcry will help. Quite the opposite. On a subsequent evening when the tsarevich comes to the theater, and afterward, with brother officers, he stops at the house to see Matilda; they are never alone together. Still, she laughs and sings and acts as if she's enjoying herself.

The tsarevich departs for Berlin. She sleeps, she eats, she dances, while all the time she is praying. Praying that the stiff, dull German princess refuses her *dushka*, and that sweet Nikolinka will return, free, and together they will set a seal on their love. Matilda has believed for so long that a great love is her destiny. Will God deny her the consummation she craves?

SERGEI MIKHAILOVICH CALLS on Tuesday, an evening when she never dances.

"I have news that will please you very much," he says, grinning. "In Berlin, Nicky has suffered. The Princess Alix was polite but distant, and avoided speaking with him."

Matilda feels giddy with relief. "Perhaps Princess Alix has someone else in mind to marry?"

Sergei Mikhailovich laughs. "Apparently not—she's happy to live at home with her brother, occupying herself with the Darmstadt knitting circle."

Matilda is confounded. How could anyone find such an existence preferable to becoming the wife of the tsarevich?

"My poor cousin is most downcast; you will have to cheer him up, little K," Sergei Mikhailovich says. "Now, give me a drink and a song!"

MATILDA HARDLY DARED hope to see Nikolinka at the theater the very first night after his return. But he's there, sitting in the imperial box, and he never takes his eyes off her.

Blast! Her carriage is delayed in picking her up. She waits in the empty lobby, nearly wild with frustration. But when she reaches home, she immediately sees his blue greatcoat hanging on the stand in the hall, and her heart takes wing.

Their first encounter is so tender, so sweet, so careful, but by the end they are both breathless, shaken by the force of their union.

As she always suspected, she is the most passionate of women, and love is her *raison d'être*.

BETWEEN THEIR MEETINGS, time is burdensome; Matilda lives only to see Nikolinka again. In her bedroom, they find exquisite ways to give and take pleasure. It's like discovering different paths through the woods that lead to the prettiest glades. The world outside and everyone in it shrinks away—even the tsar and tsarina become distant, toy-size people. No one can intrude. They dance a dance they can only dance with each other.

She shivers at the touch of his faintly rough fingertips. She adores him, every single inch. Narrow hips, flat belly, angular shoulders. A naked male body is bulkier than she expected, and Nikolinka, although not a large man, has a pleasing sturdiness to him. And his smell! Fresh like grass, with a musky undertone of leather.

After he falls asleep, she likes to slip out of bed, to write a little note to him, recalling their lovemaking. She puts it in his trouser pocket for him to find later.

Nikolinka gives her a diamond brooch, then a diamond necklace, then a set of eight emerald-encrusted vodka glasses. They toast each other, in the evenings, in their cozy nest on the English Prospekt.

IN SEPTEMBER, THE Italian ballerina Pierina Legnani comes to dance *Cinderella* at the Mariyinsky. Legnani can turn thirty-two *fouettes* in a single spot—a tour-de-force out of the reach of all the dancers in Petersburg, including Matilda.

She resolves to be the first to equal the Italian. Some other ballerinas race to the studio of Cecchetti, the Italian ballet master, and beg for instruction. But Matilda seeks out her old ballet school friend Nikolai Legat, who partners Legnani when her usual Italian partner is ill.

What is Legnani's secret? She must know.

"She holds her upper body perfectly steady as it rotates while she whips her head around," Legat explains.

"Show me."

The first day, she manages a dozen turns. After a week she's at twenty. A fortnight of work and she's surpassed her rival and can do thirty-four. She tells Nikolinka to come to the Mariyinsky on a certain evening, promising a special treat. She's dancing Aurora in *Sleeping Beauty*, and during the performance, with Petipa's permission, she includes the thirty-four *fouettes*.

The audience's applause is deafening—it goes on and on, the cheering and the whistling and the stamping until, yes, she performs thirty-four more, faultlessly.

At home alone together, she asks him, "Do you know why I did it?"

"Because you are the prima ballerina?"

"No. Because I haven't the funds to buy you lavish presents like you give me."

"So?" He seems neither to care nor understand. If she didn't love him so, Matilda would say her precious Nikolinka is a tiny bit witless.

"I learned as a gift to you, which is also a gift to Russia. Russian ballet must be unrivaled in Europe."

Now he looks pleased. "Who did you say taught you?"

"Nikolai Gustavovich Legat."

"Let me send him a token of appreciation. Do you think he'd like a gold cigar case?"

"I do." And she smiles. She longs to ask him for something more: *Tell me you will love me always.*

But no, she knows her *dushka*. He's not ready to say it—yet.

Chapter Twenty-Two

※※※※※※※※※※※※※※※※※※※※※※※※※※※※※※

Remonstrating

St. Petersburg and Darmstadt, October 1893

*E*lla waits for the empress in her lavish private sitting room at the Anichkov Palace, where the walls are covered in raspberry silk and every surface crowded with precious objets d'art.

When last she was invited here, four years ago, Minnie admonished her for imagining that Alix might ever be the bride of her precious son. And since then Minnie has kept her distance, always gracious when they meet, but not warm. From the amiable tone of Minnie's note, requesting that she call, Ella senses a desire for rapprochement. Could this have something to do with a certain ballerina? Ella's friend Zinaida Yusupova tells her that rumors of Nicky's affair with the dancer Kschessinska alarm and distress the empress. What if the girl falls pregnant? Two of Sasha's uncles have children with dancers, and several of his cousins. Minnie does not want this for her boy. He must be married, and married soon.

Minnie did not allude to Nicky's amorous entanglement in her short message, only that she's heard Ella is in town en route from Moscow to her old home in Darmstadt. Might they confer on "family matters" before she departs?

Sitting on a low mahogany sofa, Ella realizes she hasn't missed Minnie's affectionate regard. In truth, she's become rather contemptuous of her sister-in-law. At Easter two years ago, in the chapel of the Sergievsky Palace, wearing sandals and a simple white robe, hair loose down her back, Ella embraced Orthodoxy formally. She's astonished by the depth of her belief now that she has left behind dry Lutheran observance for the elaborate rites of her new church. In contrast, Minnie, the empress, a woman looked up to by millions, never thinks seriously about faith. What are her true interests beyond husband and children? Fashion and gossip—that's all.

Ella will be cordial. She'll overlook the empress's nasty remarks when last they spoke privately. Minnie is the supplicant now—seeking Ella's help in bringing about a match she once vehemently opposed.

Will the empress want to go over the events at Margaret's wedding earlier in the year? How when Nicky tried to speak with Alix, she rebuffed him—and, complaining of earache, left the banquet early? Later, at a family dinner hosted by Irène and Henry, Alix requested to be seated at the opposite end of the table from the tsarevich. The entire time in Berlin, Alix looked so woebegone, and so ill, Ella hadn't the heart to reprimand her. She did write to Alix afterward, urging her to get reacquainted with Nicky in June, at the London wedding of their mutual cousin George to May of Teck. But Alix declined her invitation to that occasion. So frustrating!

What should Ella say about her sister's current state of mind? Alix's letters are not revealing. She's still deliberating this when Minnie sweeps into the room, wearing an elaborate gown of violet wool, with a black vest and black belt. The bruise-like hue of the dress rather clashes with the deep pink on the walls.

She kisses Ella on both cheeks and sits down on a tall chair. Maybe it's the discordant colors, or the angle from which Ella is looking up at Minnie's face, but the empress looks puffy, sallow, and for the first time, most definitely middle-aged.

"You've heard about my darling Georgy," Minnie says after a quick exchange of greetings.

"Only that he's been quite ill."

"The doctors are certain now, it's tuberculosis. He must go to live at Abass-Tuman in Georgia, where the dry air will be better for him."

"How terrible for the poor boy, for the whole family."

"Yes, you cannot possibly understand. Witnessing your child suffer—it's unendurable." Minnie closes her eyes.

This remark rankles, but Ella doesn't react, merely asks evenly, "And Sasha? Serge mentioned headaches?"

"My dear, they plague him! He works much too hard. We went to Livadia for six weeks and Sasha sat on the balcony looking at the sea all the day long."

"Did he find the holiday restorative?"

"Very! But once we returned to Petersburg, Sasha immediately caught a cold, which turned into influenza." Minnie shakes her head. "Only in the last few days has he been meeting his ministers again."

"I pray the dear man regains full strength soon," Ella says.

"If only Xenia would stop pestering him—pestering both of us. She wants to be engaged to Sandro."

"Don't you like Sandro? He seems to me a fine young man. I like him best of all the Mikhailovichi."

The empress flicks her fingers impatiently. "Xenia is only eighteen—there's no hurry. And, certainly, she cannot marry before her elder brother does!"

Minnie looks down at Ella reproachfully. Having listed all her troubles, she has reached the one connected with Ella. "We're at an impasse! And we notice your sister takes pains to avoid Nicky!"

"In Berlin, she was still deep in mourning for dear Papa. I should have warned Nicky she was not herself."

Minnie arches a single brow.

"My brother tells me she is brighter now," Ella continues. "Ernie and she went on a tour of Italy in the spring, which they both enjoyed."

"But then she failed to appear at George and May's wedding!" Minnie exclaims.

"She said she couldn't afford the journey."

"Yet she had funds to travel in Italy."

"I wish she'd made a different choice," Ella concedes. "Without parents, Alix has no one to guide her properly. I'm traveling to Darmstadt now to meet my sister Victoria there. We intend to speak to Alix, and to Ernie, about their futures. Perhaps you heard how our grandmother threw Ernie together with our cousin Ducky this summer at Balmoral?"

"I did hear!" Minnie smiles. "How the queen loves to match her relations to one another."

"Although Ducky is still very young."

"A year younger than Xenia, and quite stormy-tempered. Is your brother prepared for that?"

"I'll ask him," Ella answers lightly. In fact, both she and Victoria have grave concerns about Ducky's suitability—but that's none of Minnie's business.

"What will you say to Alix? Can she be moved?"

"She's always cared deeply for Nicky." Ella feels confident of this much.

"Then return to Russia with her," the empress demands, nostrils flaring. "Let Serge manage on his own in Moscow, and have Alix reside with you at the Sergievsky Palace for the winter season."

Having once banished Alix, now Minnie orders her carted back to Petersburg? Ready to receive Nicky when he breaks off relations with his dancer? No, Ella won't agree.

"I prefer a different plan," Ella says. "At home Alix will feel at ease, more receptive to advice. I can discuss everything with her, assure her of Nicky's ardent devotion, and discuss the religion here. Once I'm certain she is ready to receive a proposal, I will cable from Darmstadt and Nicky can follow me there."

Minnie frowns. "It would be undignified for the tsarevich to make a mad dash across Europe upon the whim of a girl who last time they met declined to speak with him!"

"You don't believe he'd be willing to travel?" Ella inquires mildly.

"That's hardly the issue."

"I'll only invite him once I am confident Alix will accept," Ella says.

The empress shakes her head. "I don't like it. We must ask Sasha."

OVER DINNER THE tsar—weary, pouches under his dark eyes—is very short with Ella. "I hate how this business is dragging on. Your sister refuses to talk to Nicky. Nicky refuses to consider anyone else. And meanwhile he capers about, out at midnight suppers, visiting the new clubs, drinking too much, cavorting with all sorts of unsuitable persons."

And who but his parents are to blame for this? Ella thinks. Aloud she says, "I hope we can resolve everything in Darmstadt."

"You believe you'll be able to persuade Alix?" Sasha asks. He's drumming the table impatiently with the tips of his fingers.

"I will do my best."

"If your sister's prepared to accept him, I dare say the boy can journey there."

"Thank you, dear Sasha. Before I leave, I will explain to Nicky how it's been for Alix, all these sad months."

"Good luck laying your hands on him," Sasha answers, scowling. "We rarely see him these days."

ELLA SENDS A message to Nicky, and word comes back that he is too busy to call at the Sergievsky Palace.

Ella, surprised, sends a second note: *You have no time for your poor old Tetinka? In Petersburg for a mere four days?*

He turns up the next afternoon—too late for luncheon, and he wants no tea.

"I have only a short while," he says, faintly truculent. "Sandro and I have an engagement."

Off to see his mistress? Why else would he be so impatient? Ella feels irked but smiles and asks him to sit.

"While I'm in Darmstadt next week I intend to speak seriously to Alix, to persuade her that changing belief need not be an impediment to marrying you."

Nicky frowns. "What makes you think she'll be open to accepting this?"

"Time has passed, she turned twenty-one in June, and I'm sure she longs to start her life properly."

Nicky looks dubious.

"Your parents have agreed, my dear boy," Ella continues. "Once I have seen Alix and know that she will consent, you can come to Darmstadt and propose—confident of her answer."

Now Nicky smiles. "A pretty thought."

"Leave it to me."

He shrugs. "I'd like to believe—but I think it unlikely. In Berlin we lived less than a mile from each other for a week, and she ignored me. Occasionally I caught her giving me a strange, chilly glances!"

"She was mired in grief then."

"But just imagine! For years I have hoped to marry Alix, and when finally Papa and Mama allow me to approach her, and I travel to Berlin imagining my dream close to being realized, and instead I find the curtains drawn! She appeared to actually dislike me. I felt completely beaten down!"

Petulance doesn't suit Nicky.

He goes on. "I know you dearly desire to see Alix as my wife, Tetinka. But that's not enough—she must want it too."

"Of course. But remember, dear Papa collapsed in front of Alix—losing her sole remaining parent was a terrible shock. And now she has got a fixed idea in her head, that out of loyalty to our father, she can never change faiths. There's no one close to her in Darmstadt to remove the obstacle—only I can do this."

"I wish you success," Nicky says with a sigh. "Whenever I look into our garden at the Anichkov I always think of those lovely times with Alix, on the ice."

"Trust in God."

"Yes, I must I suppose," he says, his voice doubtful.

PRINCE ISENBURG AND the rest of Papa's crusty old *Kamaraden* are nowhere to be seen at the Neues Palais. Ernie counts among his closest friends artists, musicians, and writers. On the first evening of their visit, Ernie takes Ella and Victoria, along with Alix, to the *Staatstheater* to see *Charley's Tante*, the German version of a very amusing play by Brandon Thomas, translated by one of Ernie's friends, Dietrich Faber, who comes back to the palace afterward for a jolly supper.

Ella and Victoria agree. The happy mood of their reunion, the lighthearted conviviality amongst the four of them is lovely— but they mustn't put off for long the vital conversations.

When Alix goes out to visit her friend Toni the next afternoon, Ella and Victoria invite Ernie to sit with them in the library.

"You both look so stern," their bother says with a merry

smile. "Have you uncovered some mischief? Detected impropriety you insist be addressed? I promise you, Alix and I live a very staid existence here."

"I doubt staid," says Ella. "You appear to be leading a cultural revival in Darmstadt."

He chuckles—this praise clearly pleases him.

"But we must ask you something," says Ella, her tone graver.

"Do you really care for Ducky, or are you just going along to please Grandmama?" Victoria asks.

"A bit of both. I have to marry someone," Ernie answers. "Everyone says so."

"I don't think you do—at least not now. You've made a wonderful start as grand duke," says Ella.

"I'd like to have children. As we've discussed, Victoria, I need an heir." Ernie snaps open a silver box on the side table and takes out a cigarette. "Mustn't delay too long."

Ella and her sister exchange a look. Is this the attitude of a man in love?

"Ducky is only seventeen," Ella says. "And I fear a bit spoiled—Uncle Affie and Aunt Marie are such indulgent parents."

"Also, she's our first cousin," Victoria puts in.

He shrugs.

"Ernie, we can't escape the truth that our family should avoid closely intermarrying," Victoria goes on. "Think about it: Uncle Leo, Frittie, now Toddie . . ."

Irène's son, a boy of four, has the bleeding disease that caused the deaths of both their uncle and their brother.

"Is that what's worrying you?" Ernie waves his cigarette at them. "Both of you are married to cousins of Papa's."

"Louis and I aren't first cousins," Victoria says. "And even so, two London specialists have told us that Alice's deafness may well be the result of her parents' close kinship."

"Alice is beautiful, and clever enough to compensate for her mild deficit."

"Mild! I have lost sleep over it, staring at the ceiling in despair!" Victoria exclaims.

"Don't be silly," says Ernie.

"Once you are a father, you'll understand such feelings are not in the least *silly*," says Victoria, vehement. "It's awful to believe you've caused harm to your child."

"Don't you think it's the duty of a man in your position to have healthy descendants?" Ella asks.

"I think a man in my position has limited choice in brides, and Ducky is lively and she seems keen on me." He gives them an admonishing look. "Do let's choose another subject."

"Alix," says Ella immediately.

"What about her?" Ernie says, brightening.

"Can we not persuade her to accept Nicky?"

"Try if you like," says Ernie. "I never mention him. She only makes a scene."

"She quarrels with you?" Ella is surprised.

"No, she performs a soliloquy—sometimes shorter, sometimes longer—but always along the same lines: No one should imagine she would ever betray Papa."

"Does she still care for Nicky?"

"I'd say yes, but our dear sister is constantly caught up with self-examination, weighing her own actions. What is the right thing to do? What is wrong? She always asks herself this. And marrying Nicky? Well, that counts, most definitely, as wrong."

THE NEXT MORNING, Ella and Victoria confer.

"I will speak to Alix alone," Ella says. "As it's a question of religious conviction."

"Better—yes," says Victoria.

"What tranquil setting should I choose?"

"Take a walk up to the Rosenhöhe?" suggests Victoria.

"No, too gloomy," says Ella. "Alix never needs reminding of all she has lost."

"What about the Schepp Allee?" says Victoria.

"Good idea," Ella answers. She loves this public avenue, lined with pines pushed into whimsical shapes, that their forefather Landgrave Ernst Ludwig laid out as an elegant place for Darmstädters to take the air.

When Ella proposes the outing after luncheon, Alix appears guarded, but agrees.

They haven't gone far before Alix says, "I know what you're planning to say to me."

"How's that?"

"You have a particularly annoying expression on your face, indicating you're on the brink of delivering a reproving lecture."

"Reproving? Never."

"An improving one then. You aim to instruct me on life."

Ella smiles. "Dear girl, I only want the best for you. Why have you been avoiding Nicky? Why won't you speak to him at least?"

"It's better that I don't."

"His parents tell me he drifts around aimlessly, in regrettable company. He hasn't agreed to court anyone else."

"Is this my concern? I should commit a sin, so Nicky might be happy?" Alix swings her rolled parasol forcibly as she walks.

"It wouldn't be a sin—as I've tried to explain. You would be laying down a second path to God over the first one."

"You make it sound like putting on an overcoat. You know it's much more serious than that."

"Of course it's serious."

"I would be forced to publicly renounce my belief and ever

after pretend to love the faith I'd been made to take on, all the while desperately missing the one I left behind."

"I'm sure you will come to love—"

"And how cruel of you to say I am ruining his life," Alix interjects. "I find it hard enough as it is. I never want to hurt him."

"You do care for him, then?"

Alix stays silent for a long moment, and then she sighs. "I was surprised to see in Berlin that he wears a beard now. You never told me. It suits him. The deep expression in his eyes is exactly the same—and I've always loved that."

Ella feels a surge of elation. This pairing is meant to be, she knows it—the interlocking of two souls that will be a rich blessing for each of them, and a gift to Russia. "How overjoyed I would be to see you married, living together in perfect happiness!"

"If my happiness mattered to you, you wouldn't nag at me constantly," Alix snaps back.

"Constantly? I have not seen you in ten months."

"But now you've come all this way to badger me in person."

"I'm also here in Darmstadt because I worry about Ducky as Ernie's wife."

"Ernie has to marry someone."

"So he says, but must it be Ducky?"

"I like Ducky—she has a lot of 'go.'"

Ella sighs. "Dearest, please forget Ducky now, and listen. I hate to see you throwing away joy."

"Only you regard it as such."

"Not only me! Victoria, Ernie, Serge, Irène, Uncle Sasha, and Aunt Minnie—we all think the same."

"You're quite sure of those last two?"

"I spoke with them in Petersburg before coming away. Nicky's parents will welcome you with open arms."

"Aunt Minnie has never liked me," Alix says grimly.

"In '89 you and Nicky were still so young, and remember in those days Aunt Alix and Grandmama hoped you'd marry Eddy. How could Minnie support a match contrary to her beloved sister's desires? It would have been disloyal."

"And what of my loyalties?" Alix asks hotly. "Why do you imagine I'd be untrue to Papa? Simply put aside his wishes now he's gone?"

"You were wonderfully devoted to Papa, Sunny dearest," she says. "Still, isn't it possible that by marrying this worthy husband, who loves you and needs you, for whom you would be an exquisite and virtuous consort, you would honor Papa in a wider way? His daughter assuming such a very important role in the world?"

"Perhaps it was always easy for you, ignoring Papa's wishes, but I find it impossible! I loved him too much."

Now Ella is stung. She's silent for a long minute, and then says, rather stiffly, "You will discover, dear girl, there comes a time in life when you must follow your own soul's commands. I am aware my conversion hurt Papa, but I believe he forgave me."

"Do you? Do you really? I'm not sure I can!"

"Oh, Alix, don't say that."

They have reached the Schepp Allee. But, preoccupied, neither of them comments on the pines.

Next Alix says in a low, insistent voice: "You never accept that I have my own ideals. To which I am entitled, just as you are yours."

Ella sighs. Has Alix always been such a mule? And how difficult to argue against "ideals" when they disguise a deeper truth. She tries again. "Dearest, I can appreciate the prospect of living in Russia is an intimidating one. I myself felt rather frightened before I moved there, but I will be close by to help and support you, and Nicky will be such a devoted husband. Do you imagine there is someone you could love more?"

"No one." Alix's voice trembles.

"For Nicky's sake you must pray to God for the courage to do a thing which at the moment seems impossible."

"I cannot." Alix halts and turns to face her, hastily brushing away a tear.

"Avoiding him—that is most unbecoming and unworthy of you," Ella says sternly.

Alix sniffs.

"And I am tired of being the go-between," Ella adds.

"No one asked you to be such!"

Ella feels her patience at an end. "Alix, if you are really so adamant in your refusal, then you must write to him and explain. Describe those ideals of yours!"

Her sister crosses her arms in front of her chest, and, still holding her parasol in one hand, scowls at Ella.

When have I seen her like this before? It comes back to Ella in a rush—Alix aged six, sulky when scolded, lips pouting, eyes indignant. Ella almost laughs. Oh dear, will her contrary little sister ever see sense?

"Once I write this letter to Nicky, will it then be a finished thing?" Alix asks.

"If that's what you so desire."

ON THEIR LAST morning together in Darmstadt, Victoria and Ella walk up to the Rosenhöhe to lay flowers at Papa's and Mama's tombs.

"Imagine Mama alive, coping with her grown children," says Victoria, as they stroll through the park gates on the way home.

"That's difficult, she's been gone so long," Ella says.

"She'd probably have felt as frustrated as we do," Victoria says.

Ernie has permitted no more discussion of his possible marriage to Ducky. And Alix has penned her letter to Nicky, rejecting his suit forever, and wordlessly passed the sealed envelope to Ella.

"I'm certain Mama's advice would have carried more weight than mine, especially with Alix," Ella says, sighing.

"Don't blame yourself, Ellie; you've done all you can for the girl," says Victoria.

"Have I?"

"Of course you have. And it's likely for the best."

"Is it?"

"She says she loves Nicky, wants no other husband, yet still she refuses him? That's more than moral scruples—she's frightened of life there. Best she doesn't take it on."

"Nicky will need a strong wife to bolster him," Ella says. "And I'd like the next empress to be a serious-minded lady. The current one has a fundamentally frivolous character."

"Oh, come now. Minnie is high-spirited, perhaps a trifle vain, but never malicious."

"Russia deserves better."

"So you *haven't* given up on the idea?" Victoria looks skeptical.

"Imagine if Alix could be persuaded that by marrying Nicky she'd be acting virtuously? I'm quite sure she wants to accept him—she just doesn't know how. She needs a way to cancel out what in her mind is a great evil—breaking her vow to Papa."

"Alix's obstinacy is wearisome. Don't waste more time arguing with her."

"I don't plan to. For the moment she won't listen to me, as I am a vile sinner for betraying Papa."

"Hardly a generous, sisterly attitude."

"This prevents me from getting through to her—but another might."

"Not me, if that's who you mean!" Victoria exclaims. "I'm

still not convinced she should marry the man. It's an intimidating thing, agreeing to be a Romanov, empress one day, sitting at the top of that savage, archaic regime."

"It wasn't you I had in mind, dearest," Ella says tartly. She dislikes Victoria voicing her anti-Russian opinions. She sounds too much like Grandmama.

"Do you intend to urge Nicky to make an appeal to her conscience?"

"No, Alix doesn't see it as her duty to rescue him."

"And I suppose Nicky's parents are out?"

"Sasha won't stoop to appeal to Alix, and Alix is suspicious of Minnie, whom she senses, correctly enough, has never favored her."

"Who then?"

"I'm still thinking."

Chapter Twenty-Three

Yearning

Königliches Schloss, Kiel, December 31, 1893

When, two months ago, Alix sat down to write to Nicky she was flooded by a passionate sense of righteousness.

She had looked at it in every possible light, she explained to him, but she finds it impossible to go against her conscience and become his wife. A marriage needs to begin with the real blessing of God. And to convert would be acting a lie to Nicky, to his religion, and to God Himself. They mustn't go on torturing themselves hoping for something that can never be.

At first, passing the letter on to Ella, she felt relieved—at peace and proud of herself. In refusing to be shaken from her convictions or break her vow, she not only behaved virtuously, she appeased her terrible suspicion that she hastened Papa's death by loving him as much as she did. God will recognize her sacrifice and preserve others whom she loves. And to put one's conscience ahead of one's earthly desires, isn't that the definition of virtue?

But for five long weeks, during which she had no answer from Nicky, her thoughts began to drift down another path. Has she done him wrong? Is he furious with her? Does he think her hateful? Is he wishing they'd never met?

More likely he is diverting himself with others and trying to forget her. Which is as it should be. And yet . . .

And yet every day she had no reply she felt crushed.

Then it arrived: a most beautiful response. Ever since those winter weeks they spent together in Petersburg, he wrote, he has loved her, and the sad letter he has received from her will not change this. No happiness in the world exists for him without her.

And then he begged her forgiveness. *Please don't be angry at me for telling you all this.*

Angry? How could Alix ever be angry over this? Their love is hopeless, impossible on the earth. But to hold in her hand the paper onto which he confessed his undying passion thrills her. She remembers him at Peterhof, that charming boy—playful and affectionate. And meeting him again, transformed into a dashing, teasing young man with whom she danced and skated and frolicked so happily. Who can forget sliding down the ice hill side by side on the wooden board? Or walking the streets of St. Petersburg, incognito, conspiring to steal time together? In Berlin, she didn't like to look at him directly too often, wary of encouraging him. But she glanced at him often enough to admire his trimmed auburn beard, which gives his handsome face a pleasing maturity. And she noticed him passing his hand through his thick hair from time to time, a nervous gesture, but such a sweet one.

What would it be like to kiss him? And more, to love him as a wife does a husband? She blushes to picture it, although, alone in bed, she imagines he is there, that she can roll toward him and embrace and caress him. What rapture. She holds out her arms sometimes, longing for his invisible figure. She wishes fervently to dream of him and frequently gets her wish. In one dream she is riding a horse astride, behind him, her arms around his waist, and she hugs him against her, tighter and tighter. She awoke from this dream, her body shuddering, tremors washing over her—so odd, but so pleasurable too.

Her furtive, romantic yearnings won't come to anything, though. She'll never know what it is like to embrace Nicky. And while she treasures his letter, and carries it with her everywhere, she does not answer it. What more is there to say?

TONIGHT, IN THE last hour of the year, she sits up late in her chilly bedroom in Irène and Henry's castle home, where she and Ernie have come for the Christmas season.

She finishes writing a letter to Grandmama, sending best wishes for 1894. Sealing the envelope, she wonders: Why exactly do people celebrate the arrival of a new year? Do they give no thought to the sorrows awaiting them in the months to come? The difficulties, tragedies, and losses as yet unforeseen?

And what does the New Year promise for her? She still misses Papa every day. And now that darling Ernie plans to marry Ducky, she will soon be *de trop* in Darmstadt.

Irène insists she'll always have a home here in Kiel. "Henry considers you his own sister," she told Alix. "Toddie, especially, hopes you will never leave."

Henry and Irène's little boy is a great duck, with adorable chubby limbs and a dimpled smile.

"I love you, I do," Toddie told her as they walked hand-in-hand along the icy garden path yesterday. He is four now and he has the same trouble with his blood vessels as Frittie and Uncle Leo did. But his parents take his condition quite matter-of-factly. Irène has sewn soft cotton pads to tie around Toddie's knees to protect them when he stumbles.

Victoria is also anxious to help Alix. Won't she come to England in the spring? *We've taken a lovely little house in Walton-on-Thames*, her sister wrote last week. *And I know your craze for sweet children, Sunny—come and dote on your nieces and baby nephew.*

Yes, she has choices. She will go to England directly after

Ernie's wedding in Coburg in April. She might return to Kiel for the autumn. She doesn't dare go to Ella in Russia for at least a year, maybe two. It would be far too painful for Nicky—and also for her.

Ernie gave Alix a bullfinch as a Christmas gift. She's named him Bully. He has a beautiful red chest, black head, and gray wings tipped with black. He's a fine mimic—she's already taught him a few bars of "Twinkle, Twinkle, Little Star." Now as she watches him whistle and skip around in his cage, she realizes what 1894 holds in store for her—fond sisters rallying round, nieces and nephews to cherish, a number of comfortable homes where she will be welcome.

But at the end of each day she will be alone, with only a bird for company.

Chapter Twenty-Four

The Kaiser Plays Cupid

Coburg, April 1894

William has been kaiser for nearly six years now, and he's proud of all he's accomplished. He booted out Bismarck to become sole master of the Reich, and he's the vigorous, forward-thinking leader the German people deserve.

Still, from time to time, he reflects on what life might have been like had he been born a private man.

He wouldn't have married Dona, certainly. The older he gets the more he looks down on his wife. Docile yes, but hopelessly clingy, and empty-headed. He can't discuss important matters with her, never seeks her counsel, and hates how she's perpetually complaining about his long absences. If home offered more satisfactory company, he wouldn't travel as much.

Ella, his first love, would have suited him far better. He's sure of it. Since his ascension he's only encountered her a handful of times. In '88 they spent the day together with the tsar's retinue aboard the *Hohenzollern*, riding at anchor off Peterhof. He marveled: Most women fade with time, but the loveliness of a small few grows and deepens. Dona has come to resemble an anxious ferret with her bulging round eyes, twitchy nose and mouth, while Ella in maturity is like a Madonna—luminous skin, tranquil expression, her elegant head set atop a swanlike neck. That awful creep she's married to, Grand Duke Serge—William can barely stand to look at him. It turns his stomach to think of what poor Ella has had to put up with all these years.

On that sunny afternoon in Russia William longed to ask her: *Do you think of me sometimes? You haven't forgotten our childish attachment, have you? Perhaps there's a corner of your heart that still belongs to me?* But he abstained. Too many people about. And Mama was correct to press him to forsake Ella. The risk was too high. Look at his brother Henry—he's married to Ella's sister and his son has the bleeding disease, while Dona has given birth to six healthy boys.

Nevertheless, William will always revere Ella. It's one of his soul's secrets.

Such a wonderful surprise to receive a letter from her last month. And to discover she's eager for his help! Ella's younger sister Alix loves the Russian tsarevich, but can't see her way clear to marrying him. William will be at her brother Ernie's wedding in Coburg, won't he? Ducky's parents plan to invite the entire family—the Royal Mob, as Grandmama calls them. Perhaps he might speak privately with Alix on that occasion? Ella imagines William would be pleased to have his young cousin married to the future emperor of Russia. Of course, if he, as a faithful Lutheran, has misgivings about the match—and her sister's necessary change of faith—Ella will understand.

How like her, to see him not just as a sovereign, but as a man of belief! It's this grace, this tender regard for himself, which she demonstrated even as a girl, that so touches him.

Yes, certainly, he replied—he will make it his business to persuade Alix.

Mama and Grandmama insist the girl will never say yes to Nicky, because of some vow she made to her father. But Ludwig—such a negligible person in life—has been dead two years now. William doesn't know Alix well, but why would this cousin be content as second lady in the insignificant duchy of Hesse, when she could be empress of Russia one day?

No, he can fix this and he intends to. The tsar isn't coming to Coburg. William will play the paternal role in his stead— making Nicky's match for him. And, at the same time, impressing upon the tsarevich how the new pact the tsar signed with France is an insidious thing! Russia's most natural ally is Germany, and the former alliance between the two should be restored in full!

And he'll explain to Alix that it's her duty—as a German princess, and his own close relation—to play her part in reestablishing the German Empire's crucial bond with its giant neighbor to the east.

He looks forward to his double triumph. And, even more, to being praised by the exquisite Ella.

NICKY KNOWS IT now. Coming here to Coburg was a grave error.

Yesterday on the station platform, Alix wouldn't even meet his eye, although she was among the party welcoming the Russian guests to her brother's wedding. Instantly, he understood. She intends to spurn him again, as she did in Berlin.

And proper warning had been given! After his parents announced that Nicky would represent them at Ernie's wedding, Alix sent Xenia a telegram. His sister must remind Nicky that her mind is made up—she can never change belief.

"Alix would clearly prefer not to see you," his sister told him, waving the yellow slip in front of his eyes.

He went immediately to speak with Mama.

"To chase after Alix when she's adamant in her refusal would be unseemly," he explained. His mother so often harps on about decorum. "I will not be going."

"But now you're expected," his mother replied, looking distraught. "And Ella tells us there's a real chance Alix will accept you this time. The queen will also be there. Appeal to her!"

"I thought the queen hated the idea of Alix marrying me."

"Ha!" said Mama, for a moment triumphant. "According to my sister, the queen frets there will be no place in Darmstadt for her favorite granddaughter once her brother is married. Please, Nicky, don't lose this opportunity!"

"No, I refuse to be humiliated." He felt pleased with his assertiveness.

Leaving his mother's sitting room, he resolved to move immediately to camp at Krasnoye Selo—and sneak back into town to visit little K in the evenings.

An hour later, while packing up his kit, Nicky received a summons to his father's office.

"Don't you see your mother weeping over this?" Papa shouted. "What a wastrel you are! Weak-willed and irresponsible! I agree, you will most likely fail, but you must try, as you've insisted for years that this is the woman you desire. Board the train as planned. That's an order."

Nicky did, and now he's here, and only agony has ensued.

This morning Ernie brought Alix to Schloss Ehrenburg, where Nicky is lodged with Ella and Serge. She looked lovelier than ever, but very sad. Left alone with Alix for an hour, Nicky spoke as gently as possible. Please couldn't she put her objections aside? Accept him and a new faith? Make him the happiest of men?

Weeping, she whispered over and over again: "I cannot."

She declined to stay for luncheon. He felt sulky at the table—more so when Ella announced that after the meal he must take a walk with the kaiser.

"Why? I loathe that execrable fellow."

She frowned. "Don't shirk your responsibilities."

"I know him—he'll spend the whole time expounding on his political views."

"To which you will listen, as the tsar's representative," she answered, brusquely.

Once Ella was his fond Tetinka, someone he could relax with, and now she's like Mama—always faintly disapproving, quick to tell him how he should behave.

NICKY MEETS WILLIAM in the *Schlossplatz*, and they walk along a cobbled lane toward the center of the town. A small, noisy company of guards, boots tramping, swords rattling, trail in their wake. Does the kaiser go everywhere with a ridiculous show of force? It's not as if he needs to. Imperial rule in Germany is secure.

As Nicky expected, William pontificates. His subject is the unbreakable ties of friendship between Russia and Germany, along with some other drivel. Nicky nods along, barely listening. He is silently calculating how many days must pass before he can escape from Coburg. Is it four? Or maybe three, if he orders the train to leave in the middle of the night?

Nicky only snaps to attention when William asks: "Do you really love my cousin Alix?"

"Of course!"

"She's been keeping you waiting a long while, old chap." William chortles in a way that makes Nicky long to clip him.

"She has a serious nature, and has suffered over the decision to change her religion," Nicky replies stiffly.

"I will speak with her," says William in his lordly manner. "The barrier mustn't be allowed to stand."

That this ridiculous booby thinks he has a chance to persuade Alix irks Nicky no end. But everything about his position today is infuriating.

WHEN WILLIAM CALLS, two hours later, at the Palais Edinburgh, Ella tells him Alix is waiting upstairs for him. She will summon Nicky from Schloss Ehrenburg to wait down the hall while William speaks with her sister.

Alix is sitting in a small, white-walled room, apparently an infrequently used sitting room. Her face blotchy and red, her spine slumped, and, as he enters, she looks up at William morosely.

God help him, she's a damp and miserable thing. Is this really the woman Nicky wants for his wife?

He sits down and gets right to it.

"None of us in our family are ordinary people, dear Alix," William begins. "You cannot behave like an ordinary person."

She eyes him doubtfully, saying nothing.

"You understand that on the European continent Germany and Russia are the most important powers?"

"I allow so, yes."

"Then you should understand it would be a most constructive thing for you to marry the Russian tsarevich."

"Reasons of conscience prohibit it," she says, her face hardening.

"Religious ones?"

"Yes."

"But what is the Lord's wish for the world? That peace should prevail, true?"

She nods reluctantly.

"I spoke with Nicky earlier and he agrees; things are drifting in the wrong direction. You must do your part by binding Germany and Russia closer, which preserves the European peace."

"I can't see how," she remarks, rather waspishly.

"That's because you lack my vision," William answers. "There are always tensions—even between the best of friends. Germany and Russia should be the best of friends. Having you, a German, in St. Petersburg, will help heal the current discord and ease any conflicts in future."

She shakes her head. Silly girl.

"Don't be blind, Alix!" he says forcefully. "You believe we were all put on this earth for a purpose, don't you?"

"Purpose?"

"Those of us of rank possess the most important purposes. This afternoon I enjoyed a wide-ranging and sympathetic discussion with the tsarevich—a very intimate exchange of views. I heard from Nicky directly how he feels about you. He loves you deeply. Facing all that he will face in the future—isn't it your duty to return his love?"

She offers up a small smile. He is working his charm.

"I don't regard loving Nicky as my duty," says Alix in a soft voice. "He is simply the person I care for most in the world."

"And that's lovely. Regard him however you like—but marry him!"

"No, Cousin William, you ask too much. Do you know what is required? To convert, I will be forced to renounce our German church as heresy."

What the devil is she talking about? He stares at her, confused.

"Yes, it's true and most dreadful," she continues, reading his expression. "At the moment of accepting the new faith I would be obligated to spit three times to repudiate Lutheranism. I can't do that—not even for Nicky."

"This is mandatory?" William asks.

"Yes."

"Only this prevents you from accepting him?"

"Also, my vow to my father. I promised Papa never to change belief."

"My dear, your father, were he alive today, would also be deeply concerned about the prospect of a bloody war should Germany and Russia drift any further apart. He would expect you to grasp the opportunity you have been given to prevent any such estrangement!"

She frowns.

"As a woman you can't be expected to understand," William says breezily, waving his hand. "Take my word for it. Now, on this spitting issue, let's see what I can do. Wait here."

LEFT ALONE, ALIX feels rather odd—pushed off-balance. Might the answer come back: yes, she's excused?

This possibility seems so unlikely that for a moment she's angry. *Don't get lured in!* But no, she can't help it. She longs to be released. She remembers dear Nicky this morning, appealing to her repeatedly, his tender eyes imploring. And she kept saying no, while her guilt and her sadness wound around her like ropes—constricting her chest. She could barely breathe. Compelled to deny those eyes, she hated herself. How has it come to this? That to give in would be odious, but to resist is to inflict misery upon a most precious soul? She felt as if she were torturing him, stabbing his spirit with a dagger, time after time. What a cruel beast she is. .

The door of the room swings open and William bounds in—this buffoon, this self-important oaf. How Papa abhorred him. But he looks very pleased with himself. Will her Prussian cousin be the angel of her deliverance?

"I've spoken to Nicky. The family will not insist on the formal renunciation. It will be left out of the ceremony," the kaiser declares.

Now Alix feels the skeptical edge of reason take over. If the requirement can so easily be dismissed, why wasn't this obstacle removed earlier?

"Are you certain?" she asks.

"I've just negotiated it! No one will dare go back on their word to me." Cousin William sounds annoyed.

"Tell me exactly what Nicky said."

"At first, he did not believe an exception could be made, but his uncle Grand Duke Vladimir was in the room also, come over to see what progress has been made. Everyone wishes you to accept the dear boy! Vladimir urged Nicky to act decisively. He knows Sasha desires your union, and the tsar heads the church and can command the priests as he sees fit. Vladimir instructed Nicky to agree, so he did. And here we are."

Alix's mind races. The world has shifted. New laws of nature apply. She will be allowed to marry Nicky? To love him, to live with him, to sleep alongside him?

"Don't be nervous," William says. "Nicky is so unhappy—we mustn't keep him waiting any longer. Are you prepared to accept him?"

She stares at her cousin, dazed. She's been granted what she most desires, apparently, and yet she resists absorbing this. Does she believe she isn't entitled to the gift? That a future so sunlit, so companionable, can't possibly be allowed to someone as unfortunate as she? The small girl robbed of her mother? The Sunny who lost dearest May? The orphaned young woman still mourning her adoring father?

The kaiser admonishes, "Come now. It is not often that a lady, in following her own inclinations, has such an opportunity to perform a wider good."

Ugh—she can listen to no more of William's absurd sermonizing. Nor does she need to! The ropes are unwinding. Fear and doubt are releasing their grip on her. She feels suddenly carefree.

"Might you ask Nicky to come in?" she proposes.

William grins and is gone.

Alix finds herself staring out the open window, marveling at the tall trees, bright green in first leaf. Today is her favorite sort of day—a trace of coolness remains in the crystalline spring air. And what a beautiful place Coburg is. Even this plain room and the matting on the floor, smelling of fresh straw, delight her.

She hears the door open, and she turns her head to meet Nicky's eyes. Never again does she have to torture the dear boy.

He approaches and says, "Darling Alix, is it true, do you consent?"

"I do." She stands; he embraces her.

Holding him, she feels his chest heaving with sobs. She begins to cry, too, her joy spilling over into tears.

"Do you think me a dribbling idiot for loving you as much as I do?" he asks, pulling away, showing her his wet face.

"How could I? I'm the same sort of idiot."

He leans in to kiss her. His mouth is soft, but pleasantly insistent. Her first kiss.

"I've dreamt of it—but I never believed I'd get a kiss from you," Alix whispers.

"So many more to come," he tells her.

"Say it again."

"For you, my bride, the kisses will never cease."

Chapter Twenty-Five

The Tsarevich Confesses

Coburg, Peterhof, England, April–July 1894

*N*icky's aunt, Marie, always claims the queen is square—as wide as she is tall. But having spent a few days now in the old lady's company, Nicky sees this isn't exactly true. Rather, Alix's grandmother is a round ball, propped up on short, unsteady legs. And on her last day before quitting Coburg, the queen takes Nicky aside.

"Alicky is wonderful, but so delicate, requiring a great deal of peace and quiet," she tells him sternly. "Her dear father's death, her brother's ascension, and all the subsequent anxiety about her future—these have tried her nerves terribly."

Nicky nods, straining to appear responsible and grave, the ideal future husband, protector, and helpmate.

"She is aware her new position in Russia will be full of trials and difficulties—she admits this to me," the queen goes on. "You've chosen to marry the only princess in Europe who has no interest in your wealth or your position. She is marrying you for love."

"Yes." Nicky is still incredulous that he and Alix will live together on intimate terms for the rest of their lives.

"Given this," the queen continues, "your duty will be to care for her most tenderly."

"And I always will." He bows.

"Now, Alicky tells me you would like to join her in England

for some weeks this summer. I will permit this, but only after she takes a cure." The queen has arranged for Alix to travel to Harrogate, a place in the north of England, for the sulfur baths. "That terrible pain in her back and legs must be remedied before she is married!"

"I agree," he says, nodding earnestly. In truth, Nicky dreads the prospect of being apart from Alix for seven weeks.

"And I understand you are willing to wait a year? The marriage will take place next spring?"

"Yes, as Alix desires time to study her new belief."

The old lady sighs, gazes disconsolately at Nicky, and shakes her head. "You are an appealing young man. I hope Alicky finds this sufficient compensation for the *many* sacrifices she must make to become your wife."

The queen pauses. "You may kiss my hand," she says, and he quickly grasps the plump white fingers she extends toward him, and brings them to his lips.

BACK AT PETERHOF, everyone hurries to congratulate Nicky. Even the servants, down to the youngest, shyest chambermaid, have kind words for him. Georgy has traveled from his home in the south to wish him joy in person. Mama desires to send Alix a gift—does Nicky know if she prefers rubies or emeralds? Only Xenia is put out. His sister has been engaged to their cousin Sandro for three months, but their mother refuses to set a date for the wedding.

"Yesterday I overheard Mama telling Lili Vorontsova there's no reason for you and Alix to wait! The sooner the better! Tell me, where's the justice in that?"

"It doesn't matter what she thinks; we won't marry for a year, as that is Alix's preference," Nicky explains.

Xenia scowls. "Watch, Mama will insist Sandro and I wait until after that. Which will be unbearable!"

Nicky understands how she feels. "I'll find an opportunity to speak with Papa, alone."

Looking up from his desk at the Lower Dacha, his father appears tired, and his cheeks are sunken—has he lost weight? But Papa gives Nicky a benign smile, and as they stroll out for a short walk along the shore Nicky finds his father in an expansive mood.

"I admit I did not believe the possibility of such a happy result for you, my boy."

"I am overjoyed."

"Is she quite set on waiting until next spring?"

"Yes."

"A shame."

"Necessary with all the preparation she must do, and she will pass the summer with her English family. So, Papa, you know, for Xenia—"

"I know, I know," he cuts in, laughing. "Your sister is impatient. I'll speak with your mother. Maybe Xenia's wedding can take place at the end of July."

"And in that case, will you agree I can go to England to see Alix for a few weeks beforehand?"

"Yes." Papa nods. "Now, what about that other business of yours?"

It takes Nicky a moment to understand. His father is referring to Matilda.

"I plan to buy the house on the English Prospekt and give it to her as a gift," Nicky says hurriedly. "That should end things in a nice way."

"You can't be certain—no woman enjoys being replaced," his father says.

"Sergei Mikhailovich has always admired her. I discussed it with him last night, and he's agreed to take care of Matilda. He will set her up in Strega for the summer. She'll be out of the way out there."

Papa nods. "Good. And I'll have Vorontsov send her father 100,000 rubles—as further guarantee of discretion."

FROM HARROGATE, ALIX sends Nicky the most loving letters— she finds it as unendurable as he does to be separated. But the baths are doing her good, and Ella has sent her books to read about the Orthodox religion.

Only the newspapermen disturb her peace. Having discovered her living in a quiet guesthouse, under the name Baroness Starkenburg, Alix and her lady companion, Gretchen von Fabrice, are now followed wherever they go—by reporters and curious townspeople both. She wishes, she tells him, to stick her tongue out at all these rude people.

It seems an endless time until the day Nicky boards the imperial yacht *Polar Star*—generously put at his disposal by Papa. He lands at Gravesend on the morning of June 20, in the pouring rain. Accompanied only by his valet, Nicky catches a train to London Bridge, where Alix's brother-in-law, Louis Battenberg, meets him. Together, unrecognized, they cross town to Waterloo Station and travel down to Walton-on-Thames.

And there—standing on a cheap flowered carpet, in front of a small coal fire, in the poky parlor of an undistinguished house—is his darling girlie.

"AT GRANDMAMA'S WE can't act like this," says Alix. Nicky and she sit together on a blanket under an elm tree in the Walton garden. "She never approves of such carrying-on."

"She'll have second thoughts about me, then," Nicky says, leaning over to kiss Alix. It's very decent of Victoria and Louis to leave them completely alone. Earlier in the day they walked along the high street, arm in arm, just the two of them.

"You must take care to restrain yourself at Windsor, Boysy dear."

Nicky laughs. "Did I tell you what happened the other week? Xenia perpetually hangs her arms around Sandro's neck, and they are constantly kissing in front of everyone—the mad creatures. This time they were playing Mama and Papa—as Georgy calls it—lying one on top of the other on an ottoman. And they broke it!"

Alix looks shocked.

"Georgy and I had to make up a story for Mama, about bouncing on it. Good thing it's not much longer until *that* wedding!" And he laughs again.

"How very indecorous of Xenia!"

"I blame Mama, she should have allowed those two to get married long since."

Little blonde Alice, Alix's niece, comes running out of the house and across the grass. She calls out, "Mama says if you don't mind the interruption, can you come in for tea?"

WHEN A LARGE black landau, with two outriders clad in the chocolate-brown livery of the queen's household, arrives to fetch them, the Walton neighbors emerge from their homes to stand in the street and gawk.

"No one suspected we had such important people stopping with us," says Victoria as she kisses Alix and Nicky goodbye.

They are driven over to Windsor, where they stay two days before traveling with the queen to Osborne. At least he and Alix are together, but Nicky sorely misses the hours of undisturbed intimacy at Walton. Even when they stroll down to the private white-sand beach, or drive out in the brake, through the woods, someone always accompanies them—one of Alix's giddy Holstein cousins, or the enormously fat Duchess of Teck.

He's delighted when, after a long, dull lunch with too many

elderly guests, Alix whispers to him, "Let's go out and sit by the fountain."

Maybe she will agree to go farther—and find a secluded spot on the grounds where they can be alone.

The afternoon is hot, and on the parterre there's little shade from the glaring sun.

Alix leads the way to an iron bench, and pulls out of her pocket what appear to be letters.

"Look at these," she says, passing them over.

One glance and his heart lurches. That rounded script—once so familiar, and so welcome, when he would find her notes in his pocket—appears now threatening and evil. The envelopes bear Russian stamps, and are addressed:

Princess Alix of Hesse
The Buckingham Palace
London, England.

Someone has scrawled beneath in red: *Forward to Osborne House.*

"Do you have any idea of the sender?" Alix asks. "They are not signed."

He unfolds one and then another. They are written in French. Phrases jump out:

You should know your fiancé loves another.

He only agrees to marry you because he is compelled to.

The tsarevich is false—he has given his heart already and will betray you.

He glances at Alix beside him. He feels ill. He can hardly speak.

"I am well acquainted with the person who wrote these letters," he says, forcing himself to fully meet her eyes.

Alix presses her lips together anxiously. She must anticipate what is coming.

"She's a ballet dancer called Matilda Kschessinska. She performed at camp, and I would see her also dance at the Mariyinsky Theater. You remember, we went there together for the ballet? In '89? That was before I knew Matilda."

Alix nods soberly.

"I found her pretty and nice, and yes, we flirted, but for a long time it was just that."

He sighs. He cannot avoid the painful revelation. "Last year, when I returned home from Berlin, when I thought you would never be mine, I succumbed to temptation, and she—I—we . . ."

"Oh no," she says, her eyes broad and horrified. "Do you love her?"

"No, of course not—I never loved her as I do you."

She flinches.

"I didn't intend to tell you about her. I hoped I wouldn't need to," he says, miserable. "But perhaps it's for the best that you know."

"Yes." But she still looks so unhappy.

"As soon as you accepted me, I arranged things. She was given a house, and her father received 100,000 rubles. Sergei Mikhailovich, my cousin, who has always liked her, will look after her from now on."

"Did you see her again, when you were back in Russia, after Coburg?" Her voice quavers.

"I did agree to meet her one more time, to say goodbye. But I did not go to her home. We met on the Volokhonsky Highway, a short ride from Krasnoye Selo. She cried a lot, but I thought she understood."

"Understood what?"

"How I have known you and loved you for so long. And that my marriage, someday, was inevitable."

"You hadn't promised her anything? She didn't imagine there would be more between you?"

"No."

Alix clutches her hands in her lap and looks away, off toward the sea.

"I was so weak; I am sorry," Nicky says. He's desperate for her to turn back to him, to smile. He wishes to lay his forehead on her shoulder and beg for her forgiveness.

I know I am a poor creature, but I am also your slave. Please stretch out a fond hand to me.

Finally, she turns and regards him silently. In the strong light, her eyes are like blue glass.

He must try to speak calmly. "Has this ruined everything? Have your feelings changed?" His voice is tremulous.

She shakes her head. "I was a beast, putting you through all that I did."

Sweet relief buoys him. "You're an angel." He reaches out and picks up her clenched hands, and cupping them in his own, attempts to bring them to his lips to kiss.

She pulls her hands away and stands up.

"Grandmama must be looking for us."

FOR THE REST of that day, Nicky watches Alix closely. She appears composed, but inside she must be reflecting on his detestable behavior. If only he were unblemished. Might she reconsider their marriage, now she knows the truth? She seems to have said no. Still Nicky yearns to read her thoughts.

He sleeps poorly and wakes early. Nervously pacing in his room, he notices his journal lying open on the desk. He didn't leave it so—he's written nothing for several days. He looks carefully, and sees lines written in Alix's hand. He's astounded. How did she find time last evening to slip into his room?

Have faith in your girlie dear, who loves you more deeply and devotedly than she can ever say. We are all tempted in this world, but as long as we repent God forgives us.

He hurries down to breakfast. She is already sitting at the table, and she beams at him as he slips into the chair next to hers. She leans over and whispers in his ear. "We'll never keep secrets from each other, will we?"

"No, we won't, dearest Sunny," he whispers back. Since their stay at Walton, he's been permitted to use the family nickname.

"I find I love you even more since you told me that little story," she says, and squeezes his hand.

FOR THEIR FINAL week together in England, Nicky and Alix visit Uncle Bertie and Aunt Alix at Sandringham.

Nicky admires the grounds of this house—the emerald-green lawns, the great clumps of azaleas and rhododendrons backed up against firs—but he doesn't much like the cramped over-furnished rooms inside, nor the strange crowd. Uncle Bertie has invited a lot of uncouth businessmen and their braying wives. The men are so coarse; the women wear too much paint on their faces. Thank goodness Alix agrees to take many long walks with him, and they share burning kisses.

If only he could take her by the hand, and lead her upstairs, there to undress her, see her body properly, touch her everywhere.

She seems to understand. "I know you're impatient, Boysy," she says on their last day. "But think how sweet it will be when we are married."

"Nine endless months from now," he teases.

"Yes, but you'll manage to come to Darmstadt in the autumn, won't you? We'll spend time together then."

He agrees.

"Without you I will be more Rainy than Sunny," she tells him the next day, when they part.

Chapter Twenty-Six

The Tsar Falls Gravely Ill

Darmstadt and the Crimea, September–October 1894

*A*lix is delighted that Ducky expects a baby in the spring. But she can't go to Russia to be married until Ernie is free to take her. When Alix writes to tell Nicky the news, she suggests their wedding take place at the end of June. Or July, perhaps? She hopes her Boysy doesn't find this further postponement too disheartening. Meanwhile, her Russian language is improving and she's learning so much during her religious instruction. And she's trying on the smart undergarments and nightgowns that will be part of her trousseau. Is he shocked she would mention this?

I suppose I ought to be shyer and primmer with you, like with others, but somehow I can't be.

She's disappointed when there's nothing flirtatious about Nicky's reply sent from the imperial family's Polish hunting lodge at Spala. He's very low. They've done no shooting—his father has been unwell since they arrived. A doctor from Berlin, a Dr. Leyden, has been summoned, and he says the tsar suffers from an inflammation of the kidneys, plus nervous exhaustion. Six months of complete rest in a warm climate is advised.

Rather than fly to Alix's side in Darmstadt as he so longs to, Nicky must sacrifice his own happiness to accompany his parents to Corfu, where the king of Greece has offered them a palace for the winter.

Alix feels too miserable for words at the thought they might not see each other for months.

"POOR UNCLE SASHA," says Ernie when he hears the latest. "He's normally so strong. It must be especially aggravating for him to feel unwell."

"And Nicky had so looked forward to some bison hunting. They never got out, not for a single day!" Alix tells her brother.

"Why worry," remarks Ducky, getting up from her chair and walking toward the sitting-room door. "A winter in the sun will restore Uncle Sasha."

"Of course one worries," says Ernie, quite sharply, to his wife. And he frowns at Alix behind Ducky's retreating back.

It concerns Alix that the newlyweds are not always in harmony—indeed often quarrel in heated tones. Alix can't imagine she and Nicky ever having such rows. But at least both Ernie and Ducky are very excited about the pending arrival.

IN HIS NEXT letter, from the Livadia Palace, Nicky reports his father struggles to walk on his swollen feet, suffers terrible headaches, and isn't up to traveling farther. They will stay here in the Crimea a month to allow the sea air to strengthen his dear Papa before sailing for Greece.

On October 17 a telegram from Nicky arrives at the Neues Palais. The tsar has fallen gravely ill. Will Alix come immediately?

Ernie insists Alix cannot travel alone. Ducky insists Ernie cannot leave her. Victoria, who happens to be staying with her children and Aunt Julie at Heiligenberg, agrees to accompany Alix as far as Warsaw. From there, Alix argues, she can manage on her own with Gretchen. But Ernie prevails on his adjunct,

Lieutenant General Claus Wernher, to go along. The four of them set off on October 19 via the night service to Berlin.

In the morning, waiting for them on the station platform is Cousin William.

"You must tell Nicky that he can depend on me, Alicky," the kaiser says to Alix, a strange, zealous look on this face. "I can advise him on everything—as I did at Coburg. Whatever he needs, he need only to ask me. I am his true friend."

Maybe because she's hardly slept on the train, Alix is bewildered. What is their cousin suggesting?

William escorts them onto the connecting train for Warsaw. Alix waits until he's left the compartment to ask her sister, sitting opposite: "What help does William imagine he might offer? Is he, too, planning to come to the Crimea? No one will want to see him!"

Victoria shakes her head. "William believes that when Nicky is tsar, he will feel at a loss and reach out to him for help. Such nonsense! Willy's dreaming! Serge and the rest of Sasha's brothers won't stand for any interference by the German kaiser."

Alix is still in a muddle. "William imagines Nicky will be tsar soon?"

Victoria nods sadly. "The Berlin newspapers report that Sasha has something called nephritis, a serious, often mortal kidney condition."

Alix regards her sister incredulously. How can something so monumental be announced as just another news report? "But Uncle Sasha won't die now?"

"We will pray not," says Victoria. "Still, dearest, I think you must prepare yourself for the worst."

Once, when she was seven or eight, Alix tumbled out of a hayloft at the farm at Heiligenberg—and fell eight feet down. She landed flat on her back and, knocked hard, stared up at the wooden roof dazed and unable to catch her breath.

She feels this again—stupefied. *Uncle Sasha dead? Nicky tsar?* It's a disaster, an end to everything, the ripping away of years and years that she and Nicky were to live in peace and quiet, have children, raise them without crushing pressure. And now—what? Will they be immediately thrust into the center of things, their lives no longer their own, always burdened, always watched?

She feels a shudder of fear, and black dread descends upon her. She has caused this. She brought Nicky bad luck. She's a *Pechvogel*—he should have stayed away.

She senses Victoria watching her closely.

"Should this happen, dearest Sunny," Victoria says, "do not imagine you will buckle. I know you. I know your strength of will."

Alix nods. Victoria has no idea what really frightens her.

"You can only lose your way if you obsess over things morbidly or sink into melancholy. And we all know you are quite capable of that."

Alix scowls at Victoria. How nasty of her sister to be patronizing and critical at this dire moment.

"You must remain rational. Put Nicky first. Stay calm. Think of what he needs."

"Of course I am thinking of my poor darling Boysy!" Alix exclaims. Does her older sister believe her selfish? Or hysterical? Unwilling to do whatever is necessary to support Nicky? Alix will always hold him tight in her arms, she will defend him unto death, and she will never forsake him.

She stares fiercely at Victoria and snaps, "How can you believe anything different?"

Victoria smiles. "Good, you are rising to occasion. As you must."

That evening, when they reach Warsaw, Alix still feels rather disgruntled with her sister. Still, it's a terrible wrench to wave goodbye to Victoria and watch her cross the station, heading for the hotel where she will spend the night before returning in the morning to Germany.

Alone in her narrow berth, the train rattling south through the night, Alix weeps.

LOOKING OUT THE window the next day at the miles and miles of scenery—tussocky fields and small, brown-roofed villages and huddles of dark wooden shacks set next to pastures—Alix thinks only of Nicky. What must he be feeling, her poor, sweet, precious darling? That this terrible fate might befall him when he is so young and inexperienced—it's ghastly.

But she mustn't lament, or curse fate. Duty calls. She will be with him. His troubles will be hers. They will share the burden. Certainly, they can't wait until next summer to be married. It must happen sooner. She looks down at the maroon-colored wool dress she has on. *I will be married in this if necessary.* First, she must be received into the Orthodox faith. She can tell Nicky as soon as she arrives—how the priest in Darmstadt said she has made so much progress. She is ready.

ON THE MORNING of the third day, she and Gretchen and Lieutenant General Wernher alight from the train at a dusty place called Simferopol. The shabby station reminds Alix of the one she saw at Verzhbolova, on her first morning in Russia, ten years ago now.

There is yet farther to go to see Nicky—a three-hour ride by coach to Alushta—along a winding road through the mountains. They pass white stone villages with square church towers that remind Alix a bit of the hill towns outside Florence. Finally, they catch a glimpse of blue-green water—the Black Sea.

Twenty minutes later, their coach stops in front of an inn, where Nicky and Serge wait with a half dozen guards.

Her Boysy is wearing a dark-green uniform and the round, black, tight-fitting astrakhan hat of the Russian army. When she sees his dear face, the forlorn expression shocks her. Nicky has never looked so small.

"What joy to be here with you, even in these circumstances," she whispers in his ear after they embrace.

"I feel half my cares and worries lifting off my shoulders," he whispers back.

They have a carriage to themselves for the two-hour journey to Livadia. When, along the way, Alix tells him of her resolution to be received into his faith immediately, so they can marry soon, without impediment, Nicky drops his face into his hands, overcome.

She reaches out to pull on both his wrists. She wants to gaze directly into his eyes. "Boysy, from now on you must look upon me as a part of yourself, and trust me fully."

THERE ARE TWO residences on the imperial estate, a larger stone one and a smaller wooden one. It's the second—the Maly Palace, a villa with Moorish fretwork balconies, overgrown with honeysuckle and vines—that Uncle Sasha has always preferred. Nicky's father declared this morning that he would be getting out of bed and putting on his full uniform to properly receive the future empress of Russia.

"But he might not have managed it—he's so weak," Nicky warns as they approach the front entrance.

They ascend the stairs to meet the tsar in his room, and find Uncle Sasha *is* up and dressed. Pale and gaunt, he looks like a ghost of himself. He struggles to rise to greet her—Aunt Minnie holding him by one arm, and Nicky rushing to take the other. On his feet he sways unsteadily. He kisses Alix on both her cheeks and collapses back down into his chair.

She is full of alarm. Surely, the tsar will not live long.

A WIDE, SOFT bed is so welcome after many nights on the train. The next morning Nicky comes to eat breakfast with her on her room's small covered balcony. Rain pours down. She smells the wet woodwork and hears the gutters run. Uncle Sasha, Nicky reports, is very pleased by her plan to change religions promptly. His personal confessor, Father John of Kronstadt, will meet with her later this morning to give her final instruction.

They wait together for the priest's arrival.

Alix is hurrying to finish some needlework she started in Darmstadt, an embroidered cover for the chalice, white lilies on pink satin. She wants it done in time for the service at which she will embrace her new belief.

Nicky sits across from her, watching listlessly.

"How is your father this morning?" she asks.

"I don't know. Dr. Leyden never tells me anything."

"What do you mean?"

"He reports only to Mama and Uncle Vladimir, sometimes Serge."

Alix feels instantly very angry. "As heir you should be first to know! You must be firm with Leyden about this."

Nicky shrugs. "He's preoccupied."

"Which doesn't matter. Let's go and speak to him now."

They find Dr. Leyden standing in a small room off the upstairs passageway, conferring with a nurse. He appears surprised to see them.

"We have come to know the details of His Imperial Majesty's condition," Alix says, in clipped German.

"He's eaten quite well, and spent a quiet night. I gave him a sleeping draught," the doctor replies. A tall, imperious man of about sixty, he has a long nose and bushy brows. He assesses Alix with a shrewd eye. She refuses to be intimidated.

"What are the prospects for his recovery?" she asks sharply.

The doctor cocks his head. "He may gain some strength, but he will never be the man he was."

Alix looks pointedly at Nicky, to prompt him.

"I must have more frequent reports from you," Nicky says in a tentative voice.

The doctor's expression softens a bit, and he bows his head at Nicky, "Certainly, Your Imperial Highness."

As they walk away Alix whispers, "Remember, show your own mind, and never let others forget who you are."

THE SUN COMES out in the afternoon. The breeze is moist and mild, and the smell of flowers is everywhere. She wishes Ernie, too, were here to see lovely Livadia.

They walk down the cliff path, following the tight turns above the steep drop. Once on the beach, they remove their shoes. Walking across the small stones makes Alix's feet slightly ache. The water slips in with a quiet sigh, breaks in a long line, and slips out again, hissing against the pebbles. Clear at the edge, it extends to the horizon, an ever deepening blue.

Little more than a week ago, the future was a calm sea of years stretching out before her and Nicky—as far as they could see. No longer.

IN THE EVENING they sit together again on her balcony. By candlelight, Nicky is signing papers, reminding Alix of Papa. From time to time, he looks up and smiles at her, as if reassured by her presence.

Occasionally she feels like her heart might burst with love for Nicky. And they have been gay today, in snatched moments.

Alone with Nicky she is never uncomfortable, never ill at ease—she's a chatterbox, actually. If only she could feel more relaxed with the rest of his family. This residence and the other are crowded with all of the tsar's relations. Many of whom she barely knows, and all of whom she struggles to speak with naturally. Will she ever lose her terrible shyness? Ernie always advises she take a deep, calming breath before beginning to converse. But even so, her mouth feels frozen, her teeth sealed together, and when she does speak her voice wavers, and makes odd swoops up and down in register.

She must compel herself to do better. Her new life will demand it.

ONLY ELLA AND Serge are present with Alix and Nicky in the chapel the next afternoon when Father John receives her into the Orthodox Church. Her sister looks quietly ecstatic—her whole face radiant. She's affectionate toward Alix but seemingly more wrapped up in her own experience of this exalted moment, than in what Alix feels.

One might think the service is for Ella, not me.

Alix immediately rebukes herself—she mustn't harbor unkind thoughts on a sacred day. And she does feel a profound sense of rightness when she's anointed with the holy oil. She's done this for Nicky, and for that reason it's no sacrifice. It's a privilege. She prays to God to help her be always a good Christian, and show her how to best serve Him in her new faith.

She and Nicky, with Ella and Serge, take communion together.

ON HIS FINAL day, Uncle Sasha speaks only to Aunt Minnie.

His skin is gray, his eyes bulge in his face, and his legs are very swollen. But rather than lie in bed, he prefers to sit up, by the window.

Roses are brought to him, the thorns snipped off at his request. He keeps the flowers in his lap, and wordlessly he distributes them, one by one, to those who come into the room to say goodbye.

When he passes a pink rose to Alix, she finds herself tongue-tied. She had planned to ask Uncle Sasha to pray for them. To bless Nicky and her, specially, with an appeal to God for His protection as they embark on their treacherous future.

But, inevitably, she's struck mute. She gazes into the tsar's eyes and sees there his quiet, wistful regret. He is leaving them to their fate, because he cannot do otherwise.

Chapter Twenty-Seven

The Prince of Wales Takes Charge

Livadia Palace, October 1894

*T*hree days and three nights on the train, with a sea voyage to follow—to Bertie's mind it is the most arduous and miserable journey he has ever undertaken.

Having departed London with a single goal, to see Sasha alive once more, he and his wife, Alix, reach Vienna only to learn that the tsar has breathed his last. "My poor sister, my dearest Minnie, left a widow and not even fifty years old," his wife moans.

Onward. Ever eastward. By rail to Sevastopol and then by boat for four hours to Yalta—a small place, nestled within an amphitheater of gray, cypress-studded hills, with tall mountains beyond.

As they disembark Bertie hears, as he did when touring Egypt, the chants of the muezzin summoning the faithful to prayer. Sasha's youngest brother, Paul, has come to collect them. The grand duke looks very glum.

"We're in chaos without Sasha," Paul admits as they drive along a road lined with palms. "Minnie is distraught and exhausted, Nicky is overwhelmed, and my brothers quarrel constantly amongst themselves, and with Nicky, and clash with the court minister Vorontsov."

"What are these disputes over?" Bertie asks.

"Funeral arrangements mostly, and also Nicky's desire to be married immediately."

"Not here?"

"Yes, here. Your niece Alix was received into the Orthodox Church the day before Sasha died, and Nicky refuses to allow her to return to Darmstadt. He wants the wedding to take place while Sasha's body is still with us. Poor boy, he longs for the comfort of a wife. He never wished to be tsar, he's told me, and he looks sick with dread."

"But to hold a tsar's wedding privately? *En famille?*"

"Yes, it's an absurd idea, only Minnie supports it. She's worried Nicky can't cope otherwise."

"My sister must be in despair. What does Alicky say?" asks his wife quietly.

"She will do whatever Nicky wants. Your niece remains admirably composed, unlike our new sovereign."

Bertie sighs and shakes his head. When Nicky and Alicky stayed at Sandringham in July, they appeared intoxicated with each other—always sidling out of rooms, gone for hours. "The love birds," Louise and Maud called them. Bertie found the young man pleasant enough, although oddly immature. Too much time behind palace walls, not enough rough-and-tumble with ordinary folk—that's Bertie's view.

At Victoria Station, seeing them off, Gladstone said: "Your Highness, should the worst happen, if the tsar should die, we must keep his son on side with us, and away from the kaiser."

"The tsarevich and I got on well this summer, and I'll be on the spot to provide advice and direction," Bertie assured the prime minister. Now he's arrived he wonders what form, exactly, this guidance should take.

MINNIE IS WAITING in the dark and dank drawing room of the Maly Palace. Bertie's wife and she fall into each other's arms and begin sobbing loudly.

"Dearest Sasha told me I must remain calm, but how can I?" Minnie wails.

So strange, really. On the one hand, Sasha was a double-dyed reactionary and something of a sadist. And yet on the other, a devoted husband and father—plus an amiable brother-in-law. On holiday together in Denmark, Bertie and Sasha shared plenty of jokes about the challenges of being married to a pair of very excitable sisters.

Nicky and Alicky emerge out of a far corner of the room. Bertie kisses his niece on both cheeks. Black does not suit her—she appears pallid and stone-eyed. Nicky looks haunted, and he speaks in a tremulous voice. "Uncle Bertie," he says. "How will I manage? I know nothing about the business of ruling."

"You will learn, my boy. You will learn. But first things first. What are the funeral plans?"

"Nothing has been decided. My uncles aren't agreeing—"

"Nicky's uncles consider themselves in charge of everything, which is quite wrong," Alicky says, cutting in. "They don't have enough respect for their new tsar, especially Vladimir."

Sharp and furious, she's a much more commanding presence than her fiancé.

"Where are your uncles, Nicky?"

"Now? In the chapel, I believe. We moved Papa there just this morning," he answers.

"You two will show me."

"Can we first talk about . . ." Nicky trails off and glances over anxiously at Alicky.

"Nicky would like us to be married here, now—this evening, or tomorrow," she explains.

Bertie shakes his head. "On balance an ill-advised idea, I fear, my dears."

"And why?" she demands.

"The wedding of the tsar should take place in the capital, in suitable surroundings, with the appropriate guest list. The people will expect it."

"The people will understand," she answers.

Bertie smiles. "You have been living in Russia for how long, Alicky?"

She frowns. "Nicky's express wishes should not be denied."

"We can discuss this later," says Bertie. "I need to see Sasha first."

Leaving his wife to comfort her sister, Bertie crosses the lawn with the two young people.

"Dear Sasha passed peacefully?" he asks Nicky.

"Yes, thank God. Papa had a serene smile on his face when he died—it was remarkable," he reports. "But then last night he swelled out dreadfully; his stomach became enormous. There's a smell . . ."

Bertie stares at the new emperor of Russia. "The body has not been embalmed?"

"Men were delayed in coming from Sevastopol, and I'm not sure how good a job they did."

Inside the marble chapel, the walls are draped in black. The mortal remains of his brother-in-law lie in an open coffin in front of the altar. There's a definite whiff of putrefaction in the air.

Good God, the embalmers muffed it.

A dozen or so Romanov men, dressed in full uniform, stand about, a few kneeling in front of the casket. Bertie has never been able to keep Sasha's multitudinous relatives straight.

Surprised looks, a murmur of approbation, and then striding toward him comes a thickset individual Bertie recognizes as Grand Duke Vladimir, Sasha's oldest surviving brother—the haughty Grand Duke Serge a step behind.

"By God, it's wonderful to see you," Vladimir says, and Serge gives him a sharp nod. Bertie has never warmed to his niece Ella's husband—he recoils from the gleam of fanaticism in that man's eyes. And why does this Serge wear his clothes so tight?

"What a terrible loss; I grieve with you," Bertie says.

"An enormous tragedy has befallen all of Russia," Vladimir replies.

"We will struggle to go on without my brother," Serge adds.

"Facing the many challenges that we do," Vladimir continues.

Nicky is standing beside Bertie, but the two grand dukes speak directly to him, without acknowledging their new sovereign. Bertie can see why Alicky is infuriated.

"What plans for the funeral?" Bertie asks.

"Still to be arranged. There has been a distracting discussion about a wedding." Now Vladimir glares at Nicky and Alicky. The new tsar looks down at the floor. His niece boldly returns the grand duke's hostile stare, but the color rises in her cheeks.

"Let me wash up, and shall we confer on everything?" Bertie suggests. "Funeral *and* wedding? As the bride has no father living, I will represent her interests. We'll take up the funeral first?"

"Definitely funeral first," Vladimir bellows.

Bertie holds up his hand in a gesture of acknowledgment, which is also a plea for restraint. "We can talk this over calmly, can we not? In the bigger palace in an hour, say? Is there a suitable room there, with a table and chairs?"

Vladimir agrees there is, and Bertie exits the chapel with the engaged couple.

"Thank you, Uncle Bertie," Alicky says immediately.

"Don't thank me yet. I'm not sure the Romanovs will listen to me."

"They will. You're the Prince of Wales," says Alicky, sounding perfectly confident.

"Which may count for nothing here," he replies, rueful.

"Nicky will follow your lead, won't you, dearest?" she prods.

"Certainly," Nicky says. "But please, Uncle, I don't want to wait a year to be married."

"No, you shouldn't have to," says Bertie. "Perhaps the ceremony can take place this winter?"

Nicky looks stricken. "The Christmas fast begins in a few weeks' time. No weddings are permitted—we'd have to wait until mid-January."

"Isn't it simpler to celebrate the marriage here, quickly and quietly?" Alicky says.

He smiles at her. "Simpler yes, proper no."

Alicky nods sadly. Maybe she sees sense. Nicky, meanwhile, is grinding the back of his hand into his mouth.

Have some dignity, man! With effort, Bertie keeps himself from shouting at the new tsar.

"Come, Boysy, let's take a short walk while Uncle prepares," Alicky says, and, reaching for her fiancé's hand, leads him away.

NEVER, BERTIE REFLECTS, has he attended a meeting with so many clenched fists thumping on the table, making such a tremendous racket.

The new tsar's four uncles—Vladimir, Alexis, Serge, and Paul—are all large men, and they prefer to communicate with one another by shouting, even when they essentially agree. The minister of the imperial court, Count Vorontsov, has, quite reasonably, been getting on with arrangements for the funeral and lying in state, first in Moscow and then in St. Petersburg. This incenses the grand dukes. How very irregular! Most unfitting! All details should have been approved by the late tsar's brothers first. The minister has gone behind their backs!

Bertie is forced to declare loudly, several times, "In English, please, gentlemen!"

Vorontsov stays calm, a placid look on his face. Bertie admires his sangfroid.

After allowing the grand dukes to shout for a quarter of an hour, Bertie puts his hand in the air and says, "I have a modest proposal."

They quiet immediately. He continues: "Shall we commend the court minister for his efforts? Shall we ask him to circulate a paper outlining the arrangements he's made thus far? Those of you with objections may submit them, in writing, by ten o'clock tomorrow morning. And Count Vorontsov will address them. How would that be?"

Sasha's brothers exchange looks and nods, and then Vladimir announces, "This is acceptable to us."

Bertie suspects that, when it comes to it, the grand dukes will have no objections.

He poses his own question to Vorontsov: "Will you send for new embalmers? I think the need is clear."

The man assents immediately.

"Next, we must decide, when should Nicky and Alicky's wedding take place?" Bertie asks. His niece has not been invited to this conference, but the young groom-to-be sits to Bertie's right, tense.

"Not here, and not now," says Vladimir.

"The Russian people would feel cheated if the ceremony is private," Paul says.

"They might doubt the validity of the marriage, or suspect that the bride has some defect, or something to hide," Alexis declares.

"And after the death of the tsar, court mourning always lasts for a full year," puts in Serge.

"That's a long time," says Bertie. "Mourning could not be lifted for a day?"

"We must not hold the wedding here!" repeats Vladimir.

"No, I think the couple will concede the ceremony must be held in St. Petersburg," Bertie says, and turns to give Nicky a meaningful look.

The young man gazes back at him, dejected. "This is contrary to my wishes," he says quietly.

"Perhaps on Minnie's birthday . . ." Paul says, ignoring Nicky.

"And when is her birthday?" asks Bertie.

"November fourteenth, here in Russia conveniently the day before the Christmas fast begins," says Serge.

"That's it, then, let's hold the wedding on that day," says Bertie. "Count Vorontsov, what do you think? Can the arrangements be made in time?"

"For the religious service, yes. If there were to be a banquet—"

"There will be no banquet, you idiot. Not with the court in mourning," Vladimir growls.

The minister answers serenely, "Of course, Your Imperial Highness, just as you say."

"Nicky, you will agree?" asks Bertie.

The new tsar sighs, and says, "Yes."

Meeting adjourned. Bertie feels in dire need of a drink, or two.

MINNIE DESCRIBES HOW, during the last days of his life, looking out from his window, Sasha admired a new warship, *Pamiat Merkuria*, riding at anchor in the Yalta Harbor. Now this ship has the sad task of bearing Sasha's body, and all the rest of them, to Sevastopol for the first segment of what will be a five-day, sixteen-hundred-mile-long journey to St. Petersburg.

The lengthy train, draped with black bunting, inches north. At every station, peasants throng the platform. They fall to their knees as the train slowly passes—women keening, men twisting their caps in their hands.

The second day of the journey is Bertie's fifty-third birthday. Nicky and Alicky come to his compartment to offer their congratulations. The young man appears very cast down. His fiancée looks tired and on edge.

"I do wish people wouldn't call me Your Majesty—it sounds like a bad joke," Nicky says.

"You'll grow accustomed to this," Bertie replies.

"I suppose I must," says Nicky, bleak. "Uncle Bertie, I know nothing. Papa never foresaw his death, and did not include me in any state business."

Foolish of Sasha to leave the young man so unprepared. "Take time to learn," Bertie counsels. "To start, choose amongst your father's men the ones you most trust, and rely on them. Quiz them closely—why are they supporting one policy rather than another? Allow debate in your presence so you have a full picture of the issues. Your uncles will be eager to share their opinions, but don't feel obligated to do as they say. Once you make a decision, stick to it. Should you discover you've chosen unwisely, admit it, and change course. I warn you to be suspicious of the kaiser, who will immediately try to get you to see things his way—when it comes to the French, the Balkans, the Straits, et cetera."

For a moment, Nicky looks resolute. "Papa disliked William, and never trusted him."

"With good reason. Don't allow William to presume on the family connection to conduct state business directly with you. Force him to go through your ministers."

"*My* ministers. Even that sounds inconceivable," says Nicky.

Alicky gives her intended a worried look. She is beautiful, this niece, Bertie has always thought it. He remembers how besotted poor dear Eddy was with her, for a brief time. Only her habitual hard expression detracts from an otherwise delicate, flawless face.

"If you follow your father's example in all things, and do what he would do, all will be well, Boysy," Alicky says.

"Up to a point," puts in Bertie, quickly. He is duty-bound to help these children. "Grant yourself a short apprenticeship, Nicky. Once you've been in post for a year, begin to think about the future. How best to rule, as a sovereign, in this modern age. Devise a program of reform."

Nicky looks baffled.

"Not on your own, naturally—with your trusted team," Bertie says, a tad impatient.

"Papa always said change would only create chaos," Nicky answers.

"Russia is nothing like England, Uncle," Alix says. "I have been reading about this, and have had several long discussions with Serge. The Russian people revere their tsar as their 'little father.' To them he's a sacred figure. To interfere with autocratic rule, ordained by God, would be disastrous."

She looks at Bertie sternly.

He nearly laughs. This girl, educated to be a glorified *Hausfrau*, to make dinner conversation with the grandees of Darmstadt, presumes to lecture him on statecraft? His sister Vicky has always said it. The Hesse girls think too highly of themselves—having lost their sensible and intelligent mother while still very young. Never has he seen this so clearly!

"My dear Alicky," he says, his tone sharper, "all thrones are vulnerable nowadays. The Russian one, the Prussian, even ours at home. Consider your primary task to make a comfortable and welcoming home. If you hope to support your husband with his work, urge him to find and retain competent and loyal advisers. Governance is best left to them."

He turns to Nicky. "And for your part, Nicky, the job is to keep up the dignity of the crown while evolving it. You will need the finest minds in Russia to help you do that."

The new tsar gazes back at him with an uncertain expression on his face—as if he can't quite follow. His niece just looks annoyed.

Jesus, save us.

THE NEXT EVENING, they reach Moscow, where the tsar's body lies in state for twenty hours at the Kremlin. They pass another night on the train before arriving in Petersburg. From the station they go in a slow procession of carriages behind the funeral cortege to the Peter and Paul Fortress. Four hours are required to cover little more than three miles. The coffin is placed on a catafalque, and each member of the family must ascend the five steps to kiss the corpse. The air is heavy with incense. A band of priests drone on—*Gospodi pomiloui . . . Gospodi pomiloui . . . Gospodi pomiloui*—a relentless, melancholy chant.

When it's Bertie's turn to kiss Sasha's cheek, he sees the dead tsar's face has turned black.

Chapter Twenty-Eight

Their Majesties, the August Newlyweds

St. Petersburg, November 14, 1894

*A*fter days and days of standing in church, of praying and listening to prayers, Alix will do the same today—except today she will wear white instead of black.

Last evening, leaving her at the Sergievsky palace, Nicky whispered, "This must be someone else's wedding, because how could ours be happening in such melancholy circumstances?"

And now, as Alix stands in front of the same gilded mirror as Ella did when she was married, in the same enormous Malachite Room of the Winter Palace, and clad in a near-identical dress—white brocade edged with ermine at the neck and along the hem—she struggles not to weep. Her sister's wedding was a joyous occasion—this one cannot be, without Papa or Uncle Sasha.

Leaving Darmstadt a month ago, she carried two cases. An army of seamstresses here in St. Petersburg hastily stitched up the wedding dress, and several additional black gowns for her, because tomorrow, with the wedding behind them, the entire imperial family will resume wearing full mourning.

Ella has helped her pull on white lace stockings, wriggle into six wide, starched petticoats, and then don the gown itself—although the job of supervising her nuptial toilette is properly Aunt Minnie's.

Nicky's mother, very frail, looks on from a gilt chair to the side. She has trouble standing for any length of time. Her eyes are red and swollen, and she says barely a word. Her white velvet court gown is trimmed with gold lace, and she wears a pearl-and-diamond tiara and heavy matching necklace, but the ornate garb swamps her. She's like a flower with a broken stem, head drooping, shoulders slumping, a balled-up handkerchief clutched in her hand.

"If only Minnie could have stayed at home," Alix whispers to Ella, with a glance at Nicky's mother.

Her sister shakes her head. "Impossible—although I feel for her."

Ella circles Alix, pulling on the skirt so it lies smoothly over the underskirt of silver tissue. Scanning the room, crowded with grand duchesses and various chattering Romanov maids of honor, Ella asks: "Where is Monsieur Delcroix? He was due an hour ago."

The hairdresser, a thin and languid man, had called yesterday at the Sergievsky Palace to meet Alix and match her natural hair color with a range of false curls he brought along. He's not kept his promise to be prompt.

"I'll be late to my own wedding. On top of everything else," Alix says.

"You mustn't worry," answers Ella, her tone faintly chiding. "Clear your mind and think only of the sacred vows you are soon to make."

The hairdresser's absence fits in with the day's undercurrent of grief and disarray. Perhaps Ella could float above this, but Alix feels agitated and uneasy, although for the moment her part to play is a passive one. She's required to stand still, in front of the mirror, like a giant doll, and let others make her ready. She has to give herself over to something much bigger than she is. Tears prick the corners of her eyes.

Stop, you mustn't. No self-pity, no tears, be reasonable.
Nicky deserves a composed bride.

IT WAS A misunderstanding at the palace gates, apparently.
A sentry on duty suspected Monsieur Delcroix's pass to be a
forgery. When the hairdresser began arguing loudly, guards
threatened him with arrest. Just then, thank goodness, Nicky's
cousin, Grand Duke Konstantin, arrived with his wife, who recognized Delcroix and had him admitted.

Now the hairdresser is working rapidly, pulling on Alix's
hair, coiling it into a bun high on the back of her head. On
either side of her are Ella and Aunt Marie, posed like two tur-
baned servant boys presenting pillows laden with treasure—in
this case, Catherine the Great's jewels, the elaborate pieces
Alix remembers Ella wearing.

"We have only to get these on, the crown, and the veil," Ella
says. "We will be a mere forty minutes behind time."

Aunt Marie exclaims, "And the mantle!"

Alix won't wear a red velvet mantle as Ella did—cloth-of-
gold is thought more appropriate for the bride of an emperor.

"To be pinned on last thing," Ella directs. "We'll need to
summon the pages to carry it once it's attached."

NICKY, WAITING OUTSIDE the Malachite Room flanked by
Georgy and Misha, wears a happy smile. Good. Alix is relieved
he has put aside his low mood of yesterday—even if she finds
it impossible to do the same. She forces herself to return his
smile.

Now someone in the crowded corridor is waving at her. A
beaming, cheery face. Who on earth could this be? Oh, it's
Ernie. He grins and waggles his eyebrows at her in a comic way.
She feels her shoulders and her neck relax, she lifts her chin in
acknowledgment, and quickly rolls her eyes at him.

He laughs. Her brother understands—it's all so much to endure but what can she do?

Her spirit lighter, Alix takes her place at the front of the procession, as directed by the master of ceremonies. With sorrowing Aunt Minnie beside her, Nicky directly behind—handsome in his red Hussar uniform, a white dolman slung across his shoulder—and a troop of forty family members and foreign royals following, they begin to process to the palace church. Because there isn't room for everybody inside, and no banquet will follow the ceremony, observing the procession is the day's spectacle for most of the guests.

A ribbon of red carpet winds through one enfiladed room after another. At the entrance of each cavernous chamber, a guard of honor noisily draws out sabers and holds them high. The ensuing wave of curtsying and bowing recalls for Alix a strong wind gusting across a field of tall grain. But the atmosphere is neither fresh nor airy. Although lilies brought from the greenhouses at Tsarskoye Selo are banked against the walls, the crowded rooms smell not of fresh flowers but of cologne and of camphor—so many ladies have brought out their best furs for the occasion.

AT THE ALTAR, Alix trembles, her cheeks burn, and her mouth quivers. She finds by lowering her head, tucking her chin, and looking up at the Metropolitan from this angle, her agitation lessens and her responses come out evenly enough. Nicky, she notices, has to be prompted to complete aloud each line of his vows.

She instructs herself to breathe slowly in and out. The smoky incense makes her dizzy, but she mustn't fall over. On this cold, clear day sunlight streams in the high windows—rays catching the facets of a thousand gemstones. Astonishing, really, the riches on display, adorning the head and neck and arms of every woman present. Although what did she expect? The world she is joining is one of fantastic wealth. As a child the drama of Russia amazed her—the sheer scale of everything, the ornate, sprawling palaces, the vast distances, the extremes of light and darkness. Now she is older, she's shocked by the prodigality of the Romanovs, their negligence and moral haphazardness, their disdain for moderation. Her home with Nicky mustn't be like that. If she has one resolution for her marriage, beyond loving Nicky with every fiber of her being, it is to create a sphere apart, away from his family, where order, humility, and simple, good manners will prevail. This she can give him, and also children, dear little ones they will protect and nurture.

The Metropolitan recites the benediction, the choir bursts into a Te Deum, and the long service comes quite abruptly to an end. She's swept along with Nicky, in a wave of people, out of the church and into the lofty 1812 gallery.

Once there, somehow, in the crush of bodies, they are separated. Family and friends cluster around Nicky, calling out congratulations. His uncles pound him on the back. This raucous group, Nicky at its center, advances into the adjoining blue-and-white St. George's Hall, leaving Alix behind. The six pages charged with carrying her mantle have vanished. Without them, when she tries to step forward, she cannot. The cloth-of-gold hanging from her shoulders, like a weighty anchor, pins her to the spot. As the gallery rapidly empties and no one looks back, she strains to advance. It's impossible. Now this is too much—she has come to the end of her endurance. Trapped, alone, and abandoned, she feels dread flood through her. She has been acquired only to be discarded? How long will she be left here forlorn? Why do they all care so little for her?

Alix begins to sob. She shudders. She can't catch her breath properly. Just as she thinks she will sink to the floor she spies

Ernie approaching. "Here you are! What's the matter?" her brother asks. "Are you plotting an escape?"

"No," she replies, teary. "This wretched mantle prevents me from moving—it's so heavy on top of the gown."

"Oh, my dear. I hadn't . . . Let me go and get help."

"Don't leave me here alone!"

"It will only take a moment to fetch—"

"Sunny?" She hears Nicky's voice. Her new husband is walking quickly toward her. "Dearest, I lost sight of you. Aren't you coming?"

A balm like no other—the tender look in those splendid eyes. It takes a moment for the fear to subside, her breath to steady, her heart to unclench. But then she smiles.

"I would, but I'm held fast. Won't you set me free?"

The marriage of Nicky and Alix was a supremely happy one, and their love endured until their final, violent hour.

As empress, Alix was not a success. Russians never warmed to her. And her health collapsed under many pressures, particularly the illness of her only son.

Nor did Nicky prove equal to the gargantuan task thrust upon him, aged twenty-six, when his father died. He clung to the autocratic principles Sasha had espoused, despite calls for reform from all corners of society. Alix supported him in this, stubbornly believing that a mystical bond between the Russian peasantry and their "little father," the tsar, would keep the throne safe.

Their tragedy began at home. Alix had four daughters and then finally, in 1904, gave birth to a son and heir. Immediately, baby Alexei showed symptoms of hemophilia. Like her sister Irène, her mother Alice, and her grandmother Queen Victoria, Alix was a carrier of the disease, which at that time could not be effectively treated.

Revolution first broke out in Russia in the winter of 1905, and on February 17, Serge was blown to pieces outside the Kremlin by a terrorist's bomb tossed into his lap as he sat in his carriage. Hearing the explosion, suspecting what it meant, Ella ran out on to the street, where shocked but composed, she helped to gather up her husband's remains. Over the next few years she sold off her property, including all her jewels, and used the funds to found a hospital and a convent, installing herself as abbess.

Alix and Ella met for the final time in December 1916, when Ella traveled from Moscow to Tsarskoye Selo to beg her sister to banish Rasputin, the self-proclaimed holy man and healer who had already badly damaged her reputation. Alix, convinced only Rasputin could keep Alexei alive, refused.

Nicky was forced to abdicate in March 1917. Alix and Nicky and their five children were kept under house arrest until the Bolsheviks seized power in October, after which they were transported to Tobolsk in Siberia, and later moved to Yekaterinburg.

In March 1918, Kaiser Wilhelm, through the German ambassador in Moscow, negotiated for Ella's safe passage out of Russia. But she refused to leave Moscow, and continued to minister to the poor and the sick. Lenin ordered her arrest in May, and she, too, was sent east.

On the night of July 16, 1918, Nicky and Alix and their children were shot and bayoneted to death in the basement of the house where they had been confined in Yekaterinburg. The next night Ella was beaten and thrown into an abandoned mine near Alapayevsk, along with five other Romanovs, including Grand Duke Sergei Mikhailovich, the former lover of dancer Matilda Kschessinska. The executioners next hurled grenades down the shaft, suspecting their victims might not yet be dead. How long Ella survived at the bottom of the mine is not known.

Lenin allegedly remarked that Ella's murder was necessary, because "virtue with the crown on it is a greater enemy to the world revolution than a hundred tyrant tsars."

In 1921, Victoria and Louis Mountbatten (they were compelled to Anglicize the German Battenberg name during World War I), having learned that Ella's body had been recovered and taken by a faithful priest to the Russian Orthodox Mission in Peking, arranged for her grave there to be dug up and her remains to travel by ship to Port Said. From there, the Mountbattens accompanied Ella's coffin by road to Jerusalem, where Ella was laid to rest in the Church of Mary Magdalene—the church she and Serge saw consecrated in 1888.

Victoria lived until 1950. Her eldest daughter, Alice, later a princess of Greece and Denmark, was the mother of Prince Philip, Duke of Edinburgh. On December 15, 1948, Victoria attended the christening of her great-grandson, the future King Charles III, as one of his eight godparents.

Sources

$\mathscr{A}$lix's correspondence with her brother Ernie, beginning with the notes they sent each other as children while recovering from diphtheria, has been assembled in a single volume, and ably annotated by Petra Kleinpenning. Another remarkable book that aided in the writing of this novel is *A Lifelong Passion: Nicholas and Alexandra, Their Own Story*, compiled by Andrei Maylunas and Sergei Mironenko, which includes not only letters Nicky and Alix wrote to each other, but selections from their diaries, and the letters and diaries of those who knew them best. Many of these documents became available only after the fall of the Soviet regime in 1991. It's unfortunate that Serge ordered his correspondence burned, so his bond with his wife, Ella, which was the subject of much speculation during their lifetimes, remains something of a mystery. I found in Christopher Warwick's excellent biography of Ella, *The Life and Death of Ella, Grand Duchess of Russia*, excerpts from Ella's revealing letters to her father at the time of her conversion to Orthodoxy. *Bread of Exile: A Russian Family*, by Dimitri Obolensky, includes two fascinating testimonials—the memoirs of his grandmother Countess Sandra Shuvalova and Great-Aunt Sofka Demidov—which I drew upon for the chapter recounting Alix's fateful winter visit to St. Petersburg in 1889.

For a full list of the memoirs, biographies, and historical accounts upon which I relied, see my website, claremchugh.com.

Acknowledgments

A Royal Air Force raid on the night of September 11–12, 1944, destroyed the Neues Palais and much of central Darmstadt, but Jagdschloss Wolfsgarten still stands. I am grateful to Donatus, Landgrave of Hesse, for allowing me to visit Wolfsgarten, where on a tranquil afternoon in May, I felt I only had to turn in one direction to spy Ella and Serge walking across the meadow, and turn another to see Alix and Ernie chasing Tyrus the dog around the grassy court. Many thanks to Claudia Brueckner in the office of the Hessische Hausstiftung, who kindly coordinated my visit, and to Michele McAloon for accompanying me there.

Kate Kazin, my dear friend, was for two years via Zoom my invaluable writing partner. I relied, too, on Sandra Newman, for her discernment and generous encouragement. I am indebted to Paul McHugh for his unstinting support, to Wendy Greenbaum, Jacqueline Laurence, Lucia Macro, Beth McHattie, Faith Moore, and Colette Willis for their comments on early versions of the manuscript, and to Marc Denison, who improved both the English and German prose.

Everyone who works with Mark Lasswell knows of his extraordinary skill as an editor. I am no exception. And I am grateful, too, for his companionship, which enlivens every day.

READ MORE BY
CLARE McHUGH

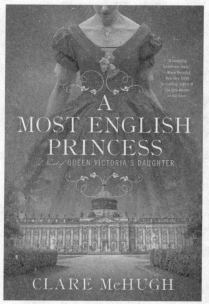

Perfect for fans of the BBC's *Victoria*, Allison Pataki's *The Accidental Empress*, and Daisy Goodwin's *Victoria*, this debut novel tells the gripping and tragic story of Queen Victoria's eldest daughter, Victoria, Princess Royal.

To the world, she was Princess Victoria, daughter of a queen, wife of an emperor, and mother of Kaiser Wilhelm. Her family just called her Vicky…smart, pretty, and self-assured, she changed the course of the world.

January 1858: Princess Victoria glides down the aisle of St. James Chapel to the waiting arms of her beloved, Fritz, Prince Friedrich, heir to the powerful kingdom of Prussia. Although theirs is no mere political match, Vicky is determined that she and Fritz will lead by example, just as her parents Victoria and Albert had done, and also bring about a liberal and united Germany.

Brought up to believe in the rightness of her cause, Vicky nonetheless struggles to thrive in the constrained Prussian court, where each day she seems to take a wrong step. And her status as the eldest daughter of Queen Victoria does little to smooth over the conflicts she faces.

But handsome, gallant Fritz is always by her side as they navigate court intrigue and challenge the cunning Chancellor Otto von Bismarck while fighting for the throne—and the soul of a nation. At home they endure tragedy, including their son, Wilhelm, rejecting all they stand for.

DISCOVER GREAT AUTHORS, EXCLUSIVE OFFERS, AND MORE AT HC.COM.
Available wherever books are sold.